MY TWO LIVES

MY TWO LIVES

JAN HUNTER

www.6e.net

First published in paperback in 2013
by Sixth Element Publishing on behalf of Jan Hunter
Arthur Robinson House
13-14 The Green
Billingham TS23 1EU
Tel: 01642 360253

ISBN 978-1-908299-49-9

British Library Cataloguing in Publication Data. A catalogue record for this book
is available from the British Library.

Jan Hunter asserts the moral right to be identified as the author of this work.

Printed in Great Britain.

www.6e.net

All characters appearing in this work are fictitious.
Any resemblance to real persons, living or dead, is purely coincidental.

For Tim, Helena and Tim for their love, support
and continuous encouragement.

With many thanks to The Hon. Simon Howard for his support, and for allowing me to use Castle Howard as both my inspiration and location for My Two Lives.

CHAPTER ONE

I thought and hoped that today was going to be a normal day in the life of a comprehensive school teacher, if ever there is such a thing. However, my life was to change so dramatically in a split second, that as I am writing about it now, it seems too unbelievable to have actually happened.

It seemed to be such an ordinary day at first. It was the first day back at work after the half term break. I climbed out of bed, bleary eyed from a heavy night's sleep, and skirted round the damp rucksack and muddy walking gear which I had flung on the floor of my flat at midnight.

I was always reluctant to leave the Lake District. It was a little oasis of calm in my somewhat chaotic existence. I was a teacher, the bringer of literature to children whose ears were stuffed with headphones and whose brains were full of reality TV. The fells seemed to be full of stressed teachers at the beginning of the week, who slowly became human beings again by Sunday. Willingly I joined the exodus, and returned home refreshed, my mind stilled by nature.

I turned on the shower and glanced idly at my steamy reflection in the bathroom mirror. Yes, I still looked the same. I hadn't transformed into a super model overnight, but the Cumbrian air had given a healthy glow to my cheeks. I felt satisfied I could give some of these so-called celebrities a run for their money, except that I seemed to have twigs in my hair.

I was late. Not good for a teacher. Not good for a thirty plus soon-to-be divorcee who had been given a new start in a new school and was determined to inhabit an office in the corridor of power at some point in her career.

For breakfast there was a stick of celery in my fridge and six

1

bottles of wine. I was pondering how the celery got there as I squeezed my little Corsa into a parking space outside the bakery. I was late and I was hungry, and the hunger won, as it always did.

The bakery was full to the brim with prams, pushchairs and agitated commuters, but the warm, succulent smell of pastries and good coffee drew me in. Two very large mothers whom I recognised from my last and rather fractious parents' evening were blocking the doorway.

"Bloody teachers!" The mother of one of my more reluctant learners threw a venomous glare in my general direction. "What does he want to learn bloody French for, he can't even speak proper English. He's a soft get that Mr Paradis, and he's French, taking our jobs them foreigners, coming over here…"

Her voice trailed away as I weaved past them with a polite smile, only to get the elbow of a sharply-dressed commuter jammed into my ribs. I did have a little more padding due to my frequent visits to this establishment, but it didn't stop me giving a withering look to what looked like a child in a suit who had hair so highly waxed that he looked permanently surprised.

I breathed in the aroma as I neared the counter, making a mental note to self that tomorrow I would have muesli instead. A very shaky work-life balance and a pending divorce had seen unwelcome expansions to my good self, through hasty en-route breakfasts of un-skinny lattes and croissants. But I had no remorse. If you had to face what and whom I had to face each morning, one croissant would never be enough.

She was there amidst the pungent aromas, white cap askew and pencilled eyebrows disappearing under a diagonal fringe which seemed to be glued to her head.

"Anyfink else?" The cracked, purple nail varnish twinkled as she held out the stark, white bag to me.

"Any floury baps?"

I didn't really give her a second glance. How was I to know under what circumstances we would meet again?

My teeth sank into the croissant and I went into grateful submission as I exited the shop. The two mothers at the door were well into their character assassinations of my colleagues, but I was lucky. This morning my name was not mentioned.

Balancing the coffee on the bonnet, I opened the car door and stacked my breakfast on various shelves before speeding off again towards Primrose Meadows, my place of work.

Primrose Meadows; the name conjures up light, space and colour, but it wasn't like that. Firstly, in my experience, primroses don't grow in meadows. So which well meaning, but slightly dim member of the council had suggested that bloomer? One can only imagine the bright day when the ribbon was cut during the Summer of Love in '67, and the children of the sixties surged in breathing love and harmony. So what went wrong? Primrose Meadows was now a mass of teenage hormones and worn out, cynical staff.

It loomed above me, blocking out the light as I turned into the shabby street full of litter. This school was a concrete rabbit warren stuck in the middle of endless blocks of high-rise flats, all built by an architect with no imagination.

There were no parking places so I double parked and raced through the grimy glass doors, balancing books and bags on my arms. I ignored the frosty-faced bursar who glared at me through her glass window, after pointedly looking at the clock. I bumped into the headmistress who was striding out of assembly where, incidentally, I should have been with my class ten minutes ago. They were sixth formers. They wouldn't know if I was there or not as most of them didn't wake up until after lunch. However, she looked at me covered in croissant crumbs and then at her watch. She sighed, raised her eyebrows and said, "History cover, room one, period one," and disappeared into her office accompanied by my chances of promotion in the near future.

Damn it! My precious free period gone thanks to Simon, who preferred to spend Monday morning in bed with the Guardian newspaper, and whoever else was around, rather than facing Year 9. Thank you, Simon.

As ever, the class was in chaos and there was no work left for them, so I weaved through the mayhem to the history cupboard, to find some work sheets on the Victorians. A lesson on how grateful they should be that they were not down the mines or up the chimneys would soon shut them up.

Dust was everywhere. The shelves were grey and thick with it and books were piled up in such a haphazard way I was almost afraid to touch anything in case I caused a landslide. It was obvious that Simon hadn't cleaned or sorted out his stockroom for twenty five years. I found some yellowing worksheets and tried unsuccessfully to tug at a red-bound book, high on the top shelf, entitled Love and Sex in Victorian England. That should settle the testosterone levels for a few minutes.

I tugged so hard that I fell back quite forcefully and banged the back of my head on the wooden shelf behind me. A strange mist started to seep around me and I felt faint and weak and found myself flat on the floor unable to open my eyes. It was the smell that drove into my subconscious and woke me. It was a miasma of all things rotting, flesh, food and waste. The stale, damp air pervaded my nostrils and made me gag.

"Miss, Miss, is you hurt or anyfink?" An urgent voice swirled above me.

I opened my eyes quickly, red hot embarrassment pouring through me. Had I been unconscious? What was happening to my class? And what was that smell? Surely I hadn't, I couldn't? Oh God!

A pink face, framed by a curly white cap came into focus. It was the girl from the bakery. I couldn't make any sense of this. How did I get to the bakery? Why was I lying on the floor? Soft hands lifted me gently. Sunlight hit me, blinded me as I got to my feet, but I couldn't stand up. My legs were tangled in cloth. Cool water in some kind of small bucket touched my lips. I glanced at my feet, which didn't appear to be where they should be. Instead, yards of cloth covered my legs.

I panicked, glancing quickly around, my eyes still blurred by a thin mist. The foetid smell was so strong in my nostrils, but my vision was clearing. I was in a street, an old alleyway, flanked by brown brick walls. Standing squarely in front of me, her hands gripping my arms tightly, was the girl from the bakery, in a long black dress and white pinafore, a shawl wrapped around her shoulders.

"You awright, Miss? You fainted." Her pale blue eyes stared straight at me.

I opened my mouth to reply, but my jaw was constricted. I reached up to touch what felt like a ribbon, which appeared to be tied tightly around my chin. My hands explored further. My head was encased in a hat or a bonnet. A bonnet?

I fell back against the wall, scraping my knuckles, and her hands scrabbled for me. I felt dizzy, my head was whirling. I grasped and scratched at the walls, trying to find something to steady me. The bricks dissolved and my hand clutched something. Was it a loose brick, or a book? I couldn't see. Whirling mist seemed to blur my vision again. When it slowly cleared, I found myself back in the history stockroom, leaning on the shelf I had fallen against, my hands grasping the book I had tried to reach.

I stumbled out of the stockroom, my mind in pieces. What had happened to me? A silent, empty room yawned at me. Motes of dust were twinkling in the shafts of sunlight that streamed in from the windows. Books and papers littered the floor. Where was the class? I sat down suddenly at the nearest desk and glanced at my watch.

It was 10.20am, the end of period one. I had gone into the stockroom at the beginning of the lesson. It couldn't have been later than 9.15am. So where had that hour gone? What had happened to me in that time? Where had I been?

A wave of panic hit the pit of my stomach with a jolt and then started crawling up my body. My heart was thudding as I tried to rationalise the situation. I must have knocked myself out. I must have been unconscious for all that time. What had the class been doing while I was in the stockroom? Why did nobody come to find me?

But nothing hurt. My head felt fine, but the bun I had hastily assembled this morning had come loose. Tentatively I probed at my skull with my fingertips, but there were no signs of injury. I stood up quickly, placing my hands firmly on the desk. I was fine. I'd had an accident, and the class had coped without me. There may have been general mayhem and slaughter, but they had gone and here was I perfectly well, and ready and late for period two. I slung my bag over my shoulder and grasped the door handle.

I froze. My fingers were scraped and bleeding. In my unconscious state, I had fallen against a wall in the alleyway. I remember reaching out and grazing my hand. I shook my head in disbelief, then laughed at my stupidity. I'd hurt myself when I fell. That stockroom contained twenty five years worth of accumulated rubbish. Simon probably had a medieval man trap in there or some instrument of torture I had fallen against. I hurried down the corridor to my next class, making a mental note to find someone from 9GL at break, to see how they had got on without me.

The day passed by in a bit of a haze. I was too busy to think of anything else, other than the job in hand. However, a hasty phone call meant that at 4.30pm I was walking out of the doctors with a clean bill of health and some advice which is standard for all teachers; work life balance, coping with stress, having 'me' time and so on. I knew all this. My visits to the doctors had been so frequent over the past years that we were on first name terms and we were almost up to the point in our relationship where we were swapping recipes. I know I work too hard. Stress and I were constant companions, but after what had happened that morning, I thought I would check.

As I walked towards my car, having settled in my mind that all was well, a hearty, "Hey Miss!" hurled across the air towards me. My heart sank. I had been spotted and there was no escape. I recognised the voices instantly. My group of Year 9 boys were a tricky bunch and we didn't seem to share a passion for Shakespeare. However, they always got very involved in the sword fight between Romeo and Mercutio. I did try to ban them from fighting on top of the desks but they didn't use real swords and only sustained minor injuries from the bamboo canes.

Generally, not including that minor hiccough, I was gaining a reputation as a force to be reckoned with inside the classroom, but not everyone thought that way and two examples were now bulldozing their way towards me. These particular two had been targeted in the 'Every Child Matters' campaign which was a new initiative, pioneered by several bright young teachers in the school who were eager to be fast tracked to the corridors of power.

These particular pupils had been given all kinds of mentoring, but still felt they had to tell every teacher to go and fuck themselves at every opportunity. They sauntered over to me, their baggy jeans giving them a feral-like gait. They squinted up at me through their long fringes and I sighed and fixed a friendly, welcoming smile, which was part of the new initiative.

"Hello, Damien, Wayne," I said, brightly.

As usual they invaded my personal space so much that I could smell the midget gems and cheese and onion crisps they had been devouring, and were there faint traces of smoke and alcohol underneath the fumes?

"Hey, Miss, how come you skived our lesson?" Damien offered me a midget gem from a grey-looking paper bag.

"What do you mean, Damien?" I enquired, taking a sweet from the bottom of the bag and promising to save it for later.

"Our history class this morning." Wayne had a particularly piercing voice, so I moved slightly out of his radar, which meant I was stuck with Damien and the midget gems.

"You went in the stockroom and didn't come out. We went looking for you but you weren't there. You must be like him off the telly who disappears." Wayne snorted at his wit and looked to Damien for approval.

The smile remained pasted onto my face, but inside my heart started racing and I felt my legs beginning to give way. I stared at them, needing, but not wanting to hear any more.

"Nah, she climbed out the window. Scared of teaching us, weren't you, Miss. We 'ad a right laugh with no teacher there."

The lads sniggered.

"See ya, Miss." They swaggered off laughing.

I don't know how long I stood there, feeling light-headed and faintly sick. Eventually, I got in the car and drove home. I don't remember the journey. I don't remember how I got back to my flat. Now I was worried and I needed time to myself to find a rational explanation for this. I needed to think. I needed to work this out.

I turned the key in the front door, hoping that Jeff, the painter and decorator, had left. I started my new job last year, which meant a pay rise, and when my husband moved out, I immediately called Jeff, a friend of a friend, and asked him to redecorate the whole of my apartment. This was a job my now ex-husband and I had been meaning to complete for the past eight years but somehow neither of us had got round to it. This was perhaps indicative that something was not right between us. Now I needed a new life, a new start and the time was right.

For the past six months Jeff had made himself at home, decorating at a pace beyond slow. I tolerated this situation because he was good company and also because he looked like a very young Robert Plant, complete with obscenely tight jeans.

As I walked into my flat, feeling tired and confused, I saw that he was seated at the kitchen table with his feet up, reading my copy of the Teacher. There wasn't a sign of a paintbrush anywhere.

"Hi, Jill, you're late. Coffee?" A grin appeared between the curtains of blond waves. "Kids bin giving you grief?"

He splashed water into the kettle, and reached for two cups. I placed my bag wearily on the floor. I felt weak and worn out.

"Isn't it time you were home, Jeff? Arlene will wonder where you are."

I sank into a chair, stretched out my arms and rested my head on the table. I was desperate for some time to myself to sort out my head, my day, and my sanity.

"Nah, it's okay," he grinned. "I'm meeting her at Crystal Therapy. She's working late."

Jeff and Arlene were into alternative healing, at least Arlene was. I think Jeff was her guinea pig. I raised my head as Jeff was cheerfully spooning coffee into two mugs.

"Jeff, I don't feel well, do you mind if you go now? I don't mean to be rude but…" My voice trailed off.

He paused, spoon in midair, and looked at me. "Sure thing,

but talk through your day if you want. It's good therapy!" Jeff was into talking. I knew things about him that you would not believe. I hoped Arlene was a good listener.

I shook my head slowly as it was starting to bang.

"No, Jeff, not this time."

"Okay." He grabbed his jacket. "But don't forget to think positive. You are beautiful inside and out and your aura is pink and gold. Good signs of healing. Oh and by the way, you have two messages on your answer phone. One from your ex-husband, who wants to see you before the decree absolute and another from a bloke selling carpets, so I rang him back and told him to go to hell. Cold callers. Bad karma."

"Jeff, I'm organising the delivery of a new carpet for when you have eventually finished my lounge. Now I'll have to ring him back. Will you please just go?"

Jeff inserted himself into a very tight leather jacket. His clothes left nothing to the imagination. I tried to focus on his face, which was, thankfully, rather beautiful. He shook his head at me as he grabbed the keys to his van.

"Hey, hostile! You know me, just trying to help. See you tomorrow."

The door banged behind him, and the silence whirled around me and settled. I could hear the clock ticking and see the fruit sitting in the bowl on the table. I glanced at the half-stripped walls, and felt the solid wood under my hands. I was alive. I was here in the present moment, but what had happened to me today?

The red graze across my fingers challenged me. There had to be an explanation, a simple and logical explanation. I reached in my bag for my car keys and in twenty minutes I was back in school.

"I've forgotten something," I shouted to the caretaker who was about to launch into a tirade about inconsiderate teachers, and fled up the stairs. I pushed open the door of the history stockroom, my heart and stomach both fluttering. That smell of dust and neglect seared through my nostrils once more.

I snapped open my glasses case, fixed the glasses onto my nose and calmly began to search the area where I had fallen.

Nothing.

Nothing to graze myself on, just shelves, papers and books. I stopped my search and my gaze travelled back up to the book with the red binding. My hands were trembling, and every logical cell in my brain was telling me that this was nonsense, but I had to know. I grasped it firmly and pulled it off the shelf, holding my breath at the same time.

Nothing happened. I remained where I was, and could hear the steps of the caretaker getting closer. I waited. No mist, no feeling of light-headedness, no pungent smell, nothing. I remained exactly where I was.

The caretaker wrenched open the door and I could hear his voice muttering at me.

"I've got to lock up and it's past five. Do you teachers never realise I have a home to go to?"

His face, set in a permanent scowl, appeared around the door. I replaced the book, feeling a small sense of relief. He held the door open for me, ungraciously, and I moved to go past him. Then I stopped dead.

The smell, it was here, the overpowering stench of decay in the alleyway. It filled my nostrils and almost made me retch.

"What's that smell?" I almost shrieked, turning to look at him.

The scowl darkened. "Cheeky cow," he grumbled. "You'd stink too if you were cleaning out the boy's toilets, but you teachers never notice what I do, you teachers…"

His voice died away as I moved slowly down the stairs, and back to the car. I could feel myself trembling and my heart was thumping. I put my hand on the roof of the car to steady myself and as I looked up, hearing footsteps behind me, the girl from the bakery walked straight past me. She glanced at me, showing no sign of recognition, but they were there, those pale eyes, the same eyes that had looked at me so closely in the alleyway. She stumbled past me in high lace-up boots, and out of her enormous handbag, which was slung carelessly over her shoulder, dropped a frilly white garment. It had to be the bonnet she was wearing in the alleyway.

Not thinking at all, I ran after her and snatched the garment from the pavement, without looking at it. She had to be the key. She would give me an explanation. She turned and stared at me blankly as I was pounding after her.

"You dropped this," I gasped, holding the garment out to her. I handed it to her, the unspoken question in my eyes, and the garment fell open. It was her apron. The one she wore in the bakery. My cheeks were flushed with embarrassment.

She frowned then looked straight at me. "Ta," she said, and tossed it back in her handbag.

I watched her go. I stared after her until she disappeared. This was crazy. I needed home, a drink and I needed to think things through. My imagination was getting the better of me, and I had tea to make and books to mark and a life to lead; a life where I was in control. I'd fought hard to get here and nothing was going to change this, especially not an over-active imagination arising from a fainting fit, and two boys whose word you wouldn't trust, not if your life depended on it.

I needed to be logical about this. I knocked myself out in the stockroom. The class would have left me there, taking advantage of the situation, as kids did. The caretaker had been cleaning out the toilets, hence the smell, although I must make a note to tell the Head there must be serious issues there. As for the girl in the bakery, she must have been on my mind for some reason and when I knocked myself out, she was there in my subconscious.

I'd proved that it was all in my imagination as I'd tackled the trigger, the book I had pulled from the shelf that had started it all. I was calm again and in control of my life, and that was the way it was going to stay.

CHAPTER TWO

Do you want to know the most boring part of a teacher's job? Exam supervision. It is soul-destroying. In this enlightened age, teachers are no longer required to patrol the aisles of the exam hall because they are too busy filling in forms. So, to give us more time for this worthy exercise, the authority employs exam supervisors.

However, on this particular day, two of the supervisors were ill, so we were short-staffed. Instead of covering someone else's class in my free period, I was selected for exam supervision. This meant that for one hour out of my life, I had to walk up and down the endless rows of desks, trying lots of different ways to stop myself from going out of my mind. I counted kids with blond hair, brown and red, those not wearing a tie, those with a tie. I did averages on how many girls had long hair and how many boys used hair gel. Eventually, I propped myself against a desk at the back of the hall, and fixed my eyes on the trees outside the window, rather than on the clock.

A week had passed by fairly uneventfully, since the strange episode. There had been no more fainting fits or dreams about the girl in the bakery. There was absolutely no change to the decor in my flat, even though Jeff had insisted that I couldn't see the careful preparation he had accomplished. I hadn't yet talked to my ex-husband about the decree absolute, but I seemed to be on the right side of the headmistress again, as I was in the throes of organising a school trip, *and* I was the first to get my sixth form reports to her. Lots of points to chalk up there, I thought.

I was just trying to work out how I could get to see my friend Liz next week when, there it was, an oasis in the desert, a hand in the air. I grabbed some extra paper and strode purposefully down the aisle before anyone else noticed the hand. Sometimes we had races to see who could get there first. I always lost, due to my highly unsuitable footwear. The PE teachers always won hands down, because of their minty white, soft-soled trainers.

The boy who was attached to the hand was writing madly with his other hand, not daring to stop, but I did, suddenly. It was a boy I hadn't seen in school before. He had thick blond hair, and his long tapering fingers clutched his pen tightly. As he looked up to give me a brief smile of thanks, I looked into the same startling blue eyes.

Chris. This boy was his double. It could have been him. I hadn't thought about Chris for so long, and as I did, the balance of my body shifted. This feeling was so strong that I had to stop walking and put a hand on the back of a chair to steady myself. I thrust some paper at him and then strode back up the hall, feeling decidedly wobbly.

"Who's that boy?" I whispered to one of the bright young things who was leaning against the stage, staring out of the window. She was the unlucky other who had drawn the short straw this morning, ending up with me, in the hall.

"Which one?" She turned eagerly, glad of the diversion.

I pointed, I hoped, discreetly.

She shrugged her shoulders. "Don't know, never seen him before."

"But you're his deputy head of year, you must know him!" I was becoming anxious.

She stared at me. "I've never seen him before. He must be new. I don't deal with new admissions." She was losing interest. "I only know the bad ones."

When the exam was over, I watched him walk out of the hall with two girls from my class, and during afternoon registration, I quizzed them.

They looked at me, startled. "We don't know who he is, Miss. He's new. We've never seen him before, but isn't he gorgeous? Bit young for you though, Miss." They giggled together; no doubt the story would be misinterpreted and whizzing round the sixth form common room by lunch time.

I spent my free period checking records. Inevitably, the head of

Year 12 was on a course, so I couldn't ask him for information. Instead, I scuttled back to the exam hall to search for the boy's name on his exam desk, but it wasn't there. My next step was to look through the new admissions file in the main office and as I was doing this, my dear friend the school bursar interrupted me.

"Parent to see you, Miss Woods."

I glanced up from my search, feeling hot and anxious. There she stood, resplendent in sage green crimpolene, a sour look on her face, glasses dangling from a string around her neck. Why did this woman dislike me so much? It might have been when I got drunk at the staff party and called her a sour-faced old cow, but I couldn't be sure.

"Who is it?" I snapped.

"Elliot Pinkney's mother. She says Elliot is being bullied."

I sighed and shook my head, closing the drawer with a snap. Elliot, who was a member of my form, was six foot three and a rugby prop for the school. I wanted to employ him as my minder when he left school. His mother was small, fussy and still thought of him as her baby. She called in once a day to see me, sometimes twice. I was usually unavailable, but she could see me through the office window and gave me a nervous little wave.

"Who would dare bully Elliot?" I muttered as I grabbed my handbag.

The bursar looked at me with a sense of triumph in her tight little smile.

"She says it's some Year 7 girls."

I gave her a look of disbelief and fixed my most welcoming smile for Mrs Pinkney.

Later, I drove home with my head spinning. Half an hour with Mrs Pinkney and Elliot after work had been hard going. Elliot was a gentle giant and he did not want to respond to little girls calling him names. He could have squashed them like bugs, but chose instead to tell his mum, who would probably be patrolling the streets with a Kalashnikov rifle after tea, in order to find them.

But I would leave Mrs Pinkney to her retribution, as I had far greater things on my mind. Seeing that boy in the exam hall had evoked all kinds of memories I'd long suppressed, and with good reason. The best and worst days of my life were my university days with Chris Beaumont, the boy I had loved and lost so many years ago. He was the simple reason why every other relationship I ever had had gone belly-up. I tried to calm myself with the idea that the boy I had seen must be new or maybe he was a relation of the Beaumonts. I couldn't find any record of him in the admission file, but with the state our school was in anyone could walk into a classroom off the street, attend classes and you would just presume they were supposed to be there. But what was so strange was that he was the absolute image of Chris, the smile, the eyes, the way he walked. I shook my head in order to dislodge the memory. I was not going to think about Chris Beaumont. Not now, not ever.

I opened the door to my flat and found Jeff making vegetable smoothies in my kitchen.

"Your pH is out of balance, Jill," he shouted above the noise of the blender. "You need to be more alkaline."

I threw my bag on the floor and sank into the chair, resting my head on the kitchen table. "Jeff," I muttered, "I really don't need you to sort me out."

He put a tumbler of green goo in front of me.

"No problem," he grinned. "You work too hard. You need more greens and more rumpy pumpy."

"What?" I raised my head, scanning the kitchen for a sign of new paint on any surface.

Jeff was wearing a very tight t-shirt which said Love Is All You Need on it.

He swallowed his goo in one gulp and sighed blissfully. "Jesus, that was good," he said, wiping his mouth across the back of his hand.

"You need more greens and more sex. You work too hard." He saw my face and grinned again. "Just a suggestion. I wasn't offering."

"I thought all you needed was love, not green slime, or sex."

"It depends on your interpretation." Jeff perched close to me on the table and I was amazed that he could sit down in those jeans. They were spray-painted on, but there was not a speck of emulsion on them. He was the cleanest decorator I had ever known.

I glanced around the kitchen. "And what exactly have you done today, Jeff?" I enquired.

"Just more prep," he said, getting his jacket. "By the way, there's another message for you on your answer phone from the ex. He sounds really pissed off that you haven't phoned him. I think you'd better. He's a nice bloke, takes a lot to piss him off. See you tomorrow."

The door rattled behind him and I made a mental note to teach him how to close a door quietly. I stared at the glass in front of me and drank it down in one gulp. It could only do me good, and I was so tired and so confused by the events of the day that any pick-me-up was welcome.

It was vile. I ran to the toilet and threw the lot back up, and as I flopped over the sink to rinse my face, I caught sight of myself in the mirror. There was something wrong with the way I looked; there was something on my head, something white, like a cap. I whirled around to see white towels neatly placed on the rack behind me.

I turned back to the mirror, and reached out to touch my reflection. All was normal. My imagination was getting the better of me again and my eyesight must be getting worse.

Feeling slightly disturbed, I made my way to my study and switched on the desk lamp. The A level papers were laid out in neat piles, all ready to be marked. I glanced out of the window at the rain sliding down in rivulets. There was a faint patter of raindrops against the glass. It sounded like someone tapping, wanting to get in. The lamp lit up my reflection and I gave a start. I grabbed hold of my hair which was loose against my shoulders, just to reassure myself. In the reflection that stared back at me, my hair was up in intricate coils. The face, which was mine, gave a slight smile and then inclined her head. This was not my reflection, although the face was my face. I let out a scream and backed towards the door. The image disappeared and I ran to the window to open it. Rain poured in, soaking my arms. There was nobody there. How could there be? I was three flights up. I slammed the window shut, and there was my true reflection, my hair down, soaking wet and plastered to my head.

I ran into the kitchen, grabbing a towel from the bathroom on my way. I poured myself a large glass of wine, towelling my hair vigorously at the same time and sat down at the kitchen table, my body trembling so much that I spilt some of the wine. It oozed across the table cloth and I stood up quickly, looking around for something to soak it up. The radio had been left on by Jeff and someone was singing quietly. I turned it right up, becoming scared of the silence.

"If you take a chance with me, be prepared to bleed," sang the radio. I gave a start. This was one of Chris's songs. He composed it when I was living with him, and he had some success as a songwriter in the States, but I hadn't heard this song since he had played it to me many years ago.

I watched the red wine spreading like a bloodstain on the embroidered cloth. Something very strange was going on and it was starting to scare me. I mopped up the mess and sat down again, taking a hefty gulp of wine as I listened to the remainder of the song. Scraps and shades of memories started to pierce my brain again, but I couldn't and wouldn't let them. I had to stop thinking about Chris and I had to solve the puzzle of the reflection in the window.

Taking the bottle of wine with me, I walked back quickly through the hall and into my study. My legs felt like jelly, but I was determined to solve the puzzle and put my mind at rest. I turned on the desk lamp and slowly my eyes travelled towards the window. The wind seemed angry and destructive. It howled round the building as if trying to get inside, and the branches of the beech tree outside my window were whirling in the gusts of wind, causing my reflection to change and become distorted. I kept staring, seeing my face and hair change shape as the branches rattled against the window. There was my explanation. More or less satisfied, I closed the curtains. My heart had stopped pounding and I no longer felt overwrought.

I banished Chris from my thoughts and turned to my work

for tonight. A couple of hours marking was required and then an early night ready for the next day. My trip to London, which I had organised in a very weak moment, had arrived. I was determined it would go well, and gain me a few more brownie points with the Head. My desk was littered with consent forms, medical forms, theatre tickets and neatly printed itineraries for all. On the trip would be me, Simon, the head of history, if he remembered to turn up and Alison, an english department colleague who was rich, well into husband number three, and teaching for pin money. But most importantly, I would be in the constant company of forty hormonal Year 9s.

I couldn't wait.

CHAPTER THREE

After three phone calls to the depot, the coach which was taking us to London eventually arrived, and we were only one hour behind schedule. It was raining, and the expectant smiles of the excited pupils were fading fast and they were becoming fractious. The boys refused to shelter because it wasn't cool to do so, and the carefully straightened hair of the fashionable crowd was starting to frizz, much to the consternation of the girls who were crowded underneath one very pink umbrella.

"It looks like a pre-war vehicle," Simon muttered as he climbed aboard and then settled himself on the front seat behind a copy of the Guardian.

"Oh, I'll get the kids on, shall I, Simon?" I growled, as the excited but soggy mass surged towards the coach door.

I thought that this was the way things would be if Simon came along, but of course the Head insisted that a senior member of staff went with us. Then, if anything went wrong, I could be officially blamed.

As I saw to luggage, settled arguments, and removed all the would-be villains off the back seat, Alison purred into the car park in an E-type Jaguar, with a bronzed and beautiful husband at the wheel.

"Jill, Jill, darling, so sorry." She climbed up the steps in impossible heels, Louis Vuitton luggage on each arm. "I completely lost track of time. I hope you haven't been waiting long. Hello, everyone, are you all excited?"

She beamed at everyone, showing at least £3,000 of dental work. I had to hand it to her, Alison had charm. She dumped her luggage on Simon's lap so he could deposit it on the luggage rack for her, and then she tottered up and down the aisle, in a cloud of Chanel, chatting to the kids and amassing a pile of sweets and magazines for the staff.

When everyone seemed to be settled, I took charge of the microphone and gave my speech about healthy eating, which included not eating sweets if you were a bad traveller and the importance of sitting towards the front of the coach if you felt ill. Most of the pupils must have been listening as we had only two stops for people to be sick. One child was a little late in her prediction of how and when, and Simon ended up with a steady stream down the back of his neck.

I listened to the story of Alison's life as far as the second service station, and then begged her copy of the Lady for a little peace. I also elected to sit next to the palest of the sickness brigade, and left Simon to listen to Alison, whilst buttoning up a clean shirt and depositing his old one in the bin.

I flipped through the magazine, but I wasn't really able to concentrate. It was such a responsibility taking students away from home, and my teacher's antennae were working overtime. The events of the last few days were fading as I had found a rational explanation for almost everything that had happened. I had been very tired recently and although very much in control of my emotions for most of the time, I did have a slight tendency to over-react when I felt stressed or under pressure. My health had been a worry over the past few years, and I knew that I should listen to the doctor about finding more time for relaxation.

"I've been there, Miss."

Pale child next to me was pointing to a page in the magazine, and I glanced down to see what she was looking at.

"That's Castle Beaumont," she said.

I looked at the familiar honey-coloured stone building in all its stately majesty, and my heart seemed to flip over.

"So have I," I said. "Many times."

Castle Beaumont, Chris's ancestral home. I hadn't been back there since Chris left England for America. I couldn't even drive through the village. Everything was too painful. Even looking at a photograph of that magnificent building brought back such vivid memories. I felt my heart beginning to pound again so I stood up quickly.

"Toilet stop, please," I said to the driver.

"Oh no," said Simon, frowning at me, "we haven't got as far as husband number two yet. It was just getting really interesting."

We pulled up into the car park of a grey slab of a service station, with much screeching of brakes.

"Don't you worry, darling," Alison beamed. "All will resume after tinkle time. Come on kids, let's go. Ten minutes only!"

We synchronised our watches and set off, the girls squealing as they stepped out into the cold. The lads clattered down the steps behind them, pushing and shoving each other in an effort to impress.

I checked that everyone had left the coach and then followed the girls into the toilets.

"Ten minutes and no more sweets!" I disappeared into a nearby cubicle, leaving the girls by the mirrors.

I locked the door quickly, and suddenly I felt really hot. I could hear a crackling sound and I spun round. What was that noise? It sounded like a fire. Was there a fire in the toilets? I reached out to the door to open it, but my hand went through it. A sharp smell burnt my nostrils and I gasped.

"She's all right, she's coming round."

The pale blue eyes of the girl in the bakery were looking at me. She was holding a bottle under my nose and I pushed it away as I gasped for breath.

There was that familiar swirling mist in front of my eyes, and then my vision started to clear. I was seated on a hard, wooden chair beside a crackling fire in a large kitchen. A black kettle hung over the fire, with threads of steam curling up from its spout.

I glanced around quickly, my nostrils full of the smells of roasting meat. The kitchen was very old fashioned, out of another time completely. Behind a long scrubbed table, her arms covered in flour, was a woman kneading pastry. There were beads of sweat on her forehead and upper lip. She was dressed in Victorian clothes, a frilly cap on a mountain of unruly curls, and a large white pinafore tied tightly around her middle.

She smiled at me, her round face crinkling. She paused in her work and wiped a floury arm across her forehead.

"You had a bit of a turn there, Miss Woods, but Jenny's given you a whiff of salts, and you've come round nicely. Give her some tea, Jenny, and then you can take her up to see the children."

I was speechless. I opened and closed my mouth like a goldfish, but no words came out.

Eventually, "Where am I?" seemed to be appropriate.

"You're back home, Miss." Jenny's pale eyes looked at me intently. "You had a bit of a turn in the alley and me and John brought you back."

I stood up quickly. "I have to get back to the children," I said, looking round wildly.

The woman at the table brushed the flour from her arms and walked over to me, her long skirts swishing against the floor.

"No you don't now, Miss. They are out with the Master. You take off your bonnet and rest. You can see the children later."

My hand flew to my head in horror. There it was. A stiff bonnet, tied under my chin with a bow. I glanced down at my legs encased in a long black skirt, and at my feet in shiny button boots.

I sat down suddenly with a small cry, and immediately found myself flying out of the cubicle door, into a crowd of Year 9 girls who were carefully applying their lipstick.

"God, Miss, you're dead white, do you want some blusher?" one of them offered helpfully.

"I'm fine, Grace, I'm fine." I staggered to the mirror. The bonnet had gone. I was in my normal clothes, but I was white as a sheet.

The girls were staring at me curiously, eye pencils and lipsticks poised like fairy wands. I turned to face them, leaning against the sink for support.

"How long was I in the toilet, girls?" I asked.

They glanced at each other. "You'd just gone in, Miss. Why?" Grace seemed to be the spokesperson today.

I ran my hand through my hair, and then managed to fix what I hoped was a reassuring smile on my face.

"Nothing, nothing." I smiled brightly. "I just felt a little faint, that's all. Now let's all get back to the coach, shall we? We're already behind schedule."

The rest of the journey was a blur. My thoughts were in turmoil. I could hear Alison's voice beside me, moaning about her kids who had everything, but no time for her. I sat in a daze, seriously concerned that I was ill. I couldn't understand what was happening to me or why. There seemed to be no logic to it. What made me suddenly quit this world and end up in another? Panic started to burn itself into my stomach, forcing its way up my throat, until I could feel myself growing nauseous. I was trembling.

I wanted to tell someone, I needed reassurance, but if I told Alison, the whole staff would know about my problem even before we returned to school, so I had to keep it to myself. If I was going mad, I had to work through it by myself.

I forced myself to concentrate on the task in hand. We were now one and a half hours behind schedule, even though the driver had decided to speed down the outside lane of the motorway, trying to make up for lost time. I became nervous when he began to overtake a series of very powerful cars, the coach rattling and shaking so much that talking above the noise was impossible. The kids were in a state beyond hyper, and I was trying to keep everyone calm. It didn't help when the driver announced that he'd never been to London before and enquired whether or not we had a map.

As we were stuck in an everlasting traffic jam, I sent one of the more responsible pupils to find a newsagents in order to buy either a map or an A to Z. I was hanging out of the door, keeping my eye on him and Alison was at the back window with the girls, making sure he was kept in sight. Just as he reached the coach door, waving a street map triumphantly, the traffic started to move again and the driver set off suddenly. We screamed at him to stop. The poor boy tried to keep up as he ran alongside the coach, waving his arms and shouting. The kids hung out of the windows yelling encouragement, and when the coach finally slowed down we had to haul him aboard, breaking every health and safety rule in the book.

Simon didn't even move from behind his paper. He just tapped his teeth with his pen as he tried to do the crossword, muttering things like, *if I had organised this trip… you can't trust women to do things correctly*, and other such unhelpful rubbish.

I was ready to kill him, but I was a professional, and I thanked Alison and the kids, very pointedly for helping with the situation.

Eventually, when the excitement had died down a little, I sat down to count the theatre tickets and ring the restaurant, where we were expected in less than half an hour. I looked up as I heard the driver shout, "Oh shit," in a very shrill way and the girls at the back started squealing. Alison came running down the aisle towards the front of the bus yelling, "The coach is on fire!"

Clouds of smoke were pouring from the engine as the coach shuddered and then stopped.

"Everyone out, and keep it nice and calm." Alison took charge as we hustled the kids out of the coach and onto the pavement.

The driver disappeared under the smoke and then started making numerous frantic phone calls. Simon stayed on the coach.

"We've got twenty minutes to get to the pizza place," I said quickly to Alison. "We can't check into the hotel, we don't have time. We'll have to walk to Pizza Planet, and then walk on to the theatre." I was thinking on my feet.

The kids were distraught. They'd bought new clothes, they wanted to change, they wanted to do their hair, and they needed the loo.

"That's fine," said Alison breezily, flashing us all one of her brilliant smiles. "The smoke seems to be clearing from the coach, so we'll rig up changing areas with towels inside the coach, and I have two pairs of battery-operated straightening irons in my case. Jill, I'll sort it," she continued as she saw my face. "You take the girls to find a loo and get Simple Simon to take the boys."

The girls scrambled for their cases, chattering with excitement and the boys tried to look cool. Throughout all this, Simon remained on the coach. I took a deep breath and marched up the steps to where he was sitting, still doing the crossword, pen poised, with a resigned look on his face. I leaned towards him.

"Simon," I said, brightly, "if you don't put that paper down and help us out here, I'm going to take it from you and ram it right up your arse."

He looked at me in astonishment. What had happened to mild mannered Miss Woods, I could hear him thinking. What a surprise for him. What a surprise for me.

"What would you like me to do?" he asked, carefully folding the paper and placing it on the seat. "I thought you had everything under control."

"Take the boys to the loo and then help Alison," I said, and turned back to exit the coach.

Some of the boys were standing on the coach steps. They grinned at me and cheered as I went past. "You go Miss!" they shouted. "You tell that wanker!"

Damn it, they weren't supposed to hear, but I couldn't help smiling, and feeling more than a little triumphant. I decided to ignore the fact that they had called him a wanker. Although not a word I would use myself, it was quite a good description of him.

The driver met me on the pavement whilst the girls hopped about beside him, desperate for the loo.

"It's not looking good," he said sheepishly, "but it should be fixed in time for me to collect you from the theatre. Oh, and by the way, your guide is on her way. She should be here soon."

"Well, I hope she knows where the nearest loos are." I placed the theatre tickets inside my bag.

"Ah, she's here." The driver seemed pleased to divert the attention away from himself.

I turned to greet her, grateful for another pair of hands, and found myself looking straight into the eyes of the cook I'd seen kneading pastry in the kitchen.

CHAPTER FOUR

"Hello." Her eyes crinkled as she gave me a warm smile. "Sorry about your coach. These things happen, but we have time to get to Pizza Planet." She rummaged in her enormous handbag, which clunked and rattled as she fished about inside it. She held a badge triumphantly for me to check, her many bracelets clinking together, as she did so. She smiled at me from underneath a cloud of corkscrew curls.

I stared at her in astonishment. I was so shocked I didn't know what to say. Luckily Alison stepped in.

"We're ready to go. Can we do a quick toilet diversion? Lead on, Miss er...?"

"Sorry, sorry, Julia," said the guide, smiling as she threw her numerous scarves over one shoulder. "Follow me."

It was chaos at Pizza Planet. The management thought that we were arriving an hour later, and then all the orders were wrong. The kids complained loudly. Someone couldn't eat cheese and there were two vegetarians whose salads didn't arrive. Two boys sneaked out to the McDonalds next door and did quite a good trade at selling fries at an inflated price. I was past caring. Good for them for being enterprising, I thought as I gave out the theatre tickets, leaving the kids to fight it out as regards who was sitting near whom.

"I'm going to the bar," I announced to Simon, as his nose looked like it was going to take him in that general direction. "Look after the kids and get them into their seats while I have a drink, otherwise I may kill someone."

I hurried through the foyer before Simon could respond, hoping that Julia would follow and I could try to make some kind of sense of what was happening to me. Maybe she would have some answers.

26

She didn't know me, so it didn't really matter whether she thought I was barking or not. I was renouncing my responsibilities for ten minutes and, if I was going mad, I would go there with alcohol inside me.

Julia was at my elbow as we waited at the bar, which was reasonably quiet. We were served quickly and found a table near the window, which overlooked the busy street below. Daylight was fading and the streetlights gave off a golden glow. We could hear the bustle and noise of the London traffic.

"You need to take off your coat and rest, you look so tired," said Julia, shrugging off her scarves. "You can see the children later."

I felt my body go cold. That is what the cook had said to me in the kitchen, almost the very same words. I stared at her. Who was this woman? Was she real or was I imagining her too?

"Julia, I have to say this," I blurted out, after a hefty gulp of wine, "I'm sure I've seen you before, or I could have dreamt about you as I'm really not sure what is reality anymore. This may seem crazy to you, but when I met you before, you said those same words to me, but we met in another time, another place."

Words just kept tumbling out of my mouth, and I wasn't sure if I was making any sense. Well how could I be? The whole thing was stupid, ridiculous, unreal. It couldn't happen, especially not to someone like me. I looked up at her, feeling anxious and concerned, and hoping that she might have some kind of explanation. She raised her eyebrows and looked at me, her expression not giving me any clues as to what she was thinking.

"I don't know what is wrong with me," I continued. "Twice now, in daylight, and not when I am asleep, I seem to have visited another time. It sounds unbelievable I know, but it's so vivid and clear, and so real." I felt really hot and foolish and my palms were sweating, but I ploughed on. "I'm certain that there is a logical explanation for this and I'm going to find out what it is in a calm and rational way, but just let me run these events past you."

I paused to take a breath and to see if there was any reaction, but there was none. Julia had fixed me with an unwavering stare. This unnerved me, but I was known to be calm in a crisis so I took another gulp of wine to calm my fluttering stomach, and pressed on.

"The first time it happened I was in the history stockroom at work, and the second was today, in a motorway toilet. Suddenly, I found myself in another time and place. I was in the stockroom and then I ended up in an alleyway and the second time I was in a kitchen. I was wearing Victorian clothes, and *you* were there. Why were you there?"

She still didn't say anything. "You think I'm mad don't you," I said, leaning back in my chair. "Maybe I am, maybe I'm having another breakdown. Oh, God, nobody knows about that… jeez, what am I saying?"

My voice was becoming quite shrill. I felt on the verge of tears. Panic was starting to get the better of me, and I sighed wearily, rubbing my face with my hand as if trying to clear my head. "Oh God, what is happening to me?" I downed the rest of the wine, waiting and hoping for some reaction.

"Well," she said eventually, as she looked at me levelly, "it does sound very strange, I admit."

She continued to stare at me, but then she smiled, leaned towards me and patted my hand. "You might have ESP," she said. "Some people do. You may be sensitive to atmosphere, or maybe you're being sent messages from a different time."

"What?" I withdrew my hand. "That's nonsense. Come on! Sorry, but I really don't believe in all that stuff."

Julia smiled and took a sip of her wine. "Well, what would you like me to say, that I think you're losing your mind?"

"Is that what you think?" I looked up sharply.

"No," she said quietly, "but not everything can be explained by science and logic. Humans are limited in their perceptions. We don't know everything. How could we? Strange things do happen to people."

"Now I'm really spooked." I sat back in my chair. "What is happening to me sounds like an episode of the X Files, entertaining but not in the least believable." I glanced at her. "Do you believe in this stuff? Are you a clairvoyant or a medium or something?"

Julia shook her head, "No, but I do read about other people's experiences and beliefs. Where I worked before, I had to organise body, mind and spirit weekends, and it was interesting to find out what different people believe."

"I thought you were a London guide." I drained my glass, desperate for another drink, but I was aware of the time, *and* my responsibilities.

"I am now, since I moved to London." Julia gathered her many accessories together. "I used to be an events organiser in a stately home in Yorkshire. I also did my dissertation there for my history degree. Such a strange and interesting past the family have."

She glanced at her ticket and gave me a brief smile. "It was Castle Beaumont, such a beautiful place. I was sorry I had to leave."

She disappeared into the crowd before I could react to what she had said. I pushed my way after her but she was gone, her seat right at the other end of the theatre to mine.

I was unable to concentrate fully on the show, and I moved quickly towards her seat as soon as the lights went up again. She excused herself, before I had a chance to talk to her. She had a text message and had to leave quickly, but she would see us at our hotel the next day.

"Enjoy the rest of the show..." Her voice trailed off as she disappeared into the crowd once more. Enjoy it? That was a difficult one.

Miss Saigon, a tale of unrequited love, partings, disappointments and betrayal. It was all there for me to absorb and remember, yet another reminder of my life with Chris Beaumont. I began to get angry with myself and the events of the past few days. Before these strange things began to happen, I was becoming more content with my life. I'd had to deal with some very dark times in my early twenties but I'd found a way through. I was currently sailing through a divorce with my emotions intact, and my feet were firmly placed on the career ladder. Life was as I chose it to be and I was determined that nothing was going to shake me out of the world I had built for myself.

I dried my eyes before the lights went up, only to find girls weeping all over the boys who looked proud and manly and responsible. We waited outside for the coach to arrive. And waited, and waited.

The seamier side of London life was now appearing on the streets, and the Year 9 boys became very interested in items which were on sale out of large black bin bags. The girls were propping each other up and complaining about being tired. Alison was pacing up and down in her incredible heels, ear glued to her mobile whilst she shouted at Simon to do something.

He set off reluctantly to search the surrounding streets, and two hours later our coach driver arrived, minus coach, and was met by a stony silence. He was almost in tears. Simon appeared behind him.

"Well?" Alison stood blazing in front of him.

"It's been towed away," he mumbled, staring at the ground.

"What?" Simon pushed through the kids to face him.

"I parked it on unauthorised ground. I couldn't find anywhere to leave it. It's been towed away by the police."

I felt almost sorry for him as he felt the full wrath of our head of history come down on his head. Simon and the driver set off for the nearest police station, and after a rather stressful journey walking through the streets of London at two o'clock in the morning, Alison and I got the kids into their hotel beds by three.

I collapsed onto my bed, glad to be in a room on my own. It was peaceful and still and smelt of clean sheets and air-freshener. My room was at the back of the hotel so there were no sounds of the constant London traffic. I would have a quick cup of tea and check on the kids before I went to sleep.

I filled the kettle and switched it on. The events of the day were still swimming around in my head. I drew back the curtains and propped myself up on the window seat, looking out onto a dark street, old fashioned lamps leaving yellow pools of light on the wet cobbles below.

Wet? I didn't remember any rainfall. The streets were dry on the walk back to the hotel. Maybe the streets had been cleaned. Maybe there'd been a shower of rain and I just hadn't noticed. I wiped the condensation off the window with my hand. The room suddenly felt cold. Then I stopped, looking at my arm in terror. I wasn't wearing my M&S pyjamas anymore. A frill of cotton was around my wrist. I jumped up and my legs tangled in the long nightgown I was wearing.

Where was the light? Where was the light? Candle wax and smoke and the smell of damp filled my nostrils, as I stumbled around the room which was dimly lit by the street lamps. I sat down on a hard bed and my eyes grew accustomed to the gloom. There was no TV or telephone. Where was the kettle I had just filled? The room had completely changed. I couldn't find a light switch and my feet were freezing on the cold floor. I screamed in terror and grasped the doorknob which turned stiffly in my hand. I found myself in a long, dimly lit corridor. It was icy cold.

A figure, holding a branch of candlesticks, was walking along the corridor towards me. I could see dark shiny boots and glimpses of white ruffles at the neck. The boots echoed on the polished wooden floor. The hotel had disappeared. I could only see the light and shadows the candles cast on the walls, as they bobbed towards me, illuminating portraits, statues and numerous other doors. I held my breath as the figure reached me. I could see the fine white linen of a shirt and smell the leather from his riding boots. I could hear him breathing and the candles were swept up to illuminate my face.

"Ah," said a voice, "you must be the new governess. I thought I heard someone cry out. Why did you wake the household in the middle of the night?"

I felt my whole body go cold with fear. I knew that voice. I reached up and gently moved the candles away from me so I could see who it was. The face was shadowy at first, but as a draught blew down the icy corridor, the candles brightened.

I was looking into the face of Chris Beaumont.

CHAPTER FIVE

I stared into those familiar blue eyes, the eyes of the boy I had seen in the exam hall, the eyes of the man I had loved so desperately so many years ago. He had the same sculptured cheekbones and slightly haughty expression which made him look both beautiful and dangerous. I forgot the lack of logic in this moment. I forgot that in reality this could not be happening. I was absorbed in looking at that beloved face again. Despite tearing up all the photographs, I never forgot the way he looked. His image was imprinted in every cell of me, despite all my efforts in trying to erase him from my mind. I could see there were slight differences, but this must be Chris, sent back in time as I was. It had to be.

The smell of wax, candle smoke and polish filled my nostrils. My feet were so cold on the wooden floor. I touched the cloth of my nightgown, feeling the fabric cool and coarse between my fingers. I was breathing. I was real. The breath filled my lungs and I sighed it out, becoming aware of the beating of my heart, the coldness of the atmosphere.

Chris continued to scrutinise me. "You *are* the new governess, I presume?" He moved the candles towards me to illuminate my face once more. His tone was impatient, and I thought, quite unfriendly. He had that same cut-glass aristocratic voice as my Chris but his was colder.

"Where am I, Chris? What's happening?" I found my voice, and I continued to look at him, desperate for him to show some kind of recognition. His eyes were icy blue and they stared back at me. I began to feel afraid. He looked at me with what seemed like contempt. Chris had certainly never looked at me that way.

"It is not the place of a governess to address the master of the house with such familiarity," he said scornfully as he swept the candles within inches of my face. "I suggest you remember your place in this household. You will wake the children early, as is the way of things here. I am sure that you will have been given your duties for the day. Goodnight."

The last part of his speech was given as he moved away from me, back the way he had come. I panicked. I didn't want to be left alone. I was scared, really scared. Why didn't he recognise me? Why was he so cold to me? Nothing made any sense to me anymore. My world was dissolving into threads around me.

I fled down the corridor after him, calling out in desperation. "Governess? How can I be a governess? Chris, what is going on? Where am I? Please tell me what's happening."

Then I tripped. There was some kind of carpet which ran down the centre of the wooden floorboards. It was dark and I missed my footing. The last thing I saw was Chris turning back to glance at me, as I fell into the darkness.

"Jesus, Jill." I heard Simon's voice. "What the hell are you doing?"

I looked up sharply. The hallway was flooded with light. The dark corridor had gone and so had Chris. Simon and the coach driver were looking down at me.

"We got the coach back," said Simon, as he helped me to my feet. "It's not worth going back to bed. It's just past seven. We'll have to get the kids out of their rooms. I've been up all night so I intend to sleep all the way back."

The poor coach driver, still dressed in his uniform, looked bedraggled and tearful.

"I can't apologise enough," he said. "Another driver is on his way to take you back."

I was trying to get my head round where I was, having seemingly been catapulted through time once more. I hadn't been to bed, but it was morning. I had lost a whole night. My feet were still freezing; I could smell vague remnants of candle smoke.

"What about the tour of London?" I was conscious of my state of mind and my state of undress, and I tried to cover myself as best I could.

Simon looked almost smug. "Just to add to the disasters of this trip," he said in his you-are-only-a-woman-and-couldn't-organise-a-thing voice, "our tour guide has been called away, so I suggest we pack up, drive through the main sights and then go home. The new coach driver is willing to do that, so we don't disappoint the kids."

I glared at him. Why did this man feel it was his duty to undermine me at every opportunity? "This is my trip," I snapped. "I would like to be consulted about any decisions."

"And don't I know it." He folded his arms and looked over his glasses at me as though I was a naughty Year 7 pupil. "This trip has been a shambles, and if it wasn't for Mrs Ditmus-Flynn and myself stepping in and taking charge, things would have been much worse. And, I suppose you have a reason for wandering the corridors in a state of undress and then falling over. Have you been drinking? Not very responsible behaviour for a teacher supposedly in charge of a school trip."

He leaned in and sniffed in my general direction.

I looked at his sneering face, with those mean little eyes, his slicked back greying hair, tousled with gel in an attempt to look trendy; his body spoke of arrogance and total contempt for me. Something welled up inside me. A feeling so strong that it coursed upwards through my veins, filling my whole body. It was anger. Anger and injustice and frustration.

I let him have it. Right on the nose with my right fist. I had never hit anyone in my life before. I saw the blood spurt from his nose, and threw my hand up to my face in horror at what I'd done. My fist was throbbing.

He gave me a look of utter disbelief as his hand covered his nose. Blood oozed through his fingers and we both watched it drip onto the carpet. The coach driver beat a hasty retreat to his room just as Simon turned on his heel and swept down the corridor to his room, slamming the door behind him. I knew then he would never forgive me, and I couldn't understand why I had lashed out like that. It was so out of character and so unprofessional of me. If I'd been thinking more clearly, I could have waited until I got home and made a voodoo doll of him and stuck pins in it.

Shit! What had I done?

The journey home was horrendous. Simon abjured all responsibility and sat behind his paper nursing a swollen, purple nose. He snapped at the kids as they asked him continuously what had happened to him. The more he snapped, the more they asked him. Simon had no knowledge of what a wind-up was.

Alison was shocked and surprised by what I had done but took my side, saying that I had only done what half the staff wanted to do anyway, and I would be a hero when I got back to work. I swore her to secrecy, which was a bit of a joke as she was the town crier of the staffroom.

I felt I owed it to Simon to explain why I had hit him, and I so wanted to tell someone about what had been happening to me, whoever it was. Perhaps Simon would understand why I felt so stressed and had lashed out like that. So, in the next motorway service station while the kids stuffed themselves full of burgers and fried chicken, I told a disbelieving Simon and Alison all about my experiences in the last few days.

When I had finished, they said nothing, but continued to look at me, perhaps waiting for me to burst out laughing and tell them it was a joke, or failing that, maybe run round the restaurant in my underwear.

Simon dabbed at his nose with his handkerchief; he was really making a meal of this.

"And you say it started in my stockroom." He continued to stare at me over his handkerchief, his voice echoing with disbelief and his expression one of extreme dislike.

I put my teacup down and ran my fingers through my hair. "Look, I know it sounds weird." I looked from one to the other, willing them to believe me. "But why would I make something like this up? It keeps happening. Simon, I feel out of control of my life. *This* is why I hit you, because I am so wound up by it all. I am really, really sorry. I'd just been back in time at that moment when you found me in the corridor, and it really freaked me out. I have never ever hit anyone before. I don't know what else to say. I can't apologise enough. Shit, Simon, I am so sorry, and why am I swearing? I don't swear. I'm an english teacher. I have enough vocabulary without… oh *shit*."

My voice petered out. Was this man made of stone? No wonder my fist hurt. And as for Alison, normally you couldn't shut her up, but she was just looking at me, stirring her Earl Grey until it slopped over the side of her cup.

Eventually, she put her spoon down. A small frown appeared on her expensively tanned face.

"I think you should see a doctor," she said, eventually. "It isn't that I don't believe you, but it could be that when you are having blackouts your brain is getting confused and you are seeing people you know in a different setting. People do *not* travel back in time. That's just science fiction. See the doctor and he will give you something. Maybe you are tired. You know what this job is like."

She stood up. "It's time we went," she said, gathering up her expensive wallet and designer glasses, and putting them in the Louis Vuitton shoulder bag. "The kids will be waiting at the coach."

Simon had nothing more to say but as he got up from the table he gave me a pitying look, and if he could have sent for the men in white coats there and then, he would have done so.

Well, that went well, I thought, as I climbed back into the coach. Bad move, big mistake. I should never have told them.

The rest of the journey passed quietly enough. The kids were tired, but I didn't dare sleep, frightened of closing my eyes and waking up somewhere else. Alison was chatty and friendly on the way home, lending me her magazines, and reassuring me that all would be well. I was glad to have had her on the trip, and told her so as we parted company when all the kids had been collected by their parents. Simon strode off into the night as soon as the driver put the brakes on. I was certain that my confrontation with him did not end here.

I could hardly keep my eyes open, as I climbed the stairs to my flat. I hoped Jeff wasn't there. All I wanted to do was collapse and not think of anything. It seemed as though every room in the flat was illuminated and I could hear voices from the kitchen. There was also a strong smell of paint, which was highly unusual.

I pushed open the door to the kitchen to reveal Jeff and an older man, who was covered in spatters of green paint, sitting at my kitchen table. They were playing dominoes. "Just waiting for the paint to dry," Jeff grinned at me, "and you've got a visitor."

I opened the door fully and there, standing by the table was Louis, my ex-husband, looking dark and brooding with something obviously on his mind.

CHAPTER SIX

So, here I was again, queuing for my fix in the bakery on a Monday, having been up all night wrangling with my ex-husband about our finances. Actually, it was me who was wrangling. Louis was perfectly reasonable as always.

However, he had dropped a bombshell. He wanted me to sell the flat. His current girlfriend was pregnant and he needed the money. He wouldn't let me buy him out. The flat had to go because he wanted to sell the furniture too and halve all the profits. He reminded me how I said I had never liked the place anyway, so it shouldn't be too difficult a decision for me.

So, a great start to the rest of my life. I would have no home and no furniture, I had assaulted a colleague, and I was going out of my mind.

"What can I get you?" The girl in the bakery was staring at me, hat askew as ever and a dab of flour on her cheek. The plastered fringe gleamed under the lights. I stared at her but again, there was no sign of recognition from her.

"Are you gonna get sumfin' or what?" A large pink tracksuit came into view as I whirled around. An angry face framed by the largest gold earrings on the planet was inches from mine. Normally I would have smiled politely, but not today.

"Have some manners," I shrilled at her, my voice beginning to sound slightly hysterical. "I haven't decided yet."

"Well make your bloody mind up, you dozy cow. Some of us have work to go to." She shoved her way past me, at the same time ordering two dozen pasties.

Leave some for the rest of us, I thought grimly, wondering whether they were all for her. I had no chance at all in getting past her large frame. She stood in front of me like a pink roadblock.

"This lady was first," smiled my friend in the frilly cap. "Is it your usual, croissant and coffee?" She winked at me, and I was taken aback. Did she know? Was she part of it? Was this some kind of conspiracy?

The blob in pink started to rant and rave and then the rest of the shop joined in, protesting that I was first. We mild-mannered English, who prefer to mind our own business and look away when anything embarrassing happens, suddenly started standing up for our rights. The meek were indeed inheriting the earth, I thought to myself as I staggered out of the shop, still in one piece.

I'd barely got through the school doors, which still hadn't been cleaned, when my friend the bursar stuck her head round the door of her empire and announced, with a smug smile, that the Head wanted to see me in her office right away.

I quickly brushed croissant crumbs from my coat, drained my coffee and knocked on the door. This would be about the promotion. I had interviewed well, but unusually, the governors had asked for time to decide. There wasn't anyone else with my experience. I had attended the boring but necessary courses, and I knew I was the hot favourite.

I knocked at her door whilst picking flakes of croissants from my new suede boots. They were so high I had to slope forwards when I walked. This new image of mine was not without pain. I waited and knocked again. The headmistress always made you wait outside her door. It probably gave her a feeling of power. I admired her, but didn't like her. Her aim was to turn the school around, as we didn't come out shining after the last Ofsted inspection. She had made it quite clear that you were either with her or against her in her ambitions. I had made it quite clear that I was on her side, even though I may have been late for assembly once or twice, but hey, I am a good teacher and surely that is what matters.

I was summoned in and I quietly closed the door behind me. I turned with a bright smile, which was not returned. She stood by the desk, which was bare except for a laptop. She had the most extraordinary hair which always fascinated me. The staff called her

Louis, not after my first husband, but Louis XIVth, as the hair was the same. She was standing in the same pose as the famous painting, one hand on the desk, but minus the ermine robes.

"Please sit down, Miss Woods." She made a sweeping gesture towards a chair which was considerably lower than her own, and then sat firmly behind the desk. This was not looking good.

Shouts of encouragement from the football field drifted through the open window, and on the words, "Fuck off you wanker, you're playing like a tart," she closed it firmly and turned to me.

"I want to discuss something which has come to my attention," she said, crisply. She sat down and leaned towards me from the other side of the desk, hands clasped together. "It seems as though you were ill on the trip to London." She gave me what she thought was a sympathetic smile. I thought her face might crack open.

"Get your finger out, you soft bugger. Move your arse for Christ's sake!"

She gave an impatient sigh, pushed her chair back and strode over to the window. She flung it open.

"Mr Simmons, would you please get the boys to moderate their language on the playing field!" she yelled across the pitch.

I didn't like to tell her that the voice she had heard was that of Mr Simmons, but I was too preoccupied by what she had said.

"Ill? I wasn't ill!" I exclaimed. "Who on earth told you that?"

She raised her eyebrows under the copious curls.

"So you didn't have blackouts. You didn't faint in the corridor in the hotel, or feel that you were er… going back in time?"

The eyebrows completely disappeared, and I leaned back in my chair and sighed heavily. Alison or Simon? Which one was Judas? I opened my mouth to reply, but she silenced me with a look and then stood up briskly and came round to my side of the desk.

"Miss Woods." She perched on the end of the desk so that she could look straight at me. "You are a highly respected member of staff, and your health is very important to us. I feel you may have been working a little too hard during the past few months and I believe there were one or two hiccoughs during the trip to London."

She held her hand up and shook her head as I tried to speak again. My defence was not getting a look-in.

"Fucking hell, tackle the bastard!" came a roar from the pitch.

My thoughts entirely, but I wasn't getting a chance.

"I would like you to take a week off, see your doctor and see the people at HR. You need to rest. We are aware of your past health record and starting a new job at a new school is very taxing. I have no complaints about your teaching methods and your classroom management is excellent, therefore I can only imagine that a week of complete rest will sort out the problem."

I leapt to my feet, my heart pounding. "No, I can't do that!" I shrieked, doing myself no favours by becoming almost hysterical. "I have my exam classes, and I am not ill, I assure you. Any problems which occurred on the trip were successfully dealt with."

I swallowed quickly. "And what about the head of year appointment?" I continued. "I thought that must be why you wanted to see me."

"Head of Year 9 has been offered to Mrs Ditmus-Flynn, and we have two regular supply teachers who can take your classes."

The soft and sympathetic voice was supposed to calm me, but it enraged me. Alison, the traitor, and I bet Simon was in on it somewhere.

She walked back slowly behind her desk and looked up at me suddenly. "You will be pleased to know that the head of history will not be pressing charges of assault. He is prepared to forget about the incident, for the good of the school."

"What!" I cried. "He was appalling on the trip, he did nothing but criticise me and he didn't help with any of the duties…"

"Miss Woods, go home and rest," she said sharply. "Please send a doctor's note to the office and let me know personally how you are getting on, by email. Go home and rest. That is all."

I was burning up with rage at the injustice of it all. I was so angry, I had to do something. I had to take action. I grabbed my handbag and rummaged through the pens, Tipp-Ex and tissues. My whole body was pulsating with fury. I found what I was looking for and flung a card across the table at her.

41

"And that is the telephone number of a very good hairdresser," I said, as I stormed out of the room.

I fled up the staircase to my room in the english block. It was mayhem up there. Andy, my head of department, was drowning in kids. He was being his usual unflappable self, trying to be reasonable above the persistent chatter. His hair was standing on end as it always did, and his shabby clothes looked as though they had been slept in, the result of having four children under five. Almost a biological impossibility I thought, but Andy had managed it.

"Jill, what's happening? The Head said you won't be in this week!" His voice carried above the chaos.

"What's happening here?" I waved my hands in the general direction of the disorder.

"Three staff off, no cover available, supply on their way, painters in my room and our office, and no heating in Room 5." His face was turning pink.

A convenient time to be away for a week then, I thought grimly. Good forward planning from the Head. Well done, Louis!

"You lot, shut up!" My voice boomed out. Three years of drama training on voice projection always came in useful in this job. The kids looked at me in astonishment, but they eventually became quiet.

I clicked into automatic pilot mode and filled my lungs with air once more. I put on my, I'm-in-charge-and-don't-you-forget-it face and launched into the fray.

"Year 7s in the library now. Leave your bags, chewing gum and mobile phones outside. Year 10s, set an example for heaven's sake. You are an exam class. Go to the library, keep an eye on Year 7s and find what you can on the internet about Bram Stoker and Mary Shelley. Go! Sixth form, in my room now, and switch those phones off or I will take them off you. Don't speak, don't question, leave Mr Tyler alone, and just go!"

There was a general murmuring and shuffling and I managed to reach Andy when there was a gap in the exodus. I loved him to bits. He was inspiring, a brilliant teacher and the kids adored him, but he relied on me to organise and shout when necessary. He always looked as though he could do with a good night's sleep and his limited wardrobe was always crumpled and buttoned up wrongly.

He gave me a lopsided grin, and rubbed his hand across his forehead. "Thought you were ill," he said.

"Oh, Andy," I sighed, "such a long story. I'll set work for my sixth form, and I'll email you. Oh, and by the way," I continued grimly, "do tell Alison when you see her, thanks for everything."

"See you at the book club. You can tell me everything then," he called to my retreating back.

When I reached my classroom, I found the sixth form in several stages of lounging across the desks.

"Why are you in such a strop, Miss?" asked Georgina, who was sorting out the contents of her handbag, presumably searching for her english file.

"Look, I'm going to be off this week," I said. "I'm sorry, I'm not well."

"Oh, Miss." There were murmurs of sympathy from the girls, and the boys looked hopeful of gaining some extra free time.

"My lessons are not cancelled," I continued, deflating the boys with one shot. "I want you to research the life of Dickens and find out what you can about Victorian London. Remember Dickens was a social reformer, and he had also suffered as a child himself. Find out what you can and I expect a presentation from each of you at the beginning of next week."

With that I smiled at them, trying to cover up the hurt and disappointment I felt. I hurried out of the room and down the steps before the Head could see me. I exited through the smeary doors, casting a look of venom at the bursar for good measure, then sat down on the low wall by the herb garden, and broke my heart with huge gasping sobs.

All the anchors of my life seemed to be dissolving. I was losing my flat, my furniture, my chance of promotion and perhaps even my job. I was drifting, ungrounded, living a nightmare and I didn't know what to do, or who to turn to. I buried my face in my hands as my world caved in around me.

CHAPTER SEVEN

It was moments before I became aware of it again, that damp, stagnant smell, but this time it was much worse. It filled my nostrils until I felt like choking. Suddenly, the quiet and tranquillity of the herb garden had changed. There was a rumbling and clattering that increased in volume with each breath I took.

I moved my hands slowly away from my face and my eyes snapped open. There, through a veil of faint mist, was the huge dome of St Paul's Cathedral, splendid and proud, rising high above me. The scene below took my breath away. I was sitting on a low wall outside a pawnbroker's shop. Gone was the wide thoroughfare of Ludgate Hill, and in its stead, a cobbled street jammed with horse drawn vehicles. I could smell the sweat from the bodies of the steaming horses as they passed me, pulling carriages, carts, hearses, fire engines, and smart hansom cabs. The noise was deafening; the air filled with the clatter of wooden wheels on cobbles, the snorting of horses and the shouting of humanity.

People were jammed together at the sides of the road and everyone seemed to be in a hurry. Amidst the noisy, bustling tradespeople were gentlemen sporting side whiskers and dark frock coats and women with bonnets or dainty hats decorated with feathers, perched on the side of their heads. Their bodies were swathed in an excess of material; cloaks, long skirts and petticoats trailed on the ground. A flock of sheep was holding up the traffic, adding impatient and angry voices to the cacophony. Above my head, a steam train whistled and clanked as it crossed the narrow bridge, filling the air with soot and smoke. Ragged children ran in and out of the crowds, splashing everyone with mud and debris. I put my hand to my nose to give myself relief from the terrible stench. Raw waste was piled up at the sides of buildings. It covered my shoes, and dampened the edges of my long skirts.

But even with this all going on around me, I didn't feel so afraid this time. The London of Dickens was here before me and, for whatever reason, I was a part of it, I would go with it, settle into its flow, so to speak. I had come to no harm before and had got back to my own world safely. This I wanted to savour, to enjoy, to experience. My own world was falling apart, so what did I have to lose?

The bell on the pawnbroker's shop clanged, then the door slammed shut and a young boy, looking remarkably like Jeff, my decorator, gave me a sunny smile.

"I got it back, Miss." He touched his cap. "Thank you for helping me and my family. We'd better go quick, as the mistress will be wondering where we are."

"Remind me where we're going." I got up to follow him, bunching up the cloth around my feet as I did so. There must be a more elegant way of doing this.

He pointed to a basket which was beside me on the bench.

"Feeding the poor, Miss." He coloured slightly. "And seeing my family, but Mistress says you can't tell the Master. Some of the children got the typhus, so we have to be careful."

My eyes widened in horror.

"It's not far, Miss, come on."

We joined the throng of humanity that seethed through Fleet Street. The boy dodged down narrow alleys, which were cobbled and filthy, the stones slimy underfoot. The windows of the upper stories of the buildings we passed were nearly touching and hardly any light seeped through into the street below. Filth and detritus covered the cobbles and ran down the side of the walls as waste was deposited into the streets below. Dead animals, rotting fruit, and straw, animal and human waste formed a soggy carpet and I lifted my skirts up in horror, trying to pick my way carefully through the mess and trying to keep up with the darting boy ahead of me.

We turned sharply into an even darker, narrow street. The sun that had been shining brightly by St Paul's was completely blocked out by the overhanging buildings. It seemed as though its brightness was not welcome here. There was an air of doom and desolation about the place. Gaunt, hollow-eyed children, their faces streaked with filth, stared at me from the doorways of the derelict houses, holding out their tiny hands for money, too hungry and weary to call out to me.

"Stop, please stop!" I shouted to the boy. He turned, gave me a quick glance and then ducked through a doorway, beckoning me to follow him.

I lifted my skirts and ran, slipping on the filthy street as I did so. I reached the house and bent my head to go through the narrow door. The stench of damp and intense cold hit me, and when my eyes became accustomed to the gloom, I could make out some shadowy figures in the room, a group of children sitting in a row on the bed. A woman, whom I presumed to be their mother, was talking earnestly to the lad who had accompanied me. He looked at me, expecting me to speak, but I didn't know what to say.

"The basket, Miss," he said, gently, as he saw my hesitation.

I held it out and the woman took it gratefully. She was so close to me and I could see she was very young, but so very thin; the hand clutching her shawl was like a bird's claw.

"Thank you, Mum." She bobbed a brief curtsey and emptied the basket carefully, laying bread and fruit and meat on the table. The children surrounded her and began pulling at her skirts to be fed, their faces pale with malnourishment.

I continued to stare. I'd read of the hunger and desperation of the poor but had never imagined it could be like this. There was one bed, covered by sacking and a worn blanket, the table being the only other item of furniture. It was dark and freezing cold and the only sound came from one of the children who lay whimpering on the bed. I held my handkerchief to my nose discreetly because of the stench, not to mention the fear of infection.

The woman handed the food out to the children who crammed whatever they were given into their mouths, then she gave the basket back to me with a faint smile.

"We must go back, Miss," the boy said. He moved away from the table and walked through the door, giving the briefest of goodbyes to the young woman, slipping something into her hand as he did so.

"No, stop!" I said desperately. "I'll see if I've got any money. I want to help you and your children."

I searched around my clothes but found no purse, so instead I stripped off my gloves and undid the bonnet from my head.

"Sell these," I said, pushing them into her hands. She grasped them to her as if afraid I would change my mind, and with that I followed my companion out into the daylight.

But there was no sunlight in this miserable place. It had grown darker, and it was difficult to see. A fog seemed to have descended onto the street and I shouted out to my companion.

I blinked repeatedly, my eyes watering, and when the mist started to clear, I found myself back on the low wall by the herb garden, outside the main doors to the school.

The stench of the street still lingered in my nostrils. How long had I been away?

I looked at the lavender bushes, their flowers turning brown as autumn faded into winter. The air here smelt of soft, damp earth, yet it was no more real than the stink of the London streets. I tried to think it through but there was no logic, nothing to latch on to. People didn't travel back in time. It didn't happen, and if that was the case and it was all in my head, what was happening in there? Also, who could I tell? Who could I go to? I'd lose my job. Better to go along with what the Head had suggested for appearance sake, but that didn't help my own sanity.

Why was it happening, and why were people I knew with me in the past? They didn't know me, they didn't recognise me except as Miss Woods, the governess. Miss Woods, my own name. It was like I was living in two worlds.

I sighed and buried my head in my hands as I tried to think, to work it all out. The strangest part was seeing Chris again. Why was he in my other life? There was no recognition from him, either. I started to think what the trigger could be and how I could avoid it. There must be something I did which kept sending me back, but for the life of me, I couldn't find any links. What if I got stuck there, in my other life? What if I couldn't get back? What if I was driving, or in front of a class, would I just disappear?

I gave a heavy sigh. Didn't I have just enough to deal with in my present life without having to manage two. Everything seemed to have fallen about my ears, home, ex-husband, job. I needed to get my present life in order but the question was… where to begin?

I turned to pick up my bag, when I caught a glimpse of the boy I had seen in the exam hall, poised on the steps of the main entrance to the school. He hoisted his bag on his shoulder and as he put his hand on the door in order to push it open, he turned to look straight at me. He smiled, and the likeness to Chris was so striking that I was immediately transported back to those halcyon days when I first met Chris at university. I had moved on, and deliberately suppressed those feelings but now they returned to overwhelm me. The boy was gone, but my senses were stirred and powerful emotions tumbled through my body, reawakening memories of long-forgotten passion, the kind that filled every membrane and cell of my body so that I could hardly live or breathe without it. He had been a part of everything I did. The sun was brighter because he was with me; there were not enough hours in the day to be with him. The coincidence of seeing two people, so like him, in very different circumstances, must mean something. *Was Chris the link to all this?* I made a note to find out who the boy was. That could be my starting point.

I threw my bag in the car, and set off for home, but I was so disturbed by strong memories, and my experience in the dark London streets, that my legs were trembling as I pressed the accelerator and drove away from Primrose Meadows.

CHAPTER EIGHT

I had fully intended to go home, ring my much-neglected friend Liz and seek her advice, before I did anything I might regret. So, how I came to be sitting at my kitchen table with Jeff and his rotund friend is still a mystery to me. Girlfriend Arlene was making drop scones at my stove, and coffee was flowing freely, thanks to Jeff.

When Jeff saw the state I was in when I returned home after only an hour at work, he immediately phoned Arlene, and as usual, decorating of any description was put on hold.

Jeff's friend, Rick, was called to the kitchen from the dining room where he was splattering the ceiling, and singing Elvis songs.

"Rick's got a gig tonight," explained Jeff as he flicked the switch on the kettle. "He does Elvis impersonations so he practices while he paints. I quite like to hear him really. We don't need the radio on. Saving your batteries, eh, Jill? Go on, Rick, let's have, Love me Tender!"

"No, no, thanks, not right now." I gave Rick a brief smile and sank into a chair. "Some other time."

Arlene had arrived earlier in a flurry of keys and handbags, five feet tall, dressed in vintage clothes and oozing self-confidence. She shook her hennaed head at me and announced that she could see I was a troubled soul.

"Let's hear all about it then, Jill," she boomed from the stove. You didn't expect to hear such a loud voice from such a small body.

Sometimes, I think it's easier to confide in strangers, and although I was wary after the episode with Alison and Simon, I did need someone to talk to, if only for them to tell me that things weren't as bad as I thought.

"It's flickin' amazing. Just flickin' amazing!" said Rick as he wiped his paint-encrusted hands onto my tea towels. "I saw a UFO once, and nobody would believe me. I really saw it. It's getting people to believe you that's the trouble. I got banned for a while from my bowls club, 'cos they thought I was mental."

"You also think that Elvis is still alive. This is different," said Arlene. "I think this is about regressive memory, Jill, and if you want to talk to me in private about this, these two can disappear."

Jeff and Rick looked at each other in disappointment.

"No, it's fine, Arlene," I said. "It's good of you to listen, all of you. Just explain to me what this is, explain to me what's happening if you can. If you have any theories at all, I'd be happy to hear them, please."

Arlene smiled indulgently at me and put a pile of scones in front of us and Jeff started to slap copious amounts of butter on them. My butter, of course. She pulled up a chair beside me, and sat down. She took my hand in hers and fixed me with a rather disconcerting stare from her slanting cat-like eyes.

"Well," she said, eventually, "*I* believe we've all lived before this lifetime in some capacity, and in our previous lives we've also shared our time with the same people, but the relationships may have been different."

There was a pause as we all digested this, as well as the scones.

"So, Arlene, in a past life you could have been my boss, *or* my servant?" suggested Jeff as he spooned the last of my strawberry jam onto his plate.

"Exactly," said Arlene, throwing him a quick glance. "This is why we sometimes carry baggage from our past life into this one. Our cells still contain memories from our past lives and experiences."

"Which could explain why some relationships you have with people are wrong, or don't work out, or you really feel a strong bond with others," Jeff chipped in as he took a large bite of his scone. He and Arlene were like a double act, but I am not convinced she wanted all of his suggestions as she kept giving him sideways glances when he spoke. They were the same glances I used to give Louis when I wanted him to shut up.

"I wonder what my flickin' missus was in my past life," Rick enquired, as he set about demolishing the rest of the scones.

He had a large face and very small eyes but his mouth was like an open letter box, taking in whole scones at an amazing speed. "Cos sometimes we want to kill each other," he continued.

Arlene gave him a look and his smile flickered and died, and he was quiet.

"Sorry," he whispered, spraying crumbs across the table, "carry on."

Arlene moved closer to me. "Somehow, Jill, you have found a window into your past life." She paused. "Maybe there's something you have to do, a journey you have to make, some unfinished business."

"Temporal paradox," Rick piped up.

"What?" Arlene snapped, obviously becoming tired of the interruptions.

"Isaac Asimov. You have to fix a paradox or you will fade into oblivion." He wiped his mouth and we all turned to look at him. "Someone else may have gone back in time and killed one of your ancestors, so actually you don't exist, so you have to go back to fix it so that you can exist. I read that in one of his books. The End of Eternity, I think it was."

We all looked at each other in surprise whilst trying to work out this theory.

"But I do exist," I said eventually. "I'm alive. I'm here."

"Or," suggested Jeff, "you could actually be living two lives, and one of them is in a parallel universe, in which case you do exist, but there are two of you."

Rick nodded in agreement. "Another universe where The King is still alive," he said. "Any more scones going? They're flickin' beautiful."

Arlene's eyes turned back on me. "There you are, Jill," she said, sounding none too pleased that her theory was not the only one, "three very different theories… science, science fiction and, of course, *my* more spiritual one."

She glanced sideways at the boys and I could imagine the debate going on in Jeff's house tonight whilst he made the tea and Arlene did her nails. She started to collect her belongings, signalling in an imperious way to Jeff and Rick that it was time to leave.

Rick gave me a warm handshake as he was leaving. "Don't you worry, love, if knowledge can create problems it's not through ignorance that we solve them."

I looked at him blankly.

"Asimov," he said. "I'll lend you some of his books. They're doing the rounds down our bowls club at the moment but I'll get one to you. By the way, say hello to Elvis for me, if you see him on your travels."

"Thanks, Rick, I will." I couldn't help smiling as I watched them walk down the stairs. Arlene's voice boomed out as she barked orders at Jeff about what he needed to buy for their meal tonight, and Rick kept on hinting about an invite. The outside door banged behind them. Jeff must have closed it in his own inimitable way. I sighed and went back into the kitchen.

I was alone again.

I spent the rest of the day at my computer trying to make some sense of the theories I had been given, but gave up after a while, feeling more confused than ever. I decided to visit our physics department at some point, to see what they had to say, without revealing what was happening to me, of course.

I closed the laptop with a snap and needing a distraction, I decided to phone Liz and we agreed to meet for lunch, now that I had an empty diary during the day.

I poured myself a very large glass of Merlot and curled up on the window-seat in my flat. I stared out onto the park as I watched the flickering lights of the town beyond, my thoughts far away. When I had talked to Liz, my closest friend, more and more memories from my immediate past had surfaced, and I found some of them very difficult to deal with. Liz had helped me through those terrible times when Chris had left, yet I had severely neglected her friendship, always using work as an excuse.

We had arranged to meet tomorrow after my doctor's appointment. I didn't want to see a doctor, but I had to be seen to be obeying the Head. I hadn't directly mentioned Chris in our conversation, but he was there, always there, the Adonis in the room. I shut my eyes tightly, trying not to remember... the smell of him, the warmth, his voice, the sheer beauty of him, but it was all there, locked away but now released, flooding through my whole being, the best and the worst time of my life.

CHAPTER NINE

Liz has been such a vital part of my life that it is hard to imagine living without her. A revolutionary at university, a militant feminist whose bedside reading was Erica Jong and Spare Rib Magazine, she fell madly in love with Chris's best friend Pete, opened a health shop with him instead of going into teaching, and now had three children and a business to run.

She arrived for lunch, ten minutes late, which was par for the course. Her curls were escaping from an untidy bun, which could have been assembled anytime in the last three days, a smudge of flour on her cheek and her familiar Julia Roberts's smile.

"Car broke down and I forgot my purse, so it might have to be on you." The smile widened and she kissed my cheek and dropped into the chair opposite to me with a long sigh.

"You look awful, Jill," she said, appraising me behind her round glasses. "How are you handling the divorce? It's such a shame, we so liked Louis, you know."

She had a quick glance at the menu. "Stir fry with tofu for me." She shrugged her arms out of her coat. "I've got about an hour until I pick the kids up, so how are you, sweetheart?"

She glanced at me. "Let's order," she said. "By the look of you, it could be a long lunch."

An eager young waiter appeared at our side, pencil poised as soon as Liz put the menu down.

"Tofu stir fry for me." She looked over her glasses at me. "Jill?"

"Beef stir fry, with lots of meat," I said to the waiter. I shot her an amused glance as she shuddered, "and two glasses of Shiraz."

"I'm driving, Jill," Liz protested.

"Make that two small glasses and a bottle of water," I said to the waiter who was writing everything down on his notepad. "Believe me, Liz, you'll need a glass of something when you hear what I have to say."

"Go ahead," she said, as she started to polish her glasses on her scarf. "Nothing you do, my friend, can ever surprise me."

Five minutes later Liz was still staring at me, lost for words, which was very unusual.

"Please say something," I said.

The wine arrived and she took a deep swallow, then looked at me again, as if making sure that I was still there.

"Jill, are you absolutely sure that none of this is your imagination going wild? Don't be cross with me, I'm not being patronising, but you know how ill you were after Chris left. Seeing that boy at school may have brought everything to the fore again. And don't forget that dreams can be so vivid. Sometimes I wake up and I feel I'm still in the dream, and the dream feels like real life."

I sighed and twirled the stem of my wine glass round with my fingers. All this was really happening to me, so why was it so difficult for people to understand? Why in God's name would I make anything like this up? I sat back in my chair and looked at my friend.

"Liz, you have to believe me, it is not a dream. It happens anytime, in the day or night. There's no pattern that I can see…"

Liz frowned. "So you could be shopping, watching TV, driving, or in front of a class."

"Yes," I said impatiently. "Jeff's girlfriend, Arlene, thinks it could be my memory regressing to a past life. It is so real. I can smell the streets, feel the cloth of what I am wearing, feel the heaviness of the skirts as I walk, and Chris was there, he was real, he was standing in front of me. At least, it was someone who looked so like him."

Liz looked thoughtful.

"Do people miss you when you appear and reappear in the two worlds? Do you disappear from sight?"

I shook my head. "No, I don't think so, except for the first time it happened, when I was absent from the class, but in the other times it seems as though the two lives are running parallel and I am going in and out of each of them. I have no control over it. There seems to be no trigger. The first time it happened I touched a book, but when I touched it again at another time nothing happened. Someone or something is controlling this and it isn't me, and that's what scares me."

The food arrived and we ate in silence for a while, each of us deep in thought. You could almost feel the energy fizzing, as our brains went into overdrive.

I took a deep breath, not sure what reaction I would get, but the taboo subject needed to be raised.

"Have you heard from Chris?" I asked.

She glared at me but my gaze remained level. "Have you heard from him?" I repeated. "This could be something to do with him. I need to know."

Liz sighed. "He's still living in America, with his wife. He emails us. What else do you want to know?"

I hardly heard her. As I looked at her whilst she was speaking, the room shifted focus. She was still speaking but I couldn't hear her anymore. I jammed the heels of my hands into my eyes and rubbed hard. There was a sweet smell of roses with hints of lavender, then the pungent smell of wax, perhaps furniture polish. I opened my eyes and there was Liz, but Liz with glossy ringlets and loops in her hair, tying a tiny hat onto her head, whilst speaking rapidly to me. There was a swish of silk as she moved away from me to check herself in the gilt mirror which hung over a fireplace. The cafe had gone, and I was in some kind of elegant drawing room. The light came from a log fire burning in the grate, and from the slightly hissing gas lamps, which lit up the portraits in their heavy frames. There was a richness and opulence about the room, and my eyes lighted on an ornate gold clock which chimed six o' clock. Six o'clock, when and where?

"My dear Miss Woods, the children," said the woman who looked like Liz. "We must not insult Mr Dickens by arriving late."

"Mr Dickens…?"

There was another rustle of silk as Liz came over to me, pulling on a pair of leather gloves. I was fascinated by her clothes. She wore a rich green jacket with tiny buttons over voluminous skirts, but as I looked more closely at her face, I became aware that this wasn't Liz. There was a slight difference in her features, but this woman looked so much like her.

There was a quiet knock at the door and a man who could only have been the butler entered. "The carriage is ready, your Ladyship," he announced.

She waved her hand in acknowledgement and he gave a polite nod and disappeared, and as he did so a boy and a girl burst into the room. They looked like miniature adults in the clothes they wore. The boy looked like his mother with the same dark curls, but the girl was the image of her father with those same cheekbones and vivid blue eyes.

They ran over to me, chattering together so that it was almost impossible to hear what they were saying. Their mother put out her hands to stop them and, with a hand on each shoulder she bent down in a swoosh of skirts and stared at them, her face level with theirs. "Perfect behaviour from both of you, or Papa will be cross. And so will Mr Dickens."

"Yes, Mama," they replied obediently.

Liz stood up and smoothed her skirts. "Now hold Miss Woods's hands both of you. Emma, Christopher, remember how we behave. Thank you, Miss Woods, they look beautiful."

Emma. The name made my heart flip over. She put her warm little hand into mine, and as I looked down into a pair of bright blue eyes, I felt myself welling up. I pulled myself together just as Christopher took my hand.

Her Ladyship flashed me a bright smile, Liz's Julia Roberts's smile, and I followed her out of the room and down the elegant staircase, a little child on each hand. My skirts were so heavy and my waist was so constricted that I could only breathe in little gasps. Chris was waiting for us at the bottom of the staircase, looking like every woman's dream of Mr Darcy, resplendent in evening dress and white shirt, his blond hair shining under the lamplight. This man was so like Chris, the tilt of his head as he appraised me, those high cheekbones and sculptured face.

"Your bonnet, Miss Woods?" Chris's blue eyes looked at me coldly. I had forgotten his obvious contempt for me. It was then I remembered I'd given my bonnet and gloves to the poor lady I had met, so that she could buy food. I hesitated, not knowing how to respond.

Liz turned to the girl from the bakery who was standing to attention by the door. "Jenny, my blue bonnet, quickly!" she said.

Jenny fled up the stairs and returned with a bonnet just as the butler opened the door for us. I jammed it on my head as I followed Liz out of the house. She had saved the day for me, saved me from being embarrassed and I was very grateful.

As we stepped out into the chilly night air, I looked around me, eager to drink everything in. The familiar dome of St Paul's soared above us. I was in London. Glossy black horses stood waiting patiently on the street. One was pawing the ground with his hoof, making a clattering noise. Steam rose from his flared nostrils as he snorted impatiently. The black and gold carriage squeaked as Liz was helped inside by a smart footman. The children scrambled inside after her and I took the hand of the footman as he held it out for me. I hesitated in order to look about me for a little longer, fascinated by the thick darkness of the night, and the pools of orange around the gas lamps. The lamp on the carriage threw shadows across the face of the coachman as he sat upright, whip in hand, and instead of the endless London traffic there were carriages of all sizes rumbling and clattering through the street.

I stepped into the dark interior, the smell of leather filling my nostrils and I sat down cautiously on the hard seat. Chris was the last person inside and as he sat down, he hit the roof with his cane and there was a jolt, a jangle of harness and the sound of the horses neighing as they began to move.

It is difficult to describe the complete fascination of actually being there, being present in another time. This was no BBC costume drama. This was real, and here was I on my way to see Charles Dickens perform. Charles Dickens! But, the most frightening and disturbing feeling was that I was sitting opposite to someone who was the image of a man I had loved all my adult life, and the turmoil of feelings was suffocating. He was sitting so close to me that I could feel the heat from his body, and we were breathing the same air. I tried not to stare at the immaculate long coat and waistcoat and the glittering watch chain. His long fingers were curled around those of his wife, to whom he gave every attention. He was explaining to his family about the performance we were about to see, encouraging the children not to be frightened by the ghosts.

The carriage stopped with a jolt, the door was opened and the steps unfolded. I descended into a film set. We were outside a theatre. I should have known which one, but everything looked so different. There were throngs of people climbing out of carriages and moving up the steps towards the entrance to the theatre. The men were all in black and the women fluttered around them like peacocks in their rich colours and full skirts, bonnets and feathers perched on their heads. I grabbed the children's hands and walked quickly away from the road, where carriages were moving off in every direction, the sound of their wheels and the neighing of the horses adding to the noise and confusion.

We climbed the steps of the theatre, swept up by the crowds, into a foyer thronged with people. There was a steady hum of voices, interspersed with the tinkle of women's laughter. There was an air of excitement which I felt was increasing as I moved quickly though the room, still clutching the hands of the children. I kept my employers in sight as they greeted and smiled at acquaintances. We climbed up another staircase. My eyes were everywhere; oh for my mobile phone to record the glitter of the jewels, the chandeliers, the clothes, the flowers, the wonderful spectacle of Victorian England at the theatre. I could not believe what was about to happen... we were going to see an actual real life reading by Charles Dickens. I sent up a silent prayer. Please don't let me go back yet. Let me experience it if only for a short while.

We were seated in a private box which overlooked the stage. I was with the children, a little behind Chris, so I could now gaze my fill. The children were excited by this treat. It must have been close to Christmas, but I wasn't sure of time. I was brimming with excitement myself. What would he read? What would he be like? There was a hush and such an air of anticipation. There came an enthusiastic rumble of applause, which sounded muted as everyone was wearing gloves, and there he was, a tall, thin dignified figure, striding across the stage, a bright red flower in his button hole and his hair brushed forward, which gave him a rather eccentric look. My heart was hammering and my palms felt damp. I gazed and gazed at one of my heroes, full of wonder and incomprehension as to how I came to be here at all.

He paused in front of a pair of bright red screens, by a small desk, where there was a decanter of water, a small bouquet of flowers and a book. He began, his voice booming out across the theatre.

"I would ask that you imagine you are with a small group of friends, assembled to hear a tale told."

He looked about him. The only sound was a faint hiss of gas lamps.

Dickens walked forward. "Marley was dead to begin with: there is no doubt whatever about that."

I held my breath, this could not be true. I was spellbound, totally absorbed, hardly daring to move. It was the most fascinating performance I had ever seen. I thought of all the mechanics and effects of today's theatre, yet here we were, transported by this one man. A man who became all his characters with such energy and attention to detail. He contorted his body as Mr Scrooge and when he became Marley's ghost, the children hid their heads in my lap, terrified.

Chris turned round to smile at them and I felt the glow of his warmth and love towards them reflecting on me. He reached out his hand to touch his daughter's head and I felt the soft pressure on my legs and saw the golden blond hairs on the back of his hand.

Then he was gone, and Liz was there in the cafe, finishing her tofu with a smack of her lips.

"Gorgeous," she said, throwing her napkin onto the table. "How was yours?"

CHAPTER TEN

Liz stared at me incredulously as I explained what had happened to me throughout our meal together.

"You were *here*. You were talking to me. You were telling me about what you had said to the Head. How can you have been watching Charles Dickens?" She stared at me, the trace of uncertainty in her eyes. I looked at my plate. It was clean, my meal finished, and I didn't remember one bite.

After a glance at me, and then at her watch, she pushed her chair back and planted a kiss on the top of my head. "I'll call you," she said, fleeing out of the door. Even my best friend didn't believe me. How could anyone believe me?

Jeff announced, "There's a letter from your school on the dining table," as I walked into my kitchen. "You look awful. I've just made falafel. It's a new recipe."

I sank down onto a kitchen chair and he put a cup of strong coffee in front of me. I stared at it for a while, my head still full of Chris and the performance I'd seen. I felt as if my brain was going to burst.

Eventually, I took a grateful gulp, and looked at Jeff. The jeans were particularly tight today and I didn't need any further distractions. I had a momentary vision of Jeff struggling into them each morning, lying down to zip them up. If he wasn't so good looking, would I tolerate his lack of interest in decorating my flat?

"Jeff, you're my decorator, not my cook, or PA," I said, dragging my gaze away to further up his body. He had such a lovely smile, and I smiled back. Sucker!

A plate of falafel balls and fresh green salad replaced the empty coffee cup and not remembering a thing about lunch, I tucked in gratefully.

"Louis's coming around at six." He put another plate on the table and drew up a chair, tucking his blond curls behind his ears, before proceeding to demolish his creation. "He wants to sell, you know."

"I know, I know, but I don't want to. I feel more settled here now."

Settled! Would I ever feel settled again?

"Then, you'll have to buy him out." Jeff was drowning his falafel balls in sweet chilli sauce. "I also think you should get a new shower in the bathroom before I start decorating. The water just trickles out. I hardly got wet at all."

Jeff in my shower? Oh God, I couldn't cope with this.

I glanced up at him. "I think we should put the decorating on hold, Jeff, until we know what Louis wants to do."

"Fair comment," he said as the doorbell rang. "Shall I get it?"

An hour later my ex-husband and I sat staring at each other over the table, impasse.

I looked at his dark eyes and floppy hair which was only slightly tinged with grey, and felt a sadness that engulfed me so much I could hardly speak. Every couple must ask themselves the same question, what happened? What *did* happen? We used to get on so well. He now had a fiancée and a baby on the way. Unfair advantage. Where were my supporters?

If I could sum Louis up in a word, it would be, kind. I met him when I was still a train wreck from my relationship with Chris, and he had loved me with a patience beyond belief. Now he seemed to be my enemy, and I was near to tears.

He leaned back in his chair, exasperated, and rubbed the back of his head with his hand, a familiar gesture when he was in a difficult situation. I used to tell him he would go bald if he didn't break the habit.

"I need the cash, Jill. I need somewhere to live, somewhere for the baby and Veronica. I'm still at Mike's, and a flat full of rampant divorcés is not the place for them."

"Sounds like fun to me!" I tried to lighten the atmosphere to stop myself from snivelling.

He started rubbing at his head again, encouraging the baldness I kept warning him about.

I leaned forward. "Louis, what happened to us?" I asked. "Why did we suddenly start arguing all the time? Why did you leave?"

He stopped rubbing and stared at me as if I had performed some kind of public indiscretion.

"You want to talk about feelings?" he said. "We could never discuss feelings."

I sat back quickly, stung by his words. "What do you mean? Of course we could."

He gave a snort of laughter, unexpected and hurtful. He placed his hands on the table as though he was going to either stand up or pounce on me. "Jill, I loved you, but you would never let me get close to you. I thought I could change you. That was my mistake."

I was starting to become uncomfortable. I didn't want to hear any more.

"Fine," I said, standing up, "if we can't decide what to do, if we can't agree, let's do it through our solicitors."

Louis remained seated and he looked at me sadly. "I had to leave. I was lonely. You can only love someone for so long if it's not returned."

I recoiled as if he had slapped me.

"You knew when I married you that I didn't want children," I said, my voice starting to break. I looked hard at the table so he couldn't see that I was upset.

Louis stood up and came round the table to stand next to me. "I understood, because of what had happened to you, that you didn't want them at the time, but we were very young then, and both had careers, but there's more to life than that for me." He put his hand on my arm to turn me towards him, to look at him. My eyes were welling up and so were his.

"If only you'd let me in." A small tear found its way down his cheek as he looked at me. I wanted to wipe it away. I wanted to undo all the hurt, but I stood there, rigid, watching him cry.

He wiped the back of his hand across his eyes.

"If only you'd let me talk to you like I'm doing now."

I had a momentary vision of how things might have been. Louis was a good man and he had tried to make me happy. I felt an overwhelming wave of regret.

"I really messed things up, didn't I?" I gave him a watery smile, but my heart felt like lead.

He gently took my hands. "Don't blame yourself. I was too weak, too eager to please. Maybe we weren't right together."

"And now you love someone else," I said brightly.

He let go of my hands, and looked at me steadily. "Yes, I do, but I'll always care about you too. You've been a part of my life for a long time."

He reached out to me again, as if to give me a hug, and I turned towards him. I wanted to be held. I wanted to rest my weary head against his warm, comforting shoulder again. I wanted to tell Louis everything, but suddenly the atmosphere changed. It became cold, so cold and there was that smell again, the stench of old London, the yellow fog coming down. There was a confusion of noise, people were shouting and singing. Louis's hand was still there and I reached for it through the mist, but it wasn't his hand. This one was gnarled and calloused, and it pulled at me roughly. I was outside, in a noisy backstreet. It was gloomy and narrow and the air was filled with the smell of decay. The fog swirled around me, making it difficult to see anything clearly. The noise came from some kind of alehouse which kept disgorging its inmates onto the street followed by roars from within.

I could smell the foetid breath of the man who had hold of me. He grinned showing blackened teeth and his hands were pawing at my jacket, tearing at the buttons. He shoved his hand up my skirt and pulled me towards him. I struggled but although drunk, he was very strong and laughed at my efforts, tearing at my clothes until my shoulders were bare. I screamed and kicked, fear making me strong, but he laughed even more.

"Help me!" I yelled, looking around frantically as I felt his breath on my body.

His grizzled face changed as I called for help, and he gave an angry growl.

"Who's going to help you, grandly dressed as you are?" he sneered, and his hand dealt me such a blow across the face that I screamed. I was terrified and my cheek stung. The street was filled with people; scruffily dressed women in faded shawls and tattered dresses, children and young girls were being offered to passers-by, mainly to filthy, drunken men. Nobody gave me a second glance. I may as well have been invisible. I yelled and struggled as my dress was torn away, white hot panic prickling its way through my body, when suddenly, he let go and fell to the floor like a stone.

The boy who looked like Jeff was standing behind him, a plank of wood in his hand.

He clutched my arm, and led me away, both of us stumbling past people who were shouting and grabbing at us. We fled along the crowded streets, the sound of what must have been police rattles behind us. We kept on running, the noise of pounding feet following us, relentlessly. Suddenly, Jeff pushed open a door and we both fell inside. He slammed it behind us but it just swung backwards and forwards on its one hinge, so we crawled further into the darkness, hearing the footsteps running past. We were in the same house we'd been in before, when we visited Jeff's family. As I was about to speak, the same young woman came out of the gloom and put her fingers to her lips, until the sound of footsteps died away.

Jeff clambered to his feet. "I'm going to get the Master," he said. "We've been searching for you."

I started to speak, to thank him, but he was gone, into the night. I turned back to the young woman who held out her shawl to me. It was then I realised that I had been running through the streets half naked. I wrapped it around myself gratefully, and as I did so, I caught sight of her young family peering out of her skirts at me.

I looked up at her dark shadowed eyes. "I'd like to help you." I said.

She stared blankly at me.

I got to my feet, wrapping the shawl tighter around me, as once more Jeff opened the door.

"Miss Woods, the Master is here with the carriage. We have to go, quickly."

I unwound the shawl, not caring about how I looked and handed it back to her with a grateful smile. I followed Jeff into the night, trying to cover the top half of my body with my hands.

"What is his name? The name of the master?" I panted, as I ran alongside Jeff, struggling to keep up with him. He looked at me in astonishment and stopped running.

"Why, it's Lord Beaumont. Lord Charles Beaumont. You must know that, Miss."

I nodded. Of course, it made perfect sense, and what a coincidence. Or was it?

"And his wife?" I asked.

"Lady Elizabeth, Miss." He looked at me quizically.

I ploughed on regardless. "Remind me of *your* name?" I said, giving him an apologetic smile.

"John, his Lordship's footman, but I can handle the horses better than most, so I drive his Lordship the most." He touched his cap. "We'd better hurry, Miss."

The carriage stood at the end of the street, the horses snorting, their breath steaming into the fog. Lord Charles was on the pavement, and he helped me up, slamming the door behind us, and rapping the roof with his cane. "Beaumont House," he shouted.

There was a jolt and we were off, back to the family's London home. We were alone in the carriage. He held out the travelling rug to me and I blushed, conscious that I was showing far more flesh than a governess should.

He continued to watch me as I entombed myself in the wool. I was conscious of his eyes on me and we were so close that I could see the faint rise and fall of his shoulders and hear the intake of his breath. This was no dream. This was real. He was real.

"Miss Woods…" His voice was cold. "You are employed to take care of my children, not to wander the streets of London alone at night."

"Lord Beaumont," I replied, becoming angry by his obvious lack of sympathy, "I have just had a very frightening experience. I have been attacked, almost raped. I didn't wander off deliberately; I must have become separated from the family. I do not wander the streets of London alone at night. This is not my fault and I feel it is unfair and unjust of you to blame me."

I would almost swear I saw the faint trace of a smile on his face, but it could have been my imagination. He continued to stare at me, and I was unnerved by his silence.

"You have a lot to say for a governess," he said, eventually.

"Your footman, John, rescued me," I continued. "He hit the man who attacked me with a plank and the police were chasing us. I hope he will not be in trouble on my account. He probably saved my life."

Lord Charles continued to regard me, his gaze inscrutable. "The authorities have informed me that the man who attacked you is wanted for murder," he said.

I gasped, thinking what might have been. "John didn't kill him, did he?" I asked.

He shook his head and there it was again, that faint trace of a smile.

"So, the gallant young Robinson rescued you, did he?"

Lord Charles leaned back against the seat, and tapped his finger against the top of his cane, thoughtfully.

"Yes." I sat forward on my seat, trying to steady myself against the swaying and jolting of the carriage. "I would like to reward him. I think it was his family who helped to hide me. They live in a slum. The conditions are awful, and they don't have enough to eat. They can't pay the rent and their pig of a landlord will throw them out if they can't. Can we appeal to him? Can we pay him? The money can be deducted from my wages?"

I looked at him, hopefully.

The blue eyes looked at me levelly.

"*I* am that pig of a landlord," he said.

CHAPTER ELEVEN

The rest of the journey passed in a rather awkward silence. I was aware of the sound of the horses' hooves on the cobbles and the jingling of the bridles, but there was no further conversation between us. My cheek was sore, and it felt swollen, and I was still shaking, but the nearness of Lord Charles in the carriage and the fact that we were alone made me feel nervous and uncomfortable.

I was sharing my space with the exact double of the man who had dominated my young life. But it wasn't him. I had to keep telling myself, *this man is not Chris*, but as I caught glimpses of him as he sat opposite to me, staring out of the carriage window deep in thought, it was so hard to believe that it was not him.

More importantly, what was I doing here? Despite the theories of Jeff, Arlene and Rick, I found it difficult to believe that people could travel through time. It *was* impossible, and yet here I was. I felt scared and vulnerable because it seemed to be out of my control. If I was going to lead a double life then I had to find the trigger that sent me backwards and forwards through time, and most importantly, find the reasons why.

On our arrival back at Beaumont House, Lord Charles helped me out of the carriage and then after depositing his cane and hat with the butler, he swept up the staircase, calling over his shoulder that I was to see the housekeeper immediately. He had obviously lost interest in me, and of course, I was not of his class so I was not worth spending time with. This would take a bit of getting used to.

I was directed to her rooms by the butler, who kept sniffing disapprovingly, as he climbed the stairs behind me. I certainly was not flavour of the month in this household.

I knocked politely at the door I was directed to and, after a pause, an imperious voice shouted, "Come."

I opened the door with a sinking heart, knowing I had been in this same situation in my present life only days before. It had to be her, didn't it? And yes, there she was, frizzy hair swept protesting and screaming into a severe bun, her hand on the table. A replica of my beloved headmistress.

The room was oppressive, hung with heavy dark curtains and furnishings, the lamps shedding yellow pools of light and shade, giving the room a gothic feel. She emerged from the gloom, her face severe.

"Miss Woods, our new governess, I presume. I am Miss Tibbs, the housekeeper."

I was unsure of the etiquette here. Did I shake her hand, curtsey, kiss her on both cheeks? She looked like the type who would want a curtsey, so I gave her my best. She stopped walking towards me and her face registered shock. "My dear girl, you do not curtsey to me, you are a respected senior servant," she said stiffly.

She folded her hands across her chest and stared at me in astonishment. Then she became brisk and business-like.

"Nanny has put the children to bed. Your duties will begin at 9.30 after the family breakfast; the servant's breakfast is at 7.45, followed by prayers. Your trunk is in your room, which is opposite to mine. You will find water there to bathe your face. The household is relieved you have been found relatively unharmed. I hope you find your room comfortable. Goodnight."

I was dismissed, but I wasn't into this class war I seemed to be having, so I gave her my most brilliant smile.

"Oh, goodnight, lovely to meet you too. I'm sure we'll have such fun together." I gushed. She glared at me. So, she understood sarcasm. Excellent. We were sure to be great friends.

I turned and found my way out of the gloom. I really was Miss Popular in the Beaumont household, but if there's one thing teachers do not like, it is being told what to do. We can give it out all day, no problem, but we are not used to taking it.

As I was closing the door behind me, deciding whether or not to put two fingers up at it, I heard the sound of rustling skirts and then a small gasp. I turned swiftly to see Lady Elizabeth disappearing into what I thought was my room. I opened the door cautiously and there she was standing by the window, dressed in her outdoor clothes, her finger to her lips.

"Please close the door," she whispered. "I don't want anyone to see me."

"I thought you were dining at Rules with Mr Dickens," I whispered back as I closed the door and turned to face her.

She shook her head. "When we became separated from you, my husband and his footman went to look for you, and I was sent home with the children, but I didn't go home."

She looked round quickly as if she expected someone else to be listening. "You must promise me you will say nothing. If my husband asks you anything, I was here with you, discussing the children. You did not see me come into the house."

She stripped off her tight little gloves in an agitated manner.

"Can I ask where you have been?"

She shook her head. "No, I cannot tell you, but I am asking you to tell lies for me and for that I am sorry. I will explain where I was perhaps tomorrow but now, I cannot."

She glanced up at me, and gave me a wisp of a smile, then her face changed. "You are hurt." She rustled towards me. "Your face, what happened to you?"

"I was attacked in the street. I was rescued by John, the footman. His family looked after me, and they are so poor and they live in appalling conditions. It's awful. People shouldn't live like that!" I took a deep breath and looked straight at her. "Your husband is their landlord, Lady Beaumont."

She stopped in her tracks and her face closed up. "I must go," she said, briskly. "My maid is waiting for me, she will be tired, and she may become suspicious of my whereabouts."

She left the room in a swish of silk, and I sank down onto the bed feeling exhausted. After an hour of struggling to get out of my clothes and into a voluminous nightdress, I thought smugly that if Lady Elizabeth was having an affair, I would probably seriously consider jumping on her husband at my earliest possible convenience.

But this was not to be. I was woken by my mobile phone alarm which heralded my first day back at work after my week's unofficial suspension. I had to check the news to make sure what the date was and I flew round the flat, completely disorientated as I hadn't been here to do any preparations and my mind was full of my previous life. But I *had* done preparations. Sheaves of neatly piled papers were on the top of my briefcase. My other self had got it all sorted.

I had a quick shower, and I struggled into my only suit, determined to look professional. However, the face staring back at me sported a nice red bruise just above the cheekbone, from where the would-be rapist had hit me. This threw me completely, and made the situation I was in much more real. But how could I have sustained an injury from one hundred and fifty years ago? My other self had been here, preparing for my day at work. I must be living two lives! Here was the proof, but were the worlds colliding? I made another mental note to start reading Asimov. Maybe he could sort this out for me.

I dabbed some blusher on the other cheek and imagined what I would say to anyone who asked how the bruise got there. "Well, after I had been with Lord and Lady Beaumont and their children to hear Charles Dickens read A Christmas Carol, I was attacked by a Victorian drunk who tried to rape me… by the way this is in my past life which I disappear into every now and again. I am a governess, you know."

From now on I must be very careful who I confided in. I needed help and explanations, but from the right sources. This job was everything to me and I did not want to further jeopardise my chances of promotion. It was unlikely they'd employ anyone they thought was completely barking.

I threw the rest of my make-up into my bag, grabbed my copy of A Christmas Carol and sped off to the bakery for breakfast. This was where it began. Somehow, I felt, the answer was here.

I backed into a convenient parking space and went to push open the door, my mouth watering in anticipation, but it didn't give. I looked up at the door, and read the scribbled sign.

"Closed for refurbishment until further notice."

Damn it!

Conscious of the time and the looming 9am meeting with my headmistress, I headed back to school, hungry and disappointed. As usual, there was nowhere to park. I didn't belong to the 8am swots who bagged their parking places early. Their system was to walk past the Head's office with a cheery "Hello" in order to gain a few points, and then they would watch the rest of us struggling to park, through the steam of their first coffee.

I abandoned my car by the bins, and was in the Head's office assuring her of my sanity, well before the appointed time.

"I'm going through a divorce," I explained, "and I haven't been sleeping very well. This has had no effect on my work, you understand."

"And how are you now?" The Louis XIVth wig seemed to have got even larger in my absence, and had turned a dark shade of auburn. The sun was shining on it, and it looked as though her head was on fire. If only!

"Fine, thanks. A good rest and everything's back to normal." I dragged my eyes from the auburn inferno, and gave her a reassuring smile. Then I got more serious.

"And I also owe you an apology. My rudeness to you was inexcusable."

She acknowledged my apology with a regal tilt of the head, and then said, "I hope you are fully prepared for our inspection this week, Miss Woods. I've been given very little notice, but I expect my staff to pull together for the sake of the children, and the school's reputation."

"Of course." Could I have grovelled anymore? It was embarrassing to witness myself.

I flashed her my warmest smile, which was not returned. "Absolutely," I said.

A buzzer broke the silence and I glanced round in surprise.

She stood up. "We have replaced the bell with a quiet buzzer." She *almost* smiled. "I think it will help to keep the children calmer."

"And the staff, hopefully," I mused, as I closed the door quietly and subserviently.

I fought my way to my classroom as the buzzer heralded a change of lesson and everyone was going a different way to me.

"This corridor is one way now, Miss," a cocky Year 7 girl informed me.

"Not for me, dear," I thundered, striding through the mob to my destination, battered by bags and elbows en-route.

In my absence, it seemed as though undercover detectives had trashed my classroom looking for clues. My sixth form dribbled into the room with their assortment of handbags, iPods in their ears and phones in their hand.

They greeted me in surprise, carefully unplugging and removing any items that smacked of technology from their persons. I had strict rules about that sort of thing.

"Miss, thank God you're back. We had Miss double-barrelled thingy and she was rubbish. She knows nothing about Dickens."

Alison, I thought triumphantly.

"Where are the boys?" I enquired, as the girls rifled through their enormous handbags looking for files.

"Football tournament. They tried to find you to excuse themselves."

"Mmm," I muttered, taking A Christmas Carol from my bag. "Well if that's the case I will put the presentations on hold for the moment, and instead I'm going to show you exactly how Charles Dickens would have performed his story in London in 1861. Then you're going to choose a section for yourself to perform aloud."

I was fired up for this lesson. Seeing his performance for myself had excited and inspired me.

"Imagine, girls," I said, walking towards them, "living in the age when England ruled the world in trade, inventions and discovery. Imagine a small theatre lit by gas lamps. Everyone smartly dressed, not like today. The women in long dresses, their hair coiled and curled, the men with waistcoats and side whiskers, little children dressed as miniatures of their parents. The theatre would be all gold, with plush red furnishings, and then Charles Dickens walks out on stage, a red flower in his button hole."

At this point, two men with clipboards walked into my class and sat down at the back. Inspectors, I knew it! Thank God I was ready for this.

I indicated where my lesson plans and paperwork were to be found, and they nodded, indicating for me to proceed.

"There is a smattering of polite applause from gloved hands, and then an expectant hush," I continued, "the gas lights hiss, the silk from the women's dresses rustle, and then he speaks…"

I was in full flow, longing to recreate the sight and wonder I had felt. I had the girls on board the whole time, not one sneaky glance at a phone. When I had finished, I encouraged them to create their own versions for each other, bringing the text to life. We were on fire, full of creativity and confidence. The room was buzzing with energy. At the end of the lesson, the inspectors left without a word, and the girls filed out.

I started to pack away my notes when I became aware of someone near me. I looked up sharply.

"Miss." My brightest student was standing by my desk. "Loved the lesson, but the Dickens bit was slightly over the top."

I raised my eyebrows at her. "But that's how he did it, Julie," I smiled indulgently.

She shook her head. "In my opinion," she said, as she plugged herself in to her various instruments of technology, "he would have been laughed off the stage. Just tone that bit down, Miss, just in case you do that lesson again. The rest was great. See you."

She was almost knocked over by Andy who hurtled into the room, hair on end and what looked like baby-sick on his shoulder.

"How did it go?" He rubbed his hand over his forehead. "You got seen, didn't you. They seemed to like what you did. Good feedback, Jill. I knew I could rely on you."

He grinned at me. "Are you okay now? No more visits to the past?"

I looked at him levelly. "The doctor says I'm just suffering from stress, probably because of the divorce. I'm fine now, back to normal." I trusted Andy completely, but I needed to diffuse the rumours which would be flying round the staffroom. I picked up my briefcase, wondering how much Alison had told him. "I really wanted that head of year job, I can't believe Alison told the Head what I'd told her in confidence. That's why I didn't get it, I'm sure."

Andy shrugged. "Everyone knows how good you are, especially me. Something else will come up soon, I'm sure, and I'll always put in a good word. And I am so sorry about you and Louis, you are both such nice people. Still I'm not too worried about your survival with that deadly right hook. Old Simple Simon's still got the bruise you know."

I felt my cheeks beginning to burn.

"Don't worry," Andy grinned. "Most of us have been wanting to do that to him for ages. You've earned the respect of us all."

Suddenly, Alison's head appeared around the door, sporting a new power hairstyle. "Head wants to see you, Jill."

"Oh, no!" My hand flew to my mouth. "Not more rumours about me reaching her ears, I hope!"

She had the grace to blush and disappear.

Once again I was outside the room of power. I gave a very polite knock and waited. There was a longer pause than usual. Maybe she was fawning to the inspectors and didn't want anyone to see.

"Come," was my signal to move inside.

Instead of retreating behind the desk this time, the headmistress walked towards me and indicated for me to sit down in the low chair. She then returned to her throne, sat down, and began leafing through the notes in her hand.

I waited with a patient look on my face, determined I wasn't going to screw up this time. Then I remembered the hairdresser's card, and I started to feel very hot.

"The inspectors were impressed by your lesson, Miss Woods. Interactive and informative, with every pupil fully engaged in a challenging project."

I gave a little cheer inside. *Yes! You see, you old bat. I* can *do it!*

She glanced down at me and I felt about 12 years old. I smiled at her, but as usual, it was not returned.

"The doctor's report shows that you are making a good recovery and HR has given you advice on your work-life balance."

She gathered the sheaves of paper and placed them in a folder. The folder all about me, I suppose. It looked very thick. I hope it made exciting reading. Perhaps we could discuss it at the book club next month.

She crossed her legs and leaned forward. She reminded me of a cobra; a very hairy one I admit, but I couldn't help flinching, waiting for her to strike.

"The head of history has been very professional about your recent conduct, and no charges will be made against you, as I have explained before. To cement your relationship, he has very kindly offered to let you accompany him and the sixth form on their history trip tomorrow."

"That's very kind of him." I tried to sound sincerely grateful and suitably ashamed of my past behaviour. "Where will we be going?"

"Castle Beaumont." She rose from her seat. "I suggest you go and get the details from him."

CHAPTER TWELVE

The thought of going back to an empty flat, and being alone with my thoughts for a whole evening filled me with dread. Jeff was now helping Arlene in The World Peace Cafe, whilst the decorating was temporarily suspended, so the only sensible thing to do was to go to Tesco and kill some time buying food. I couldn't remember when I last ate anything. Had I eaten anything during my past life visits? Had I eaten this morning? No, the bakery had been closed.

I walked round the bright shelves with my solitary basket. Meals for one. I felt a kind of sadness. Why had this never bothered me before? I was a career girl, independent and carefree, nobody tugging at my heartstrings. Meals for one were *fine*.

Ahead of me in the aisle, two little children were helping their mother push the shopping trolley. The mum looked harassed, as you could see that she was trying to plan and shop ahead for the week's meals and she couldn't think. The children were tiny rockets of energy. They were about the same age as my charges at Castle Beaumont. They were squabbling and demanding sweets and kept putting things in the trolley. Mum, who was obviously on a hiding-to-nothing healthy eating agenda, was trying to tempt them with fresh fruit and hummus.

I slid into the next aisle, a smug expression on my face, just as a full blown battle was about to commence. Yes, that could have been me. Meals for one were just fine. I enjoyed the tranquillity for the moment, temporarily forgetting where I was going tomorrow.

As I was examining the fresh salmon, I felt a hand on my arm. I looked round quickly and there was Louis, with heavily pregnant girlfriend in tow. Louis hated shopping. He would never go with me, and here he was with a very beautiful girl who was at least half my age, her face glowing with health and love for my husband.

He looked as though he was actually enjoying himself.

"Jill, this is Veronica," said Louis without the slightest embarrassment. The way he looked at her made me bristle like a bad tempered mongrel.

She held out a slim hand and smiled. "Hello, Jill, pleased to meet you at last."

Oh how civilized are we British. I smiled back and shook her hand, politely enquiring after her health, when all I wanted to do was stamp on her pretty red M&S pumps and call her a harlot.

"Jill, thanks so much for agreeing to sell the flat," said Louis, as he tucked her hand under his arm. "We've found a great little house, and hopefully if we can do a quick sell, we won't lose it."

My mouth dropped open, rather like one of my Year 9s when I try to explain about Brecht's staging techniques.

"I agreed?"

A slight shadow passed over Louis's face. "Yes, last night, remember? We agreed to meet at the estate agents after work tomorrow, to sort everything out."

I clamped my mouth shut and nodded. So, when Louis came round last night, and I flitted back to Victorian England, my other self had agreed to the sale. Why? What else had I said or done that I didn't know about?

I rang Liz as I was cooking my salmon that evening. It was Pete who replied. Dear Pete, Chris's best friend, who had helped me through so much. He seemed distant on the phone, not like him at all; the man who could insult the best of us for England.

"You haven't told him?" I demanded of Liz, when she came to the phone. "He'll think I'm barking."

I settled the phone under my chin as I flipped over the salmon.

"Only a little." Liz's voice was apologetic.

"So he doesn't believe it either. He'll just think I'm crazy and that I'm going to have another breakdown."

"No, Jill, no, but it is hard to take in. You were having a meal, talking to me about selling the flat, and you say you were tripping around in a crinoline."

"You don't believe me," I said flatly. "And how do you know I'm selling the flat?"

"You told me. Fresh start, you said."

I shook my head wearily. I couldn't keep up with this.

"Liz, I have to go to Castle Beaumont tomorrow on a trip."

There was a silence at the other end of the phone.

"Can't you get out of it?"

"No."

"Then you'll have to go."

"I know, but I haven't been back since…"

"You're stronger now. It was years ago. You *are* better."

"I'm afraid it'll all come back."

"You might find some answers there. You may be able to look into the history, find out about the ancestors you say you're employed by, so to speak."

"I'm afraid," I bleated.

"Don't be." Liz was always so reassuring and sensible. "If you get wobbly, I'm on the other end of the phone."

"Thanks, Liz." I hung up and went back to my salmon.

I had trouble sleeping that night. My dreams were full of Chris; my Chris turning into Lord Beaumont and him looking at me with such distain. My two lives became blurred and I half expected to be transported back during the night, but it wasn't to be, and I woke fretful and tired.

Simon was cool but polite, and the sixth form were relieved that I was on the trip with them instead of just boring old Smithers. They had named him after the cartoon character, and I could see the resemblance.

We were busy at first, collecting consent forms and last minute payments. When we had settled back into our seats at the front of the coach, Simon leaned across the aisle to talk to me. "Do you know anything about Castle Beaumont?" he asked me.

He was keen to see that I had done my homework and keen to report back that I hadn't. "Perhaps you could do an introductory talk."

He passed me the microphone with a slimy smile, one eyebrow raised. Oh dear, the bruise hadn't quite gone yet, I noticed.

I smiled back, pointedly looking at the bruise. I took the microphone, took a breath and clicked the switch.

"Okay, everyone, a little bit of background to the present family in residence at Castle Beaumont."

There was the usual shuffling.

"iPods out, all of you, I can see in the mirror."

There was a general mumbling and then quiet. I settled into my seat lulled by the windscreen wipers and the patter of the rain. I stared out of the window, remembering.

"The present owner of Castle Beaumont, Lord Christopher Beaumont, lives in New York. He is a songwriter. His younger brother Harry runs the estate jointly with Christopher, but he lives at the family home. The Dowager Duchess is French, and that is why a lot of the art you will see today, is by French impressionists. You will also notice the French influence on the furniture and furnishings. The family also have a house on The Avenue Foch in Paris where the Duchess now lives. Both her sons are bilingual. They spent their summers in the Loire Valley with their grandmother who hated all things English and used to try to beat them with a stick if they spoke English in her presence.

"Some years ago I attended a Hunt Ball at the house. If you can imagine, when we get to the driveway, lighted torches stretching right up to the Castle, which was lit by chandeliers and thousands of candles. The footmen wore scarlet liveries, and there were fires burning in all the rooms, and so much food the tables were almost bending under the weight. The fountain was illuminated and there were thousands of lights in the trees. To this day, I still believe that Castle Beaumont is the most romantic place I have ever been to. That night especially is hard to forget: the sound of the band, the lights, the gentle splash of the fountain. It was paradise."

I paused in order to bring myself back into the present moment. Then I handed the microphone back to Simon and settled into my seat with a smug smile, enjoying the silence from the sixth form and the look on Simon's face.

CHAPTER THIRTEEN

I spent the rest of the journey with my memories.

I'd had the best and worst times of my life with Chris, and now I had to be grown up and face the fact that my life had moved on. I had been desperately ill when we split up, but I had risen up and fought the battle of life alone. Living seemed to be so much simpler and calmer if there was just me in my life. However, the growing realisation that I could be now living with two of me was unsettling, if not downright frightening.

The rain suddenly stopped, and the sun shone through the raindrops on the windscreen. I felt like Saint Paul on the road to Damascus as the bright light illuminated my face. The bus turned sharply and the sun was shaded momentarily, and there it was, standing so grandly on the brow of the hill, the honey-coloured stone gleaming in the light, the sun glimmering on the lake. As always, whenever I saw it, a frisson of excitement pulsated through me. Without thinking, I grabbed the microphone.

"Unplug and regard," I said, "a sight that inspired both artists and poets alike. 'A beauty sublime methinks I am in Elysium'."

"Where's Elysium, Miss?" asked Dan, one of my more motivated students.

"Near York, cloth 'ead." Alex, one of my less motivated students who had a voice that could strip paint off walls, was sitting next to poor Dan. "My Dad took me to the Air Museum there. It was mint."

"Don't you mean Elvington?" asked Dan politely.

"No!" snapped Alex, frowning at him.

"Yes you do!" Sally and Lucy said in unison, as they crept up to the front of the coach to get a better look at the Castle.

"Elysium is near Pontefract," chirped Lucy, a doll-like romantic whom Dan loved with an unrequited passion. He started to blush as she moved near him.

"And how do you know that, Barbie?" Alex was fired up for a fight, and Lucy cowered nearer to Dan, who looked as though he was about to internally combust.

"Look!" I whirled round. "Greek Mythology. The Elysium Fields were the final resting places of the heroic and the virtuous."

There was a silence. "So where are they then? York or Pontefract?" demanded Alex.

Simon gave a snort of laughter and I glared at him. "Come closer, so you can see the house," I said to the students, "but sit down otherwise the bus driver won't be happy."

I glanced in the mirror as they settled down and leaned over their seats to take a closer look.

"Do you know the family?" asked Sally, as she balanced her phone on the back of the seat so that she could take a photograph. "I've always wanted to meet an aristocrat. All the boys I know have no manners."

There was a grumbling sound from the male contingent of our party.

"That's because of women's equality," Simon retorted. "You've got equality now, girls, so don't expect to be treated like delicate flowers."

I was about to reply but the girls were there before me, and a heated argument destroyed the tranquillity of the moment. The argument was still going strong as we descended the stairs to exit the coach, but I was elsewhere. I was with Chris, purring up the drive in his Jaguar, at the pinnacle of my happiness. Of all the girls he had met, all the girls that were falling over themselves to get him to notice them, he had chosen me.

I walked briskly towards the east wing, clutching our tickets, as the sixth form followed, chattering behind me. I tried not to glance towards the west wing – the family quarter – but I couldn't help it. A large black sign saying, *Private*, swung on a chain across the gravel drive, barring the way.

We assembled in the great hall, the massive dome with its painted ceiling towering above us. The girls clattered across the black and white tiles in their heels and the boys were buying guide books and fruit pastilles. I sat on the sofa next to the log fire. It was here that I heard the final argument between Chris and his father. The shouting, the slamming of doors, his mother crying and Chris storming down the long gallery to the great hall, leaving his ancestral home never to return; and eventually leaving me. I felt as if a wound that had healed had suddenly burst open again and the tears started pouring down my cheeks. I turned towards the fire and blew my nose. I was immediately surrounded by the girls. The boys were looking on anxiously.

"Log fires." I sniffed, smiling weakly at the anxious faces. "I seem to have an allergy to them."

Simon was calling everyone into the garden hall, and as the students began to file past us, he turned towards me. In an unexpected act of kindness, or more likely because he thought I was taking over the trip, he pointed to his watch. "See you back here in twenty minutes, then you can show them the grounds," he said.

I was now alone.

One of the boys had left his thick, glossy guidebook on the sofa next to me. I didn't feel that my legs would support me, so I started to glance through the pages. On the first page was the family tree. If I was truly going back in time, then the family I worked for would be here somewhere. Eagerly I traced my finger to the 1800s. The eighth Duke, Charles Beaumont married Elizabeth Waterson. Their children were... Emma... I snapped the book shut, not wanting to read any more. Emma; why Emma? Why that name? I swallowed hard and tried to get my breathing to return to normal. I was still trembling.

I grabbed my bag, and shakily made my way across the Garden Hall and on into the long gallery. Portraits hung from floor to ceiling on gold chains, suspended from a long pole which seemed to run the length of the room. The sun poured through the heavily draped windows, illuminating mahogany cabinets lined with books. I padded my way across the polished floor, past ancestors in wigs and brocade who seemed to be staring down at me so solemnly from their oily canvases. I searched for familiar faces. I had to know.

And, there he was, his portrait hanging over the ornate marble fireplace in the centre of the gallery, Lord Charles, my employer. There was no mistaking that finely chiselled face, the sardonic look, the incredible likeness to Chris, his great-great grandson. Next to his portrait was one of Lady Elizabeth, her sweet face framed by her elaborate hair. She looked very young and very serious. It seemed so strange staring up at them. I half-expected them to move. These were the people I worked for in another life. The situation was bizarre.

I gazed up at Lady Elizabeth. She looked so demure and innocent, the angel in the home, a true, decorative Victorian wife. I went up close to her portrait and looked at her large brown eyes. "What are you up to sneaking around at night, you minx?" I whispered to her. I stepped back and looked at them both. "And you, your Lordship, living in luxury, whilst your tenants go hungry." An old couple in matching green jackets appeared at the end of the gallery, so I moved away from the portraits and walked back to the garden hall, pushing open the French doors that led down the steps to the fountain.

One hot summer night almost sixteen years ago, Chris and I walked together through the sweet smelling rose gardens and down the steps to the fountain. The night was so hot and the air was so still. I sat on the edge of the fountain, trailing my hand in the water in order to cool myself down, whilst Chris stood in front of me, those blue eyes so serious, telling me of his dreams to be a musician, dreams his parents vehemently opposed.

I reached the fountain and those same feelings returned. The strong sense of loss was so overpowering it made me gasp. *"I have to go, Jill, I have to get away."* Those words which had sealed my fate.

I brought myself back into the present so I could enjoy the beauty of my surroundings. The water sparkled in the sunlight, the sound was hypnotic. It was early spring and the rich green lawns were covered with swaying daffodils. I walked down the steps as though it was my destiny to do so, when I felt my waist contract and my body suddenly feel like a lead weight. The change was so quick that I nearly lost my balance. My hand felt warm and I looked down and saw Lady Emma, her hand in mine, walking quietly beside me. Lord Christopher had a small hoop and a stick and was behind us, trying to keep up. I looked about me, taking in the scene, the daffodils, the gentle plashing of the fountain, the spring sunshine. It all looked the same, but how could it be?

I looked down at the little girl, walking silently beside me. I tried to still the fear I felt at being here. I was sure I would give myself away, and that scared me. Who I was and where I came from would be very difficult to explain. I'd probably end up as an exhibit in a Victorian freak show, or being dissected as a unique experiment. I must be very careful.

"Why are we here, children?" I asked, as casually as I could. "What are we doing?"

Emma looked up at me, surprised, a small frown on her little round face.

"It's our morning walk, Miss Woods, and then we have our lessons."

"Why aren't we in London?"

She would think I was a totally dumb governess, but I needed to know when, where and why. That would, perhaps, lessen the chance of any mistakes.

"Papa has work to do on the estate. He wanted us to come here as the air is good. London is smoky and foggy."

Her little feet in their button boots crunched on the gravel. She was wearing a bonnet and coat, and poor Christopher was trussed up like a small version of his father, with waistcoat and coat and a cap on his head. The atmosphere was gloomy and quiet. Christopher abandoned his hoop and took my other hand and we walked on, towards the fountain which looked brighter and newer, not covered in lichen as it was in the 21st century. We stood at the top of the hill looking down at it.

"I have an idea," I said. "If your father wants you to take the air and have exercise, let's play!"

The children dropped my hands and stared up at me in wonder.

I unfastened my bonnet and stripped off my gloves.

"Wait here," I said as I dodged behind a tree, lifting up my skirts to get rid of the infernal petticoats. "Take off your shoes and socks and your coats and hats, so you can run," I shouted.

I looked round the tree as I struggled with my boots.

"Go on then!" I commanded as they were standing exactly where I had left them, looking bewildered.

I came out from behind the tree to help them. It was obvious they didn't dress themselves and hadn't a clue what to do. As I disrobed them, they laid their surplus clothes in neat piles and continued to look at me in wonder.

"Watch!" I said as I laid myself down at the top of the hill. "Here I go!"

And with that I tucked my arms into my sides and rolled over and over down the hill, shrieking as I did so and landing with a bump at the bottom. It was wonderful. I hadn't done that for years.

I jumped up quickly and waved at them. "Come on," I yelled. "Try it, it's fun!"

They lay down obediently, then after a few furtive glances at each other, they started to roll, shrieking and laughing as they went. Eventually, they tumbled into a heap at my feet. Christopher jumped up and clapped his hands, his solemn little face now rosy with exertion. "Please, Miss Woods, would it be possible to do that again?" he asked in his serious little way.

"Absolutely, let's all do it together." I grinned. "C'mon, last one up the hill is a dipstick."

And so it went on, and there we were puffing and panting up the hill and shrieking our way down. The children's cheeks were flushed and their eyes bright as they laughed and ran and played in the vast expanse of green. We played tag, ring-a-roses and I swung them both round by their hands until we were dizzy. I felt like Julie Andrews in The Sound of Music, in fact I stole the idea of teaching musical notes by using the song, Doe a Deer, on the stone steps near the house. The children were laughing and happily played with increasing confidence and enjoyment.

I was just hitting the high notes of the end of the song, and the children were shrieking at the top of their voices, when I caught sight of Miss Tibbs, the housekeeper, standing at the top of the stone steps looking mean and disapproving.

"Miss Woods," she shouted. We all stopped dead, standing in a row like naughty children. "His Lordship wishes to speak to you in the music room. Children, collect your clothes, you are coming with me to the nursery."

"Please Miss Tibbs, is Mama there?" asked Christopher in his polite way. I saw the shadow of a sneer cross her face at the mention of Lady Elizabeth. That was interesting. Did Miss Tibbs disapprove of their mother?

"No, Lord Christopher," she replied stiffly, "your mother has visitors. Now hurry and collect your things. I will have to tidy you up. What were you thinking of, Miss Woods? The children are dirty."

"We were playing, it's what children do," I sighed.

The children went obediently to collect their outer garments, and I went to retrieve my clothes and try to make myself look presentable. I dragged myself up the steps, hating these long skirts and numerous petticoats. I was trying to get my hair back into its bun and open the French doors at the same time.

The scene which greeted me stopped me in my tracks. An army of maids in long black skirts and starched, white, lace caps and pinafores were marching through the long gallery carrying piles of sheets and towels. Shafts of sunlight poured through the tall windows, picking out the reds and golds of the carpet and the shiny polished floor. The whole gallery looked newer and fresher than I had seen it, only hours before, but instead of tourists there were Lord Beaumont's staff, polishing, shining, carrying and organising. Smartly dressed maids were arranging lilies and roses in huge Chinese vases, some were laying fires, and others struggling with pails of water, which slopped onto the floor. In the midst of it all, clutching the children by the hand, the housekeeper barked orders at everyone, and a constant stream of maids and footmen clattered up and down the staircase. The butler strode through the middle, pointing and commenting to individuals as they hurried past him.

He caught my eye and walked over to where I stood, rooted, drinking in the moment.

"His Lordship is waiting for you in the music room, Miss Woods," he said stiffly. "Shall I get one of the footmen to show you the way?"

"I know the way, thank you." I swept past him and joined the throng, turning sharply left into a corridor of stone arches lined with statues on plinths, treasures from Greece and Rome, taken from their countries by the seventh Duke.

I could hear the sound of the harpsichord as I drew closer to the music room. I stopped dead with a strong sense of déjà vu. My last memory of this room was the sight of Chris on the harpsichord playing Beatles music for me and making me sing along. Sometimes we couldn't sing for laughing so much.

Strains of Mozart filled the air as I pushed open the door. The room looked almost the same, but instead of my Chris, Lord Beaumont was playing, lost in the music. I watched, hardly daring to breathe, until he saw me, and stopped.

"Miss Woods," he said, "as you are going to teach the Lady Emma music, I need to hear you play."

He moved from the seat and gestured for me to sit down. He was wearing riding clothes which were faintly spattered with mud. The cut of the coat flattered his muscular figure, his hair was tousled from the ride and there was a tiny splash of mud on his chin.

I had to move past him to sit down and I could feel the heat of his body through my clothes. Once more something moved, shifted inside of me and I felt off balance.

I seated myself at the harpsichord aware of his eyes on me. He was standing by the mantelpiece, watching me, one booted foot resting on the fender. I had no musical ability. Chris had taught me one song and we used to play it as a duet, never seriously and only after copious amounts of wine. So in the music room of Castle Beaumont, in 19th century Victorian England, I played our version of Blueberry Hill.

I finished with a flourish, rather pleased that I'd made no mistakes. I glanced up at Lord Beaumont, and the expression on his face made my heart sink. I shut the lid gently and stood up.

"Please sit down, Miss Woods," he said, his voice hostile.

I quickly sat down and stared at my hands. I felt him walk over towards me; I could feel his disapproval reach me before he did.

"Miss Woods," he continued, "you are the governess of my children as a favour to your father. He and my father were good friends, as you know, and I have every sympathy with your present financial situation, but I must protect the education of my children."

My father!

It never occurred to me that I may have a family. So, I had a family that had fallen on hard times. I was desperate to find out more.

"You cannot expect me to approve of my children running around the grounds like street urchins," he continued. I stared at his white shirt, not daring to look at his face. "It is unseemly and it is not the way I wish them to be educated, and if that dreadful sound is your idea of music, then my daughter will be unable to play what is expected of a young woman in her social sphere."

I looked up at him; his face was so disapproving and he turned away from me swiftly, stalking back to the mantelpiece. His body was lithe and athletic beneath the tailored coat and breeches and my thoughts were a jumbled mass of fear at what he was going to say, and pure unadulterated lust. I was shocked at the strength of my feelings and stared hard at the floor.

"Perhaps we need to find another governess," he sniffed, as he tapped his fingers on the marble. "Your stay with my family so far has been naught but a series of mishaps, and you have yet to prove that you can teach them anything of worth."

I stood up and walked swiftly over to him, my skirts making my progress slower than I would have liked.

"Please give me another chance, sir," I pleaded, putting my hand on his arm. "The children were playing outside. They had exercise, fresh air and fun. I was teaching them music too. The children are getting used to me. Please, give me some more time with them. I am very well-educated and I promise that you will not be disappointed."

He looked down at my hand, which I removed quickly. I folded my hands demurely and looked at him pleadingly. I was afraid that if he cast me out, I would have nowhere to go, and the glimpses I'd had of the streets of London had filled me with fear.

He continued to tap his fingers on the marble mantelpiece.

"Miss Woods, I am a gentleman of my word. I made a promise to your father and I would not see you destitute. However, I am not a charity. I expect my children to be educated in their early years, especially my son. I expect to see results and I shall keep a sharp eye on your methods. You may go."

"Thank you, sir." I bobbed a quick curtsey, and fled the room, my heart still thumping.

I couldn't find the nursery in the maze of corridors. I had never been to this part of the house before and I quickly got lost. Luckily, Jenny, the maid who was with me in the alley, was struggling up the main staircase with her arms full of dresses, so I clattered down the stairs to help her.

"Fank you, Miss," she lisped. Her face was beaded with sweat and she wiped her hand across her brow.

"You don't look well, Jenny," I said, noticing the dark shadows under her eyes, over the pile of heavy silks and taffeta.

She glanced at me quickly. "Miss Tibbs is working us really hard, Miss, because of all the people comin' to stay. And I've not been sleeping too good."

We'd reached a corridor I recognised. It was where all the main bedrooms were. Jenny took the dresses from me. She did look exhausted.

"Why aren't you sleeping, Jenny?" I enquired. She had dark smudges under her pale eyes and her cap was askew.

She glanced at me and looked both ways before moving towards me, hoisting the dresses nearer to her body as she did so.

"Don't say nufink, Miss, but it's these dreams I keep having."

She lowered her voice to a whisper. "I keep dreaming I'm in a shop and I'm selling cakes."

A strange crawling sensation made its way up my spine.

"But, Miss, things are different and it frightens me. I'm dressed like a fallen woman. My dress is so short…"

"Jenny, stop gossiping and get on with your work!" Miss Tibbs boomed up the corridor. "Are you unable to find the nursery, Miss Woods?"

She strode towards us, and I stared at her, unable to speak, stunned by what Jenny had just told me.

"The nursery is up the staircase. The children are waiting. Jenny, come with me, and if I find you gossiping again, I will dock your wages."

She flounced off in a flurry of stiff, black cloth, Jenny trailing in her wake. I marched up the staircase, determined to talk further with Jenny. I wasn't alone, it was happening to someone else. The sense of relief was enormous.

As I reached the nursery, Lady Elizabeth was just coming out of the door. She caught my arm quickly, looking around her as she did so. She was so beautiful, her hair was set in elaborate coils and ringlets and she was wearing a white cotton day dress decorated with tiny lilac flowers. "You haven't told anyone, have you? About the night I was in your room, or the charity visit you did for me?" she whispered.

"Of course not." I smiled at her reassuringly. "You can count on me to keep a secret."

She gave the ghost of a smile. "Thank you, Miss Woods; I may require more from you when we get back to London. I cannot explain right now. I must however, be able to trust you."

I nodded and she looked around again quickly.

"I have also seen your father."

I stared at her.

"He has been moved from The Marchalsea and is now in The King's Bench, but I am trying to request a move to the new White Cross prison. This will unfortunately require more money from you, my dear. I have so little of my own, and so little influence."

Someone was turning the handle of the nursery door, so she put her finger to her lips and hurried down the corridor, her skirts swirling behind her.

So my father was in prison. And a debtor's prison at that! What other surprises were in store for me?

"Miss Woods, shall we continue with our painting?"

Emma was at the door. My heart gave a leap every time I saw her. She pushed the door aside to let me in. I had seen the nursery with Chris, full of Airfix models and footballs. The sight that greeted me was every historian's dream. The sunlit room was full of wooden toys and games, toy soldiers, rag dolls and a wooden train set which was laid out on the floor by the fireplace. A beautiful rocking horse, with a real mane, dominated the room. The children were working at a large wooden table in the centre of the carpet, and fast asleep by the crackling fire was an old lady, dressed all in black, her lace cap slipping down over her eyes and fluttering gently in rhythm with her gentle snores.

"Nanny's asleep." Emma took her place at the table, and Christopher looked up as I walked towards him. "I am trying to draw Jip, Miss Woods, but he keeps moving," he complained.

I noticed a black labrador also sleeping by the fire. It raised its head as I moved towards the children and started to growl at me.

The children looked at each other in surprise.

"He doesn't like you," said Emma as she took up her paintbrush. "Jip never growls at anyone. He likes everyone, even Grandpapa."

Oh, dog, don't give me away, I prayed.

Suddenly, there was a huge boom which came from high above us and I fell into the table in surprise. The sleeping lady's eyes shot open and with an agility that belied her years, she leapt to her feet.

"Time to go, children," she smiled, seeming totally unaware of me. "Grandpapa needs me." And with that she swept out of the room.

I gazed at the children who continued with their painting totally unaffected by the noise.

"Don't be concerned, Miss Woods," said Christopher as he splattered black paint onto his drawing. "It's only Grandpapa shooting rooks from the roof."

"Nanny goes to load the gun for him," said Emma, frowning with concentration, appraising her drawing and looking none too pleased with the result. "Nanny also sleeps in the same bed as Grandpapa and she thinks we don't know."

There wasn't really anything to add at this juncture so I continued to listen, hoping that my silence would encourage more interesting pieces of gossip.

"You should not discuss the lives of our family with the servants, Emma," Christopher said.

I raised my eyebrows at him, making a mental note to deal with this snobbery at a later date.

"Miss Woods is not a servant, she is our governess and Mama says we are to treat her with respect," Emma continued, pointing her brush at her brother. "Do you know, Miss Woods, that our father and mother used to sleep in the same bed. I think it's really silly as we have over thirty bedrooms to chose from. I think they must have been very cold. However, Papa has his own room now and he always asks for the fire to be lit. He must be more comfortable now, don't you think, but maybe he is cold without Mama?"

I suppressed a smile. An interesting snippet of information to store away, I thought as I walked towards the children.

"I think so too, Emma, so shall we start our lessons now? Pack away your paintings, which are looking very promising, by the way, and then we'll make a start with some reading."

I walked over to the window as they packed away their paints, determined I was not going to wait on them hand and foot. Christopher was reluctant at first but my teacher's glare, which had never failed in the classroom yet, soon silenced his protests, and Emma, always the bossy one, was soon trying to organise him.

The top floor had the most magnificent views across the gardens, all the way to the mausoleum in the east and the summer house in the west, both buildings made from the same honey-coloured stone. Central to it all, the fountain flowed, the drops of water catching the sunlight.

Peacocks were trailing their feathers across the lawns, and as I looked at the fountain once again, a figure moved from behind it, and started walking back towards the house. It was Charles, Lord Beaumont, my employer. I felt a catch in my throat. He was definitely

Chris's double, the way he walked, confident and purposeful, that mass of blond hair, those hypnotic eyes, even the small cleft in his chin. I was lost in admiration.

Suddenly, he stopped and looked right up at me. I couldn't move away, I was seen. He held my gaze, although it was too far away to see the expression on his face to know what he was thinking. My heart was hammering in its stiff corset. Then, all of a sudden, more figures came into view from behind the fountain. It was my sixth form boys, chatting together and swinging their digital cameras. One of them was reading out of the guide book and pointing to various things in an abstracted kind of way.

I whirled around to see a room swathed in dust sheets; no children, no table, no toys. Only the rocking horse was visible, swaying slightly as if someone had just been playing on it. I felt a frisson of fear as I quickly made my way to the door, long skirts no longer hindering my movements. Outside, the corridor was quiet. I was probably in the private apartments, with no idea of how I got here. If the students were still in the grounds, I hadn't missed the bus, but how much time had passed? How long had I been gone?

I ran down the nearest stone staircase, my hands grasping the iron balustrade, and as I descended, it seemed as though the portraits glared at me disapprovingly. How often had I felt that same disapproval from Chris's family? I wasn't one of them, I was never welcome.

As I hurried down the next staircase, and came to a curve before the final descent, I heard someone coming up the other way. I stopped dead… I couldn't go back up; I was trespassing!

The steps came closer and a figure came into view. It couldn't be. I could feel myself shaking; this was more than a coincidence. Jenny, the girl from the bakery, was coming up the staircase. It was her, the same flat fringe, the same eyes. She was dressed in a short black skirt and apron as were all the girls from the tearoom.

She glanced at me, recognition in her eyes.

"Hello," I said, shakily, finding my voice from somewhere, "I don't know if you recognise me…"

She nodded. "Yes I do, teacher, croissant and coffee, about nine o'clock."

"What are you doing here?" My voice was decidedly squeaky.

"The bakery got sold, so I got a job here, my boyfriend works in the gardens. I am so lucky. I've always wanted to work here. By the way, if you are with the kids, the coach is leavin'. Are you lookin' for the way out 'cos this staircase is only for staff?"

I nodded and she pointed to a door at the end of the next corridor.

I mumbled my thanks and fled. If I missed the coach, Simon would live on this for a year. I opened the door which led out into the entrance hall and bumped straight into Sally and Lucy.

"Miss!" cried Sally, as she peered at me over her spectacles. "Where've you been? We lost you after you showed us round the gardens and the coach is going. We've been sent to look for you."

Oh, great this is all I need, I thought, as I pictured Simon sighing and shaking his head and telling tales to the headmistress on our return.

"Go, girls, go!" I gave them a gentle push and they set off in a run and I puffed my way across the grass behind them, making a mental note that I needed to go to the gym more often. The coach was still waiting; there was no way that Simon would leave without the girls. We clambered aboard, hot, sweaty and out of breath.

"Sorry." I flashed a bright smile at everyone, deliberately not looking at Simon. "I got lost looking for the loo."

Simon told the driver to get going. He didn't even let me sit down first and I lurched forward and tumbled down the aisle, putting my hand out to try to save myself. Someone grabbed me, and as I looked up to voice my thanks, I stared straight into the eyes of the mystery boy, Chris's double, and I knew absolutely that he was not on the coach on our journey here.

CHAPTER FOURTEEN

I kept staring at the boy, until I realised I was embarrassing him, so quickly sat down in my seat. I leaned over the aisle to talk to Simon who was buried behind his Guardian newspaper, pointedly ignoring me.

"Simon, I apologise if I held up the coach. I needed the loo and got lost. Simple mistake."

He folded his newspaper slowly, keeping me waiting for his response, trying to make me feel like a naughty schoolgirl.

I didn't wait. "Who is that boy, the one sitting next to John Dalton?"

Simon gave me a contemptuous look and swirled round to look behind him. "Oh, him," he said. "The Head asked me to pick him up from here. He's on exam leave and he's got a science module this afternoon."

He picked up his newspaper again, pulled a biro out of his top pocket then folded the paper over into a neat square so that he could do the crossword. "A pity you held up the coach," he said as he tapped his biro on his teeth. "I hope you will explain to all the waiting parents why our arrival is delayed."

"Glad to," I snapped, "but this boy, what's his name?"

"No idea, but he's wearing our uniform." Simon laboriously filled in one of the answers. "The Head said you knew all about it, so I don't know why you are asking me. You've got the consent forms."

That's right, Simon, your trip, but delegate all responsibility.

I thought it was better not to pursue this. Simon was not on my side and had never forgiven me for hitting him. He could seize this as another opportunity to discredit me. The Head must have discussed this boy with me, when I was in my other world. Oh God, this was getting tricky.

I could see the boy through the driver's wing mirror and kept looking for opportunities to engage him in conversation. He was engrossed in conversation with his friends, and I could think of no reason to talk to him without it looking suspicious. However, on the way out of the coach as he passed my seat, he held out the Castle Beaumont brochure to me.

"You dropped this, Miss," he said, pushing it into my hands. "And thanks again for the lift. As I was already staying there, it was a good opportunity to get a lift to school. I hope Georgina gave you my consent form."

Staying there? He was already there? Was he a relation? Was he Chris's son? Scores of explanations went fizzing through my brain, but as I was about to ask him what he meant, he had disappeared down the steps, hastily followed by the majority of the girls.

Georgina. I needed to find Georgina in the morning. She'd shed some light on the mystery, and I made a mental note to check the consent forms as soon as I got home. As I was walking down the steps I suddenly realised that I couldn't remember buying a brochure at Castle Beaumont. Puzzled, I pushed it into my bag, and clambered out of the coach. We'd made good time and there was no reason to apologise to any parent. Feeling smug about that, I slung my bag over my shoulder and headed across the car park, trying to catch another glimpse of the mystery boy, but he had gone. I got into my car and reached in my bag for the consent forms. They weren't there. I must have left them on the coach. Damn it! I watched the tail lights of the coach disappear down the road, and sighed as I turned on the ignition.

I drove straight home, not knowing what my other self had been up to whilst I had been gone. I'd probably given Louis and Veronica my flat as a wedding present.

There was a *For Sale* sign slap in the middle of my minute front garden. It looked large and garish and obscene. Someone had been busy. Probably me! I climbed the stairs to my flat and was greeted by Jeff flinging the door open. He had a paintbrush in his hand, which was unusual.

"Sorry about the sign, Jill. They came today to put it up. Louis has been round. He gave me a call and asked me to tart up the hall a bit. You did the right thing, you know."

"Hah." I slung my bag in the corner of the kitchen and sank onto the chair, putting my head in my hands as I did so.

"I've made Moroccan mint tea and flapjacks, low sugar," Jeff said cheerily as he filled the kettle, "and you need new weighing scales, Jill. Yours are in pounds and ounces."

I lifted my head wearily. "Jeff, I don't cook. Why do I need weighing scales?"

"Eat." He placed a plate of flapjacks in front of me, and stood looking at me, hands on his very slim hips.

"What's the latest news then? Any more trips back in time?"

He poured the water into the teapot, and then sat down opposite to me.

I nodded, as I picked up a flapjack. "Jeff, do you think Arlene knows anyone who can help me. Anyone who I can talk to about this?"

Jeff poured out the tea. It looked very green. I sniffed it and took a sip. I looked at him. He was usually quick with an answer.

"Jeff?" I enquired.

He was looking down at his tea. He looked up at me. His usual ready smile was nowhere to be seen and he looked tired.

"Arlene and I, well, we… Arlene and I've had a small disagreement."

"How small?" I munched my way through one of his flapjacks, thinking that maybe I could adopt Jeff as he would be so useful to have around. He was certainly too young for me to even consider a relationship with him in any other capacity. Or was he?

He took a gulp of tea and looked at me over the rim of his mug.

"I want children," he said, "and Arlene doesn't."

"Doesn't ever, or doesn't at this moment?" I enquired.

"Doesn't ever," he said gloomily, staring into his tea.

Silence. I stopped munching as it seemed to be a bit heartless under the circumstances.

I glanced at him. He was always so cheery, lighting up my kitchen with his positive philosophy on life. He seemed crestfallen, stirring his tea. A frown had etched its way between his eyebrows, between the mass of blond curls.

"No compromise, no middle ground?" I asked, gently.

"Nope."

"So, what are you going to do?"

He shrugged. "I suppose I have to choose between having children and having her." He looked at me. "You don't want children either, do you? Tell me why, tell me what makes some women not want to have them, and maybe I can try and understand."

I was silent, I couldn't answer him.

He looked up at me and I looked away quickly, not wanting to meet his eyes.

"What is it, Jill? I'm sorry, I'm being too personal." He looked embarrassed. "Sorry," he repeated, "I was prying." He covered my hand with his.

I shook my head; my throat was constricted, so I cleared it, and swallowed. I withdrew my hand from under his and took a sip of tea. I replaced the cup carefully. "I had a child," I said, my voice quivering slightly, "when I was nineteen."

He was very still.

"A baby girl, Emma. I wanted to have her, she was so wanted; she was all I had of a boy I loved but..." I was finding this so difficult. I hadn't spoken about this for sixteen years. "She died, a cot death, she was three months old."

His hand covered mine again, but he said nothing.

"Since then," I continued, "I've hardened myself against ever wanting them. I was in the supermarket, and there were naughty kids running around and I felt relieved that I didn't have the responsibility, but then Louis was there, with Veronica, and they are so looking forward to the baby. He seems so happy now."

"And you aren't?"

I couldn't answer him.

I wiped away a solitary tear with the back of my hand, feeling cross with myself for being so weak.

"Nobody knows about this, Jeff, please tell no one." I looked at him, his face full of sympathy. He shook his head.

"I was so ill afterwards. I'd lost Chris and I'd lost Emma, and I can't help worrying that these two lives I seem to be leading means I am on the edge of another breakdown. It could be that it's not really happening, that it's all in my head, it could be hallucinations. I could be going mad. *Do you think I'm going mad?*"

I put my head in my hands. I didn't want to tell anyone this. Why had I confided in Jeff? I started to sob, wracking, heaving sobs which seemed to come from the depths of me. Something had been released and I couldn't stop. I had an overwhelming feeling of desperation and loneliness.

"No, no, dearest girl, don't cry."

This was a soft voice, a voice that was not Jeff's, but a familiar voice. The atmosphere had become cold and damp; the smell of earth and mildew surged through my nostrils.

I lifted my head to look around me. I was seated on a hard chair, my arms resting on a rickety wooden table. A hand was stroking my head. I looked up into the face of my father.

"Dad?" My eyes swept the room, taking in the bare walls, the earthen floor, the meagre bed, the mean furniture. I looked back at my father, the side whiskers, the neat but shabby shirt and waistcoat, the half moon glasses, the same twinkling eyes. My father, one hundred and fifty years ago!

"It's better here at The King's Bench, my dear girl."

His hand continued to stroke my hair, and I grasped his hand, love and compassion filling me up. I hadn't seen my real father for two years, and all the love and guilt I felt so overwhelmed me that I couldn't find the right words to say. Although this wasn't my real father, it wasn't him, I couldn't stop the strength of my feelings transferring into this moment.

He patted my hand and smiled at me, those familiar eyes twinkling as they always did, even when adolescent hormones made me into a monster.

"The money you send me helps me so much." He touched my face gently. "I am just so sorry it has come to this." A tear splashed onto my hand. "My dearest girl… a governess."

"I'm going to get you out of here." I clasped both his hands. "You shouldn't be in this place. It's not right!" Perhaps this was it, perhaps I had been sent to free him, to help him. Perhaps, because of the way I'd treated my own father, I had to help this one.

"Ah." He sat back in his chair and folded his hands across his stomach, his eyes holding mine for a moment. "My debts accumulate as we speak, my dear. I will end my days in here."

"No, father, you can't stay here, it's cold and damp." I was confused between my feelings for my own father and this old gentleman who so resembled him.

Another lonely tear trickled down his face. "It's my own fault." He wiped it away quickly, his sense of pride momentarily stronger than his emotions. "You could have married well and I have ruined your life for you. Charles and Elizabeth are kind to you, I know, but you are a governess, supporting your worthless father."

Tears were now dripping off the end of his chin and he looked embarrassed and upset. He blew his nose and wiped his reddened eyes.

I knelt beside him, the coldness of the earth floor seeping through to my knees. "I'll do something, I'll try to do something," I said, desperate to help him.

He smiled fondly and patted my head. "You can do nothing in this world, my dear, because you are a woman. Unfortunately, that is your lot in life."

CHAPTER FIFTEEN

My father's face began to fade and as I reached out to touch him, my hand landed on solid wood and the strong smell of cooking permeated my nostrils, making my eyes water. I rubbed them hard, and there was Jeff, standing at my stove, a grin on his face and the smell of onions filling my flat.

"Thanks for asking me to stay," he grinned, pushing back his Viking locks. "Didn't feel much like going home just yet."

He adjusted a pinafore around his tight jeans, and I stared at the face of Johnny Depp, a present from a well meaning friend to encourage my sad attempts at cooking.

"Jeff, I was there."

"Where?" He was sprinkling the onions with copious amounts of sweet chilli sauce, and seemed only to be half listening.

"I've just been back, back to my other life. I was sitting in the prison with my father."

"I thought you said your dad was in Canada." Mounds of chopped vegetables were thrown into the pot and Johnny's sultry looks were somewhat altered by sweet chilli sauce running down his nose.

"My *Victorian* father, I was visiting him in The King's Bench Prison. What happened to me here in the last few minutes? Was there any change? Was there any difference in my behaviour?" I jumped to my feet and went round the table to join him, as if a closer proximity to me would help him explain things better.

He glanced at me. "Well, nothing much. I convinced you that you weren't mad. You told me to forget about Arlene as there are other fish in the sea and I said, 'but who wants to go out with a tuna', and you didn't laugh. Not surprised, bad joke. Erm, then you said that after dinner we would make mad passionate love so I would forget whatever her name is…"

"Yes, sure," I said opening up the fridge door, to hide my crimson face as I contemplated what sounded like an excellent idea in theory, but life was far too complicated at the moment. Instead, I grabbed a bottle of Chardonnay.

"Are you setting up home in that fridge?" asked Jeff, as he dished up the meal, Johnny Depp now totally unrecognisable. "You're telling me that during our conversation, the conversation that we have just been having, that you were not actually here."

I stabbed at the pile of vegetables before me, whilst Jeff struggled to open the wine.

"No, I wasn't. I don't remember saying any of those things you just told me. Could you tell? Did anything happen or was I just normal?"

I opened the wine and poured it into two glasses, pushing one towards Jeff. I took a large slurp.

Jeff stared at me. "Yes, absolutely, but you're saying that you don't remember, because you weren't actually here? By the way, the passionate love thing, I made it up."

I shook my head at him and he pointed his fork at me. "Joking apart, if what you say is true, this is amazing. There was no indication that anything changed at all, not the slightest thing."

I pushed the food around my plate thoughtfully. "So, this means that these lives I'm living definitely run parallel, and I'm slipping in and out of them, being me in both of them. While I'm here, my other self, the governess, continues her life. That's why nobody notices that I've gone anywhere."

"I think that it's something to do with time," said Jeff, looking at me intensely. "You've somehow found some kind of loophole in time, and you have access to the life you lived before. It's got to be the string theory, got to be. You're living another life in a parallel universe."

I pushed my plate away after some half-hearted attempts to eat. "But why? There has to be a reason. It can't be random. Some of the people who are in my present life are there in my past life. You are there, and Chris, Emma's father, is my employer and his little girl is called Emma. She could have been my little girl. She could have been my Emma." My voice broke but I was too weary to cry. I felt exhausted.

Later that night, I wrote the names of all the people in my past life on separate pieces of paper and matched them, where I could, to the people in my present life. I shuffled them constantly around the table, trying to find some kind of logic or pattern. I was amazed by the strength of feeling being in the past had stirred in me.

I picked up the paper with 'Dad' on it, and felt a surge of love so strong that it made me tremble. I felt so guilty. My father had shown me nothing but unconditional love, and when I decided to button up my feelings against the world, I'd pushed him away too. He'd tried so hard and I'd rebuffed him repeatedly, too scared of loving anyone anymore. So, when my brother took his family to Vancouver, Dad went too. My dad needed to be loved and Paul and his family loved this gentle man, as I should've done.

I picked up the phone to call him, but my courage failed me. I stared at the phone trying to unblock this rock inside me. I took a deep breath, picked up the phone again, and dialled.

The soft burr of the Canadian ring tone filled my ears. I could hear the sound of my own ragged breathing and then there was a click.

"Hello?"

"Dad?" My voice sped across the miles. There was a pause and I heard a sharp intake of breath.

"Jill? Jill? My dear." The pleasure in my father's voice made me curl up with shame. "How are you, my love? It is so good to hear from you." No accusations, no questions; how typical.

"Dad, I'm fine."

"Is there anything wrong, dear?"

"No, no. I, er, I realised that I haven't spoken to you for a while. I wanted to know that you were all right."

"Very well, we're all well. Are you still working hard?"

I smiled. Work, always so important to me; my career, my

independence. My independence from everything and everyone.

"Have you seen your mother? Has she been in touch?"

"She wouldn't get in touch with me," I said. "I don't know where she is." Or with whom, I nearly added.

"Ah, oh well. Never mind, I'm sure she's happy."

Bound to be, I thought grimly, running off like that, trying to find herself, I hope she's damn well lost.

"Dad, I want to come over and see you, stay with you, probably in the summer. Would that be okay?"

There was a pause. "Of course. You'll have to let me know when, as we are all going to Banff in August. We all love it there."

Life has gone on without me, I thought, feeling an overwhelming sadness. My dad is part of a family and I have made myself an outsider. I have nephews and nieces I have never seen. I swallowed hard. I wanted to tell him how sorry I was. How I must have hurt him, but as before in the prison cell, I couldn't find the right words.

"Dad, can I call you again?"

"Anytime." His voice sounded as though he were smiling. "Goodbye dear, so nice to hear from you." Then there was a click, and he was gone.

I stared out of my window for a long time. Sleep was so far away. Memories of my childhood filled my head and in each one my dad was always there, always supportive. Then there was my mother, trapped in a marriage she had grown tired of, throwing away the love of such a good man, leaving him heartbroken.

I sighed and turned my attention back to the pieces of paper. I continued to shuffle them about. There must be a link. Did they all need something from me? Was I sent back to help them in some way, to put things right? I picked up the piece of paper with Jenny's name on it and turned it over and over in my hand. And then I realised a connection. She was there in the past and in the present; she talked about her dreams of another life. She was the only one who'd appeared at the same place in both time zones.

I turned the piece of paper with Chris's name on it. I thought back over the moments when I had gone back to a previous life. All except the first one were linked to him, seeing the boy who looked like Chris, talking to Liz about Chris in the cafe, talking about my life with him to Jeff, seeing a photograph of Castle Beaumont on the way to London.

Castle Beaumont. I would go there again. Surely it was there that I could find some answers.

CHAPTER SIXTEEN

It was nearly the end of term and on the first day of the holidays I planned to go to Castle Beaumont again. Actually, most teachers felt it was nearly half term on the very first day of a new term. It was a way of making sure we didn't fling ourselves into the blackboard, whiteboard, or interactive board on the first day back after a holiday. Andy had a calendar in the english office where the days were crossed off at 3.30pm each day with a thick, black, marker pen, and the holidays were always outlined in red. Ofsted didn't even warrant a mention. We had our priorities right in the english department.

It was Monday, and each Monday after teaching for five hours, we had a two hour meeting. After a hard day trying to get the sixth form to be enthusiastic about Milton and preventing Year 9s from sticking pens in each others' ears, I was listening to some bright young thing in a suit telling me how to become a better teacher. She was one of the baby teachers who had smiled at the right people and got enthusiastic about whatever ridiculous scheme the government had come up with. The latest buzz words were *In-Depth Learning* and she was the child in charge of this new concept. She didn't look long out of nappies.

Andy and I were playing hangman, our concentration broken only by interjections from Alison and others who were travelling upwards on the slippery ladder to the corridor of power.

Don't get me wrong, this job was everything to me. I had been a deputy head at a *failing school* and I had helped to turn it round with a grave cost to my health. I had always been prone to stress since I had lost both Emma and Chris, but I recovered and decided to take a job closer to home. I had taken this present post and was determined to join the gang on the ladder. Okay, so I had made a few teeny mistakes like knocking seven bells out of a senior teacher, but I knew that I was good at my job, and had a lot to offer the school.

"It's way past that child's bedtime." The head of geography folded his Guardian newspaper and began the crossword, nodding derisively at the bright young thing.

"It's just so exciting," wittered the baby teacher, getting approving looks from the management team. "It will make such a difference."

Our game of hangman was not going well as poor Andy had nodded off. The twins were constantly keeping him awake through the night.

"I think it sounds very exciting," beamed Alison, pointing a neatly manicured hand in the air, "and I would like to volunteer to be on the working party."

The baby teacher beamed, nearly bursting out of her suit with excitement. "This is wonderful," she sighed. "Anyone else?"

A gentle snore came from Andy, his head now resting contentedly on the shoulder of the head of languages, who was trying to crochet a jacket for her latest grandson.

I raised my hand sheepishly, planting my foot firmly up another rung on the ladder. "I'd like to do it," I said.

I thought the baby teacher was in the throes of an orgasm.

"Oh, that is *wonderful*," she sighed again. "Your experience will be so beneficial to us all."

"Indeed." I glanced sideways at Alison. "I hope it will."

Jeff was nowhere to be seen when I got home, and I missed him. I'd started to look forward to his culinary experiments and cheerful demeanour. I wondered where he was and how things were going with Arlene. There had been some attempt at decorating a door today, but it was half finished, seemingly abandoned. The flat was quiet and empty. For some reason I thought of how I had rolled down the hill at Castle Beaumont, and the laughter and excitement of the children. I switched on the hall light, and went from room to room, switching on lamps, trying to infuse some cheerfulness into my flat. It felt lonely and oppressive. This was my own private space, where I could retreat from the world, and it no longer felt like home. I couldn't settle to anything.

I lit some candles and slotted a CD into my new sound system. Usually I would rest in a luxurious bath with a glass of wine, but at the moment I was too restless and I prowled around the rooms. I had other flats to visit tonight, the estate agent to call, but a feeling of inertia overwhelmed me. Maybe I was just tired. I had another interview tomorrow; this one for the deputy head of sixth form. I had to prepare for it, but the enthusiasm I had felt for this opportunity seemed to have drained away. I poured myself a glass of wine, a bad habit straight after work, but it seemed to be appropriate tonight. I sank down onto the sofa, and threw off my shoes. I thought of Andy going home to a full house of children and to his adoring wife, and Louis, excited about his new baby. I thought of my dad and my brother Paul and his family, happily ensconced in Vancouver, me no longer a part of their lives. And I thought of Chris, and what might have been, and Emma, my little girl who would have been sixteen this year.

And I thought about me and my life now, my independence and freedom, and I thought about my life in the past; my life as a governess where I was surrounded by people. Was I starting to look forward to being her? Was I starting to prefer my life there? And I realised that if for once in the last sixteen years I was going to be truly honest with myself I was, I had to admit, feeling lonely.

My mind was too full that night to drop off to sleep. My thoughts were still of my father. He was of the old school, loyal and loving, for better or worse, and it didn't really get much worse with my mother. At forty she suddenly realised that she didn't want to be married or have kids any more. She wanted, like some 19th century pioneer, to set off and find herself. She had married young and had pursued my dad relentlessly, seeing in him the strength and stability we all loved about him, and which she did not possess. She was an artist and she was beautiful. My brother's friends fell in love with her, but she didn't know what love was. She used it as a source for manipulation. I remembered the way my dad used to look at her, as though he couldn't believe his luck. I remember his face when he read her note, the morning when the three of us sat around the breakfast table, trying to eat, trying to come to terms with the fact she was never coming back. My dad was so brave, smiling as he carved the turkey on the first Christmas without her, his little paper hat falling over his ears, his forced laughter at the jokes in the crackers, the big yawning gap that we all tried to fill.

Then I went to university and he struggled to fund me. I got a bar job in an upmarket village near my hall of residence, where I put up with the local leering youths and the haughty women who found me only slightly more interesting than a cockroach.

And after that the memories became blurred by my guilty tears, dad at the airport, leaving for Canada, tears trickling down his cheeks, and me, my heart now set in stone, holding him briefly and wishing him luck; no tears for this remarkable man from his only daughter.

I slept so fitfully. It seemed that I was in and out of my two lives. I was so aware of the brief conversation on the phone to my father, and how he'd been genuinely pleased to hear from me, but he had put the phone down first. This thought jerked me awake, but it wasn't just that. There was a firm hand clasped to my left breast. If this was a dream and Johnny Depp was at the end of that hand, well maybe I'd let nature take its course, but the breath on my cheek was sour, and smelt of alcohol, cigars and stale food. My eyes flew open and a shadowy face leered over me. I landed a crack on his nose that sent him reeling backwards, and felt for my bedside light. It wasn't there. I leapt out of bed, nearly tripping over my long nightdress. A single candle burned near the washstand and I grabbed it. Whoever had attacked me was slumped against the door, cursing me, and I held the candle high above my head. A skinny old man in a nightshirt stared back at me, whilst rubbing his nose. Wisps of long grey hair stood out on his head, as though he had been electrocuted, and he glared at me through rheumy eyes. "Damn filly, I'll soon tame you," he muttered, staggering towards me, his bony legs wobbling unsteadily.

Then the door to my bedroom opened and a female replica of

my attacker stood framed in the doorway, a lighted candle in her skinny hand. "Come back to bed, Kit," she said, rubbing her sparse grey hair. It was Nanny.

"Not 'til I've had this filly over the washstand!" he exclaimed as though he was announcing his desire to have a cup of milk before turning in.

Nanny shook her woolly head and gently took his arm.

"Kit, this is the governess, not a scullery maid," she said patiently.

"I know, I know," he said, his eyes not leaving me, "but she's got a fine pair of bosoms and I want to play with them. I saw her at dinner and I haven't had this one, she's new."

Me, a fine pair of bosoms? Me a size 34A? My hand grabbed at my chest and there they were, large and round and magnificent. Oh thank you, God. I always wanted huge boobs in my next life, and here they were in my previous one.

Lord Kit took a step towards me and I lifted my fist. "Piss off, you pervert!" I shouted at him in a voice that quelled the noisiest of Year 9 classes. "Don't you come near me."

He turned to look at Nanny. "Did you hear that, Nanny?" he said. "This servant is telling me what to do. Let's tie her down and throw her out of the window when we've finished with her."

"Kit, Kit." Nanny patted his arm as though they were arguing about what film to go and see at the local cinema. "This is the governess, young Gilbert's daughter, remember? They've fallen on hard times, dear. You cannot seduce her, it wouldn't be right."

"Hah." He shook off Nanny's arm. "Young Gilbert won't mind. He's not here. He'll never know. Fetch my riding crop, Nanny."

I took a step towards him. "If you come near me, I'll scream," I said through my teeth. "I mean it, I will."

"Piffle," the old man spat, "a good rogering will do you the world of good. I fought with Nelson you know. I know how to roger a pretty girl like you." He took a step towards me and I opened my mouth, took the biggest breath I could, then screamed and screamed. I was like Fay Wray in King Kong. Then I pushed past him, wrenched open the door and yelled as loudly as I could. Doors began to open and servants in long white nightshirts, papers in their hair and long shawls wrapped round them, began emptying out of doors. I heard the sound of heavy boots striding along the corridor, and the servants parted respectfully.

Lord Charles appeared in the doorway holding a branch of candlesticks, illuminating the scene. He glanced quickly around, assessed the situation, and barked at the servants to get back to bed.

"Father, back to bed," he said firmly. "Nanny, take him back to bed."

Lord Kit hung his head like a naughty schoolboy being caught stealing someone's conkers. He stuck out his lower lip. Nanny tugged at his arm.

"I was here first, boy," he said petulantly. "You find your own doxy."

Lord Charles shook his head. "Father, this is Gilbert's daughter, your friend, the Earl of Swainby. It would not be right. Nanny, please take him back to bed."

Nanny led him away gently saying in a soothing voice, "Come on Kitty, dear, we'll play some games, before we go to sleep. I'll find your riding crop."

I stared in astonishment at the couple as they retreated into the darkness. I was the daughter of an Earl, I had almost been raped again, and at this moment two over-eighties were planning the time of their lives. I became aware of Lord Charles's eyes on me and I quickly picked up my shawl and wrapped it around me. I was shivering.

"I can only apologise for my father, Miss Woods," he said quietly. His face had softened and had lost that haughty look. "There is a fire in my room and some brandy. I insist that I make sure that you are comfortable after what must have been a terrible shock."

With a sweep of his arm, he signalled for me to leave the room. I almost collided with two more people who were about to come in. I stepped back and saw the formidable figure of the housekeeper, with Jenny peeping round her, a worried look on her face. I was given an icy stare as Miss Tibbs wrapped her shawl tightly around her.

"Was it you making that dreadful noise, Miss Woods?" she asked, her voice matching the expression on her face. Then she saw Lord Charles and her face changed quickly. "Sir, is there a problem here?" she asked swiftly.

"No harm done, please explain to her Ladyship that all is well." Lord Charles nodded to her and I felt a gentle push in my back. I started to walk out of the room in front of him.

The housekeeper turned stiffly, her gaze never leaving us.

"Sir, her Ladyship is not in her room." There was a trace of malice in her voice, distinguishable to anyone who was listening. Lord Charles paused and looked at her dismissively.

"She'll be with the children. Thank you, that will be all."

I was almost frogmarched down the corridor and I could feel the eyes of the housekeeper piercing my back. The candelabra Lord Charles was holding made long shadows and shapes as we descended the staircase. He opened a large oak door at the bottom and light flooded into the room. He indicated for me to go in. The room was dominated by a large four poster with dark green damask drapes. A huge fire crackled in the grate and I went over to it, gratefully warming my chilled hands. Two labradors were stretched out on the rugs by the fire, hardly raising an eyebrow as I found a space between them. They must be getting used to me. Thankfully, there was no growling from them this time.

I heard the clink of glass and turned to see Lord Charles pouring dark liquid into two glasses. He was standing by a large desk which was covered with piles of neatly stacked papers. He walked towards me with the glass, which I took with a shy smile. I was still shivering.

"Thank you," I said as I took a gulp and felt the brandy bringing a glow to my body.

He indicated for me to sit down and I sank into a worn leather Chesterfield chair, hooking my frozen toes onto the fender. Lord Charles flipped his coat tails in one graceful gesture and sat down opposite to me.

The room was silent except for the gentle breathing of the labradors. I didn't want to break this magical atmosphere. The nearness of Lord Charles and his likeness to Chris overwhelmed me, utterly. I could feel the power of him in every breath I took. I was aware of his closeness in every cell of me. I was back, to the state of my being, seventeen years ago, when I thought I'd achieved perfect happiness and contentment. I wanted to stay here, never to leave.

One of the labradors stirred and Lord Charles leaned forward to pat him. I sent a silent prayer, *please don't send me back now, please let me experience this feeling for a little while longer.*

"Miss Woods…" Lord Charles broke the silence. I turned to look at him.

He was very close to me. I could see the blond hairs on the back of his hands. His skin was tanned and healthy, his fingers long and tapering. My heart started racing and I took a deep breath to steady myself.

"I can understand if you wish to leave my employment under the circumstances," he began. "Most of the people who live and work here *do* lock their doors at night. One can never be too careful about one's safety, but I do feel responsible. I am afraid that my father's behaviour is becoming increasingly eccentric. I…" he paused, "I do hope that he didn't harm you in any way." He turned that intense gaze on me, his face full of concern.

I shook my head and looked back into the fire, tearing my gaze away from those eyes. "No, sir, he did not, and I do hope that you will let me stay here, in your employment."

I waited. He placed his glass down on the table next to me and stood up.

I couldn't bear it if he sent me away. I knew this was not my real life, I knew all the logical reasons why I should see someone about these strange things that were happening, but I was worried that if I did, and if I ceased to go back to *this* life, I'd never see him again.

He moved to stand by the mantelpiece and placed his foot on the brass fender, only a metre away from mine.

"The children like you, Miss Woods and my wife is happy with your work. Most importantly, I promised your father that I would find you employment."

I turned to smile gratefully at him, but his face was serious. He kicked a log with his shiny boot and sparks crackled and flew up the chimney. One of the labradors grunted and yawned.

"However, there are certain conditions."

I glanced up at him.

"You must bring up my daughter so that she will make a competent wife for a gentleman, instead of filling her head with ideas she should not have. She must be able to look pretty, sew, make conversation, speak a little French, organise a household and obey her husband, and that is all."

"But sir…"

He held up his hand to silence me.

"And my son will inherit my title and my estate. He will soon have a tutor. There is a softness in him that must be hardened or else he will not survive in our world today."

"But sir, you cannot change their characters. Emma is very intelligent and she understands her rights. She could go to university."

Charles threw back his head and gave a bark of laughter. "And be a bluestocking and a spinster, I don't think so. Emma will marry well and take care of her husband and family."

I carried on; I was in full flow and I couldn't help feeling that this was the weirdest parents' consultation I had ever had.

"And Christopher will become a snob if we don't stop him. He must also be made aware of the needs of his tenants. He cannot live just in this world of privilege. As for his nature, he is a little unsure of himself at times but he'll grow out of that with increased confidence…"

He put his hand up again to stop me. "I think you heard the conditions of your employment, Miss Woods. If you do not agree with the way I want to bring up my children, then let us find you another position."

I was silent, staring into the fire. I had no choice.

The fire crackled and I bent down to stroke one of the dogs who had put its head on my foot. I marvelled at the way I could feel its furry body, the warmth of the fire. Everything was so real, a hundred and fifty years before I was born. A log dropped and the labrador woke up with a start. The light went out and when the darkness cleared I was sitting in my kitchen, the notes for my forthcoming interview strewn across the table, a cold cup of coffee in my hand.

CHAPTER SEVENTEEN

"You need to get in touch with your past life." Liz's voice hit me from across the table. I gave a start and spilled coffee over my notes.

I looked up in astonishment to see her sitting across the table from me, wearing a huge winter coat over her pyjamas, her hair corkscrewing round her face. She threw me a handful of tissues.

"What are you doing here?" I dabbed hastily at the stain, making the coffee spread even further over my notes. I sighed in frustration. "What time is it? I've got an interview today."

Liz gave one of her snorts, usually delivered when people were being excessively stupid, in her opinion. I guess today it was me.

"It's 7.30 in the morning. You phoned me and asked me to come round." She frowned at me. "Or don't you remember? Were you dancing with Lord Beaumont in the great hall?"

So, I had left my previous life in the middle of the night and it was morning here. No logic to that, either.

"No," I said quietly, "I was sitting with him by the fire in his room."

I remembered the feeling of warmth and contentment; it still lingered. The glow of the fire, the dog's head on my foot, the feeling of being in tune with the world.

"Sorry, Jill. Didn't mean to be cynical." Liz got up to make us some fresh coffee. "You sounded desperate on the phone."

"About what?" I was trying to arrange my notes into some kind of order.

She turned towards me and leaned against the work surface, waiting for the kettle to boil.

"We haven't got that far yet, but I guess it's about this time travel business. You sounded agitated." She was trying to flatten her hair and work it into some kind of bun. She sighed and gave up for a moment, in order to make the coffee.

"There's this man I know who comes into the shop," she said, as she poured water into the cups, "and he wanted to leave a card on my notice board. He does regressive therapy. You remember Leah, the other bridesmaid at my wedding? She has always suffered from chronic insomnia. This guy hypnotised her and she went back through her past lives; he played her the tape. She talked in another language for some of the time. In one of her lives she was a Roman soldier, on guard duty at night. You see the connection? Not sleeping."

She placed the cup of coffee in front of me and I blew on it before taking a sip.

"But I am going back in time, without hypnosis," I said. "I can do that all by myself. Why would I want to go to see this man?"

Liz pushed her unruly hair underneath the baseball cap she'd pulled out of her coat pocket. "Because he might be able to stop it happening, so you can lead a normal life again, or he may know why it is happening. He may have answers, he may not, but at least you won't feel so isolated. He may be someone who understands." She poured some cold water into her cup and then drained it. She picked up her car keys.

"There's his card." She threw it onto the table. "I've got to go, kids, business, blah, blah."

She pulled on her Wellingtons and opened the door.

"I hope you don't get run over looking like that," I said.

"My underwear is clean, that's the main thing," she retorted, closing the door behind her.

I twirled the card between my fingers, thoughtfully.

The problem was, did I want it to stop? In my other life I had a father who needed me, children I was fond of. I wanted to help the groom's family, and it seemed that Lady Elizabeth required my help too, and then there was Charles, the enigmatic Lord Charles.

Unfinished business perhaps; but with Charles or with Chris?

I left the card on the table then quickly showered and got ready for work, surprised by my lack of enthusiasm. I had an interview this morning, two flats to see tonight and my divorce papers to sign in my lunch hour. I felt tired and listless, not full of my usual energy and this worried me. Why was I so tired? All I wanted to do was sleep. I gathered my coat jacket and briefcase and as I opened the door, I found Lady Elizabeth standing right outside with her finger to her lips. The room had changed in a flash. I was back in my bedroom at Beaumont House.

She squeezed past me, her crinoline swaying as she did so.

"Close the door, Miss Woods," she whispered.

She was dressed in a plain coat and gloves with a veil over her face. She lifted the veil as she approached me.

"I must ask you to come with me. I am sorry, I know that it is late, but I don't know who else I can trust." She opened the door a crack and looked out into the gloom. "Please put on your outdoor clothes and meet me in the library. Be as quick as you can, I will explain in the carriage."

Then she was gone. I hastily dragged on the garments which were hanging over the one chair in my room, and flung a shawl around my shoulders. It took me ages to dress. The small buttons on the dress and the buttons on the boots were so awkward to fasten. I was still fastening my dress as I crept slowly down the stairs to the library, keeping to the wall as it was so dark. A light flickered under one of the doors off the main entrance hall.

I knocked softly, there was the sound of swishing silk, and it was opened. Lady Elizabeth pulled me inside, quickly looking around her as she did so. There was a soft glow from a lamp inside the room, and I made out the figure of the groom, John. He gave me a respectful nod, and I gave him a slight smile back.

"You have met John, I believe. I am trying to help his family, and he is in my confidence. He thinks we can trust you." She waved her hand in his direction. "Whatever we do tonight, you must tell nobody. Not my husband, Miss Tibbs, or anyone."

I nodded and glanced at John who was looking earnest and alert.

"Let's go, your Ladyship," he said, grabbing hold of the lamp and holding it high above him. "The carriage is ready."

John led us out of the library and we hurried down lots of stone steps to what must have been the basement of the house. The kitchens were silent, the rows of scrubbed, copper pans hanging above us, shining in the lamplight. The fire was still burning brightly and the room was warm and smelt of fresh bread and the remnants of the evening meal. We climbed up more steps which led out onto the street. We were at the back of the house. It was so dark. I had left my own world in the morning, as I was about to go to work, but here, it was night. The carriage was waiting, the horses standing patiently. It felt chilly and damp and there was a strong smell of smoke in the air.

John helped us to climb in and there was the familiar squeak as we settled inside, then I heard the sharp jingle of the bridles as the carriage gave a lurch and we were off.

I looked at my companion for an explanation.

She leaned forward and gave me her wide smile. "We are going to meet someone," she said in her little breathy voice. "I want you to help me."

"I will if I can…" my voice trailed off. I was imagining all kinds of things.

"I have to stress, you must not tell my husband. He would not approve."

I'll bet he wouldn't, I thought.

"I know that he is your employer, and I know he thinks your views are too, too…"

"Liberated?" I suggested.

"Yes, yes, liberated. For a woman."

"And he wants you to look beautiful, and run the house, but not to have views of your own, is that right?" I asked.

"Oh, how well you know him," she gasped.

I lifted my eyebrows "Isn't that what most Victorian men are like?"

"Victorian?" she looked puzzled.

"Isn't that it? Women are regarded as inferior. Angels of the home."

She smiled. "But we are, aren't we? Men are so much cleverer." Her smile grew wider. "But not in all things."

Suddenly the carriage stopped, and Lady Elizabeth threw me a quick glance. "I can rely on you, can't I, Miss Woods?" she said. "I cannot do this alone. If you will help me, I promise I will do everything I can for your father." She looked down quickly and then gave me a shy smile. "But even if you can't, I will still help him. He is a good man."

I sighed. Why was this woman so nice? She was making it very difficult for me to consider seducing her husband. Still, if I was aiding her in *her* love affair that kind of cancelled everything out.

I pressed her hand. "Let's go," I said.

I climbed out of the carriage behind her, and found myself on a bridge over the Thames. It was lit by lamps and I quickly scanned the skyline. There was St Paul's, but no London Eye, no brightly lit city. The South Bank was a mass of warehouses, tall, grim buildings with windows like empty eye sockets. The river was busy and bustling, and so was the bridge. Gaudily dressed women laughing and chattering were making their way across the bridge which led towards the West End. *Rather a strange place for a romantic liaison*, I thought. Then I saw John tucking a pistol into his trousers and I suddenly became frightened. Lady Elizabeth moved quickly to stand in front of a group of women who were about to cross the bridge, after warming themselves near the brazier.

"Sisters," she said in her low voice, "I can help you. I know a place where you can go, where you will be safe and you can leave this life."

They stopped and stared at her in astonishment. Then the oldest of the group who was dressed in a torn and gaudy red dress, her untidy, dirty hair escaping from a ragged bun, walked aggressively towards Lady Elizabeth. I saw John put his hand on the pistol, and I quickly moved towards the group, amazed by what was happening.

The woman put her hands on her hips and glared at us. "An' who sez I wants to go there, my Ladyship," she spat. "Are you gonna look after me and my kids?"

"Please," Lady Elizabeth put a hand on her arm. "There's a bed for you, and clothes. We will educate you, help you to lead a better life. My friend, Miss Burdett-Coutts has a house…"

The woman snorted with laughter as did the other girls. The woman leaned in to Lady Elizabeth, her foul breath making me recoil, but Elizabeth stood her ground. "But I bet there ain't any gin there, is there my lovely? You go back to your nice house, Duckie, and leave us to our lives." With a flounce of her shawl, she turned away and the women moved on, looking back at us and laughing.

There was a sudden blast of cold wind across the river. I led Lady Elizabeth to the brazier, where some of the women were huddled around the fire warming their chapped hands. They looked like shadowy black crows in the increasing darkness.

"You must stop this," I whispered to her urgently as we found a space between them. "It's dangerous."

She held her gloved hands to the fire, shaking her head at me as she did so. "They need help," she said, looking into the fire. "Nobody will help them. And I can."

A man in a shabby coat was leaning against the toll booth, smoking a foul smelling pipe and leering at Elizabeth. I glanced quickly at John, who looked uneasy as his eyes darted about, one hand on his pistol, which was hidden beneath his coat.

"My lady," he whispered. "Let's leave this place, it is not safe."

A group of shabby, dirty young girls, looking no more than twelve or thirteen, were shambling towards us, their eyes hollow with hunger and disappointment with life.

Elizabeth turned quickly and blocked their path. "My dears, come with me," she pleaded with them, her arms outstretched towards them. "I have food and a bed for the night."

I looked on in horror as the young girls stopped and glanced uncertainly at each other.

"John, the carriage," Elizabeth said over her shoulder, "quickly." She turned back to the girls. "I have food. I have a place you can go to and be warm."

"My lady," I hissed. "You can't just kidnap them."

She ignored me. "Where are you going?" she addressed the tallest one.

"To work, mum. We work the theatres."

"And your parents?"

The girl hesitated and fiddled with her shabby shawl. "Parents are dead, mum, and we don't want to go to no workhouse."

"Are these your sisters?" Elizabeth pointed to the rest of the little company.

The girl nodded.

"Then come with me," she said, triumphantly. She pointed to the carriage which had pulled up next to us. "I'll give you food and a place to sleep and you won't have to go with any men tonight."

The girls hesitated, and looked behind them, the wind whipping at their torn dresses as they shivered. John nervously glanced around him while trying to steady the horses. The man at the toll gate started to laugh, a harsh rasping sound. The stench from the river became more acute as fingers of a thick soupy fog curled around us.

"Please get into the carriage, girls." Lady Elizabeth wrenched open the door as the stinking, yellow fog started to close in. Clutching each other by the hands, the girls looked at each other and then scrambled into the coach.

There was a roar of rage and from out of the fog an enormous man emerged. Dressed in a long tattered coat and battered hat, he strode towards us, waving a gnarled stick in the air.

Lady Elizabeth and I scrambled in after the girls, slamming the door behind us as the horses took off, scattering the little knot of people who'd been watching us.

The shouts and cries of rage from the man faded into the distance, as the horses galloped across the bridge. Then we started to slow down, coming to an abrupt halt. Lady Elizabeth pulled down the window.

"What's happening, John?" she shouted up at him.

"Road's blocked, my lady, there's a cart overturned."

"But we must get through. We have to get the girls to the house. Mr Dickens is waiting for us."

"We can't, my lady. This is the only road through and it's blocked."

I noticed a few shadowy figures creeping towards the coach. "Then take us home, John. Take us to Beaumont House," she said sharply, and snapped the window shut.

"But, my lady, Lord Beaumont…" I began.

"Miss Woods." She turned to me, eyes flashing impatiently. "I want you to help me, not put obstacles in my way. These children have nowhere to go and nobody to love them. I haven't always been wealthy, and I cannot live like I do knowing that outside my house these poor creatures are roaming the streets starving and ill-used. My husband does not approve and I know I should obey him, but I cannot. He sleeps at his club tonight so he need not know." She paused. "Are you going to help me or not?"

I looked at her, so strong and determined, and at the row of sad and dirty faces in front of me. "I'm sorry," I said. "Of course I will help you."

I turned to the girls who huddled together at one side of the carriage. They were pale and terrified, giving off a stale smell of unwashed bodies.

I smiled at them. "Are you hungry?" I said to the smallest one.

She nodded her grubby head and looked up at her sisters.

"Then you shall have lots of food," smiled Elizabeth, "and a nice soft bed to sleep in."

"Will the men come?" asked the smallest one. I felt my eyes spring with tears. I took her little hand with its grimy and bitten nails.

"No, my darling, no men will come," I said, trying to sound reassuring.

Elizabeth leaned towards them. "What are your names?" she asked the oldest-looking one, taking the child's hand in her gloved one.

"I'm Nell, this is Eliza and my little sister is Molly," she said, her voice a rough whisper. She looked out of the window. "The bad man will come for us. We have to give him the money the gentlemen gives us. If we don't, we'll get a thrashing."

Elizabeth patted the girl's hands and I saw the tears glisten in her eyes. "Nobody will hurt you again, my darling." she said.

CHAPTER EIGHTEEN

We arrived back at Beaumont House through a thick, sulphurous wall of fog, which enveloped us when we climbed out of the carriage. John led the way to the kitchen, his lamp held high and as it flickered, it cast long, eerie shadows on the walls. The children were huddled together behind Lady Elizabeth. When we got to the kitchen, the fire was still burning and the children ran to it arms outstretched, the flames lighting up their grimy faces.

"John, bring Jenny, but do not rouse Miss Tibbs," Lady Elizabeth instructed, as she lit one of the lamps. "I'll get Cook. Miss Woods, stay with the children."

She disappeared up the stone steps and I hunted about for a jug of milk. I found one standing on a marble slab in the pantry, a little beaded cloth covering it. I also found three small round dishes and poured the milk into these and hurried back to the children, who snatched the dishes from my hands, choking and spilling the liquid as they drank it.

Cook clattered down the stone steps, her hair in papers. "Mercy me, Miss Woods, what has the mistress done now? And look at these waifs, they are filthy and dirtying up my kitchen!"

She reached the bottom of the stairs with lots of puffing and panting and muttering.

"They are starving," I said as they turned to look at Cook, mouths outlined with white, frothy milk. They handed the dishes back to me, keeping their eyes fixed on Cook as she bustled about finding bread and cheese, continuously giving her opinion on the night's events.

Jenny appeared at the top of the steps, her eyes heavy from sleep and her cap askew.

"Jenny, heat plenty of water and get the tin bath. These children are not moving from here until they are washed," shouted Cook, as she wielded an evil-looking knife in our general direction. She continued to mutter as she cut huge slices of cheese and bread, piling them up on a wooden board, her curls in their papers bobbing around her head like angry snakes.

Elizabeth ran down the stairs after Jenny, her arms full of children's dresses.

"Miss Woods, we will bathe the children and then dress them. These are not needed by Emma any more, and the older girl, Nell, she can wear one of my dresses."

"They'll have lice, m'lady, and God knows what else," said Cook, passing the wooden board to me.

Elizabeth ignored her as she helped me to give out the food while Jenny struggled in with the tin bath. I rushed to help her, placing it by the fire. We filled it from the huge kettles and pans which had been set to boil on the fire whilst the children stared at it in horror.

When John arrived, we wouldn't let him down the stairs as the girls were getting undressed. He was dispatched to get a message to Urania Cottage where Charles Dickens and Elizabeth's friend, Angela Coutts were waiting for the children.

As we filled the bath, Lady Elizabeth explained to me and the children about the scheme which had been set up by Dickens and Miss Coutts, to help young women and children who were in trouble.

We fell silent as we uncovered bruises and marks on the girls. They winced as we took off their faded garments, and even Cook stopped her tirade.

As little Molly sat in the bath and I was soaping her emaciated body, tears were falling down her cheeks in a steady stream. "Don't send me back, Miss," she said. "Don't send me back to the men. They hurt me."

"You're safe, sweetheart, safe here with us," I said, stroking her wet hair. "And we've got a pretty dress for you to wear."

Nell, the eldest one, was comforting Eliza as they struggled into their new dresses, helped by Jenny and Elizabeth.

"He will find us, he will. We've run away before and he beat us and locked us in a cupboard without any food," Eliza sobbed.

"Cook, we need some ointment for some of these marks," Elizabeth said quickly, "and you little one, are not to be frightened any more. That part of your life is over."

She glanced at me and I smiled at her, a bond springing up between us.

"Miss Woods," she said, "we will need to get the children out of the house and to Miss Coutts very early in the morning, before the servants awaken. There are rooms next to the nursery where the children of any guests we have, stay the night. I'd like you to…"

She stopped as there was a noise at the top of the stairs. We all looked up in horror to see Miss Tibbs, fully dressed as though expecting us, her mouth in a thin disapproving line, holding a branch of candlesticks above her.

"Miss Tibbs," I said flashing her my brightest smile, "thank goodness you are here. These children were begging outside in the street and I took them in. I…"

Miss Tibbs came carefully down the stairs. "Miss Woods, this is not your house to invite all and sundry to," she said. "What would your mistress say?"

Lady Elizabeth raised herself up, still holding onto the hand of Eliza.

"I would approve, Miss Tibbs. This is why I am here," she said, jutting her chin out and glaring at the housekeeper.

Miss Tibbs reached the bottom of the stairs and gave a thin smile. The girls clung onto our skirts, trying to lose themselves in the fabric. I could feel their little bodies trembling. Miss Tibbs put the candlestick down on the large wooden table and after a quick glance at Cook, she turned to face Elizabeth.

"Your Ladyship, your husband has employed me to take care of the house, and he is very specific about unwanted guests. I understand your family were in trade and therefore you are not used to the ways of our betters, but I know he would disapprove of this most strongly."

Elizabeth took a step towards her. I could see the anger in her face. "How *dare* you speak to me like that." Her voice was trembling. "I am mistress of this house, and I shall invite whomever I wish to stay here."

"So, you invited them, did you?" Miss Tibb's thin smile grew wider.

"No, no!" I moved between them. "Lady Elizabeth knew nothing of this…" I was interrupted by the girls starting to cry.

"Look, Miss Tibbs," I put my hand on her arm, "they're just children…"

I didn't get to finish my sentence. As her hand grasped mine, there was a small flash of light and I was in the headmistress's office, shaking her by the hand.

"Congratulations." She *almost* smiled at me. "An excellent interview, Miss Woods. Although we do have some reservations about your time keeping, your health seems to be much improved and your references were excellent. You have made a first class impression with both inspectors and your students. I am delighted to offer you the job of deputy head of sixth form on a one year contract."

I was so shocked to be back in my own time that I seemed to be frozen. I took in the room, the gaggle of governors, everyone smiling at me, except her.

I shook her hand quickly and flashed a smile. "Thank you," I said. "Thank you very much."

I almost ran out of the room in my haste to get away, in case she changed her mind. Also, my mind was with the little girls in the kitchen at Beaumont House, and I needed to catch my breath and ground myself in this world. I leaned against the door, shutting my eyes briefly.

I was deputy head of sixth form. I was moving up again; it was my dream job. I'd done it. My eyes sprang open. Then why the hell didn't I feel at all elated? Why didn't it feel right?

The school buzzer shattered the stillness. The school was on the move; it was the end of the day. There was the familiar rumble of feet and a group of children came clattering and tumbling down the stairs, pushing, laughing, and shouting. The main doors were pushed open with a bang, and the herd stampeded past me until only a few stragglers remained; those who had waited for friends, or couldn't get their lockers open or who had been speaking to teachers.

And there he was again, Chris's double. Blond and beautiful, surrounded by girls from my form, all pouting and giggling and vying for his attention. They came to a halt in front of me.

"Hey Miss, did you get the job?" Annie, whose voice could shatter windows, planted herself in front of me.

I nodded.

"Yeow, brilliant." She punched the air and the others cheered.

The boy stood silently looking at me.

"Do I know you?" I asked him, trying to sound as indifferent as possible. "Are you new here?"

He smiled at me and nodded. "Yes, I've just moved here with my mother. My parents have just got divorced."

His smile, the voice, it was so uncanny. I had to know more.

"I'm sorry if this sounds intrusive," I said, smiling. I could see the girls pricking their ears up, sensing possible scandal and they moved closer to me. "But you are so like someone I used to know a long time ago. What's your name?"

He glanced at the girls, but didn't seem at all concerned at my question.

"Charlie," he said. "I used to be called Charlie Spencer, but my mother has changed her name since the divorce."

"What are you called now?" I hardly dared ask.

"Beaumont, Charlie Beaumont."

I nearly fell back against the door. "Is your mother Helen?" I asked.

He grinned. "Yes," he said. "Do you know her?"

Did I know her? She was Chris's sister. So like her to send her boy to a state school, defying her parents. It all made sense now. Helen and I had got on so well, but had lost touch since Chris went away.

"I did. I knew your uncles too, Chris and Harry."

129

I quickly gathered up my briefcase and moved out of the way as the headteacher's door opened.

"Sorry, I have to go." I gave them a brief smile. "I have an appointment."

I don't think I breathed properly until I was in the car but when locked safely inside, I let out a long slow breath to steady myself. I had to see someone. I had to get my life back. I was drifting and felt ungrounded, moving without notice, in and out of two lives. I should have been hysterical with joy after getting this job, but my thoughts were with those poor little girls and I wanted to be back there with them, where I was needed.

Needed? Did I want to be needed? A strange and unwelcome thought drifted into my head. Who actually needed me in this life?

The answer was plain and simple.

Nobody.

I sat and watched the children leaving school, wending their way homewards in the fading light. Well-fed, loved and educated, materially so fortunate with their iPods and mobile phones and laptops. I thought of those poor mites I had helped to rescue, with their bruises and hungry faces. God alone knew what they had been through and what emotional scars they had.

I flipped open my mobile and rooted through my bag for the card Liz had given me. I felt scared, but I knew that I needed help. Life couldn't go on like this. I was losing control.

The conversation was short, I gave no details, but he was free now, and I was on my way. I cancelled my appointment with the estate agents, then switched on my satnav, praying that I would remain as me during my appointment. If I didn't think of Chris, then I might not go back.

I drove through the town, obediently following the imperious female voice. I don't know what I expected, a gothic house high on a hill shrouded in mist, perhaps? The reality was totally different as she directed me into a modern housing estate on the edge of the town. Some of the houses were still being constructed and the road was muddy. Through the gathering gloom of an early December evening the scene looked apocalyptic. Skeletons of houses reached up to the sky, casting long, spiky shadows through the orange glow of the street lights. I turned left into a recently constructed road where the pavements were streaked with sand, and that's where the satnav gave up on me. The estate was too young for it to cope with.

I pulled up outside a neat little garden. Young trees in the first flush of youth were waving their skeletal arms in the slight breeze as though they were waving me inside. It took a good five minutes for me to pluck up the courage to ring the bell of the fully illuminated semi. It was opened by one of my Year 10 pupils, a tousled redhead in oversized jeans and sweater. She grinned when she saw me.

"Hello, Miss," she said. "Have you come to see Dad?"

I nodded and she showed me into a comfortable study, where I sank into a soft leather chair. I was immediately joined by a terrier and two cats.

"Don't worry, Miss," grinned my pupil, "I'm Dad's secretary and everything is confidential. I'll get Dad." She disappeared with another grin, and I sighed and tried to get comfortable under the weight of my animal companions.

One of the problems with teaching and living in the same area is that you are famous. The young man who mended my drains was an ex-student of my former school. He had hated english and me, but he did a good job on the drains, and we managed to laugh about the time he locked me in the stockroom and threw the key down the toilet. We couldn't remember whether he was expelled for that, or for something else.

I jumped up at the sound of someone running down the stairs, spilling animals in all directions. An attractive man with a shock of wavy black hair and the most disarming smile I have ever been on the receiving end of, walked towards me.

"Hi, Miss Woods," he said. "I'm David. I remember you from parents' evenings. Welcome, please sit."

"Hello." I made a pathetic attempt at a smile. "Please call me Jill."

He sat down in a swivel chair next to an untidy desk, and turned to where I'd seated myself in the leather chair again, this time without animals.

"I have your details here. They were submitted to me by a friend of yours, Liz Henderson, in anticipation of your coming." He grinned at me. "This is unorthodox and I certainly won't use any of this without your consent. So, if you would like to look over the details."

Details? I have details? What had Liz been doing *this* time?

He passed a piece of paper to me and it was all there. How well Liz knew me. I was slightly annoyed with her, but also grateful. I would have found it difficult to relate any of this, and she knew it.

I offered the paper back to him, with a brief nod of consent. He spent a few moments reading it while I tried to keep myself in this life by focusing all my attention on him, looking at the shiny waves of blue black hair and the strong arms and hands. He was the sort of person who would look after you. I tried to relax, but the anticipation of what may happen in this room made me feel almost sick with fear. The palms of my hands were cold and damp and I clasped them together in order to stop myself from trembling.

He put the papers down, and looked straight at me. He had really dark brown eyes, almost black.

"While I am here, I may go back in time again. I may not remember what happens," I said quickly. "This may sound like nonsense, but I keep going back to another time, another life when I am a governess. The same people are around me. They are in both of my lives. It is not a dream. It doesn't happen when I'm asleep. It can happen anytime, and it's real. It is as real as you and I sitting here."

I ran out of breath and he was staring at me steadily.

He leaned forward and put my hands in his, closing his eyes as he did so, then after a moment, he opened them.

"Jill, you are a troubled soul," he said. "There is so much sadness in you." He took a deep breath which was actually more like a sigh, and his eyes filled with tears. He shook his head.

"What are you doing?" I snatched my hands away.

He didn't say anything. I thought he hadn't heard me. He gave me a reassuring smile and rested his hands on his knees as he leaned towards me. "We all have an energy field in and around us," he said. "I'm sorry, I should have explained, I was just tuning into yours, in preparation for the regression. I may have to relax or hypnotise you."

"Hypnosis?" I shrank back from him. "I don't want to be hypnotised," I said sharply.

He frowned. "I thought you would have read the brochure Liz sent to you. I'm sorry, I should have explained. I have to hypnotise you, or at least put you in a very relaxed state in order to retrieve your cell memories. That's the way it works. What is happening in this life is often rooted in unresolved past life experiences. There may be an explanation which we can find, and it may help you."

I stood up and started pacing the small room. Candles on the shelves and windowsills flickered as I walked past. "Why am I going back in time? Why is this happening to me?" I turned round to face him.

He indicated for me to sit down, but I remained where I was. "I don't know," he continued, "but there will be a reason, that's for sure. And if we can get you to regress…" Then he stopped suddenly, his gaze riveted to somewhere over my head.

"What? What? What are you looking at?" I swivelled round but there was nothing, only a closed door.

He stood up and took my hand. "Don't be afraid, please sit down and be calm." He led me back to the chair and then turned to face the door, then he looked back at me. My heart was racing and I could feel drops of sweat forming under my fringe. He put his finger to his lips as I started to speak, his eyes going back to the door.

"Jill, there is a young girl standing behind you," he said. "You may not be able to see her."

I froze in my chair, my heart now really hammering. I could feel the hairs on the back of my neck start prickling.

I saw him smile, and then he looked back at me. "She says her name is Emma, and she has a message for you."

That did it. I fled. Out of the room and out of the house. I slammed the car door and drove like a maniac, traffic lights, crossroads, everything was a blur, seen through eyes brimming with tears. I forgot about the satnav and got lost several times, each wrong turning building up the panic inside me. Tears were still pouring down my cheeks as I ran up the stairs to my flat. I could hardly get the key in the lock. The phone which was ringing from the hall sounded urgent and demanding. I ignored it and flung my handbag on the table, papers spilling out in every direction. I poured myself a large glass of wine and sat down, grabbing one of the papers. My eyes were still streaming and I could hardly read the words. I wiped my eyes with a tissue and turned my attention back to the document.

It was my decree absolute.

CHAPTER NINETEEN

I don't think that I went to bed that night. With the kind of life I was living, it was difficult to tell. The boundaries between sleeping and waking were disintegrating. Time had no logic anymore. It would be morning in one world and evening in another. I had no idea of the passing of time, and no idea of what was reality anymore.

I spent a lot of the time packing things into boxes. I had two weeks to find somewhere to live, and I hoped my other self would find me somewhere nice while I was fulfilling my duties as a governess. Louis and I had moved into this flat with such high expectations of making it into an oasis for us both, but the pressures of work and the lack of time scotched that idea. When we split up, with some snail-like help from Jeff, I had tried to make it into a real home, and just when it was starting to feel like one, I had to leave. I often felt that the place didn't have a heart, and as I sat in the window seat of my bedroom, looking out into the gloom of the long night, I started to feel the same about myself.

I've never watched the sunrise. I lived opposite to a park, but had never been in it. I'd not even noticed the birdsong before. As the sky paled from inky black to a crimson and yellow glow, and the first bird started to call, I felt that the start of this new day was somehow special and significant. The trees outside, stark and naked without their leaves, turned from black skeletons against the sky to shades of green and grey. The birdsong grew louder and more urgent, and the first car, its tyres slick against the wet road, purred past.

I made myself comfortable and started to write a list. I was a teacher. I was anal about lists. I spent my life wading through post-it notes and ticking things off as I achieved them, and now I tried to write a to-do list for my life. I abandoned it. How could I write anything as my future was so uncertain? There was only one thing

I knew I had to do immediately, and it scared me.

I swung my legs to the floor and padded across the bedroom to my phone. I took a deep breath and dialled. It was answered immediately.

"Hello."

I pictured the wavy hair and the strong reassuring hands.

I cleared my throat. "Hello, it's Jill Woods, I hope I didn't wake you. I know it's the weekend but…"

"Hello, Jill." I detected a smile in his voice. "Don't worry, I'm an early riser. Life's too short to stay in bed."

I made a mental note that there couldn't be a girlfriend around.

"I have to apologise to you for running away," I said quickly. "I got scared." I paused. "It seems that I've spent the best part of my life running away." I gave a nervous laugh.

"Don't apologise," he replied. "I probably rushed things with you. I can get things wrong too."

I hesitated. "I'd like to try again," I said.

There was a pause. "Would you feel better if I did a home visit?" he said. "Some people feel easier in their own home."

I didn't hesitate. "Yes, I would, if you could."

I heard the rustle of paper. "When would you like…?"

"As soon as possible, please."

"What are you doing now?"

"I'll see you as soon as you can get here."

"I'll be about twenty minutes."

I quickly rang Jeff. Somehow he had invited himself to go to Castle Beaumont with me today. I delayed him by an hour, and hastily showered and made myself presentable.

There was a polite knock and David was at the door. As soon as he stepped inside the flat, the atmosphere changed. There was something reassuring about him. I felt as though he took me seriously; I felt safe. Soon we were sitting across the table from each other with mugs of Jeff's green tea.

I took a breath and began. "Yesterday you saw a little girl, Emma. I am her governess in my past life. It made it all too real for me. I was afraid, I'm sorry."

Those brown eyes, so full of kindness studied me.

"No, it wasn't *that* Emma," he said quietly. "She said she was your daughter."

"Oh my God! Oh my God!" My hand flew to my mouth. I was about to stand up but his strong hands gripped mine and prevented me.

"Jill, please. If people that you have loved come back to talk to you through me, you mustn't be afraid. They want to help you."

"But she died, she was a baby… What did she say? What did…" my voice petered out.

He smiled at me. "She says not to worry, she's happy. She had only a short message for you. It was, *don't be afraid to love.* That was all."

I stared at him.

"I hope that means something to you."

I continued to stare at him, not really believing what I had just heard. "It guess it sums up my life in a nutshell," I said, my voice breaking slightly, "but she was a baby. How can this happen? How come you saw her?"

"I'm also a medium," he said. "Sometimes, people who have passed on need to contact the ones that are left behind, and vice versa. The children I have seen are older than when they died. I don't understand everything either. I am just telling you what she said."

I took a sip of tea, wishing that it was something stronger. Surely all this was just mumbo-jumbo. But what about the message from Emma, and how did he know her name? I hadn't told him and neither had Liz. It wasn't in the notes Liz had given to him either, so why would he make it up and why did that message feel so significant and relevant?

I let out a long sigh. David was still gripping my hands but they felt warm and gentle.

"I believe that we all have guardian angels," he said. "But sometimes we don't listen, or don't want to."

I made up my mind. What had I to lose?

"The regression," I said, looking up at him. "I'll do it, I'm ready."

He put his cup on the table carefully. Those deep brown eyes held mine for a few moments.

"You're not ready," he said. "There is a barrier so strong around you that I can't get through, and until you try to knock it down you won't be receptive to what I am trying to do for you."

"But what do I do?"

He stood up and reached for his coat, and I started to panic. "What can I do to get rid of it?"

"Listen to the advice of your daughter," he said, "and don't worry about going back to one of your previous lives. You are the same soul, you just have different bodies, and you've been sent back for a reason." He wrapped his coat around him. "No harm will come to you, I'm certain, or I would have seen something. There *is* a purpose to all this, although it's not clear at the moment."

I stood up. "When can I come back, when can I see you again? How much do I owe you?"

He turned to look at me again, his hand on the door handle. "Come back when the barrier has a chink I can get through, and there's no charge."

He opened the door, closed it with a faint click, and was gone.

I stood looking at the door, feeling shocked and shaken. Normally the cynic in me would have dismissed it all, but so much rang true. The message resonated so soundly and it kept churning round my brain, refusing to leave. Since I lost both Chris and Emma, I was determined never to get attached to anyone again, so I'd made my work the love of my life. It was there that I felt safe, except that work had now backfired on me too.

Jeff burst into the room, wearing his usual tight jeans and a brown leather jacket. He looked adorable, and as he deposited some strange looking cakes on my table and turned to grin at me, I caught him in my arms and hugged him.

"Whoa, what's this for?" He looked slightly embarrassed.

I gave him a kiss on a stubbly cheek.

"Thanks for being my friend." I rested my forehead against his. "Thanks, Jeff."

"My pleasure." He brushed the tip of my nose with his finger and released me, leaving the scent of a rather sensuous aftershave in his wake.

"I've borrowed my mate's sports car, so we're going to travel in style."

"The roads will be icy." I gathered up my gloves and scarf.

"We'll be fine. We'll have mulled wine and hot pies at the house. It will all be festive and warming, and on the way, I want you to look at these flats I've found for you. Arlene has just moved into them. They're by the river."

He thrust a leaflet into my hands as we clattered down the stairs. "We'll go on the way, just to have a look."

The flats were beautiful. Arlene let us see inside hers and I was smitten. The price was steep but I had a new job. With instructions to telephone after the weekend, we were soon on our way. I stuffed the information into my bag as I asked, "Do you still see Arlene? You seemed to be okay with each other."

Jeff shrugged. "Yeah, sometimes. We are still mates, I guess, but you have to move on, don't you? Anyway, there's this girl I've been seeing."

"Oh yes?" I felt a slight stab of jealousy.

He grinned. "I'll introduce you, and as a mate, you can give me your opinion. I've known her since school, but she's changed a lot. Actually I used to think she was a bit thick, but she's not. She got up one morning and decided to change her life. Bit like Eliza Doolittle. You've got to admire a girl like that."

"Can't wait to meet her," I said, as I climbed with difficulty into the tiny car.

Jeff turned on the radio and I relaxed back into my seat. Emma's words were still with me and somehow I felt strangely comforted by the fact that she may not be completely lost to me, but was watching over me.

I looked at the road ahead. I knew that I had to go back to Castle Beaumont. I was drawn to it, it felt a part of me, and maybe an answer was there. It was good to have Jeff with me, but was he another lovely man I'd let slip away? Mind, the fourteen year age gap may have been a slight stumbling block.

The snow started to fall as we reached the Castle, and the green hills surrounding it were soon coated in a white blanket, as were the horses and sheep that tried to shelter in the hedgerows. The Castle stood proudly at the top of the hill, lights blazing through the snow.

We followed the winding drive where the trees drooped as their branches filled up with snow. A clutch of red deer raised their heads to look at us as we drove by.

We parked in the rapidly filling car park, watching the tourists, who were bundled up against the cold. We walked through the freshly fallen snow to the house, the soft flakes gently falling on our faces. The entrance was warm and inviting, scented candles burning in the great hall which was hung with holly and evergreens. We paid our money and stared up at the huge Christmas tree. A fire was burning in the grate and people were warming their chilled hands.

"It's beautiful," said Jeff. "Imagine living here. I'd never be out of work if I had to decorate this place."

I suppressed a smile as I followed him, imagining Jeff making flapjacks for Chris's family. If he was their decorator, they'd have to employ him for life. He consulted the guide book and we made our way along the corridors to the main rooms. The sound of a choir singing somewhere in the depths of the house seemed ethereal and the smell of cinnamon and spices awakened the anticipation of Christmas.

"I just want to make a quick diversion." Jeff grinned mysteriously. "Come to the dining room. I'll show you where it is, I've got the map."

I smiled to myself. I knew every inch of this lower floor. I'd eaten in the dining room as the unwelcome guest of Lord and Lady Beaumont.

The girl from the bakery was on duty, talking about the portraits to a very interested old gentleman. I gave a start when I saw her again. Was she the key? What did she know? Little Jenny, Elizabeth's maid. Jenny, who was having her own disturbing dreams about the future.

She turned to greet us and beamed. "Jeff, so glad you came."

Jeff turned to me. "Jill, this is Jane," he said, "the girl I was telling you about."

The difference was incredible. The stuck-on fringe was gone. Glossy hair tied neatly in a bun had taken its place. She seemed so different, more confident.

Jane looked at me. "Hello again," she smiled. She turned to Jeff. "I know her. I used to serve Jill in the bakery and we met here when she brought her students." She turned her attention back to me. "I split with my boyfriend, he was real trouble and he got the push from here. They've taught me to speak proper as well because I have to talk to people and I've got promoted. A scullery maid no longer!"

I did a double take. "Sorry…?" I said. This had completely floored me. Jeff and Jane. This was spooky.

"Jane's going to evening classes," grinned Jeff. "She's going up in the world."

"I'll leave you two to chat for a moment," I said, wanting a little time to myself in order to absorb this new revelation. "I'll just look at the garden. I love the view of the fountain from here." I took my leave of them with a smile and then turned to look back. Jeff was grinning, talking animatedly to her while she looked up at him adoringly.

I walked back the way I'd come and stood for a while looking out of the French doors. They were festooned with evergreens and bright holly berries which framed the snowy landscape.

There was a figure standing by the fountain, dressed in a long dark coat. Suddenly it turned and strode across the lawn towards the house.

As the figure grew clearer I saw that it was Lord Beaumont. He would be on the warpath, searching for me, no doubt. I tensed my stomach muscles waiting for the tight pull of cloth around my waist. I felt his disapproval even from this far away. I wondered if he'd found out about the children we had rescued. Would I have to cover for Elizabeth? I'd let him do the talking just in case. Who knows what I might have missed while I was back in my life.

But something was wrong. He was dressed in modern clothes, and so was I. Nothing had changed. I glanced round to see Jeff and Jane still talking together, and then I stared out into the garden once more.

I swear that at that moment my heart stopped beating, just for that one second of realisation.

It was Chris.

Except it couldn't be. He was in America. But no, it *was* him and he was walking towards the entrance to the main hall. Without thinking, I fled down the corridor, my boots clattering on the marble floor. He walked in through the main doors, brushing the snow from his coat.

It was him, unmistakably him. Looking a little older, but still handsome, the same face with those aristocratic cheekbones, and the same effect on me, turning me to jelly. He was walking towards me but he hadn't seen me; one of the attendants was talking to him. I stepped out, smiled and then quickly retreated behind a pillar, changing my mind in an instant. I couldn't do it. I couldn't see him. I was shocked and I was shaking, I couldn't see him like this. I'd turned from a confident woman into a quivering schoolgirl in an instant. He was so close, I could have reached out and touched him. The power of the feelings I had for him surged through my body like a tsunami. I leaned against the cool marble pillar, not taking my eyes off him, not daring to breathe.

He walked past me, and the moment was gone.

I sat down by the fire, the seats now vacant as people had followed the distant sounds of the choir. Strains of Silent Night soared above me, filling the space with a haunting and beautiful sound. The candles on the table in front of me flickered and the smell of cinnamon filled the air.

"Miss Woods, Mama said would you like to hear the singers?"

Emma's solemn little face was looking up at me. Her small hand was resting on my knee. She gave me her toothy smile and tugged at my hand. I was in exactly the same place; the fire was burning, but the light so different. It was darker and the hall was lit by the yellow glow of gas lamps and candles, which threw deep shadows in the vast room.

"Come *on*, Miss Woods." Emma pulled my hand, and I stood up, glancing quickly to where I had left Jeff and Jane in the dining room. There was a flurry of activity as maids and footmen prepared the table for a large feast. I caught glimpses of candles, greenery and shimmering crystal.

Emma dragged me across the hall to the Christmas tree where a group of singers, muffled up in scarves and long coats and holding a variety of lanterns, were singing Silent Night.

My body tingled with excitement. This was a scene straight out of a Christmas card. The family were seated and the black-clad servants were standing around the walls. The maids, with starched white aprons, stood around in small groups listening. Some were singing, and some stood ready with trays of food and mugs of steaming ale or wine.

Emma led me over to join the family. I stood with the children, just behind Grandfather and Nanny who were sitting, their hands entwined, singing in harmony with the carol singers. A twelve bore shotgun rested on their knees and a brace of pheasants was slung across Nanny's shoulders.

I drank in the moment, wishing for my digital camera to record every beautiful detail, the sparkle of Lady Elizabeth's jewels, Lord Charles's snow white shirt, Emma's shiny ringlets bound with scarlet ribbons and the leering grin of Lord Beaumont's father as he turned to wink at me.

The singing finished, and applause rang out. Drinks and pies were given out and the carol singers dispersed. Lord Charles shook their hands, while the servants dispensed the food and drinks, and I saw large notes of money change hands.

Lady Elizabeth rose from her chair and beckoned me towards her. She gave a quick glance over to her husband and then shook her head. So, Lord Charles didn't know what we'd been doing. She led me away from the party, at first indicating that the children

143

should go with Nanny and Grandpapa. I had reservations about the twelve bore, but it was left propped up on a chair, and the family departed without it.

"Thank you, Miss Woods, thank you," she whispered, her eyes darting about as she spoke to me. "Thank you for taking those poor children this morning. They are safe. My husband thinks only that you gave them food. Miss Tibbs seems to have believed your story. However, he may speak to you about it, as I know he didn't approve of the children being in the house. I have to go to Mass, but I would like you to go to the kitchens if you would. Nanny and I will manage Lord Christopher and Lady Emma. There seems to be a problem with Cook, and I know she thinks very highly of you and may listen to you." She smiled her wide smile. "And I hope that you will join us for some refreshment when we return. We will be in the dining room."

She turned to go, her green, silk dress rippling as she did so, and I made my way to the large staircase which led down to the kitchens, wondering what task I was supposed to perform. I only remember actually meeting the cook on two occasions, but one of the confusing things about stepping in and out of two lives was that each life was continuing when I wasn't there, and I was learning to listen and learn before I spoke, trying to gauge what may have happened in my absence.

The sound of pots and pans clanking and orders being shouted, mixed with the smells of meats and sauces, became more acute as I descended the stone stairs. The wooden tables were filled with pies and juicy joints of meat shimmering with fat. Little girls with sweaty faces and mob caps were rolling out huge slabs of pastry. The fire was roaring, and pans bubbled and steamed amidst the flames. In the middle of it all stood Cook, her arms folded, her face covered with sweat and her hair unravelled from its usual bun.

Jenny was at the end of the table nearest to me polishing a massive silver dish. It seemed as though all hands were on deck. Even Miss Tibbs, her face registering total scorn, was in the kitchen barking orders whilst Cook stood like a disapproving statue, in the midst of the mayhem.

"It's Cook," Jenny whispered to me. "Her gentleman friend is arriving with the party for dinner. He's Lord Carlton's coachman and is expected any time. We are all behind, and she's angry about her hair."

"Her hair?" I looked at Jenny in astonishment.

"Yes, my hair," bellowed Cook. "Look at it!" She stormed over to me. "I've washed it and it looks like a dish rag. It's the bloody heat in this kitchen." She banged her fist on the table and the little girls turned pale. "All the food will be as good as ever, but my gentleman will not think the same about me if he sees me like this. I'm a sight not fit to be seen and nothing gets done until it's put right."

I looked at the mass of unruly hair, thinking quickly as I did so. The girls had stopped working and were watching me with eager anticipation.

"Can you spare ten minutes from your duties in the kitchen?" I asked her.

"Jenny, keep your eye on the girls," Cook barked. Jenny snapped to attention.

"You can still be here," I said to her. "I just need a heated iron, some brown paper, and some hairpins. Oh, and a bit of space on the table."

"Alice, heat up the iron. Jenny, you'll have hairpins from the mistress, and a looking glass. Get them!"

Cook lifted piles of saucepans from the table near the fire. "I've got brown paper in that drawer, Miss Woods," she indicated to me. "Now, what do you want me to do?"

"Lay your head on the table, and spread out your hair," I said as I unfolded a square of paper, "and pass me the iron, Alice. You must keep it hot."

Cook looked at me for a moment, then did as I bid her.

The iron steamed and crackled as Alice spat on it, and I took hold of the top of it with a cloth. I placed the brown paper over Cook's hair.

"I'm going to straighten your hair," I said to Cook.

"Well, don't you burn my head!" was the muffled reply.

Work was stopped momentarily, and a little knot of faces peered over the table.

"You watch them pans, my girls," Cook roared, and the faces scattered.

I pressed the iron onto the paper, moving it up and down Cook's wiry locks. They soon became softer and shiny and when I made her stand up, silky hair flowed around her shoulders.

There was a collective, "Oooohhh," from the girls and I put the finishing touches by securing the hair with pins into a loose bun. Miss Tibbs climbed back up the stairs with a disapproving sniff.

"The looking glass, quick, Alice," demanded Cook. She grabbed it from Alice's shaky hand. All the maids held their breath as Cook scrutinised herself. When the mirror was lowered, she was beaming.

"A glass of sherry for Miss Woods," she trilled.

I smiled as it looked so incongruous; a 21st century hairstyle on a 19th century woman, but Cook was pleased. She winked at me and filled up my sherry glass.

A gong sounded from up the stairs. "That's the gong; they'll be going into dinner!" Cook put down the sherry and picked up an enormous carving knife. "Alice, Lucy, upstairs to help Mr Williams serve the drinks. Jenny, you can go back to your duties. You all know what you have to do, so to your places."

I felt very much in the way as people started to move around me, and wherever I stood, someone seemed to want to be in that exact place. I climbed back up the stairs, just as the family were going along the corridor on their way to the Christmas Eve supper.

Emma and Christopher met me at the top of the stairs and led me into the wooden panelled dining room which winked and glowed with candles, crystal and glass. Scarlet berries and evergreens were looped across the walls, and a huge log fire crackled in the grate.

I felt uneasy. Even I knew that a governess never ate with the family, but then I was the daughter of an Earl. Perhaps that is why I had been invited. I was seated between the children, near Lord Beaumont, who was at the head of the table. Lady Beaumont was at the other end. There must have been about twenty people sitting down to the feast. Footmen held the chairs for the ladies, and most of the men in dark suits and gleaming white shirts, stood in small groups, until the ladies were settled. I drank in the sights, aware that I was staring.

I was fascinated by the intricacies of the ladies' hair, which was elaborately coiled in loops and plaits adorned with lace and beautiful combs. Jewels of all colours sparkled at their necks and ears, and the dresses were of such rich hues of reds, golds and purples, they barely looked real. I glanced down quickly to see what I was wearing and was surprised to see an elegant dress of dark red shot with black, tiny black lace gloves on my hands and a heavy necklace of red and gold around my neck. I tried to look at my reflection in the back of a spoon. My hair was up and it felt heavy, but I couldn't see it very well.

"You look very nice, my dear." A kindly be-whiskered gentleman sank down into the seat next to Emma. He leaned across to address me, "Anthony Ashley Cooper at your service."

I turned to look at him. "Lord Shaftesbury, the ragged schools, factory reform... oh my God!"

Here was a piece of living history, a man who had done so much to improve the plight of children.

"I am so pleased to meet you," I said stretching out my hand. "I so admire the work that you did, sorry, what you *are* doing."

He shook my hand and nodded politely, then took a cup of punch from Jenny. I did a double take as I took my glass of punch from the tray offered. Jenny's hair was straightened under her cap and she looked so like Jane it was uncanny.

I glanced up at the other maids. All had little smiles on their faces as they looked towards me. Each of them had straightened their hair and they looked like my sixth form dressed up as Victorian servants.

"I like your hair, Jenny," I whispered.

"I look like me in my dream, Miss, when I was wearing the short skirt," she whispered back.

"I'll talk to you later," I said, as she moved away down the table.

The first course arrived, which was oysters. Not sure how to eat them, or even if I wanted to, I turned my attention instead to Lord Shaftsbury. Nanny was leading the children away from the table, so I moved my seat closer to his.

"I so admire what you have done for children in the factories, Lord Shaftesbury," I said, "but are you aware of child prostitution in London? Young children, *really* young children are being exploited. They see it as a better alternative to the workhouses."

I suddenly realised that everyone had stopped talking. I looked around into a dozen enquiring eyes.

"And how would you know that, Miss Woods?" Lord Charles's blue eyes looked at me steadily. His face was expressionless. I saw Elizabeth pause with her fork halfway to her mouth. She looked terrified.

"If you remember, sir, I became separated from your party after the theatre visit. I saw the children on the streets, children as young as ten or twelve." I was flustered, but continued steadily. "Children who are trapped in poverty have no way out, other than the workhouse. What sort of life is that for a child?"

I looked at them all in their jewels and their finery. I saw the disapproving faces, and heard low whispers about the governess who didn't know her place. I didn't care. What had I to lose?

"Whilst we sit here," I continued, "young girls are being raped and abused by men and they are powerless to better themselves, to escape." There was a shocked collective gasp from the assembled parties.

Lord Charles folded his hands together, resting his elbows on the table. His gaze never left my face. "I think you will find, Miss Woods, that each of the assembled ladies will be out tomorrow on Christmas Day helping the poor, and the gentlemen will have given very generously to the needy. That is what Christmas is about in our eyes."

"But what about the rest of the year?" I exclaimed. There was no stopping me now, I was in full flight. "The poor are still starving. What will happen then? They eat well for one day of the year? That's not good enough. They live in filth and squalor. There's starvation and disease. The government is failing the disadvantaged, and the people who are rich and powerful *could* do something about it."

I could see out of the corner of my eye that Lord Shaftesbury was about to speak but Lord Charles got there before him.

He pressed his fingertips together and gave me an icy smile. "Thank you for expressing your views, Miss Woods, but the children have need of you. I hope you will be able to join us later."

I was dismissed. I rose from the table, aware that the maids' eyes were all watching me. I nodded politely to the party and walked out of the room, my head held high. I could hear the voices following me out. They were unimpressed, in fact they sounded scandalised. They really had no sense of responsibility. I was livid.

Peace and goodwill to all men, my backside, I thought crossly, *and if Lord Beaumont calls me in for another bollocking, I'll give him as good as I get.*

CHAPTER TWENTY

When I left the dining room, I walked through the corridor on the way to the grand staircase. Candles blazed from sconces on the walls which were decked with loops and boughs of holly and pine, and marble statues, standing proudly on their plinths, were adorned with wreaths and brilliant scarlet berries. I stood for a moment, absorbing it all, my senses filled with the smells and sounds of a traditional Christmas.

My thoughts went immediately to Christmas in my own time. Having no family to speak of in this country, and politely declining the invitations of good friends, I had spent most of my Christmases in luxurious hotels, in any country that promised sunshine. The only companions I needed were my books.

I would arrive back at school, tanned and relaxed whilst friends spoke of endless trips to relations, mounting expense and discarded toys. I didn't listen to the stories of families reunited, of love and fun, and the whole British spirit of Christmas, which was about having good quality time with the people you care about.

I sank down on a seat in one of the recesses, thinking of the people who cared about me and how I chose to run away from them. I was lost in my own thoughts until I heard footsteps at the far end of the corridor. A procession of servants was making its way towards me, with Cook at its head. She was holding a huge flaming pudding aloft, Emma and Christopher running alongside her, squealing with excitement.

Emma saw me and bounded towards me, ringlets flying. "Miss Woods, it's the pudding, it's the pudding! Papa said we can see it being brought in and have some in the nursery!"

"You go ahead." I patted her cheek. "I'll be along shortly."

Somehow, I didn't think I would be welcome in the dining room.

I went into the main hall where the Christmas tree stood in its blazing glory. Paper flowers and presents, porcelain ornaments, striped candy bars and candles made it alive with light and colour. It was all so real. I reached out my hand and rubbed the prickly needles between my fingers. The smell was exquisite.

"My father used to tell me how your family had the biggest Christmas tree in London."

I whirled around. Lord Charles was standing by the fireplace, with one foot resting on the fender, his usual stance. The dogs, who must have followed him in, settled themselves by the fire.

"Well, not anymore." I turned to face him. "Not with my father in prison."

Charles kicked at the logs with the edge of his foot, and stared into the flames, his arm resting on the mantelpiece. He looked so like Chris it was uncanny. It wasn't just the tilt of his head, or that rich public school voice, but his smile. He turned to smile at me for the first time and I heard myself breathing out slowly in order not to give myself away. When he looked straight at me with those piercing blue eyes, I could feel my body chemistry reacting. I'd never seen Charles smile before, and it totally threw me off balance. For once in my life, I was speechless.

"I have seen to it that the prison has a substantial donation from my family this year," he said. "John has taken provisions for your father. I believe you are spending the day with him tomorrow?" He raised his eyebrows at me and I nodded obligingly.

"I'm sorry if I spoke out of turn in front of your guests," I managed to say.

He looked amused. "I have come to realise, Miss Woods, that because of your education you have opinions, but you must not in any way, try to influence my children with them," he said. "Lord Shaftsbury was somewhat impressed with your views. You caused something of a debate over supper. However, it is not thought correct to speak about prostitutes in polite society."

"Even though most of polite society has a use for them?" I retorted.

His face darkened slightly, and he moved his foot from the fender and turned towards me. I felt a little afraid by the look on his face.

"I didn't mean to cause offence," I stuttered, "but it is a well known fact that most of the male population in what you would call 'polite society' have a mistress."

He walked slowly towards me, and all I could think of was what is he going to do, and what am I going to do? My eyes fell on the poker as a possible weapon, and then I turned to stare at him, unflinching, as he stood directly in front of me. He was so close that I could feel the heat from his body, see his eyes looking straight into mine. The air around him seemed to crackle with electricity. He was so incredibly beautiful, and so like the love of my life. Time didn't exist. It was suspended and I momentarily forgot which world I was in.

His arms slid around me and I felt his lips on mine in the most passionate kiss I had ever experienced. His arms tightened around me and I pressed him closer to me, my body a mass of tingling energy. I lost myself in him, in time, in my life, as everything stood still. I breathed him in, and the love I'd kept hidden for years absorbed me again.

And then it was over. He released me, touched my face briefly, and was gone, down the corridor towards the dining room. I watched him walking, the sound of his footsteps on the tiled floor fading as he moved further away from me.

My mind was numb. I couldn't think. I turned back to the Christmas tree, but it had changed. No longer the Victorian tree, it sparkled with electric starlight and coloured baubles. I glanced at the fire. It looked the same, the logs crackling in the grate, candles burning on the mantelpiece. I sank down on one of the chairs and put my hand to my lips. I could still feel the strength of his arms around me, the touch of his lips on mine.

"Have a good look round?" Jeff sat himself beside me, pushing back his curls with his hands. He grinned at me. "I *did* have an ulterior motive for coming here, sorry. I should have said."

I felt dizzy and disorientated. I seemed to be suspended between the two worlds, my mind in neither. I shook my head in order to clear it.

"I thought her boyfriend worked here and that's why she was here. I didn't realise that you and her were an item," I said, as I stared at the fire. If I looked at Jeff, he would see the flush and confusion on my face.

"Ex-boyfriend," he said. "She told you, remember! I've known Jane for ages. Always wanting to better herself. I used to be in a band with George, her ex." He stretched his legs out in front of him. "He was a real tosser; I don't know what she saw in him. He hasn't done a day's work in his life."

"Oh, really?" I mused, pot and kettle coming to mind.

I still felt far away, only just taking in what he was saying, unable to think properly at all. I wanted to get back to my past life. I wanted to see Lady Elizabeth, to put things right, to see Charles, to be with the children, to help those poor little girls, to experience Christmas. I didn't want to be here, in this life, which held nothing for me. The sight of Chris after so many years had filled me with such an overwhelming sense of loss that I wanted to run away, somewhere… anywhere… far away from here, far away from my empty life.

By the time I got home, I was determined to have another go at the regression again. I poured myself a glass of wine, and eventually plucked up the courage to ring David. He said he would call round here the next day, after I had been to see the estate agent about buying the flat by the river. I was half-hearted about buying it, even though I had loved it on sight. In fact I realised I was half-hearted about everything in my present life.

I poured myself another glass of wine and thought about Chris and what might have been. I knew when I saw him that my feelings for him were as strong as ever. Perhaps I should have spoken to him, but I was afraid, although of what I wasn't sure. And Charles, oh dear God! What had I done? Did I feel the way I did about him, because of my feelings for his great-great grandson? And what of Elizabeth? Had I betrayed my friendship with her? My head was spinning. It was hard enough having one life to worry about. It was impossible with two.

Tomorrow was Monday and the start of my new job. I made a small attempt at getting ready for work and then went to bed with a pile of books I'd borrowed from the history department on Victorian England. I wanted to be sure I didn't mention anything which was not yet invented and give myself away. I found myself wondering if little Emma would become a suffragette, and then my thoughts turned to young Christopher. He would be too old to fight in the Great War, but if he had children, they would not.

I drifted off to sleep and was surprised to find myself still in the present when I awoke to the sound of my alarm. After checking the time and date on my mobile, I realised that in this life, Christmas was still two weeks away and I hadn't yet made any plans, which was unlike me. Somehow the thought of a remote beach with a pile of books didn't seem so inviting.

For once, I was at work early and I felt quite smug as I pulled into the car park, wondering which of the bright young things would be left without a space. I'd worn a suit again today, determined to start my new job looking professional. The grime on the glass doors was getting beyond a joke. I tapped on the window of the office and was gazed at disapprovingly over a pair of tortoiseshell glasses. She moved as slowly as she could and moved the glass reluctantly aside.

"Yes, Miss Woods." Her face looked as though she had swallowed a wasp.

"Could you please call someone to clean the entrance doors," I said imperiously. "They are a disgrace and give a very poor impression of the school."

Her face twisted into some kind of smirk, and she pushed back her hair, a shiny wedding ring glinting on her finger. *God*, I thought, *some poor bloke actually sleeps with her.*

"Miss Woods," she said, as though addressing a five year old. "Only senior members of staff can authorise that kind of thing."

"Well, well," I said, pushing my face very close to hers, "then, as the deputy head of sixth form, I authorise it. Get it done."

And with that I flounced up the stairs emitting a loud, "Yes," as soon as she was out of hearing.

I opened the door of the english office, and found, amidst an explosion of papers, Andy asleep with his head on the desk, a cup of cold coffee next to him. He woke with a start and smiled wearily at me, suit all crumpled and hair on end. I shifted bundles of exam papers to one side and put my bag on the long desk.

"Andy, what time did you get here, or haven't you been home?" I glanced at him as I filled the kettle. "You look terrible."

He grinned and tried to flatten his hair.

"Sally was up all night being sick, and now I think Sue and the twins have got it, so I left them all in bed as I've got these exam papers to mark." He shuffled through them. "Although actually, it doesn't look as though I have marked any." He looked at me guiltily. "Oh dear."

"I've got a free first thing," I said, spooning coffee into the mugs. "I was going to sort my desk out in the sixth form office, but I'll make a start on them for you, if you like."

A big grin crept over his face and he came over to give me a bear-like hug.

"Oh, God! Yes, of course, congratulations." He gathered me up again nearly squeezing the breath out of me.

"Oooohhh, Sir, Miss!" Two Year 11s, hardly recognisable under three inches of make-up, were standing in the doorway. Andy blushed crimson and went back to shuffling papers about.

"And which part of the 'Do Not Disturb' sign on the door don't you understand, girls?" I said crisply, handing a coffee to Andy. "And the hug that you just witnessed was a congratulatory one as I have just received a promotion, so scram."

I shut the door and sank into a chair with my coffee.

"Thanks, Jill." Andy handed me a large pile of crumpled papers which he'd just been asleep on. He leaned against the desk and took a grateful slurp of coffee.

"Thank God it's nearly the end of term," he sighed. "So what exotic place are you jetting off to this time? Which beach will you be lazing on while I'm feeding the objectionable in-laws?"

I took a sip of coffee and looked at him. "I want to see my Dad," I said. "I think I'll go to Vancouver, *if* he wants me to go."

"I thought you were estranged from him?" Andy looked puzzled. "I thought you'd lost contact."

I put my coffee down and sighed as I ran my fingers through my hair. There were now two of us at it. I made a mental note to get a haircut, although I didn't want to be popping back into 1860 in the middle of it in case the final results were disastrous.

"I've been stupid, Andy. I've been stupid about a lot of things." I gave him a small smile.

There was an urgent banging at the door of the office and the telephone rang at the same time. I got to my feet, smoothing down my skirt as I did so. "We must be really failing as a department, Andy," I said, walking towards the door, "if these kids can't even read 'Do Not Disturb'."

He grinned as he picked up the phone.

"Well?" I asked the gaggle of Year 7 boys, all newly brushed and shiny, who were standing at the door.

"Miss, it's George Pettit," said the smallest boy, who had traces of sherbet around his mouth. He kept pointing towards my classroom. "He's going to jump out of the window."

"What?" I pushed past them hoping that they were joking.

But they were quite right. George Pettit was indeed going to jump out of the window. When I wrenched open the door of my classroom, boys tumbling around me like a set of hounds, I was met by the sight of George, all four-foot ten of him, standing on the window ledge, clinging onto the frame with a look of determined fright on his face, wind whipping at his hair.

"George!" I managed, routing wildly around in my brain, and fighting a wave of panic as I desperately tried to remember something in his notes that would help me. Was there a recent divorce or a medical condition I should know about? Was he being bullied? He started to sway a little and I made my mind up quickly. If I got this wrong, I'd be up there on the sill with him.

"Bit chilly up there, George," I said. "Do you want to come down; it's getting a bit cold in the classroom with the window open."

"I'm going to jump, Miss," he said, looking at me with wild eyes.

I inched my way across the room. "George, can we have a little talk before you decide what to do?" I said, continuing to edge very carefully towards him. "There's lots of people who would be very sad if you did that."

I glanced behind me at Andy who was standing in the doorway, the phone in his hand. I mouthed, "Ring home," and he nodded, putting the receiver to his ear.

George looked down at the ground beneath him. I looked at his grimy hands clinging to the window frame, his knuckles white and bony. He looked desperate and so vulnerable.

"I'm thick me, Miss, I can't do the work. Everyone calls me Thicko." He looked back at me, his eyes red-rimmed.

"*I* don't," I said, giving him my warmest smile, "and I'm sure your Mum doesn't."

Andy threw me the phone, and mouthed the word, *Mum*.

"George, your Mum is on the phone," I said, gently. "She loves you and is worried about you."

He hesitated and looked back at me, a tiny trace of hope in his eyes.

I put the phone to my ear. "Mrs Pettit, this is Miss Woods, I think Mr Tyler has explained the situation to you. I wondered if you could come to the school at once, please."

I smiled encouragingly at George and he continued to look at me.

"What's he doing threatening to jump out of the window, the silly little bugger." A piercing voice on the other end of the line threatened to shatter my eardrums, but I continued to smile encouragingly at George.

"I can't come to no school," it continued to shriek. "I've got the carpet fitters coming at ten." There was an intake of breath. "And you can tell him from me that there'll be no jumping out of no windows, else I'll tan his hide."

There was a click and the phone went dead.

"Lovely," I said to the silent phone. "I'll tell him. He'll be so pleased to know that."

"What did she say, what did she say?" George looked frantic and started to wobble.

I inched a little closer and suddenly grabbed his arm, at the same time throwing the phone onto a nearby desk. Andy ran across the room and grabbed his other arm, and we lifted him down.

"She doesn't want you to jump, George. Neither do we. And look at your friends who are here to support you. They're so worried about you."

I sat him down at the desk, and the three boys crowded round him, patting him on the back and on the shoulders. I bent down until my eyes were level with his.

"Do you know, George, that I failed my maths exam three times? I also know that Mr Pickard says that you're the best artist in your year. We can't always be good at everything, and you've got to learn to take no notice if people are not nice to you. It's their problem, not yours." I gave him a reassuring smile.

He gave me a weak one back.

"Promise me, George," I continued, "that if ever you feel like this again, you'll come and see me first. Your friends are going to take good care of you today, aren't you boys?" They all nodded furiously. "And I'm going to see Mrs Braithwaite to see if she can slot you in for a little extra help with your maths and english. How does that sound?"

He gave me a nod. I handed him his school bag.

"And George, come and see me at the end of the day, and I want your friends to come with you." They all nodded again.

Andy and I stood together, watching them walk out of the room.

George turned and looked over his shoulder. "Thanks, Miss," he said.

Andy and I looked at each other when they'd gone. I let out a sigh and slumped down into the nearest chair.

"You may have been stupid about some things – your words not mine," said Andy, "but you're bloody brilliant at others." He grinned at me. "By the way, you've got the flat; it's yours. That was the estate agent on the phone."

CHAPTER TWENTY ONE

I signed the papers, and they handed me the keys, so I could look around and measure up. I was due to move in after Christmas. It was as simple as that. Jeff insisted he accompany me, and together we made plans for the flat's decoration. I kind of got sucked into his enthusiasm. He'd help me move in and I'd employ him to decorate.

I liked the flat. It overlooked the river and had a huge picture window so you almost felt as though you were suspended in the air over the water. I felt that somehow this move would signal a new start in my life. Over Jeff's date and walnut flapjacks, I agreed to have him start to decorate as soon as the festivities had ended.

I still didn't know where I was going to spend Christmas. I'd tried three times to call my Dad but all I got was an answer phone message each time.

Reluctantly, I drove to David's after a hasty dinner of left-over flapjacks. I was apprehensive and rather scared again. I didn't feel quite so confident now the time had come to see him, and I waited in the car outside his brightly lit house, trying to pluck up the courage to go in. Instead he came out to me, tapping lightly on the window, his cheery face putting me at ease. He wore a pale blue shirt, his hair clean and shiny and his smile engaging. There was something quite calming about him, and soon I was settled into the chair in his study, my hands cupped around a welcoming coffee.

"There's no need to be afraid," he said, resting his chin on his hands, as he looked at me. He gave me a warm smile.

"What's happening to you is unusual, but you've no need to be afraid of it. Not many of us get the chance to see what life was like for us years ago. I envy you. It must be a wonderful experience."

I took a sip of coffee, and put the cup down on the table next to me.

"I don't understand it," I said. "I don't get why this is happening to me, how it's happening and why now?"

He shrugged his shoulders slightly. "It could be something to do with your daughter's message." He leaned back in his chair and looked thoughtful. "In my opinion, it could be that you have been sent back to put something right, or to learn something which will help you with this life. Have you noticed a pattern? Is there some kind of trigger you have recognised which makes you go back?"

I nodded. "It's when I think about Chris, a boy I used to know. I saw him for the first time in sixteen years, since we split up. The effect seeing him again had on me was just…"

I stopped. I couldn't put it into words.

He nodded deep in thought, and then he leaned forward again and gave me a slight smile. "There is not such a wall around you today, perhaps we may be able to go back successfully. We may find an answer, we may not, but it's worth a try."

His words sent a shiver down my spine.

"Do you want me to try?"

I nodded.

"Do you want me to record your experience?"

I shook my head. "Oh God, no, just tell me. Tell me what happens."

I wanted to get it over with and I wanted him to give me answers. He got up and indicated for me to lie down on a soft blanket on the floor. I put the coffee down and settled myself down. I closed my eyes and could hear his voice quite close to me.

"Are you ready? Don't be afraid."

I nodded, and as he spoke to me I began to feel sleepy and relaxed. I shut my eyes briefly and opened them quickly, almost immediately, as the noise around me was deafening. I glanced at my surroundings. I was in a train, sitting opposite to Lady Elizabeth and the children. I was in a compartment, with a sliding door, sitting on a hard green leather seat. I was dressed for the outdoors in a bonnet and tightly fitting long, green coat. The noise from the train was so loud! It rattled and banged as we rolled along, clouds of steam billowing past the window. The children were jumping up and down with excitement and crawling over Nanny who was asleep with her mouth open, in the corner of the carriage.

I glanced at Elizabeth, who looked a little distressed, but was obviously trying to put on a brave face for the children.

"Nanny," she said sharply. There was a snort from the corner.

"Children, wake Nanny!" she said.

The children started to shout her name very loudly, giggling as they did so. Nanny opened her eyes with a start, snorting even more loudly as she did so.

"Nanny," Elizabeth said sharply, clasping and unclasping her gloved hands, "please take the children to look out of the window opposite to our carriage, whilst I talk to Miss Woods in private."

Nanny snorted again, and the children burst into fits of giggles.

My excitement on being on a real steam train was soon dampened by the look on Elizabeth's face. She looked exquisite in dark green silk, her beautiful hair coiled elaborately under a tiny hat.

As Nanny stumbled out behind the children and the door shut with a click, Elizabeth turned to me and leaned across the carriage in order to clasp my hands.

"Charles knows," she said, her eyes filling with tears as she looked at me. "Miss Tibbs must have found out what we've been doing. He knows we go to Waterloo Bridge to help the girls and he knows that I've been giving his tenants food." She looked distraught and her voice was shaky. "How could I not, Miss Woods? How could I not help John's family and those poor girls. I, who have so much. When my father made his fortune from cotton, he sent me away to be educated, and when I came home, we used to help his workers, those who were too poor to help themselves. We refused to employ children and…" she stopped, her voice breaking.

I clasped her hands. "What did he say to you?" I asked. "I thought Miss Tibbs believed my story."

She gave a little sigh. "I thought so too, but she must have been watching us. Miss Tibbs will do everything she can to discredit me. She's been with the family for years and has never liked me because my background is trade. And my dear husband! He is so angry with me; I don't know what he'll do. He *will* stop me from helping others.

He's so ashamed of me." A tear rolled down her face.

"Ashamed of you?" I exclaimed loudly. "He should be proud of you. You're not just a decoration. You are actively helping those who need your compassion and care."

"If people are poor, my husband thinks it's their fault. It's their lot. He feels the same about you too. You are our governess now and we must call you Miss Woods, when you are really Lady Swainby. He believes that the servants cannot know your background and you are with us because your father is now poor and cannot provide for you. Charles made a promise, but he blames your father for your predicament."

She sighed, dabbing at the tears with her handkerchief. "He knows that we visit your father, and some of his less fortunate tenants, and he indulges me in this, but now he knows about my other work, our work, and he wants me to stop."

She looked at me pleadingly. "Miss Woods, I cannot not do it. I cannot stop. I cannot live in comfort and luxury whilst other people starve, even if it means disobeying my husband."

I looked at her in admiration, feeling pangs of guilt about kissing her husband. I was determined it wouldn't happen again. It wasn't fair to her. "You're so kind," I said. "And all the people you are helping are going to live a better life because of you, including my father."

I squeezed her hand again. "Don't worry. We'll think of some way of making this work." I gave her an encouraging smile. "If only I had money to pay off my father's debts. I wish I knew how much he owed and to whom."

Lady Elizabeth let go of my hand and looked down at her immaculate leather gloves.

"I thought you knew," she said looking at me, a small frown on her face. "Your father owes my husband thousands of pounds in gambling debts, and he will be in prison until the debts are paid. I have tried to reason with him, but he won't listen to me, especially not now."

At that moment the children burst back into the carriage, so I had to hide my shock as best I could. A small knot of anger fixed itself in the middle of my chest. Gambling debts! I had lost my home, and my father was in prison because Charles would not write off his gambling debts.

I sat the children next to me with a tight smile on my face.

"We're coming into the station!" Little Emma bounced up and down, her face pink with excitement. "Papa says he has put lots and lots of money into the railways so we must travel on them." She looked eagerly at their mother. "When are we going to visit the poor people, Mama? Is it now?"

I glanced at Elizabeth. "My children need to know that there are people less fortunate than themselves," she said firmly. "They are coming with me today to visit my husband's tenants and to give them gifts. This is what we do at Christmas. My husband *does* approve of this. I am allowed to dispense food and gifts for one day of the year."

"With the children?" I queried.

Elizabeth ignored me, and stood up as the train started to screech and rattle to a halt. "John will bring the carriage for us, and he will call a hackney carriage for you, Miss Woods. I will send the carriage to the pr... to where your father is, to collect you, as soon as we arrive home. Jenny and Nanny will accompany you. Jenny will meet us on the platform."

The carriage door was opened by a smart looking porter, and Elizabeth was helped down the steps. I made sure that the children did not fall through the gap and I followed behind them.

The sign on the station platform said King's Cross, but this was not the station I knew with its electronic boards and coffee bars. The same iron pillars soaring up to the roof were ornate and sparkling with newness. Clouds of steam hissed and sighed from the train as we descended, so everything was viewed through a swirling mist. The huge wheels and body of the train were gleaming, and there were porters in smart little suits and hats, wheeling cases and boxes through the crowds of people. We were surrounded by women in long dresses and furs who were giving orders to servants and porters. Their husbands stood by in long, dark coats, and shiny top hats, their faces encased in side whiskers. And there was so much noise. Whistling and shouting and the hissing and clanking of the trains. I was lost in the wonder of it. History was alive for me and I felt so privileged and proud to be there.

"Miss Woods," said Lady Elizabeth, moving away from me, the children's hands clasped firmly in hers and John at her side, "follow me. John will hail you a hackney carriage."

I glanced behind me at Nanny and Jenny, who had joined us. They were making slow progress. We were soon outside, where the heavy roar of Victorian London, the carriages, the horses and the shouting of servants and street vendors enveloped us.

"Miss Woods?" John said as he stood beside the carriage door he had opened for us. The splendid Beaumont carriage was in front of it, the little faces of the children peeping out. They waved at me, and I smiled at them as we made our way to our carriage and were helped inside.

"There may be some delay, Miss," said John as he helped me inside. "Some of the roads are being dug up because of the new sewers and the underground railway."

My heart gave a little leap. They were just building the underground! I gave him a quick nod in acknowledgment and sat down in the carriage next to Jenny.

"King's Bench!" John shouted up to the driver and slammed the door. With a jolt we were off, making slow progress through the busy streets.

I was aware of Nanny scrutinising me and Jenny's eyes fixed on the ground. It was obvious that she was afraid of Nanny and didn't want to look at her. I smoothed my long skirt and tried to get comfortable. There seemed to be so many things digging into my body and I was hot and uncomfortable. I found it so difficult to breathe in the tight corset and I loosened the ribbons of my bonnet for a bit of relief.

"Thank you both for coming with me today." I smiled at them politely and Jenny beamed back. "Her Ladyship didn't want you to go on your own, Miss," she said.

Nanny continued her scrutiny.

"I wanted to see him," she said, her little eyes staring at me through the folds of flesh. "I want to see your father before I die."

Cheery, I thought, as I gave her a brief smile.

She folded her lace-gloved hands in her lap. "I was your father's paramour when he was an officer fighting Napoleon," she said in her croaky voice, "but he gave me away on the turn of a card, and I became the property of Lord Kit."

Jenny and I stared at her in astonishment. She wrinkled up her button nose and then gave a dreamy smile. "I was very beautiful then and in order to keep me in the house, I became nanny to Lord Kit's children." She sighed and turned to look out of the window. "But I always preferred your father. I always loved him the best. A pity he married your mother. He did it for her money. I was far more beautiful. I know he preferred me."

And with that, her eyes closed and she leaned her head against the window, the lace of her bonnet gently lifting with each gentle snore.

Jenny gave a little giggle and I turned to her. "Well," I said, "you learn something new every day."

The carriage rattled along Borough Road, which was almost totally unrecognisable. I caught a glimpse of the bridge and the iron struts of the market. It was fascinating to see the old London and to be a part of it, the noise, the bustle and the dirt. All around were signs of building and construction, the massive industrial progress of Victorian England galloping forward.

The high walls of the King's Bench Prison came into view, just as Jenny tugged at my sleeve. "I'm still having dreams, Miss, and they are making me frightened," she whispered.

I glanced at her little round face. Her hair flattened by the iron looked incongruous under the little bonnet.

"Miss, you're in them and John the groom, and," she swallowed, "and I feel that something is going to happen!"

"What sort of thing, Jenny?" A little tendril of fear crept around my chest. She shook her head. "I don't know, Miss, but I'm afraid. It makes me very afraid."

I looked at her, the tendril pulling tighter, but we were interrupted by a sudden jolt of the cab, and we stopped.

"King's Bench, Mum!" came a shout, and Nanny's eyes snapped open. She descended at great speed, eager to see her lost lover, I suppose. Jenny and I were helped out, and with a crack of the whip, the carriage set off back across the Thames.

The large prison gates loomed above us, and Nanny was arguing with a be-whiskered man in a uniform. Jenny and I hurried towards them. A small knot of people were gathered outside the gates, mostly women in their long skirts and shawls, baskets of food over their arm.

"Outbreak of typhus in the prison." The red-faced official put up his hand as a barrier to stop us moving forward. "Nobody allowed in. Nobody allowed out," he snorted.

"How do I know if my husband ain't taken bad?" cried a small woman with a straggle of tiny children clinging to her skirts. "If he is, how can I help him if I'm out here?"

"Name?" The official put on a small pair of glasses and consulted his sheaf of papers.

"Bartholomew, Sam Bartholomew," said the woman in a strong cockney accent, as she wiped her hands on her grubby apron.

"He's alive. The typhus is not where he is."

"Swainby, the Earl of Swainby," trembled Nanny.

The man gave us a quick glance and surveyed his list. "Sorry, ma'am, died this morning."

Nanny gave a wail, and my hand flew to my mouth. "Where is he?" I asked, feeling Jenny's hand creep into mine.

"Put in the pit this morning with the rest." The man put his glasses back in his pocket, and turned his attention to the rest of the little crowd. "Anyone else?" he asked.

I closed my eyes against the pain, feeling an overwhelming sense of sadness for this man who was my father. I felt Jenny squeeze my hand, and when I opened my eyes, tears were streaming down my cheeks and David was sitting opposite me, his hands on my arms. He reached over and passed me a tissue.

"My father died in prison," I said, blowing my nose. I wiped my eyes with the tissue, black mascara staining the white.

"So what happened then?" I crumpled the tissue into a ball. "I went back in time, could you tell? But what happened to me in this life? Did you know that I had regressed?"

He nodded.

"And…?" I looked at him expectantly.

He sat down behind his desk. "I made some notes on what you said, and it was as you described it. You were a governess to the Beaumont family until your death."

"My death?" I was shocked. Of course I would have died in my past life, but it was something I had not considered. I leaned forward. "You know how I died?"

He nodded. "But do *you* want to know?"

I shook my head vigorously. "Did you find out why, why I keep going back?"

He frowned and leaned back in his chair. "I can only guess, Jill, but there is something you have to do there and something you have to learn, so that you can enjoy the life you have now."

I bristled. "And who says I'm not enjoying my life now?"

He raised his eyebrows at me. "Things have happened in your life as a governess which have greatly influenced your life now. We didn't get to the bottom of it, *in this session*. You spoke a lot about unfinished business, which is why the past is calling you back."

I looked at him. "You saw me die?"

He shook his head, "No I didn't, but I know how it happens."

I stood up quickly. I didn't want to know any more. I didn't want this man knowing too much about me either. "Well, thank you," I said briskly. "How much will that be?"

He stood up and looked at me. "Let's talk about that when you're satisfied with the session."

I took out my purse, but he moved away from me to open the door.

"Come and see me again," he said, "but in the meantime I have a final message from your daughter."

I felt the hair on the backs of my arms prickle.

"She came to see me just before you got here."

167

I couldn't speak.

"She says you're to stop running."

CHAPTER TWENTY TWO

Although it was early evening, as soon as I got back to the flat I flipped open a bottle of Prosecco. I sat, with the glass of fizz in my hand staring out of the window, watching the dusk settle over the park. The lights which lined the road started to glow through the gathering gloom. The only sounds were the quiet fizz of the bubbles in my glass and the pure sound of a blackbird claiming its territory. My mind was numb and refused to think for me.

The shock of being reminded that my little girl could be existing in another dimension and was communicating with me, watching over me, was a little too much for me to deal with. That her father was back in the country was also a huge shock to me and I wasn't ready to cope with it. Not forgetting, of course, that I was also living two lives. I took a sip of the wine and felt it sparkle on my tongue. I lay back against the cushions and watched the sky darken, becoming more aware of my reflection in the window as the light faded. I stood up and walked nearer to the window watching myself coming closer. My hand reached out and touched the glass, meeting its own reflection. I looked up and saw a shadowy face, my face, but a face with long hair that was looped and braided. A cold shiver crawled down my spine. She was staring at me and her mouth was moving, but I couldn't hear what she was saying. I was quivering with fright as her expression became more urgent and her mouth continued to move.

"Tell me; tell me, what do you want? What are you trying to say to me?" I pressed my ear against the cold glass, but there was nothing, no sound except for the song of the blackbird. Her face faded as she seemed to grow more anguished, then the popping of the bubbles in my glass grew increasingly loud until it was almost deafening. Then, all was silent.

I drew back quickly, dropping my glass as I did so, but she was gone. My reflection stared back at me, wild eyed and frightened. I sank down onto the sofa, taking deep breaths in order to calm myself down. My heart was racing. I jumped up again and hurriedly drew the heavy curtains across the glass. It would be a long time before I'd have the courage to look out of the window again, into the darkness. I wanted another glass of wine, but after what had just happened, I was too frightened. What had my other self been trying to tell me? I lay back against the cushions and closed my eyes. I tried a few more deep breaths and felt myself beginning to relax. David seemed sure that what was happening wouldn't harm me, so I had to go with that as best I could.

My laptop beeped as the battery began to die, and that gave me an idea. I plugged it into the mains and balanced it on top of one of the many boxes which were packed and ready to go. I tapped in '*Flights to Canada*'. I was lucky. There was one going out the day after we broke up for Christmas. Without thinking, I booked it, and a return flight for ten days later. Delighted with myself, I rang my Dad while trying to work out what time it would be in Vancouver. No problem. Dad was always a late riser. I should catch him in.

After two rings it was answered. I was so glad to hear his voice. The pain of losing my father in my past life was still with me. I so wanted to make things right between us. I had been so wrong and thoughtless in my treatment of him in the past. I also felt ashamed.

"Dad, it's Jill. I've booked a flight!" I said cheerily. "I'm going to be with you for Christmas."

There was a silence before he answered.

"Oh, my dear girl," he said, a trace of Canadian accent in his soft voice. "I won't be here."

"What?" I was stunned. Dad always spent Christmas with Paul and his family, and this year I would be with him too. I would be able to put things right.

"Oh dear, I wish you'd called earlier, Jill. I'm going to Whistler with a friend. We have only just booked it. What a pity."

What did he mean, 'What a pity'? I was his daughter. I was

surprising him, making his Christmas for him. I hadn't seen him for years, or my brother.

"Well, your friend won't mind, will they, Dad? I mean, I haven't seen you for ages." I was slightly annoyed.

"Jill." There was a pause. "My friend is a lady, we've become very close. I've finally stopped thinking that your mother will come back. Oh my dear, I'm not lonely any more. She makes me very happy, and we really want to spend Christmas together."

I couldn't think of anything to say.

"Come at Easter," he said. "Come and stay with me then."

My fourteen year old petulant self rose to the surface and I opened my mouth to speak, but then I stopped myself. I took a breath. "Dad, I'm really happy for you," I said. "I'll come at Easter. I would love to see you."

"But ring me before then," he said, sounding anxious. "Ring me again soon. Let me know the dates when you're coming. Let me know how you are."

"I will, Dad, I will," I said.

"That's lovely," he said. "Are you all right, my dear, are you happy? How's Louis?"

"Fine, fine." I just hadn't the heart to tell him.

"Goodbye, my dear, please stay in touch." The phone gave a soft click.

"Goodbye, Dad. I will." I put down the phone.

I felt strangely empty; as though every feeling I'd ever had was drained from me. I was just a husk, a shell. I became mesmerised by the steam coming out of the kettle. I couldn't even remember filling it with water or switching it on. The steam curled slowly towards the ceiling in a transparent vapour and then disappeared in a fine mist. It was so silent in my flat. The absence of noise was a huge yawning gap. What to do for Christmas? Where to go? What was I going to do?

An inertia took a strong hold over me and I couldn't even be bothered to make the cup of coffee, to find something for dinner or mop up the spilt wine. I leaned against my kitchen units and thought about finding some good deals for somewhere warm and beautiful to spend my Christmas, but I didn't want to. Things had changed, and for once I didn't want to be on my own. My Dad had moved on. I couldn't expect to slot into his life again so quickly, but I was disappointed.

I thought about Emma's messages to me. Did I believe them? Was I running? And if so, from what? From whom? I'd certainly held back from loving Louis and then I'd let him go. He was a gem, he was a wonderful man. He had found me broken and in despair and had tried to fix me back together, caring for me all the way. But I didn't love him the way a man like that deserved to be loved, and I was happy he had found someone to reciprocate all the love he had to give.

And what about David? Did I believe in him, or did I just like looking into those chocolate brown eyes? How could he have known about Emma? How did he know her name? Was she trying to offer help to her stubborn mother? My head was pounding with all the unanswered questions, just as the doorbell broke the silence. I pressed the buzzer which opened the main door, without asking who it was. Jehovah's Witness, man selling double glazing, I didn't care. At least I'd have someone to talk to.

There was a gentle tap and Andy's tousled head appeared around the door, and the rest of his crumpled body joined it. "Shouldn't leave your door open, Jill." He shook his head at me, and looked doubtfully at my jeans and shabby sweatshirt. "Are you ready then?"

"For what?"

He grinned. "Don't say you've forgotten. It's the book club's Christmas do. Got your wine and your copy of Bleak House?"

He shook a bottle of Shiraz at me. "Come on, get ready, let's go!"

It took me five minutes to change and to grab a bottle of something from the wine rack. Andy had already found a copy of Bleak House on my shelves. I hadn't got round to packing up my beloved books. I had them all in alphabetical order. You can't get much more anal than that. I must have been really bored one wet Sunday afternoon.

On the way to the venue in Andy's battered Saab, he told me of his very complicated Christmas arrangements which seemed to involve hundreds of great aunts and in-laws, and flying about the motorways of England.

I was perched on a dog's rug and kept finding plastic toys underneath me as we swerved round corners. Andy would not be my first choice of chauffeur.

"Tell me, where *you* are going then?" He grinned at me as we manoeuvred a roundabout in a very unusual way. "Have you made your mind up? Is it to be Vancouver?"

"Nope." I let go of the door handle as we escaped the roundabout and I started picking long white hairs off my black trousers. "I still haven't made up my mind."

We drove the rest of the way in silence as it was quite difficult to talk above the rattling of the engine. We arrived at Alison's show palace and clanked through the ornate gates.

"Gone with the Wind," I hissed to Andy as we swept up the curved drive.

He smiled. Andy needed lessons in how to be bitchy about people. He didn't know how and he always made me feel bad about doing it. I kept forgetting about the response I'd get when I was in full flow to Andy. It was like playing tennis with someone who caught the ball and kept it.

"They both work very hard," he said as he pulled on the handbrake. "I hope they like my wine. It wasn't very expensive. We're having a bit of a thin month."

I took the wine out of his hands, and replaced it with my bottle.

"Well, mine was. A present from long ago, so pretend it's yours. You know what she's like, you'll be judged on your wine and your outfit."

"That's me down the ladder, then." He rang the bright brass doorbell, which tinkled a Christmas refrain.

"Join me at the bottom." I fixed a smile as the door was opened.

Alison was radiant in killer heels and a black sheath dress which fit her every curve perfectly. As we wandered into a hall the size of

173

my flat, our feet sank into a plush beige carpet, and a huge, silver Christmas tree soared to the ceiling, twinkling with silver stars.

"This way." Alison waved her hand airily and we followed her into a palatial room with chocolate leather sofas. One wall was all glass, and it looked out onto a paved patio which surrounded a pool. Dozens of hidden lamps lit up the blue water. All was tasteful minimalism. There were a few expensive looking pieces of modern art on the walls and a discreet wide screen television. The rest of the book club were lost in the vast expanse of room, drowning in the softness of the sofas whilst clutching flutes of champagne and looking rather bewildered. I was surprised to see David amongst our members. He was chatting to Simon and he raised his glass at me. I flashed him a brief smile.

"Now we're all here, let's go to the library." Alison clapped her hands and we all followed her like an infant class. Liz waited behind for me.

"Have you hung your coat on your peg?" she whispered.

I giggled. "I think Andy had some mud or chocolate on his shoe when we came in. It's all over the hall."

We giggled as we followed the rest of the unenthusiastic guests.

I suddenly had a thought and stopped and turned to my friend.

"By the way, Liz, the man who does the regressive therapy is here, David. You didn't invite him, did you?"

"I might have done," said Liz airily, her attention caught by a painting which she suddenly found very interesting.

"Will you stop match-making. I'm not even divorced yet. And stop looking at pictures of nude men, or I'll tell Pete."

She laughed and floated into the library in front of me. She was dressed in a silky antique creation, her hair caught up in braids and bands. Liz always scrubbed up well. "Congrats on the new job by the way," she said. "We must go out and celebrate before you go off to wherever you're going."

"I'm going nowhere," I replied, as I took my seat at the polished oak table, being careful to put my champagne down on a coaster.

"Then you're coming to us," Liz said firmly as she reached into her bottomless bag for her glasses and copy of Bleak House. As I opened my mouth to reply, she put up her hand. "There's nothing else to say about it," she said. "It's not up for discussion."

I stared at her. She was so like Lady Elizabeth, it was uncanny. It was her eyes, and her big generous smile, and of course the unending kindness and caring that made her my best friend.

"Drink your champagne," she whispered. "Let's get pissed. You won't be getting this at our house, so make the most of it."

"Bleak House." Alison's perfect face shone in the candlelight. "What do we think the main theme is? What is Dickens saying to us, do you think?"

Andy cleared his throat. "Well," he said, "I think that primarily Dickens is exposing the justice system of the time, but one of the central themes is class." He flattened his hair with one hand as he looked round for a response.

It was my turn. I could never stay quiet for long. "As a social reformer, he is also writing about poverty. He exposes places like Tom-all-Alones," I offered, before taking another gulp of champagne.

Simon leaned back in his chair. He always did this when he was about to prove to his class, or to a silly woman (his words, not mine) that they were talking nonsense and he was the only person who knew the answers.

"Ah, but was he a social reformer, or did he just write about it, living as he did quite comfortably on his earnings? Dickens was a very rich man."

I leaned towards Simon. "Of course he was a reformer." I smiled icily. "He founded Urania Cottage with Angela Burdett-Coutts. He tried to rescue prostitutes, give them a better chance in life." *So put that in your pipe and smoke it, dickhead*, I thought, fleetingly wondering why I seemed to be building a store of ripe language.

Simon smiled his self-satisfied I-am-glad-I-am-a-man-smile.

"It is a well known fact," he said, "that all Victorian gentlemen believed that if people were poor, that was their lot in life."

"Is that why there were so many social reformers in the 19th century, many of whom were men?" enquired Liz, smiling charmingly at Simon over her glass.

"And did you know that Dickens personally scoured penitentiaries and workhouses looking for women to help?" Andy chipped in.

"Women used to stream over the London bridges at night, making for the West End," I said, "not only women but children too. There was no other hope for them. It was either prostitution or the workhouse, and in the workhouse the families were split up. Prostitution meant that families could stay together."

Simon raised his eyebrows. "Speaking from experience, are we, Jill?" he smirked. "Have you been time-travelling again?"

There was a shocked pause in the conversation. Most people in the room knew about what I had confided to Simon and Alison, but it had been glossed over at work and explained away as part of my previous illness. I'd done my best to make light of it and hoped it had been forgotten about. However, here was Simon, raising it again, and in front of everyone. I didn't know what to say, or how to respond.

A figure leaned forward out of the gloom. David was sitting next to Alison. Of course he was. He was the most handsome man here and Alison would be drooling over him.

"We seem to be getting off the point a little here," he said, "but can I please make one thing very clear. As a new member, I only wanted really to listen tonight, but I think this needs to be said in light of the previous comment. I think it's unfair to bring up personal comments about other members, and it displays a lack of trust and respect. Surely we're here to discuss a book and to socialise. For someone like me who is new to the area, it is an opportunity to meet people and to discuss a mutual love of books." He gave an apologetic smile, to us all. "Sorry if I have spoken out of turn," he continued, his gaze resting for a moment on Simon's apoplectic face.

"Told you," hissed Liz. "He fancies the pants off you, and he's gorgeous."

"You have such a way with words," I whispered back, giving David a grateful smile at the same time.

Simon leaned forward trying to intimidate David. He gave one of his sighs and then one of his best patronising smiles.

"It's no secret here that Jill believes that she has a former life. Everyone knows this," he said.

"I do think we are getting off the point here." Alison rose to her feet. "More champagne anyone?" Credit to Alison, I thought. Maybe she does have some good points.

Nobody replied. The battle was far more interesting than discussing the novel and we all wanted to see Simon shot down in flames. However I was becoming very uncomfortable about being the object of the discussion.

"How do *you* know for certain that we haven't lived before?" Liz asked Simon. I knew it wouldn't be long before she waded into the argument. "Many religions believe that is the case. I thought that *teachers* were supposed to be open-minded and teach their pupils to respect other beliefs."

There was a murmur from some of our members. Liz knew how to go for the jugular.

Simon turned his gaze on Liz but she stared at him levelly. "Absolutely, all *sane* teachers do," he smiled. "Now, shall we get on with the discussion? I believe that is why we are here."

Liz stared at him with her mouth open, too stunned to say anything. "Leave it, Liz, he's a tosser," I said loudly. "I'll show him how mad I am in a minute. I'll turn him into a toad. Oh sorry, impossible. He already is one."

"Please, please," Alison had returned with more twinkling glasses of champagne and juice. "Let's get on with the book, shall we?"

There was a silence.

"I think I've lived before," Andy said, taking a glass of fruit juice from Alison. "There's a place near where my parents-in-law live. Mount Grace Priory. When I visited there I got such a strong sense of déjà vu, it was weird. I knew that I'd never been there before, but I felt I knew it."

Some people murmured in agreement. I smiled to myself. I could just imagine Andy in a robe, tending to his plants.

David leaned forward again. "I have taken part in regressive therapy," he said, "and in my opinion I believe that we live more than one life. Parts of our previous lives are embedded within our

177

cell memory, and sometimes we can recall things from our past lives. Vividly, in some cases."

"How interesting!" cooed Alison, as she leaned towards David, revealing more cleavage than was strictly necessary.

"How ridiculous," Simon retorted as a few people started to snigger. Simon was sitting next to our head of physics, Pete Welford. Pete and I avoided each other, mainly due to an embarrassing episode in his stockroom during the last staff party, the same party where I had insulted the school bursar. We had both got really drunk on his homemade wine and I'd sort of lost my perspective and my inhibitions. Pete was an interesting man and he was as passionate about literature as he was about physics, but there was a faint chemical smell about him which had halted the stockroom episode and also halted any further episodes of same.

He was frowning, possibly at Simon, and then he spoke. "I know that we are somewhat off the point here," he said, "but I hope you don't mind me giving my perspective on this from a scientific point of view. For many years now, scientists have believed that there are hidden worlds beyond the human senses. Since the 1980s, research has shown that matter is not particles but strings, consequently these strings can exist in different places at different times."

"The string theory," David said, and a few people nodded. I remembered the conversation with Jeff and Rick.

"That's right," said Pete. "To put it simply, we believe that our universe is just one bubble amongst many more. Some believe that there are parallel universes where our history exists but with a different outcome... so Hitler could have conquered Britain, Napoleon could have beaten us at Waterloo. That kind of thing."

Simon gave a snort of laughter, but he was the only one. When science speaks, people seem to listen.

"So you are saying that everyone around this table could be living a different life in a parallel dimension. What utter bollocks!" he spluttered.

"I don't see why it's bollocks, just because we don't fully understand it," retorted David.

"Bollocks!" Simon was becoming red-faced. "I came here to

discuss literature not hocus pocus," he said.

David shrugged his shoulders and picked up his glass. The discussion was over but before the end of the night he would be hugged to within an inch of his life for trying to stick up for me; that is if Alison didn't get there first.

I took the opportunity to sneak out, with the excuse of going to the loo, when Alison began to deliver a monologue on why Esther should have married the wealthy John Jarndyce instead of the impoverished Alan Woodcourt. I saw Liz make her excuses too. We had an unspoken signalling system. I wanted to lick my wounds in private and also have a look at Alison's kitchen, not that I had the slightest interest in cooking, I was just nosey. When I got there, I found her mouse-like but very wealthy husband putting the finishing touches to a feast. I stopped in the doorway and immediately Liz bumped into me.

"Oh, hello, sorry," I mumbled. "I was looking for the loo. My, you've been busy." Liz dug me in the ribs and I gave a muffled squeak.

The mouse turned. He was a tanned and very successful looking mouse, dressed in a very expensive suit.

"Not me, the cook." He pushed his round glasses further up his nose. "I have been left in charge of the oven… you couldn't just… for a second?"

"Sure," we both said.

"Thanks," he said, moving past us. "I just need to check my iPad, and it's in the den. I'll be a minute, if that. There's something in the oven that needs taking out when it pings."

"You can rely on us. We'll listen for the ping," beamed Liz.

We looked in awed silence at the state-of-the-art kitchen and when the expected 'ping' rang out, we fell over each other to get to the oven. Liz took charge as she was the expert, not me. I leaned against the worktop, looking up at the rows of gleaming pans which were hanging from the ceiling. How different from the kitchens at the Castle and Beaumont House.

"Some interesting theories delivered by two knights in shining armour," said Liz as she walked across the kitchen to examine the food. I changed the subject.

"I saw Chris at Castle Beaumont," I said, watching Liz arranging some prawn-like objects on a silver dish.

She glanced up at me.

"I didn't know he was back," I continued. "He swore he'd never come back while his father was still alive."

"Well, there you have it." Liz was rinsing her hands under the tap. "His father died and he is now officially Earl Beaumont."

"Have you seen him?" I asked, knowing full well the answer to the question. Her husband, Pete, was Chris's closest friend.

She turned to look at me as she reached for a towel to dry her hands. "We stayed with him at the Castle last weekend." She replaced the towel.

"And you didn't think to tell me?"

She ignored my peevish question. Liz didn't believe in going over old ground. "Did you speak to him?" she asked.

I shook my head. "Was his wife there?"

"No." Liz folded her arms and looked at me. "She's filming."

"I'm over him, Liz," I lied, "and I have also made contact with my Dad. I'm going to see him at Easter."

Liz smiled her huge smile, looking so like Lady Elizabeth, it made me shiver slightly.

"Brilliant," she said, linking her arm through mine. "That is so brilliant."

"He's also got a lady friend." We looked at each other and grinned.

"Fantastic, so he's stopped waiting for your errant mother to return then?" Liz pushed open the door.

"I wonder where she is," I mused, "and whether she has found what she is looking for."

"Have any of us?" Liz laughed as we walked back to the library.

David, accompanied by an attentive Alison, was walking towards us along the hallway.

He seemed to be looking very closely at Liz. "Elizabeth?" he asked.

She nodded. "Well, nobody calls me that," she laughed. "It's Liz. Don't you recognise me from the health shop? I phoned to invite you here, remember?" She threw me a guilty glance.

He seemed confused for a moment and smiled apologetically. "Sorry, yes. Must be too much champagne!" His smile faded quickly and he glanced at me. He looked disturbed, troubled. I dragged him away from the party on the pretext of getting my diary to make another appointment with him.

"What is it?" I said as we reached a quiet corner of the corridor.

He gave me a brief smile, but he was frowning.

"Please don't worry," he said, "but it's your friend, Liz. Is she Lady Elizabeth? You talked about her so much during your regression."

"Yes, well I would, she's the wife of my employer."

He seemed as though he was trying to tell me something, but he didn't know how. His eyes were troubled and he ran his hands through his dark hair.

"Tell me, David," I said, catching hold of his arm and thinking fleetingly of how warm and strong he felt.

He turned to face me. "She's the link, Jill. One of the reasons you keep going back. It's to change something." He frowned again and put his hand to his forehead. "You have to go back to stop something happening." He paused. "I didn't think that one could do that. I didn't think it was possible to change things but..."

My skin started to prickle and I kept hold of his arm. "There's more, I know there's more. Tell me!" I grabbed hold of his other arm. I almost wanted to squeeze the truth out of him.

"There's a tragedy, Jill," he said simply. "You have to stop it. That's all I know."

CHAPTER TWENTY THREE

There was a strong smell of old wood and polish, and David's face faded. My hands were no longer holding his, but were holding the round brass knob of a door. I heard the sound of raised voices and I pushed it open. I was in Lady Elizabeth's sitting room at Castle Beaumont. The family must have returned to Yorkshire. I recognised the turquoise embossed wallpaper and gilt chairs. It was warm, and a fire crackled in the grate. A little gold clock on the mantelpiece chimed six o'clock. Charles was standing by the fireplace. I hadn't seen him since he'd kissed me, and I felt uncomfortable, especially as I caught a glance of Elizabeth sitting by the fireplace, dressed entirely in black, her face streaked with tears.

She ran over to me, her skirts rustling as she did so. The gas lamps flickered and hissed, and I was enveloped in her arms, crushed against her stiff body.

"My dear Miss Woods, I am so, so sorry about your father." She took my hands in her lace-clad ones. I glanced down at my dress which was also made of heavy, black material.

"My condolences, Miss Woods," Charles said from the fireplace. "Your father and mine were great friends."

I glared at him. "If he hadn't been in prison, this wouldn't have happened," I said stiffly, holding my head up. "My father is now in a pauper's grave without a proper funeral. He died alone. Why wasn't I told? John must have known, he took food to my father."

"John was turned away, and wasn't told why." Elizabeth led me to the fire and sat me down in her seat. "We didn't know anything else."

I stood up so that I was on a level with Charles. His face had softened and he looked at me with sympathy. Despite my anger towards him, the air between us seemed to crackle with such raw energy. I felt my body begin to burn under the suffocating clothes, but there were questions I wanted answers to, so I looked straight at him, unflinching.

"Is it true he owed you money?" I asked coldly.

He nodded. "You know your father's weakness, Miss Woods. It was the cards. The same is true of my own father."

"Could you not have forgiven him his debts?" I asked as I stared at him, my voice cold. "Did we have to lose our home, because he owed you money for a card game? Did he have to die a horrible death because you could not overlook money which was won? Money which you had neither earned nor inherited. Money which you did not need."

A shadow passed across his face and he looked disconcerted. He turned to look in the fire, avoiding my steady gaze. I heard Elizabeth give a little sigh of sympathy. He glanced at her, and then at me.

"I thought you knew, Miss Woods. Your father had an obsession, and it was gambling. He borrowed money from my father to pay off his debts, and then of course, Swainby House, your home, was lost in a game of Baccarat. All the money which was brought to the marriage through your mother was lost on the turn of a card."

"But he was your father's friend. You let him go to prison!" I could feel the tears pricking my eyelids. "And me, how has that left me? What prospects are there for me as a governess?"

Charles glanced at me. His expression darkened. "I paid off the last of his debts, and he promised for your sake to give it up. He didn't and was taken to prison owing more than anyone could afford to pay. You will not starve, Miss Woods, so long as you remain in my employment. However, when you are more composed, I wish to speak with you about another pressing matter, namely the excursions you and my wife have been making to Waterloo Bridge." His voice was becoming distinctly unfriendly and Elizabeth looked terrified. "I have heard my wife's version of events, and I wish to hear yours, later this evening."

He took his foot off the fender and gave us both a hostile glance. "I wish you both good evening. Elizabeth... Miss Woods."

And with that he strode out of the room. There was a silence except for the ticking of the little clock. Elizabeth was staring into the fire, her body rigid.

"He says that I'm bringing disgrace upon the family," she said quietly.

"Through helping others?" I gave a snort of disdain.

She turned her gaze on me, her bottom lip trembling. "Miss Woods, I fear he may dismiss you from your post, if you continue to defy him, and I won't be able to stop him. You can no longer be involved in helping me. I must do this alone. *I* must defy my dear husband. I cannot sleep knowing these poor children are being so misused when I have the means to help them."

A solitary tear glided down her cheek. "Miss Woods, you have become a dear friend to me, and the children love you. I will miss you."

My heart gave a jolt. Where would I go, what would I do? The streets of Victorian London started to look threatening and dangerous. Maybe I would be able to persuade him to let me stay. I walked over to her and knelt beside her, taking her hands in mine.

"Why does Miss Tibbs dislike us so much? Could we not talk to her, try to win her round?"

Elizabeth gave a weak smile and shook her head. She touched my cheek briefly with her lace-clad hand. "She has always hated me because I am not of noble birth. I think I have told you before; she has been with Charles's family for many years and did not approve of our marriage. We eloped you see, but our parents forgave us. We were very young." She pressed my hand and smiled at the look of surprise on my face. I could not imagine Charles being so impetuous.

She gave a nervous laugh. "You are of noble birth, Miss Woods; perhaps it is time we told the servants instead of keeping it from them. I know that is what we thought was the right thing to do at the time, but you should be treated with the respect your rank deserves."

I stood up and started to pace the room, thinking furiously, feeling like one of the Brontë sisters as they paced their dining room, sharing ideas for their books.

I was about to speak and the door was flung open by Earl Beaumont, Charles's father. He stood in the doorway with Nanny two paces behind. His whole appearance was in disarray as though he had been put in a bag, shaken up, and tipped out again. Nanny was wailing loudly. He strode over to me, his grey hair on end, and I backed towards Elizabeth, remembering our last encounter.

"My dear little Alicia." My eyes darted around me, but it must be me he was talking to. I hadn't known my first name, now I did. His bony hands grasped my arms. "My dear girl, your poor, poor father." He crushed me to him as Nanny continued to cry noisily. "I didn't know it was you, they never told me you were his daughter. We thought you were a servant. Oh, my dear."

"Kit, I kept telling you," wailed Nanny.

He ignored her and let go of me suddenly and fished in his pocket for a grubby looking handkerchief, blowing his nose loudly. "I am now your protector, my dear child," he sniffed, replacing the handkerchief in his pocket. "For Gilbert's sake. Come Nanny, we are going to get drunk in memory of my dear friend Gilbert. Tell the butler I want a fire in the library and three bottles of good port. And Nanny, wear your French can-can dress."

And with that he left as suddenly as he appeared, roaring instructions all the way down the corridor to anyone who would listen, Nanny wailing in his wake.

I felt Elizabeth's hand on my arm. She was just about to speak when Miss Tibbs appeared around the door. Her face was sour and pinched, her hair scraped back into a tight wire knot. She looked dried up of all goodness and compassion.

"And what good news and joy have you got for us today?" I stared at her tight little body, encased in dull brown fabric, her hands clenched tightly together.

She wrinkled her nose at me. "Lord Beaumont wishes to see you in the nursery, Miss Woods." She looked triumphant, in expectation of my dismissal I expect.

"Ah, that's because you have been telling tales, Miss Tibbs," I said haughtily. "You would rather see innocent children abused and you would like to put an end to her Ladyship's kindnesses. You do know how to spread sunshine and happiness, don't you, you dried up old spinster."

Elizabeth gave a gasp, and her hand flew to her mouth. Miss Tibbs looked as though she was about to explode, just like Cripps in Bleak House, through internal combustion.

I walked towards her. "And I am *Lady Swainby* to you, Miss Tibbs, governess or not, and see to it that you treat my lady with respect from now on or you'll have me to answer to."

I pushed past her wishing that I could have just one punch, just a small one, but I guess that I had a little too much to contend with at that moment. I nearly fell over Jenny and John who seemed to have been listening at the door. They straightened up suddenly, grinning at me. I also noticed their hands were entwined. I shook my head, Jenny and John and Jeff and Jane. There were just too many coincidences.

I made my way up the grand staircase, past the solemn-looking portraits of long ago Beaumonts. I wished they could talk, like in the Harry Potter films, but they remained still, haughty and disapproving, their eyes following me in my ascent. I lifted my skirts with one hand, grasping the polished handrail with the other, wondering what the next few minutes would bring. Whatever happened I was now very aware of David's warning. I had to stop a tragedy. Was that my destiny?

I ran my hands along the polished handrail. When I reached the top, I looked over the balcony to the floor below. The staircase was wide and sweeping, curving down to the black and white tiles of the entrance hall. I looked around and then hoisted my leg over the rail, dragging my skirts behind me. Then I let go, and with a whoop of delight slid all the way down to the bottom, my speed increasing along the way. I bumped onto the lintel and stopped. It was magnificent! I reached under my skirts to detach some of the petticoats, flinging them up the stairs as I ran to the top again. This time I wasn't so nervous, and I seemed to fly all the way down.

I laughed with delight, but as I reached the bottom I glanced up and caught sight of Christopher and Emma surveying me very solemnly from the top of the stairs. Both were clutching large pieces of paper.

"We've finished our sketches, Miss Woods." Christopher's face was puzzled. "Papa has sent us to find you."

"Do you want a go?" I hoisted myself off the banister and raised my eyebrows at them. They looked quickly at each other, and then their faces broke into smiles and they nodded.

I ran back up the stairs to them. "I will be with you all the way down," I said reassuringly. I bent down and took their sketches, putting them on the large window seat. "You won't fall. Now, who is going first?"

"Me, me…" Emma jumped up and down.

I lifted her onto the rail, but kept my arms around her. "Now slowly let your hands go, I've got you."

We made a steady descent and the more confident she became, the faster we slid along. She gave a cry of triumph when we reached the end. I lifted her down and we raced to the top of the stairs. Christopher was far more cautious, but his solemn little face kept breaking into smiles as we made our way to the bottom. We became more and more confident with each run and started screaming and whooping as we became more adventurous, and more excited. A little knot of below-stairs maids had come out of the dining room, and they laughed and clapped their hands as they watched us.

On the final run, they both went down together, which took all my concentration to make sure they were safe. However, quite near to the bottom, Emma was going too fast for me to keep up with her, and I could see what was going to happen. I was filled with panic as I had visions of her falling onto the hard floor. She banged into the lintel and went flying off the side of the banister. I shot out an arm and somehow managed to catch her, putting my other hand out to catch Christopher, and we fell in a heap at the bottom of the staircase. I took the force of the fall, but we weren't hurt. We were laughing with excitement as we lay there and Emma put her little hands around my neck and said, "We love you,

Miss Woods. You make us happy." And with that she gave me a gentle kiss. Christopher put his head on my chest and I hugged him. I hugged them both, feeling overwhelmed with love for these two little people.

Suddenly, the atmosphere changed. The maids scuttled back into the dining room. I looked up and there was Charles, standing at the top of the staircase, his expression unreadable, and my discarded petticoats in his hand.

I gave the children a quick kiss each and told them in a whisper to go back to the nursery. They scrambled to their feet and ran up the stairs to their father.

"Father, we do very interesting things with Miss Woods," Christopher said solemnly.

Charles bent down and patted their heads. "Go to the nursery, children," he said, "and Emma, wash your face. You are very flushed."

The children trotted along the corridor and I got to my feet, smoothing my skirts as I did so, trying to regain a little dignity. I looked up at him, standing there at the top of the stairs, brooding and beautiful. There was something erotic about him holding my underskirts in his hand.

However, I knew I had really blown it this time. My last chance had gone.

"I don't have to come up to the nursery to know I am dismissed," I said, standing my ground beneath the crystal chandelier as I looked up at him. "You can tell me from where you are now. However, your father did tell me that he would be my protector, so does that change things?"

"My father has no assets anymore," he said coldly. "Everything belongs to me."

He started to walk down the stairs towards me, flinging the petticoats to one side as he did so. At the same time, Jenny appeared out of the dining room, carrying a tray of silver to be cleaned.

"Jenny, bring Miss Wood's shawl." Charles continued his descent. "I think we will take the air before dinner, Miss Woods. We have serious matters to discuss."

At that moment Elizabeth appeared from her sitting room holding a bunch of letters.

"Have you written to Mr Dickens, my dear?" Charles enquired.

She stopped when she saw us, a faint flush spreading across her cheeks. She gave a quick nod. "Yes," she replied.

Charles turned to me. "Unfortunately Mr Dickens has made his wife leave their marital home, as he has begun an association with an actress. It seems as though Miss Coutts and he have severed their relationship. There will be no more saving of ladies, and Mr Dickens may find many doors are now closed to him." He looked at his wife and then held out his hand to her.

"My dear, Miss Woods and I have things to discuss. We will return shortly. The children are in the nursery." He kissed her hand and she gave him her big smile, looking both relieved and delighted. It looked as though all was forgiven, and I was glad. Not so sure about me though.

After Jenny had appeared with my shawl, Charles and I walked side by side along the corridor to the Garden Hall, where the winter sun was streaming in through the tall windows.

He held open the door for me and we stepped outside. The view from the top of these steps always took my breath away. Castle Beaumont stood on the crest of a hill and the rolling hills and dales of Yorkshire unfurled before us, a light coating of snow making the landscape a swirl of green and white. The air was still and clear and perhaps because of the sunshine, the birdsong was a frenzied cacophony of shrill calls and melodies. The thin spire of the village church rose to the left of us, little houses clustered around it. The view was almost unchanged from the 21st century, except for the rose garden. A few late blooms made splashes of colour as a contrast to the dark earth. The gravel path swept down to the fountain, which looked brighter and cleaner. Atlas was holding up a brighter and cleaner world.

Charles held out his arm for me and I rested my hand on the top of it, as I had seen ladies do in the costume dramas I had watched on TV. The sense of déjà vu was so strong, but in reverse. Here

I was in the past, walking down the steps towards the fountain at Castle Beaumont with Chris's great-great grandfather. The touch and nearness of Charles, the completeness I felt being with him, totally obliterated any other part of my life. Never before, except when being with Chris, had I felt myself totally in the here and now, not wanting to be anywhere else. I had a faint ray of hope. Would he be walking with me if he was going to dismiss me? There had been enough warnings, but just to experience this moment, made everything else seem unimportant.

Charles broke the silence. "I am sure that you know by now that I must ask you to leave your employment with us," he said.

I didn't look at him. My heart sank, and all I heard was the soft crunch of our feet on the gravel path. He led me around the back of the fountain and stopped. He leaned against the grey stone, and I looked up at him haloed by the splashing drops of water, his face not unkind. There was something there that I couldn't read.

"Your ways of education do not fit the way in which my children need to be educated." He looked at me, as though waiting for a response. "My children must know the roles they are expected to play in this world. Their education must be taken seriously, and I fear there is too much attention to playing in your methods."

I took a breath, and launched into the fray. "Lord Charles, your world is changing. The rich will not always rule the world; the poor will not always be so neglected. Men will go to war and women will run the country. Soon women will vote, go out to work and people will be more aware of their responsibilities toward each other. The children must be educated to cope with these changes and embrace them."

He frowned at me, but I carried on. "This is an age of great discovery. Things will be invented which will change our lives completely. We will be able to communicate in ways we never thought was possible, we will fly through the air in planes, there is so much that..." I stopped suddenly.

I was in full flow, as though in the classroom, and I had nearly given myself away.

He raised his eyebrows a fraction. "The Great Exhibition did make us feel that our country is moving forward, Miss Woods, but I think you are letting your imagination take control of you. And, as for the role of women, they are the mothers and homemakers of our nation. Their role is important in the home. How else would men be able to go out in the world?"

"And what if women want to go out in the world?" I threw back at him.

He smiled and leisurely crossed his feet, folding his arms as he did so. "I think you will now see how our ideas of education are so opposed, Miss Woods."

"So," I folded my arms and lifted my chin, "because of that, you are throwing me out into the world. I will live in poverty, despite how you told me I wouldn't starve. I'll be just like the tenants you have in London."

He looked up at me, his face grave. "By no means," he said. "Firstly, I have a very good manager who looks after my tenants, and the business side of my life is not your concern, and secondly, I have a proposal to put to you."

I looked at him, feeling a little relieved. If I was to stay in this world for a while, before my task was completed, I didn't want to be on the streets of London, so maybe I was safe for now.

Suddenly, he reached for my hand and pulled me closer to him. My hand was cold and his was warm and comforting but the nearness of him set my pulse racing again, and I could feel a slow flush crawling up my body. I tried to steady myself, and look straight at him, but he must have been able to feel me shaking.

"Lady Swainby, I have something to ask you and I want you to consider it carefully." His voice was gentle and he looked at me the way I had seen him look at his wife.

I nodded my head, wondering if I would be able to breathe normally through the next few minutes. It was bad enough trying to breathe in this damned corset but Charles was so close to me, there was a strong possibility of me expiring in front of him before I heard what he had to say. I focused on his eyes as he pulled me even closer to him, and he continued to speak.

"I love my wife dearly. I married her against the wishes of my family as she is, shall we say, not well born." He hesitated. "After the birth of my daughter, the doctor told me that my wife must have no more children... there were complications during the birth, enough to cause a threat to her life if she was ever with child again."

He looked slightly embarrassed and my heart warmed to him. I had seen a sensitive side to him, when he touched the children or smiled at his wife, but I was unsure of what was coming next.

"Lady Swainby, dear Alicia, my wife and I are no longer able to have the relations a man and wife should have. I have long felt an attraction to you, your intelligence, your spirit, your beauty. I would find you a home and give you everything you want, if you would agree to becoming..."

"Your mistress?" I said, interrupting him, the light dawning. "You want me to... but what about Elizabeth? What about her feelings? This would break her heart. Have you not heard of contraception? Oh my God. What are you suggesting here?"

I broke away from him in horror, staring in disbelief, and ashamed of the feelings his proposal had unleashed. I was torn, so torn, between my friendship with Elizabeth and my attraction for this man. But it wasn't right. In fact it was almost comical. There would be three of us in the marriage. Where had I heard this before?

He dropped my hand suddenly, and turned away. "Our religion does not permit what I think you are suggesting." He turned to look at me again, and after a slight hesitation he took my hand once more, and I couldn't tear my gaze away from those hypnotic eyes.

"My dear Alicia, Elizabeth and I have agreed that under the circumstances I should look elsewhere for those needs, but I am to be discreet and she does not want to know who it will be."

I stared at him in horror. "Oh my God, you bastard!" I shrieked at him. "How could you even think of it?" I turned away from him, and paced up and down the grass in front of the fountain. "You would do this to your wife? All she wants is to help others, and you won't let her, yet you would screw someone else and break her heart. You total, total bastard!"

I flew at him but he was too quick for me, pinning my hands

behind me. "Alicia," he said urgently, as I struggled. "Stop… please, stop this."

He let go of my hands and pulled me closer to him and I felt the heat of his hands on my waist, then on my back. He brushed his lips against mine and I stopped struggling. I couldn't help it. I was lost, totally and utterly, once again, under the Beaumont spell.

CHAPTER TWENTY FOUR

But the spell was broken.

We could hear someone calling for Charles and then for me. It was Jenny's voice. Charles released me, and walked around the fountain until he could see the house again. I followed behind him, trying not to look guilty, smoothing down my skirts as I did so.

Jenny arrived, red faced and panting.

"Sir, it's Lady Emma," she said trying to catch her breath as she reached us. "John went for the doctor. We couldn't find you in the garden. Your Lordship, she's taken really bad."

"Oh my God." I gathered my skirts in my hand and fled in the direction of the house, following behind Charles as he set off running, without a word to either of us. Jenny was panting behind us both.

The servants were milling about the Garden Hall in little groups, talking in hushed voices. They watched us as we ran in, looking unsure and anxious as Miss Tibbs tried to get them to go back to their posts. We raced up the two staircases, and once again I cursed the heavy skirts which slowed me down.

Charles flung open the nursery door and went straight over to the bed, where little Emma lay in her mother's arms, red faced and trembling. A white haired old gentleman with a slight stoop, carrying a battered leather portmanteau, strode purposefully over to the bed.

"Your Lordship, Lady Beaumont, please stand aside, whilst I perform my examination," he said as he snapped open the leather case.

Charles led Elizabeth to the fireplace and put his arm round her. We watched the doctor examine Emma's hot little body. She was crying quietly.

"This is very sudden?" Charles asked his wife. "When did this happen?"

"She complained of being hot." Elizabeth looked anxiously at her daughter. "And then suddenly she became feverish, so we sent for Doctor Haigh." She noticed the doctor putting his stethoscope away and she walked quickly to the bed.

"I'm afraid it's typhus, my lady." Doctor Haigh shut his bag with a snap. "Has she been in contact with any other children?"

Elizabeth gave a gasp. "We were in London yesterday, visiting my husband's tenants." She threw an anguished glance at her husband. "Are you sure it's typhus? Oh dear God, my Emma!"

She sank down on her knees by the bed and I moved forward, kneeling beside her. "I'll nurse her, my lady. You must all leave as it's infectious. You may give it to Christopher. I'll nurse her and Jenny can bring me what I need and leave it by the door."

If I was going to die in this life, it might as well be for a good cause, and the sight of Emma's suffering filled me with compassion.

Charles moved over to his wife and lifted her up. "Come, my dear, Lady Swainby is right." He looked at the doctor who nodded as he picked up his case.

"Keep her cool and make her drink lots of fluids," he said to me. "I'll call again tomorrow."

Lord Christopher was standing by the door, looking terrified. His mother took him by the hand, and looked at me anxiously. "Miss Woods, Lady Swainby, I can't let you do this. You may become ill yourself. It should be me who nurses my child."

I smiled at her. "You have your family to take care of," I said, as I dipped my handkerchief in water and began to sponge Emma's forehead. "I'll be fine."

Her eyes filled with tears. "You are a true friend," she said as she stumbled out of the room.

Charles gave me a quick glance. "Thank you," he said, pausing by the doorway. "My family is in your debt. I will send Jenny to you, and you must tell her what you need."

He held my gaze for a moment and then I turned back to Emma.

"Miss Woods, I am so hot," she whimpered.

"I know, sweetheart, I'll get you some water, and I'll open a window for some fresh air." I gave her a kiss on her forehead and walked to the window, drawing back the thick, heavy drapes.

So this must be it. I had to save Emma. I needed to get back to the present, to get on the internet and find the cure. That should be easy enough. But what if my past self didn't look after her properly whilst I was away? What if I found a cure but it was not available in my past life?

And Charles. What to do about Charles? My feelings for him were so strong, so overwhelming, that I felt that I had come to life again. *But, enough of that.* There were more pressing things to consider. How to save the life of this precious little girl? I could not save my own daughter, but I would do my best to save this one.

Jenny appeared in the doorway, and I snapped out of my reverie. What to ask for? There were no antibiotics; I would have to make do with what I had learned from Liz, and what I had read in the Victorian books.

I walked over to Jenny, wiping my hands on my skirts as I did so. She stepped into the room.

"Go back, Jenny." I put my hand out to stop her. "You must not come into the room or touch anything. We must keep this door closed at all times and you must knock when you bring me supplies." I glanced around the dark corridor outside. "Bring that table over here and put it by the door. When you bring anything to me, leave it on the table, and when you are taking anything away, wear gloves and wash your hands all the time. Do you understand me, Jenny?"

She nodded, her face anxious, "Miss, Master says that John will fetch you what you need. He'll ride to the village."

I nodded and moved over to where a pile of Emma's toys lay, and picked up a slate.

Emma started to whimper.

"Sshh, sweetheart, I'm just getting you some things that will make you more comfortable," I said quietly.

I scrawled on the slate, whilst talking to Jenny. "I need lots of boiling water, Jenny. I'm going to strip the bed and all Emma's clothes, so you must bring a bag and not touch them. They must be burnt or boiled. I need soap and honey, lemons, ginger, thyme, any herbs that Cook has which are antibacterial." I glanced at her puzzled face. "We need to kill the germs."

I gestured for Jenny to move back and I propped the slate on the table.

"Can you read?" I asked.

She nodded. "A bit, Miss, but John is the scholar in the kitchen."

"Bring him up, I need these things." I walked back to the bed. "And set the kettles to boil."

She scampered away and I went back to the bed. The breeze from the window lifted the curtains gently, ruffling Emma's curls which were damp with sweat.

I lifted up her hot little body and gently stripped off her nightgown, whilst she continued to whimper. I knew that typhus was caused by lice and I had to find them. I searched her hair first, then under her arms. Bingo! I remembered how we used to try to detach them from the dog when we had been in the fields, a pull and a twist. Emma gave a little moan when it came free. I took my shoe off, killed it and then threw it out of the window. After more careful searching, I found three more and disposed of them in the same way.

Just then I saw Jenny staggering with the water bowl, John following with two more pails. They left them on the table and I brought the bowl to the dresser. I wrapped Emma in a blanket and then put her in the chair by the fire. I stripped the bed, and found clean sheets and blankets in a chest at the bottom of the bed, and a clean nightgown.

Jenny came back with soap, herbs and lemons which were cut into pieces. I took them from the table, gave her a nod of thanks and closed the door. Immediately I immersed them in the water.

The sweat was dripping off me by now. I scrubbed my hands with the soap and bathed Emma's body with the infusion, and put

197

a clean nightdress on her. I placed her between the clean sheets. Cleanliness and fresh air, was that what Florence Nightingale had said? I mixed the lemons and honey with warm water and tried to make her drink it. I put the boiled water in the jugs to cool, and sat by the bed, holding her hand and sponging her face, all the time wondering if I was doing the right thing.

I needed to get back to my time, to ask Liz what to do. There were no antibiotics yet invented in Victorian England and some doctors still believed in medieval bleeding as a cure. She was so weak, that would kill her for sure.

Eventually she fell asleep and I leaned against the bedhead, exhausted and upset. *Please don't let her die*; the tears were filling my eyes, *not this sweet child. Not another Emma.*

I leaned my head against hers for a moment and closed my eyes, willing her with all the strength I had, to get well. Suddenly I became aware of a change in the atmosphere. I could no longer feel Emma close to me and I snapped my eyes open. I didn't recognise where I was as I was in a strange bed, a strange room, but where and which life? I stared at the ceiling above, which seemed full of swirling mist. Out of the mist I saw aeroplanes, Spitfires and Messerschmitts. I leapt out of bed with a cry, then realised they were models, dangling on strings above my head. They reminded me of the ones in the nursery at Castle Beaumont in Chris's time, but I knew I wasn't there. The light from a computer winked at me from a desk strewn with paper. It took a few seconds, and then I realised. I was in Joe's room at Liz's house. It must be Christmas. I must have accepted Liz's invitation. An illuminated clock on the bedside table showed that it was 5am.

I threw back the duvet and climbed out of bed, making for the computer, nearly falling over my suitcase as I did so.

I switched it on and it hummed into life but there was something else. My ears became attuned to another sound. I listened, my entire senses alert. The sound was so quiet and I strained my ears to hear it, my fingers unmoving on the keyboard. It was the sound of sobbing, and such a desperate sound I felt the hairs on the back of my neck start to stand up.

I left the computer and made for the door, feeling my way in the darkness. The light from the computer switched itself off as the sobbing grew louder, and I was plunged into darkness. I found the doorknob and wrenched it open. A cold draught plunged into the room, and there was someone outside the door holding a candle.

There was a dark shape, slumped against the table which separated Emma and me from the outside world. The body was shaking with sobs. It was Elizabeth.

"Lady Elizabeth," I called out, and she turned, her face chalk white against the black of her dress. "What's the matter? Oh dear God, no!" I turned quickly back into the room and ran to the bed which was illuminated by candles from the nearby dresser. I stared down at Emma and touched her body. She was hot. I could hear her ragged breathing. How long had passed since I was last here? I was only in the present for a few minutes, and then catapulted back. Why? Why was I now more in the past than the present? I put a cool cloth on Emma's forehead and she stirred but didn't wake. She was still alive.

I picked up the candelabra and found my way through the shadows back to the door.

"Lady Elizabeth," I called softly into the darkness. "Emma is fine. She's sleeping."

I heard the rustle of her dress, as she got to her feet, but I put my arm across the doorway. "You must not come in," I said firmly. "Think of Christopher."

She was trembling, her eyes full of unshed tears.

"It's my fault," she said, her voice a whisper. "I wanted to help John's family. I wanted the children to be aware that not everyone is comfortable and happy. I wanted them to give some of their toys to those poor children, but Emma wanted to play with them and to hold the baby."

"It is not your fault," I whispered back, concerned about waking Emma. "You did what you thought was right, and it *was* right. The poor need help and those people are living in squalor, with *your* husband as their landlord."

She shook her head. "He doesn't know," she said, as she dabbed at her eyes with a scrap of lace. "He has a manager and he relies on him to collect the rents and to see to the houses."

"It's his responsibility to know," I said firmly, then quickly changed the subject, realising this was neither the time nor the place. "Emma is sleeping. You must let *me* nurse her."

In the candlelight her face was white, her eyes huge and dark. "I love my husband." Her voice was a whisper. "But I cannot give up helping others." She stared at me earnestly, her hands twisting the scrap of lace. "I cannot live this life, having every comfort whilst others have to steal so they can eat, or send their children out into the streets. Yet by doing this I have put my own child's life in danger, and I will never forgive myself." She stretched out her hand to me, and I saw for the first time the rings, diamonds and rubies glinting on her fingers. "My dear friend, Alicia," she said with a sob in her throat, "please help my little girl, and I will be forever in your debt."

Then she was gone into the darkness, and I hurried back to the bed.

Emma was still sleeping but was hot and feverish. A red rash had started to creep over her body. I started to sponge her down, willing her to live, to get well with every fibre of my body. I made promises to God and to myself, to anyone who would listen, then settled down to wait. There was little else I could do. When she woke, I made her drink a tisane of lemon juice, honey and herbs. I brought her favourite doll to the bed. I talked to her, sang to her, the first and only little Victorian girl to hear songs by the Beatles.

Yet still she worsened, and I continued through the night, sponging, talking, singing, making her drink fluids, holding her, loving her, trying to transfer some of my energy and strength into her little body. Finally, exhaustion got the better of me, and I fell into a deep sleep with her in my arms.

I awoke to a cacophony of noise. I was surrounded by children, Liz's children and her assortment of aunts, uncles and Christmas waifs and strays, who had nowhere else to go at Christmas. We were elbow to elbow at her old wooden kitchen table which was sagging under the weight of a steaming Christmas feast. Elbows and arms were everywhere as people chattered and laughed and piled their plates high, and in the midst of it all my best friend, hair askew, Santa Claus earrings bobbing, was heaping the table with more food, lighting up the room with her Julia Roberts's smile.

I breathed in the rich scent of goose and gravy, crispy potatoes and the sharp, spicy smell of stuffing. Shiny sprouts were being piled on my plate by Liz's husband, Pete.

"Get this down you, lass," he ordered, locks of dark hair falling over his brow as he continued to spoon vegetables onto my plate. "There's more fat on a chip than on you. You're more like a stick insect than the sex goddess you used to be."

I laughed. He must know some chunky stick insects! I had always loved Pete, even though in the dark days there'd been a little bit of tension between us, because as Chris's best friend there had been divided loyalties.

The doorbell shrilled out. "Oh bollocks," said Pete, "probably more from the Sally Army, knowing my wife."

"Pete, we've had a good year at the shop," said Liz, hitting him on the head with her spoon as she passed behind us, "and if we have the means to help others, then that's what we should do."

I did a double take. Almost the same words had just been said to me by Lady Elizabeth.

"I'll get the door," I said, realising that nobody else seemed inclined to do so. "Do I invite them in?"

"Yes," said Liz as she finally sat down. "Of course."

I weaved my way along the narrow hall of their Victorian terrace, avoiding half-erected Christmas presents and bikes. I opened the door and the quick movement made my party hat fall over my eyes. I then trod on some pieces of Lego which dug into my stockinged feet. My hat fell down over both eyes as I started hopping around. "Oh bollocks, bollocks, my bloody foot," I cried, pushing my hat back up, ready with my apologies for the Salvation Army.

There, standing framed in the doorway, in a long black coat, his face tanned, those cornflower blue eyes as magnetic as ever, was Chris Beaumont.

CHAPTER TWENTY FIVE

I was nineteen again. I was living with a man I adored, enjoying a happiness nobody has any right to expect.

What was so strange was that neither of us could speak. The atmosphere was charged with so many unsaid words and emotions. I was so shocked to see him, and it seemed he felt the same way as we just stared at each other for the longest time, until his face broke into that little boy grin, and my heart broke all over again.

"Jill?"

He put down the many bags and parcels he was carrying and enveloped me in the familiar hug which had always made me feel so loved and safe. Tears pricked the back of my eyelids and my arms went round him, trying to hug away the years of hurt and loneliness.

My dreams used to be full of this moment. Chris returning home to me, telling me he had made a mistake and that he loved me. All I wanted to do was to take him by the hand and take him home with me and tell him all that had happened since he'd gone, and for us to start all over again.

I withdrew from him suddenly and defensively, knowing that it would never be like that, and that's what it was, a dream.

"I didn't know you'd be here," he said in his familiar casual way, gathering up the parcels. "I'm spending Christmas with Helen, she's just moved into a new flat around the corner and…"

He stopped as Pete came striding through the door and enveloped him in his great bear hug. "Aren't you going to invite the man in?" Pete turned to me, his arm still round Chris. "Come in, mate, come in."

I was left to close the door. I followed the shrieks of excitement back to the kitchen and stood in the corner watching the Beaumont charm at work. The kids were crawling all over him, tearing open presents and shouting with excitement. His presence filled the room. He had a way of making everyone feel special, and everyone wanted to be near him, to be a part of him.

I saw Liz watching me anxiously. *This* was obviously unplanned. I smiled and shook my head at her, telling her she needn't worry. It was *I* who needed to worry.

I left the room quietly, my appetite gone. As much as I wanted to stay where Chris was, I knew I had to find out more about typhus before I returned to the past again and, not knowing when that would be, I had to act quickly. Seeing Chris could easily trigger a quick exit back and I was worried sick about little Emma. A familiar feeling of doom oozed its way through my body.

I fired up Liz's computer in the study. It was old and slow and I tapped my foot against the desk, impatiently. I realised that I was breathing in short gasps and my body was quivering. I could feel the strength and presence of Chris in the next room. It was such a powerful force. It seemed to fill the whole house.

Liz burst in the room, giving me a shock as she tumbled in, shutting the door behind her and pressing her back against it, as though shutting Chris out and away from me.

"I didn't know, I didn't know," she breathed, rubbing the back of her hand across her forehead. "I thought he was spending Christmas at the Castle."

"Liz, it's okay." I smiled at her, trying to convince myself. "It really is okay."

She continued to lean against the door, running her hand through her unruly hair. "He called in on the off chance. He's just going to Helen's for Christmas lunch." Then she frowned. "Why are you on my computer? It's Christmas Day, and there's a feast to be demolished."

I became serious, my smile fading. "The girl I am taking care of, one of my charges in my past life, has typhus. I need to know the cure before I go back."

She stared at me blankly. "But, Jill, I don't understand. Is this still happening? Do you feel…?" Her voice faded as she saw the look on my face.

I stood up and walked towards her. "I am a governess. I keep going back to my past life, you *know* that, and you *have* to believe what I am saying as I need your help. Emma might die. I need a cure. Oh God, Liz. I am not making this up."

She continued to stare at me and then she seemed to spring into life.

"Right, yes, I'm thinking, antibiotics, penicillin? They weren't yet discovered, so we need herbs. We need to fight the infection. Oh Jesus, Jill, what am I saying? This is crazy."

"Liz, trust me!" I pleaded, taking hold of her hands. "I need to save this little girl's life. I need to know before I go back and it could be anytime. I might be able to save her. Help me, please."

"Ermm." Liz continued to run her hands through her hair, looking distracted. "Anti-viral herbs and lemons. Can't you take some antibiotics back with you?"

I shook my head. "It doesn't work like that. I'm different, a different body. The lives are parallel, but…" Then I remembered the scratch on my hand when I first went back, the black eye from the man in the alley. I'd carried both injuries forward in time with me. Was there a moment when the two times collided? Could there be a slight chance that I could transport something back with me?

"Have you got any antibiotics? I might just try something."

"Medicine cabinet, bathroom." She waved her hand in the general direction. "I'll have to go back, Jill, we're halfway through the meal."

I nodded and dashed out of the door, taking the stairs two at a time. Nobody was in the bathroom. The winter sunshine slanted through the blinds lighting up the medicine cabinet as though it was the Holy Grail.

I couldn't remember the name of the antibiotics prescribed on the Internet, was it doxy something? Would Liz have the right ones, and if they weren't the right ones might they do more harm than good?

Bingo! Amoxicillin. I grabbed the packet and shoved it into the pocket of my jeans. I had to be really aware of when I was moving through time again. I had to get it right, to time it just right.

As I ran back down the stairs, I was aware of Chris and Pete in the hallway. Chris was saying goodbye. A shrill stab of panic filled me. I hadn't seen him properly. I needed to talk to him. He looked up as I reached the bottom of the stairs and gave me the little boy smile that used to melt me. It still did.

"Sorry, it's a flying visit," he said. "I'm home because of my father's funeral. Things to sort out."

We continued to look at each other. There was too much to say and neither of us could say any of it.

"I hope we can meet again, Jill," he said, "before I go back to the States."

I nodded. "Yes, I hope so too."

And with a brief smile, he was gone.

I stared at the closed door. I felt that a light had gone out. My life felt flat again.

Pete put an arm around my shoulder. "You okay, sexy?" he said, kissing the top of my head.

"Dad, the pudding, the pudding!" The twins, my godchildren whom I hardly ever saw, were jumping up and down in the doorway and I got another jolt of déjà vu.

We entered the room where Liz was just bringing the flaming pudding to the table, amidst the shrieks of the children as they saw the flames. Liz, looking hot and somewhat stressed, started to dole it into bowls which were held by outstretched hands. She was an excellent cook, and there were murmurs of approval as everyone tucked in.

"How amazing was that," Liz said, swamping her portion in thick brandy sauce. "You weren't here, Jill, when we were discussing what I've found out so far about my ancestors, so you don't know."

She put the jug down and looked at me. "Pete bought me a 'Find your Ancestors' kit for my birthday," she said. "I've gone right back to the Civil War, but the most interesting thing I found out was that I am actually related to Chris, distantly, I may add, but we are related. I've just shown him my discoveries."

I glanced up sharply. "How are you related?" I asked.

She looked at me pointedly. "One of Chris's ancestors was a real mover and shaker in Victorian England. He invested in the railways, the new sewerage system and so on. Anyway, he was married to Elizabeth, who was the daughter of a factory owner, and they had three children."

My heart felt as though it was turning to stone. I'd stopped breathing in order to listen more closely. I quickly took a breath and asked, "Three children?"

She nodded. "Yes, Christopher, Emma and Alicia. That's as far as I can get at this stage, but we have the same great-great grandfather. Strange coincidence, eh, Jill?" She raised her eyebrows at me, and took a mouthful of pudding.

I felt a hot flush crawling up my body. Three children? Alicia? It wasn't possible. Elizabeth could have no more children. Had Charles been lying to me? I was about to speak and I felt the familiar distancing from my surroundings. I felt in my pocket for the box of antibiotics, and rose from the table with an apologetic smile. As I turned away from the table, I quickly shoved a square of foil-wrapped pills into my mouth and suddenly became aware of the sound of crying. I started to cough. I felt I was choking and once again I was surrounded by a thin mist. I caught my breath and my vision cleared.

Elizabeth was seated on the bed, holding Emma in her arms, sobbing, her lovely hair falling on the little girl's flushed face.

"Elizabeth, you shouldn't be here," I said, striding over to her. "We agreed that I would look after her."

She turned a tear-streaked face to look at me. "She's dying," she sobbed. "You were here when the doctor told us. There's nothing more to be done."

I reeled in shock from her words, staring at her in disbelief before I realised that our one last hope was gone. My mouth was empty. The antibiotics were not there.

"No," I said, "no, we mustn't give up. The doctor could be wrong."

I knelt down beside them both and felt Emma's forehead.

She was on fire and moaning softly. I felt such an overwhelming sense of love and hopelessness. There must be a chance, there must. I could not watch another child die.

I looked up at Elizabeth. "We must keep her cool. Sponge her down with cold water. I'll get her herbs to drink."

The tisane was where I had left it. I stumbled over my skirts in my haste.

Lady Elizabeth laid Emma on the bed and began to sponge her little body, murmuring endearments.

"Her heartbeat is so weak." Her voice broke, but she continued to apply cooling water to Emma's burning body. I brought the drink to Emma and Elizabeth held her up so that she could drink it. She turned her head away.

"You must drink this, my darling," I said. "It is to make you well."

She moaned and shook her head. One of Elizabeth's tears fell softly onto my hand, and as I moved closer for one last effort to make her drink, I noticed something silvery clutched in Elizabeth's hand.

"What's that?" I touched her hand lightly.

She looked down. "You know what it is, Alicia," she said almost impatiently. "You nearly choked. The doctor…"

I snatched the pills out of her hand. It couldn't be true. But it was. The antibiotics were in my hand. I tore at the foil. "She has to take these," I said urgently to Elizabeth. "They may save her life. We have to make her take these tablets and drink water."

Elizabeth thought for a moment and then moved quickly across the room to a large bureau. After opening several drawers, she gave a cry of triumph and held aloft an old fashioned baby's bottle. She rinsed it and then poured water from the jug into the bottle and pressed the teat firmly into place.

"Give her the medicine, Alicia, and I'll pour the water into her mouth if she won't drink it." She moved quickly towards the bed, elegant and poised even in a crisis, her skirts swishing as she did so.

I held Emma's head and opened her mouth. "Swallow, sweetheart, swallow," I whispered, as I put the tablet into her mouth.

Elizabeth dribbled the water into her mouth, trying to encourage her to suck on the bottle. Through instinct or self-preservation, we suddenly saw her lips move and she started to suck. The bottle was soon empty and Elizabeth quickly refilled it.

"Good girl, Emma," I said, as she fell back exhausted onto the bed. I pulled the sheets up to her chin.

"What do we do now?" Elizabeth said.

I stroked Emma's forehead. "Wait," I replied.

CHAPTER TWENTY SIX

It was the longest night.

I remember the sound of the nursery clock ticking. Was it ticking the minutes away of Emma's life or marking her journey back to health? Elizabeth and I lay on either side of her, taking it in turns to bathe her, change her sheets and give her sips of water. I gave her another antibiotic in the early hours of the morning.

Many times during the night, Charles would tap quietly at the door. At first he was angry with Elizabeth and tried to persuade her to leave, but in the end he seemed to understand and only looked saddened and concerned when he stood in the doorway, usually accompanied by a white-faced Jenny, who would bring us food we couldn't eat.

As dawn broke, Emma seemed to be worse and a worried John, who was always a few steps behind Jenny, was sent to get the doctor. Cook arrived and scolded us for not eating. She brought with her more boiling water and a little spray of dried lavender which we laid on Emma's chest so the scent would soothe her. I dozed off at one point and awoke to find my hand clasped in Elizabeth's. She too was dozing, her hair glossy but dishevelled, the love and pain she felt etched on her face, even when she was sleeping. I squeezed her hand, feeling again a strong bond with her and a feeling of deep affection.

The only person we did not see was Miss Tibbs. No doubt she was seeing to the smooth running of the house, doing her job, her duty. She had no need to spy on us now. The doctor arrived while it was still dark and announced that he would bleed Emma, to get rid of the poison inside her. Both Elizabeth and I were like tigresses, loud in our protestations of how this would weaken her further.

We sent him away with a flea in his ear. I heard something about

209

women not knowing anything as he stumbled from the room, but I let it pass.

I tried to stay awake, to keep watch with Elizabeth, but I was so exhausted that I must have fallen asleep at some point. I awoke with a start as the birds were singing loudly and winter sunshine was filtering through the heavy drapes. I pushed myself up quickly, panic filling my body, worried sick about what I might find.

I turned, reluctantly. Emma was sitting up, held in her mother's arms. She gave me a little smile. "Please may I have some water, Miss Woods?" she said.

Elizabeth raised her head to look at me. She had dark circles under her eyes and she looked exhausted. She gave me a beaming smile that lit up her face, and reached over to clasp my hand.

"My friend," she said. "My dear friend," as a tear slid down her cheek.

I passed Emma her bottle from on top of the bureau and she gave a weak little laugh. "Miss Woods, I am not a baby!" she said indignantly.

Elizabeth and I smiled at each other. "No, of course not," I said, handing her a little bowl of water instead.

"How are you? No symptoms?" I asked Elizabeth, as she stood up to straighten her clothes.

"I'm just tired," she said wearily, "so tired."

"Go and get some rest, then." I put my hand on her arm. She glanced up at me as she tried to pin her hair into place.

"Oh no, *you* must rest," she said. "You have looked after Emma for the longest time. I will be forever grateful to you, but as her mother, this is my place."

I leaned towards Emma and refilled her little bowl with fresh water, giving her another antibiotic as I did so. "Swallow this tablet, Emma," I said. "It will make you well."

She took it obediently just as Charles appeared at the door. His handsome face looked drained and tired but when he saw Emma he covered the room in three strides and gathered her up in his arms.

I left the room, leaving the family to themselves, desperately wanting a hot shower and knowing that it would be a tin bath or nothing. The servants were scurrying about as word got round the house that Emma had recovered. The rooms came to life again and there was the sound of chatter and laughter. Little Christopher, looking very serious, walked up to me as I was just about to go down the staircase.

"Miss Woods, may I see my sister now?" he asked solemnly, his little face so earnest.

I nodded and gave him a smile. "Of course," I said. He grinned and ran towards the nursery.

Jenny and Cook were making their way up the stairs towards me, their faces wreathed in smiles.

"The Mistress has asked Jenny to draw you a hot bath, Miss Woods," said Cook, stopping as she reached me in order to catch her breath. "Alice and Mary have put clean sheets on your bed and lit a fire for you. Miss Tibbs should have organised all this for you, but since Lady Emma took ill she hasn't been seen. Run away, frightened of the typhus." Her face darkened. "The Master has told us not to let her back in the house."

That was a surprise. Miss Tibbs, who had been with the family for years, bolts at the first sign of a crisis. Oh well, they say that good things often come after bad!

"Is everyone else all right?" I asked, wearily, feeling my eyelids drooping.

"Yes, Miss," answered Jenny. "The Master says it was you that acted in good time and saved us all."

"That'll do, Jenny," Cook said sharply, not wanting to be upstaged. "You follow Jenny, Miss, to the mistress's bathroom, and I'll put some bread and cold meat in your room for you. You look all in."

She gave my arm a quick pat, tears glistening in her eyes as she turned to go down the stairs again. We had all done a lot of crying in the last few days.

I felt so loved and pampered. I had a little family here, and I loved it. I thought suddenly that if my mission was to stop a tragedy, I had completed my task and I might never come back here again. This might be the last time.

Jenny pushed open the door of the bathroom. I could just about make out a huge Victorian bath on claw feet with an intricate set of pipes and taps, through the steam. The plumbing was noisy, banging and clanking as the bath filled up.

Jenny switched off the taps and wiped her hands on her apron before handing me some towels and a long bathrobe.

"Jenny, help me with these buttons, please," I asked. I still hadn't quite got the hang of the hooks and buttons and corsets. I would be asleep before I got down to my petticoat if I didn't have help.

Jenny left with my clothes over her arm and I sank into the luxurious water, disappearing into the steam. I let out a long sigh and sank deeper, closing my eyes as I did so, feeling exhausted but overjoyed that Emma was still alive.

Suddenly, the temperature of the water changed. It was slightly hotter, and a strong scent of lavender seeped into my nostrils. I opened my eyes, and could see clearly, as there was no steam. I was in a different bath, in a different place. I panicked. *Where the hell was I?* This wasn't Liz's house.

I clambered out of the tub, wrapping a towel around me, looking around at the modern appliances. I opened the door and nearly fell over a pile of boxes. There were boxes all over the hallway and it suddenly clicked. I was in my new flat. Momentarily relieved, I padded my way through the hall to the bedroom, where my clothes were strewn across the bed. Just as I was dressing, the phone broke the silence, and it took me a while to find it, as it was buried, as usual, inside my handbag.

"Hello," I managed, out of breath from mountaineering over boxes.

"Jill, is that you?" It was Chris's voice.

I sank down onto the floor, my legs like jelly.

"Yes, yes, it is." My voice was squeaky and I cleared my throat, feeling foolish.

"It's Chris. We're having a small dinner party at the Castle on Friday, January 9th, before I go back to the States, and wondered if you'd like to join us. Pete and Liz are coming, and my sister, Helen, who you may remember." He paused.

"It would be nice to see you, if you can make it."

My head was spinning. What should I do? Could I cope with seeing him again? My feelings for him were as strong as ever, but things had changed. He was married. Could my poor shredded heart cope?

"I... I don't know, I'll check my diary and call you back," I said, my throat dry. "Thanks for the invite, I'd love to but I haven't got my diary. It's in a box somewhere."

"How was the move?" he asked cheerily. "I believe Pete did his back in with all the lifting."

"Fine," I said, not having a clue about how the move went, as I wasn't physically there at the time.

"My sister lives in the same block, in the penthouse," he continued. "It's good to know there's someone to borrow milk from when you get home from work."

"Oh, yes, right, I'll go and see her at some point," I said.

"Well, give me a call and let me know about Friday, when you find your diary," he said. "I'm in London until Wednesday, but you can get me on my cell; I'll text you the number. Cheers, Jill, hope you can make it."

With that he was gone, and I was a quivering heap on the floor.

"Bastard, bastard!" I yelled, my face in my new beige carpet. "You think you can just click your fingers, you shit! You bastard! You left me, I had your baby. You can sod off, you fucking, bloody, horrible, sodding bastard!"

"Hello," said a voice from the doorway, "I believe we're neighbours."

"Oh shit!" I sank my face into the carpet for a moment, and then turned my head.

A slim blonde woman with fashionably cropped hair and beautifully fitting designer jeans was standing in my doorway, holding a huge bunch of white lilies.

"Bad timing?" She had one of those beautiful cut-glass accents. She raised a perfectly-shaped eyebrow at me. "Shall I come back later?"

"Helen?" I scrambled to my feet.

She frowned and looked at me, not recognising me, which was hardly surprising as when you've just travelled over one hundred and fifty years, you tend not to look your best.

"It's Jill. I used to live with your brother, Chris, many years ago."

Her face broke into a smile of recognition. "Jill, of course I remember you. What a coincidence."

She held out the lilies to me. "A 'Welcome to your New Home' gift. I saw you moving in. I recognised Pete but I didn't know it was you. Charlie says you're his teacher."

"One of them, yes." I took the lilies from her. "Thank you very much. Do come in, please, can I offer you a drink?"

"Oh, no thanks, I've got work to do. I'm the landlady round here. I've got some tenants to visit."

She stretched out her hand to clasp mine. "It's nice to see you, Jill, and I always thought you and Chris were so good together, if you don't mind me saying so. It threw him a little when he came back from the States and found out you were married." She gave a wave of her red tipped fingers. "Bye now. Let's have a drink sometime."

I stared after her, trying to make sense of her words.

Chris came back? He came back to see me and I didn't know. Why did he come back? Had Liz and Pete known? I must have just got married to Louis, and now Chris was married. The timing was all wrong. Star crossed lovers indeed.

I found my way through the obstacle course of boxes into my new kitchen. The wine rack was as full as ever. Nothing to eat but plenty to drink! I had a sneaking feeling I was drinking far too much, but like Scarlet O'Hara, I'd think about that tomorrow.

I poured myself a hefty glass of Minervois, sat on a handy box gazing out at the glorious view of the river, and dialled.

Liz answered with her usual breathless, "Hello," as though she had just run a half marathon.

"Liz, you didn't tell me Chris came back and wanted to see me when I was married to Louis."

"What? Jill, I've got a shop full of customers, for God's sake. Will you let it go? It was years ago. You were on your honeymoon, what was I supposed to do? Break up your marriage?"

"You should have given me the option. My marriage broke up anyway." I was furious.

"Because you didn't *want* it to work. You never gave it a chance," Liz retorted. "*Louis* didn't have a chance. Will you let it all go and get on with your life, for Christ's sake!" And she put the phone down on me.

Liz had never put the phone down on me. She was my best friend. We never argued. We loved each other dearly. And the other thing was, she was usually right. I *had* been unfair to Louis. I *should* never have married him. I was a poisoned chalice. I had brought far too much baggage to the relationship. Liz was right. I could no longer kid myself. I had been the bad guy.

I pressed the numbers on my telephone.

"Louis?" I asked when his voice replied. "Have you got a minute?"

"Sure, Jill," he said. "I'm doing reports ready for next term, anything to interrupt me. Is everything all right?"

"Yes," I said simply, twirling my hair around my fingers which I always did when I felt awkward or nervous. "What I have to say is probably years too late but I want to say that I'm sorry, Louis. Sorry for being responsible that our marriage didn't work out." I paused. "Louis, I was selfish and mean and never thought enough about you. You're a good man and deserve far more happiness than I could ever give you."

There was a long pause. For a moment I thought he had hung up on me.

"Jill, what you've said means a lot. But you were not completely responsible. I married you thinking I could fix you. I took you on as a challenge. I loved you, I still do, but we were wrong for each other. I see that now."

This was so hard for me. I found it so difficult to express my feelings, but Louis was kind and good and had helped me through part of the crazy journey of my life. He was the sort of man who surrounded himself with lame ducks and tried to teach them how to fly again. This one had drowned.

"Louis, I wish you all the best, and I hope you'll be happy," I said, trying to keep my voice even.

"I *am* happy." I could hear the smile in his voice. "And I wish the same for you."

"Thanks, Louis."

"Bye, Jill."

I breathed a long sigh and then tapped in my last number, quickly, checking my watch before I did so. A voicemail answered.

"Hi, Dad," I said. "You might still be in Whistler. If so, I hope you are having a great time with your new lady and it works out for you. I'll email you my new address and my mobile number. If you'd still like me to come over at Easter, can you let me know, and I'll look at flights. Happy New Year, Dad, and hopefully, I'll see you very soon."

I clicked off the phone and threw it on the sofa.

I had come to the serious conclusion that I'd behaved like a complete and utter selfish cow. So why was it that in my previous life, I seemed to think about other people much more? In the 1860s, I was surrounded by a house full of people who cared about me, and whom I wanted to help, and here I was in the present in my beautiful flat, all alone. Something told me that it was not rocket science to work out where I had gone wrong. I missed Emma and Christopher and Elizabeth, who'd become a real friend. I missed the fact that people depended on me. I missed the busy household… Cook, Jenny and the housemaids, loyal John and of course, Charles, who had given me a proposition which filled me with excitement, yet an overwhelming sense of guilt.

However, if my task was done, I may never go back there, never see any of them again. Stuck with my meals for one, my bottles of wine, my continuous love for an unobtainable man, and this independent lifestyle I had always craved.

I drained my glass as I watched the swans floating serenely down the river, the winter sun sparkling on the water.

I had some serious thinking to do.

CHAPTER TWENTY SEVEN

I had a habit of dozing off these days, especially after a glass or two of wine, and my dreams were all of Chris. He seemed to be dominating my life again and it was disturbing me. When I awoke, I was back in my room at Castle Beaumont, standing in front of a long mirror, and staring at my reflection. This was the first time I had ever seen myself in my past life and it was startling, as I looked so different. I was more voluptuous and curvy and my long dark hair tumbled right down my back. My face was longer and more angular, but my eyes were huge and really dark. This was a better version of me by a long chalk. In fact I was quite stunning. I knew that I wasn't bad looking in the present, but one or two marriages through the generations had resulted in not such an attractive version.

There was a commotion at the door and a good deal of shouting, then Lord Kit, Charles's father strode into the room wearing muddy riding boots, his hair on end as usual. He propped his twelve bore against the bed.

"Aha, Lady Alicia." He smacked his lips. "A fine filly to ride."

He grabbed hold of me and forced open my robe, his hands grabbing at my breasts.

"Beautiful, beautiful!" His whiskery chin was tickling me and he nuzzled his grizzled old head into my neck. "Nanny, come and look, she's beautiful. My little protégé."

"No!" I shoved him away with all the strength I had. I was getting tired of being pawed about by Victorian men. He fell flat on his back, and shouted with glee, kicking his legs in the air.

"Nanny, she wants a fight this one. Come on, my beauty." He staggered to his feet, but I was ready for him. The gun was heavy but I pointed it straight at him.

Nanny appeared in the doorway, looking a little bleary-eyed and dishevelled.

"No, no, Kit! What have you been doing?" She stumbled over to him and slapped him on his head. "This is Gilbert's daughter. We are taking care of her for Gilbert."

There was a sudden loud cawing from outside the window, which made us all jump.

"Ahh, rooks. The damn things. How dare you come near my home!"

Lord Kit sprang to his feet and before I knew it, had wrenched the gun out of my hands.

"Nanny, window!" he instructed.

Nanny wobbled over to the sash window and with all her strength pushed it open.

"Ladies, stand back!" His Lordship slung the gun expertly onto his shoulder and fired. The sound was deafening and he was flung back with the force. He recovered quickly and then ran to the window and peered out.

"Got you, you little blighter!" he said triumphantly. "Come, Nanny, time for a nightcap before bed. Your servant, Lady Swainby. Beautiful, beautiful. Fine, fine breasts!"

And with that he slung the gun over his shoulder and marched out of the room. Nanny followed, throwing me an apologetic smile as she went. Elizabeth appeared in the doorway, giving a polite knock at the same time. There was an anxious look on her face.

"My dear, Alicia, I must apologise for my father-in-law. Did he startle you?"

I shook my head, and pulled my robe tightly about me.

"How's Emma?" I asked her.

She beamed. "Well, so well, thanks to you. And sleeping soundly. I've left Jenny to sit with her."

She sat down by the fire and indicated for me to do the same. I poured us both a sherry from the decanter in my room, noticing the crumbs from the feast Cook had left me. At least I'd eaten something. I handed Elizabeth a glass and sat down opposite to her.

She took a sip of sherry and leaned towards me. She looked tired. Her long, glossy hair was loose and she had a simple black gown on. I remembered that we were still in mourning for my father.

"Alicia," she said, looking at me with an earnest expression on her face, "I know that my husband has dismissed you as the children's governess, because your views as regards education are so different to his. I haven't discussed this idea with my husband yet, but I am sure that he will agree as we are both so grateful to you for saving Emma's life." She smiled. "Now that Miss Tibbs has disappeared, we have no housekeeper. There is nobody running our household at present except me, and I can't do it alone. Would you, dear Alicia, consider being my housekeeper?"

The fire crackled and the flames lit up Lady Elizabeth's face. Her long jet earrings sparkled as she reached out her hand to me.

"I'll certainly think about it, and I thank you for your kind offer." I clasped her hand briefly. "I'm just so tired at the moment, I can't really think straight."

The smile faded from her face, and she stood up. "Of course, how selfish of me! You must have some rest." She seemed agitated and walked hurriedly towards the door. As she reached it, she turned. "This message is from my husband and myself, Alicia. We will always take care of you and can never repay what you have done for us, by saving our beloved little girl."

And with that she was gone, closing the door quietly behind her.

I turned the key in the door, just in case Lord Kit was on the prowl again and climbed up into the bed, sinking into snowy white sheets with a long sigh. In my dreams I floated between the two worlds. People I knew from the past and the present merged and collided. Chris and Charles stood together and I was walking towards them, trying to reach them but I couldn't. They started to move further away from me, and I started running, begging them to stop. Emma was running after me, calling my name and when I looked around, she didn't look like little Emma. She was grown up, a teenager, the same age as my dear daughter would have been. She was holding out her hand to me and smiling.

I woke with a start, sweat pouring from my body. But I wasn't in bed; I was sitting by the fire in the kitchens of Castle Beaumont. The fire crackled, throwing out a tremendous heat into the room.

I looked around quickly. The maids were gathered round the huge scrubbed table and Cook was sitting opposite to me, a glass of something in her hand, her stockinged feet propped up on the fender. Time must have jumped ahead. I hadn't gone back to my own world, but fast forwarded in this one. I felt dizzy and disorientated and slightly frightened. What if I couldn't go back to my own world? What if I was stuck in this one?

"A top up, Miss Woods?" asked Cook. "I do like a little nightcap when all the meals are done for the day."

I smiled and shook my head, moving away from the fire which was making me so hot.

"What's everyone doing?" I asked Cook, as I tried to peer over the shoulders of the maids.

"It's Jenny, she'll be telling fortunes. She's got the gift," replied Cook, stretching out her toes.

"Ohhh!" came a cry from the table. "How did you know that, Jenny?"

The maids parted for me as I tried to see what Jenny was doing. One of the maids was moving away from her, chattering excitedly to the others.

Jenny looked up at me. "Do you want me to tell your fortune, Miss Woods?" she asked. "Since I've been having these dreams, Miss," she said in a lower tone, "I can see the future. Do you want to sit down or somethink and I'll read your palm?"

The maids were very encouraging and even Cook stood up and joined in. I sat down reluctantly, and Jenny took my hand, and closed her eyes. All around was silent as the maids waited expectantly. She opened her eyes quickly and looked at me, her mouth working, but no words coming out. She dropped my hand, a shadow passing across her face.

"It's gone," she said. "I can't read no more tonight."

I grabbed hold of her arm to stop her from walking away.

"You saw something, Jenny," I said urgently. "I know you did, what was it?"

"No, I didn't, Miss, no, I never." She snatched her arm from my grasp, looking distressed. "I can't see nothink at the moment, only dark."

I stood up. "Jenny, tell me!" I raised my voice. "I know you saw something."

"Jenny," Cook's voice held a warning note. "Miss Woods has a right to know if you saw something that's going to happen."

Jenny looked wildly around at us, then she gave a sob and tears sprang into her eyes.

"Miss Woods, I saw you die," she cried, and then with an almighty shove she made a pathway through the maids and ran up the kitchen stairs.

There were gasps of horror from the maids and they parted to let me through, as I stumbled up the stairs after Jenny, tripping over these infernal skirts as I did so.

"Jenny, stop!" I yelled, as she ran along the corridor full of statues. I could hear the frantic tapping of her shoes on the marble floor. I heard Cook puffing and panting behind me. She reached the top of the stairs and leaned over the banister rail to catch her breath.

"Jenny!" she yelled, her voice booming out.

Jenny stopped dead.

"You come here, my girl, or you'll have me to contend with."

Jenny turned and made her way meekly back to us, her frightened face pale under her frilly white cap. Cook watched her, arms folded across her chest, as her breathing returned to normal. Jenny stood before us looking at the floor, twisting her rough little hands.

Cook wagged a finger in her face. "Now, you talk to Miss Woods and don't run away again. The library has a fire and his Lordship is not due back until this evening. Go in there."

With that, she turned and made her descent to the kitchen, muttering about good for nothing servants. Jenny stood before me, unmoving.

"Jenny, it's all right. I don't want to know how I die. It's something that happens to everyone and I don't want you to talk about that.

Don't worry, I'm not upset. I just want to know what else you have seen about me. Let's go to the library, shall we?"

She turned and walked across the corridor and into the library. I followed her and beckoned her to sit by the fire. I took the chair opposite to her. The large ornate gold clock on the mantelpiece tinkled nine o'clock.

I took the poker and stirred the fire, waiting for Jenny to speak.

"Don't be frightened, Jenny," I said reassuringly, as I replaced the poker. "I see things too, you're not alone."

She glanced up, her face still frightened.

"You do, Miss?"

"Yes," I said. "I know that in your future life you work in a bakery, then at Castle Beaumont, and that you are dating a friend of mine."

"Dating?" she looked puzzled.

"Ermm, you have a gentleman caller?"

"I've seen that too," she said with obvious relief. "Oh Miss Woods, it's not me going mad then? I can see the future, but I can see it for others too."

I leaned towards her. "You have a gift. Not many people have it. It makes you special but not mad. I believe we live more than one life. In fact, I know it."

I looked at Jenny's innocent face. Should I tell her? I was longing to tell someone but Jenny might not be the right person, and what would happen if the family found out? I had read about the Victorian attitudes to mental illness in my books. If my secret got out, it would not be believed. I'd be in a straightjacket before you could say Freud.

I seemed to have gained Jenny's confidence as she leaned towards me. "Miss," she said in a quiet voice, "when I see the future, I see you. There is me and a man with fair hair; it's quite long and curly. We are sitting at a table and we are high up. The wall is all window. It's all glass. We are by a river."

My heart started hammering. "Go on, Jenny," I urged.

"There's another man in the kitchen but I can never see his face, but he has a little boy with him. He is sitting at the table with us. We are laughing and happy, but our clothes are strange, not decent."

I stared into the fire. *Jenny, Jeff and who else, and whose was the boy? Mine? Did I have a son?*

We were interrupted by Alice, one of the other maids. She popped her head round the door.

"Jenny, Lord Beaumont is back and he wants to use the library. You have to serve him tea. He's got that brute of a manager with him. Begging your pardon, Miss Woods."

We both stood up at the same time, and walked towards the door. I was trying to get my head around this information when we almost collided with Charles and a rough-looking man who looked as though he had been squeezed into a suit two sizes too small. He had mean eyes and a self-important air about him and lo and behold, he looked like Simon. He leered at me as I walked towards him and I shot him my most withering look. Charles gave me a little bow of acknowledgement and I stopped in front of him.

"Lady Swainby, I would like you to meet the manager of my properties in London," he said. "Mr Grimshaw, Lady Swainby."

I gave a small incline of my head as I had seen the Bennett sisters do in Pride and Prejudice, and he took my hand and held it briefly to his lips.

"Lady Swainby," he said, "please accept my condolences on the death of your father. Tragic, tragic."

He didn't seem inclined to let go of my hand, so I pulled it away.

"Mr Grimshaw," I said, feeling bold. "If you manage the London estate, could you please tell me why Lord Beaumont's tenants are living in squalor?"

He stared at me menacingly with his mean piggy eyes, but I simply stared back at him, refusing to be intimidated.

He gave a snort of laughter. "And what do you mean by worrying your pretty little head about that?" he said contemptuously, walking towards the fire. "As if you'd know about people in squalor, your Ladyship."

I glanced at Charles. He was watching me, but his face was

unreadable. He didn't stop me, so I pressed on.

"I know because I have visited a poor family there. There is no running water, no heating and hardly any furniture. The place is damp and not fit to live in. What pray, are you doing to ensure their health and safety?"

"Have you heard this, your Lordship?" Mr Grimshaw laughed again and inclined his head in my direction. "Do you know, your Ladyship, that our rents are the cheapest in London?"

"Because the conditions are the worst," I snapped back. "The streets are full of filth and disease spreads. Why should people live in those conditions?"

He swung round to face me, obviously rattled. "Because they choose to."

"They choose to!?" I yelled. "That is absolute nonsense. It is because their families are poor that they have no opportunity to change. It's a disgrace. You should be improving their homes for them and reporting to his Lordship…"

"Thank you for your views, Lady Swainby." Charles cut me off in mid-sentence. "Now without seeming impolite, Mr Grimshaw and I have business to discuss."

I turned to go, but not without seeing a look of pure hatred on the face of Mr Grimshaw. As I put my hand on the door to leave, I turned to Charles.

"Come with me and see," I said to him. "When we go back to London, see for yourself." And with that I walked out of the room and straight into the school hall.

The change-over was so quick that I nearly lost my balance. I was growing so used to the heavy skirts that I almost fell over when I was back in trousers and heels.

"Watcha Miss, have you been on the booze in the staffroom?" One of my perky sixth formers was trying to gain points with his girlfriend by being amusing. He had his guitar slung nonchalantly over his shoulder, his hair carefully trained to look like a seventies rock star, and his clothes to look as though they had been slept in.

"And you are here because?" I asked him.

"Auditions, Miss. School review. If I give you a fiver, will you let me in?"

His girlfriend sniggered at his boldness. She stood gazing up at him adoringly, legs up to her armpits and hair in fashionable tatty strands. How I hated the fashion of the day. A sure sign I was getting old. I ignored him and took my seat between Alison and Andy.

"God, I hate these things," I sighed as I shoved my briefcase under the table. "I don't like to destroy the thin bubble of confidence some of these young people have."

"Most of them have more than a bubble," said Andy grimly, shuffling through the list of acts. "The one we've just seen had a block of concrete. He was angry that nobody laughed at his jokes. It was our fault."

Alison leaned back in her chair and tapped her shiny red nails on the desk.

"Who's next?" she asked Andy.

As usual Andy's papers were in complete disarray. I took them from him gently, and tried to organise them.

"Colin and his talking chimpanzee," I said helpfully. "Please tell me this is not Colin Bennett."

It was. Colin Bennett shuffled onto the stage with a tatty looking woollen chimpanzee. There was a discreet but audible groan from the rest of the watchers, who were dotted about the hall in various dancers' costumes and funky rock musician's attire.

Colin had a slower pace than most people and he spent ages getting his stool in exactly the right place. His audience were becoming restless.

"Colin, we have a lot of people to see yet," said Andy, patiently. "Could you get started as soon as you can?"

"Yes, sir," said Colin, and then he spent another two minutes trying to find where his hand should go in order to work his woolly friend.

"Okay, Colin." I smiled brightly. "Ready when you are."

"Right, Miss." He sat on the stool and we looked at him encouragingly. There was a mumble from between Colin's closed lips.

"Colin, could you speak up, please?" Alison asked, cheerfully. "You're not quite reaching us."

"Colin," Andy asked above the muffled giggles of the surrounding pupils, "is your friend supposed to have a mouth that works when you are speaking?"

"It's broken, sir," said Colin helpfully.

By this time my shoulders were shaking and I could feel Alison next to me, having the same problem. There was no way we could lose it in front of Colin, and the kids sniggering behind us were making things very difficult.

"Thanks, Colin," said Andy, who was the only one within a hundred metres who wasn't doubled up with suppressed laughter. "Just work on not moving your own mouth when it is supposed to be er…"

"Dominic," said Colin.

"Er, when Dominic is supposed to be speaking. Enjoyed it, Colin, but it needs a little more rehearsal, a little more work, not quite ready yet but getting there."

"Okay, Andy, don't milk it, he's got the picture," I whispered. "I think he's so bad, he's brilliant. We should let him in. Next!"

CHAPTER TWENTY EIGHT

As I turned on the ignition in my car, I checked the date. I seemed to have missed the rest of the Christmas holidays as I was back at work. It was unusual to skip such a large amount of time, and it made me nervous. I was getting used to having two lives in a very weird kind of way, but if I was skipping huge chunks of time, well... that could bring with it all sorts of problems. It was now Friday, January 9th. The last date I remembered was Christmas Day. I'd missed all that time. Where had it gone? How had I spent New Year? Had I completed my reports? I'd missed at least one parents' evening. Oh well, maybe there were some advantages.

I checked my diary. Another visit to David? Oh no, he was coming to me. *David, pick me up 7.30pm* was written in large print followed by, *Do I want to do this*, and multiple question marks. Oh God, what had happened between us over the Christmas period? We might be bonking each other stupid for all I knew, but I had no time to think. I had one hour.

When I walked into my flat, I was amazed by the changes. I had a new leather suite, new bed, and some new clothes. I suppose I had to have confidence in the other me to get on with my life as best I could. The absurdity of that was not lost on me.

I quickly showered and changed, grabbing a quick sandwich whilst I tidied up, noticing in passing that my reports were completed and stacked neatly on my desk. *Still as organised as ever*, I thought. However the next reports were to be done online, and I'd have to grab a techy to do them for me, as the thought filled me with horror. Our IT guys at work were outstanding to watch but they talked a different language to me, and always lost me in their enthusiasm and computer speak.

The doorbell rang, and there was David, dressed in a smart suit, looking quite gorgeous, I had to admit.

"Wow, where are you going afterwards?" I asked, stepping back to let him in.

He frowned then nodded his head slowly. "I think you should check the diary, Jill. You and I are going to a dinner party. I am escorting both you and Liz, remember? You both asked me last week."

"I don't remember my life in the past two weeks," I said as I nervously checked myself in the mirror. "I'm getting worried."

He smiled at me. "Your memories will still be there. You just need to retrieve them. I'll talk to you on the way there, as it's a long drive. We'll see what we can do."

He gave my clothes a quick appraisal. He didn't look too impressed. "You did tell me what to wear. Smart dress code, you said. Dinner is always a formal affair at Castle Beaumont, you said. Oh, and we are picking up Liz in fifteen minutes."

I flew into my bedroom. How could I have forgotten? I was going to be with Chris. How could I have forgotten a date that must have been scrawled all over my memory; something I had hoped and prayed would happen for years? Be still my beating heart, and down a bottle of wine to give me confidence. Also, I had ten minutes to look dazzling. Bugger!

Fifteen minutes later I climbed into David's Mini, looking not quite as glamorous as I would have liked. I must have bought the little black number just for this occasion, but I could have done with another hour to see to the hair and make-up.

"I must ask this, David, and please don't be offended, but why are you coming? Do you know Chris?" I asked as I clicked my seatbelt into place.

"You asked me," he said.

I turned to look at him. "I did? But you could be making that up. I have no memory of the last two weeks."

He laughed. "Yes, I could, couldn't I, but why would I?"

"I thought you were married."

"Divorced."

"Ah, so even you couldn't see that coming."

He laughed again. "No. You obviously don't remember our plan, hatched at Liz's New Year's party. You wanted me to come with you as you wanted Chris to think you had a partner, and I wanted to take you out, so in a way, we both won."

I felt a little glow, feeling rather flattered that such a good looking man would be interested in me. "Yes, I can see why I would do that," I agreed. "I'd feel much safer. You do know my feelings for him, don't you, David. I'm pretty sure I've told you the history of it all."

He nodded.

"I was a bit cheeky, though, wasn't I, asking you to do that?" I glanced at him.

He shrugged his shoulders slightly.

"I think you were very drunk."

"Highly likely," I sighed. "Now, how do I get back the last fortnight?"

"Relax like I showed you, shut your eyes and let the memories come."

I leaned back in my seat, emptying my mind and breathing slowly. Scraps of memories started to come back as I relaxed more into it. Liz's party, although most of that was a blur, watching TV by myself and stuffing myself with M&S Christmas food, doing my reports. It was strange, a re-run of the past days, like a speeded up soap opera.

"Hello, hello." Liz broke the silence and climbed into the car, bracelets jangling. "Knew you'd be late."

"Where's Pete?" I asked.

"I told you on the phone," she said impatiently. "One of the twins is ill. He's going over tomorrow to spend the day with Chris instead. Now I hope we all have our best clothes on. I am so looking forward to this. I used to love staying the weekend when we were at uni, and the weekend we had there last month was just wonderful. Like old times. Oh!" She put her hand on my shoulder. "Are you sure you'll be okay, Jill? I'm sorry. You *are* brave going. You couldn't have done this six months ago."

"I'll be fine," I said, hoping I would be, but knowing I wouldn't be. My heart was racing already.

I was glad Liz dominated the conversation for most of the journey. I wanted to think about how to react to Chris. Should I be cool, convince him that my life was good? Should I tell him about Emma? No, that was a definite no. What good would that do? Should I tell him I still loved him? No, I guess that would be a hiding to nothing. He was married to a famous and very beautiful American actress. Perhaps I would just go and enjoy the evening, reminisce about the good times and try to forget the fact that I'd had two breakdowns because I couldn't get over him, not to mention messing up my life and my marriage. And David? Where did he fit in? He wanted to take me out, and this seemed like an opportunity for him? I needed to find out a little more about the plan. What had I said or done, and what had I agreed to?

I came out of my daydream as the car turned left and the lights of Castle Beaumont appeared on the hill, sparkling through the darkness of the winter night. The car headlights illuminated the long curved drive, the trees on either side looking like black skeletons in their winter sparseness.

"Chris said to go right up to the main door," said Liz as she leaned over the back of my seat. "The car will be parked for us."

"Yes, my lady," I said.

Liz ignored me. "Now, remember our plan," she said. "We have to see if Chris will let us look at some of the archives so we can find the time you keep going back to. I have mentioned it to him, but I haven't told him about the time travel. You said not to."

"And I have to pretend to be Jill's partner," said David as he drew up to the main door.

"Yes, David. Bless you. It's better that way, in case Jill gets any ideas of taking up with a married man, and who knows what might blossom."

"So," I said, "this is your idea? Why am I not surprised? All this deception and subterfuge."

"Of course," she said, opening the car door, "and David here is very happy to play along."

I glanced at David, who was suppressing a smile.

I leaned over to him. "No hanky panky," I said warningly.

"Can't promise," he threw at me as he climbed out of the car. "It may be part of the therapy." He handed his car keys to the waiting footman.

I looked up at the Castle, took a deep breath… then steeling myself, walked up the stone steps, my heart doing backflips all the way up.

Halfway up, David linked arms with both Liz and I. There certainly was something very comforting about being with him.

"Paradise," he said. "Two beautiful women, one on each arm."

The door was opened for us, and we entered the splendid hall with the painted dome soaring above us. Chandeliers glinted and our feet echoed on the marble floor. The gentleman who met us asked us to follow him, but I was so nervous I needed the ladies and was pointed in the general direction.

"I'll catch you up," I said. "Where are we going?"

"The turquoise sitting room," the man in black said stiffly.

Lady Elizabeth's room.

"I know where it is. Don't wait." I smiled at them both, and headed off.

Anyone watching me would have thought I had a compulsive disorder. I checked and rechecked myself in the mirror. I put my hair up, then let it down. I applied a different lipstick and then scrubbed it off. I sprayed myself with so much perfume I had a sneezing fit and all my mascara started to run.

Get a grip, I said to myself crossly, as I went to the loo for a second time. I appraised myself one more time in the mirror and stepped out into who knows what…

I walked back down the corridor flanked by statues, and found myself in the great hall once more. A log fire was burning brightly in the grate and a little boy was sitting on one of the red embroidered sofas, close to the fire, swinging his legs and staring at the ceiling.

Normally in my previous anti-children state, I would have given him a brief smile and moved on, not wanting to get at all involved.

Children were my job and my social life did not include them.

"Hello," I said.

He looked at me with dark blue eyes.

"Hi," he replied, with a strong trace of an American accent.

"Can I sit down for a while?" I asked. "Is there enough fire for both of us?"

"Sure." He moved along to make room for me. "It sure is cold in this house," he said. "I keep coming here to warm myself."

"Are you Chris's son?" I asked.

"Yep," he said. "Dad's got people over from his life in England. My cousins are here too."

"I'm Jill," I said.

"I'm William," he said, "or Will, as they call me back home. You must be my Dad's girlfriend before my Mom. I've see pictures of you."

If my heart did any more backflips I would have a heart attack.

"I've see lots of pictures of your Mom," I said, trying to keep my voice steady.

He nodded. "Yes, she's famous. She's in lots of films, and I don't get to see her much. Everyone says it must be real cool to have a famous Mom. It is in some ways, as we have really cool people to stay. I've met Tom Hanks, Johnny Depp, and even Clint Eastwood."

"Oh, Johnny Depp," I sighed.

"All the girls say that," he said, looking into the fire.

"What do you think of England?" I asked.

"Cold," he said, "but I like it here 'cos I've got cousins and I have a real cool time with my Dad. We played hide and seek at Christmas and there are so many places to hide. You should see the nursery; it's got my Dad's old toys and some real old stuff. My best cousin Charlie isn't here though. He's staying at home as he's got exams."

Yes, I thought grimly, and I'll be marking them.

He turned to look at me. "Why did you and my Dad split up?" he asked.

"He went to America," I said simply.

"Did you not want to go with him?"

"I couldn't. I was eighteen."

"That's so old," he said.

I gave him a smile. "But if I had gone, you wouldn't be here."

"Guess not," he said.

"There you are, Will."

Chris was walking towards us, breathtakingly handsome in a dark suit. I wanted time to stop. Not to race ahead or to go back, just to stop. I wanted time to be frozen in this moment. This moment when Chris was walking towards me, smiling his smile just for me.

"I've been talking to Jill." Will jumped up.

"So I see," Chris grinned. "How about some food, Will?"

"Sure," he said. "Can I sit next to Jill, as we are still talking about stuff?" He took hold of his father's hand.

"I guess so, if Jill is okay with that." He looked at me and I nodded, trying to get a what-might-have-been picture of Chris and me with our child walking through the Castle.

"Glad you could come." He smiled at me. "It's good to see you again."

I returned his smile and turned to follow them, Chris striding through his ancestral home with Will running beside him, chattering non-stop. Our footsteps resounded on the floor.

They paused to wait for me at the end of hallway.

"Still wearing shoes you can't walk in, Jill?" Chris had an amused look on his face.

"Still walking ahead, doing your dominant male act?"

We grinned at each other and somehow the ice was broken, but Will was off tugging at his father's hand, and there was no time for any more conversation. We passed through the vast rooms where huge Chinese vases filled with lilies seemed to adorn every plinth. The pungent smell filled my nostrils and I had a feeling that I would never be able to smell them again without remembering this moment.

We arrived at the sitting room, with its familiar turquoise wallpaper and upholstered gold and turquoise chairs. One hundred and fifty years had gone by, yet the same clock was ticking on the same marble mantelpiece, and a fire was burning in the same grate.

Hardly anything had changed, but the people were different. There was Helen with her brood all around her, and Chris and Will were immediately enveloped in nephews and cousins. Chris's brother, Harry, was talking to a leggy blond, whom I didn't know. He gave me a wink from across the room, reminding me of a drunken hunt ball and a moment of madness. I gave him a thin smile and saw that Liz and David were chatting together by the fireplace. I'd just grabbed a drink from a passing waiter when dinner was announced.

Instead of walking around the scarlet ropes as a tourist, not being allowed to touch, but only to stare, we were seated at the long polished dinner table which was decked with fresh flowers, crystal glasses and sparkling cutlery. I was seated next to David and near Chris. Will was between us. David began to play his role as the attentive boyfriend by holding my hand as the soup was being served. I tried to respond but my eyes were on Chris and I was half listening to Will's comments to his Dad about how cold his bedroom was. I picked up the heavy spoon, scooping up the liquid, thinking of the last time I'd sat at this table, Christmas Eve 1860.

"My dear Alicia." I glanced up sharply to see Charles seated at the head of the table. "My proposal still stands."

I glanced round, and saw that we were alone at the table. My soup had disappeared and there were signs that the rest of the family had eaten with us, but they were gone too. With a wave of his hand, Charles dismissed the servants. They scurried out and he turned to look at me, his gaze so compelling that I couldn't look away.

"Lady Elizabeth," I said, acclimatising myself to my past world. "She's my friend. I cannot betray her and neither can you."

He sighed and leaned back in his chair. "She gives her blessing."

"Yes, I know, but as long as she doesn't know who the person is." I was starting to feel very hot and uncomfortable.

"Quite," he said.

"But she wants me to be her housekeeper."

He continued to look at me so intensely that I felt I was going to melt. I felt such a strong attraction for him that it was taking every ounce of willpower for me to resist him.

"It is, of course, your choice," he said, taking a sip of wine.

"Either way, you will always be under my protection, as I have promised. I will give you a week to consider."

I nodded slowly, a germ of an idea making its way into my confused brain. "Very well, I will consider what you've said." I stared back at him. "But only if within that week, you and I visit your tenants in London," I said, boldly. "Please would you consider that?"

He nodded. "I will, but I think it is only fair to warn you that you have made an enemy of my estate manager."

"Huh," I snorted. "Perhaps you should investigate his dealings with your tenants. Somebody is making money out of those people."

His face darkened. "What are you suggesting?" he asked, as he leaned towards me.

"I don't trust him." I said. "Perhaps you should..."

"And perhaps you should..." He leaned over to me and held out his hand.

His fist was closed. He was looking straight at me. He opened his fist and inside were the remnants of the antibiotics I'd given to Emma. My eyes widened in horror. He continued to stare at me, demanding an answer.

"These have been looked at by various doctors in London. They have never seen this substance before, or understand what this coating is. Also, nobody can recognise the material in which they are wrapped. Where did you get them, Alicia, and how did you know they would save my daughter's life?"

CHAPTER TWENTY NINE

I swallowed hard and looked down at the table. What could I say? How could I answer him? I rubbed my hands across my eyes, trying to clear my head so that I could think about what to say, when I was suddenly aware of the strong smell of lilies again. I was in the library at Castle Beaumont. I was back in the present. Chris and I were standing on either side of the fireplace.

"I had to see you alone, Jill, I hope you don't mind. There was no chance to talk over dinner."

I was feeling dizzy from the sudden change in time and in the nearness of him. I shook my head, and moved away from the fire. I was hot and confused. I'd longed for sixteen years to see him again, never coming to terms with losing him, but I was scared of what he was going to say, scared that he'd leave me again, but knowing that he would. We had slipped so easily into our familiar banter, but now he looked so serious.

He watched me walking away. I sat down on a nearby chair and tried to bring my breathing back to normal. I felt disorientated and totally overwhelmed by the situation.

"I didn't know that you were pregnant when I left England," he said. "I had no idea."

I was so taken aback by his words, I couldn't answer him. I clung onto the side of the chair and searched his face for any clue of how he was feeling.

His expression was sympathetic and concerned. "Jill?" he said quietly, when I didn't reply right away.

"How did you find out?" I asked, trying to make my voice seem calm and controlled.

"Pete let it slip. He didn't mean to. We were drunk, reminiscing. Why didn't you tell me?"

I swallowed, afraid of how the words would come out when I told him.

"I called her Emma. She died when she was three months old. It was a cot death. Nobody could have saved her. Nobody was to blame." My voice started to quiver so I stopped talking. I folded my hands in my lap and looked straight at him.

He didn't reply straight away. "She died?"

I nodded. "So Pete didn't tell you that bit."

"No, he clammed up when he realised he shouldn't have told me. I thought she would be living with you. I didn't know… Jesus, Jill, why didn't you let me know?"

He walked towards me but I stopped him with a look.

"You left me remember. In no uncertain terms, it was over. There was no way I was going to tell you. You'd made up your mind. You wanted out."

"It wasn't like that, you know it."

He crouched down next to me and took my hand in both of his. He was so near me I felt I was losing control and it scared me so much that I started to tremble. I had loved this man unconditionally. I wanted to reach out and touch his blond hair, to wrap my arms around him and tell him how I felt, so he would stay with me and be my life again. I looked at him and wanted so much to stretch out my hand and touch his cheek. Instead, he did that to me.

"I am so sorry. Sorry that we lost our little girl, sorry that you felt I had abandoned you. I had to get out, you know that and I had to do it on my own."

"And you came back."

"Yes, I came back. I ran away, but I still loved you. I was not arrogant enough to think that you would be waiting for me. You were married, away on your honeymoon, so I returned to the States. I didn't see my family, I couldn't. Things were still very difficult. I came back to see you but it didn't work out. I had made a life for myself in New York, so I went back."

"Oh, Chris." Tears were trickling down my cheeks, and he wiped them gently away with the tip of his finger.

237

"Hey, Dad! Found you! And Jill! Two in one go." The moment was gone. Will was standing in the doorway looked hot and flustered.

Chris straightened himself up. "You took your time finding us," he said.

"Aunt Helen found nobody at all, and she was supposed to be helping me." He sighed and his little shoulders sagged. "She's been talking to David and Aunt Liz and they've been looking at old papers, boring stuff."

"And where are your cousins?" I asked.

"Oh, they were put to bed ages ago," he replied, plonking himself into a chair. "Aunt Helen sure is strict, Dad."

Chris reached down and picked him up. "It's late," he said. "I don't want Aunt Helen to think I'm a bad father, so it's bed for you too."

Will put his hands on either side of Chris's face. "You're the best, Dad, but I do want a brother or sister. It gets kinda lonely and my cousins have so much fun. Will you hurry and get one when we get back home?"

"Maybe," Chris rubbed his nose against his son's. "Say goodnight, Will."

"Goodnight Will," he giggled and then he gave me a wave. "Goodnight, Jill. Come visit again," he said, still waving over his father's shoulder until they disappeared.

There was the sound of voices along the corridor and short barks of laughter, then Liz and David appeared in the doorway.

"We did good!" Liz waved a sheaf of paper at me. "We've got lots of info on the family in the 1860s!"

"We didn't play hide and seek very well," David said regretfully. "Too busy scanning the archives."

"You okay?" asked Liz, as they walked towards me. "You look like you've been crying."

I shook my head. "I said what I wanted to say and I feel better." I took a deep breath and let all the tension go. "Sorry David, I've neglected you. I don't think we convinced anyone we're an item."

"No but they probably think we are," laughed Liz. "I think the party's breaking up, shall we find our hosts and go?"

I nodded and turned to David. "Thanks so much for your support tonight."

"I will keep you to that drink," he said, holding the door open for me.

For some reason I turned to look once more back into the room, and got the shock of my life when I saw Charles was standing in his usual place by the fire. He was looking into the flames and seemed to be unaware of my presence. I felt the familiar constriction at my waist which always let me know that I was back in time. He looked up as though he'd heard a sound, his face serious.

"I am still waiting for an explanation," he said, firmly. "Here I am in the library as you requested. My wife is indisposed and cannot be here, so you will just have to tell me. Sit please, Alicia."

I remained standing where I was. He seemed surprised that I didn't move.

"Alicia, please." He indicated a chair by the fire, so I sat, obediently.

There was no escape. I was going to have to tell him and take the consequences, whatever they might be.

"You say that you are my protector, but can I trust you completely?" I looked at him but he declined to answer, so I continued. "I am going to tell you something that you may not believe, or you may find it almost impossible to believe, but it is true."

He waited. "Go on," he said, eventually.

I looked up at him. "Charles, I am living two lives. I am here in 1861 as your governess, housekeeper or would-be-mistress, but I also live in the 21st century. I'm a teacher and for some reason I've been sent back through time to this house, to be with your family. In short, I travel through time."

He continued to watch me, saying nothing. His face was expressionless.

"It's true," I said. "I knew you wouldn't believe me."

There was another silence as he continued to stare at me. "Give me proof that what you say is true," he said.

"The pills you have are antibiotics which kill infection. The

239

substance they are wrapped in is called silver foil. Alexander Fleming will discover penicillin in your lifetime; it could be in the next ten years." I was always a bit shaky on dates. "This will help to fight infection. It is a breakthrough in medicine. This is similar to what I gave to Emma, but in my lifetime they have been tested and proven to work."

He moved over to a crystal decanter and poured two glasses of whisky, then he walked back over to the fireplace and handed me one. I took a sip and nearly choked, but it tasted good and helped to steady me.

"I find this difficult to believe," he said after draining his glass and putting it on the mantelpiece. "You are saying that you have the ability to move from one time to another. This sounds like fiction."

"Too soon for HG Wells," I said, regretfully. I raised my hand in a semi hopeless gesture.

"Why would I lie to you?" I continued. "My name is Jill Woods. I even have the same surname."

"Alicia, I cannot believe what you're telling me." He began to pace up and down the room. "How can this be? It's impossible."

I racked my brains to think of a way he would believe me. What event was going to happen soon? Was there something that I could predict? In my mind I scanned the chapters of the Victorian books I had by my bed at home.

"Surely the pills are proof," I said. "I brought them back with me, through putting them in my mouth just at the right time." I hesitated, remembering a fact, wondering if it would help to convince him. "I know what happens this year!" I continued. "Prince Albert dies in December. December 14th 1861."

"What?" Charles looked at me doubtfully. "He is forty one years old and in good health. I know him, I work with him on many projects for the improvements of the city. How can you say…?"

"Okay, here goes," I said. "The underground railways were championed by Charles Pearson, solicitor to The City of London Corporation. He persuaded them to fund the scheme. Joseph Bazalgette was the chief engineer for the new drainage system in

London. You have to believe me, Charles, how would I know all this except from history books?"

He shook his head at me in disbelief.

"Charles, I have so much to tell you. In your lifetime, the telephone will be invented. You will be able to talk to people all over the world."

I walked towards him, feeling excited by what I was telling him. "Slums will be cleared and children of all classes will be educated and general health and medicine will improve. In my lifetime, I can travel through the air on a plane and be in America in five hours... I ca..."

He held up his hand to stop me. "Alicia, no, stop, you don't know what you are saying. This is madness."

I took a step towards him and took his hands in mine. "Charles, in my life in the 21st century, I am in love with your great-great grandson, Christopher. We lived together, we had a child together. I go backwards and forwards from one time zone to another. I've been told it is to stop a tragedy. A tragedy almost certainly involving you and your family."

He looked up at me. "To save the life of my child," he said.

"I thought that too, but I'm still here, so I can't have accomplished what I have been sent here to do. I've come back again, even though Emma is now well."

We continued to stare at each other, his face showing incredulity and disbelief, and then there was something else. He took my face between his hands and kissed me, and I kissed him back. His arms went around me, the contours of my body fusing so naturally into his.

"Don't go back," he whispered into my hair. "Please don't go back ever again."

And then I saw her. As I looked up at Charles, I caught sight of her standing in the doorway, her face frozen with shock. My friend, Elizabeth, witnessing our betrayal.

I broke away from Charles and gave a small cry of shock. We stood together, looking at her, willing for her to speak first. What could we have said to make things any better? She said nothing but simply turned and left the room. I could hear her footsteps on the marble floor, she was running, and then I heard the sound of a cry, a sob; the sound of a heart breaking. I ran too, falling over my skirts as I did so, lifting them high to tear after her. I heard the sound of Lord Charles behind me.

"Elizabeth," he cried, as she fled up the main staircase, colliding with a group of maids as she did so.

He overtook me just as she reached the door to her room. She pushed him away from her. "Get away from me," she kept repeating, her voice cracking.

She tried to close the door on him but he pushed his way inside, holding on to her as he did so. He closed the door behind him with a slam that echoed down the vast corridor and then there was silence.

I sank to the floor. How could we have done this? How could I have betrayed her friendship and her love for me? I hated myself. I leaned against the banister rail, not wanting to move. I had to know that she was all right. I had to try to stop the pain she did not deserve. I closed my eyes and waited. I would stay here for as long as it took. I had to see her. I had to explain.

CHAPTER THIRTY

"Feel the weight of this little gizmo I picked up."

"Did you get Adobe Reader like I said?"

"If you disable Sky it works much better."

I hardly dared open my eyes. I knew exactly where I was. I loved our techy-boys. They were like angels descending from heaven in a crisis, but to be with more than one at a time when they were talking techy-speak, 'did my head in', as the kids would say. I tried to acclimatise myself quickly to the moment and forget the distress I'd left behind. If this time travel had done anything at all, it had made me get used to living in the here and now.

"You know, he should write an agony column in a computer magazine, he's so good. No, no Bri, go into options and disable it first."

I interrupted their flow. "Boys, boys, just show me how to put my reports online. I can't do it, talk simple to me."

Stu, who was head of IT, was a genius as regards fixing computers. He was tousle-haired and cheerful, and when mending my aging laptop, he would give forth a stream of what seemed to me pure gobbledegook, and it would ping into action again, regarding me disdainfully with its blinking eye.

"Okay, write on Word, then do this, press this, shrink it, fit to the page. Done."

"No, Stu." I shook my head. "Me no understand. You too fast. Me arty-farty teacher of english. Explain."

"Tell you what…" Stu leaned back in his chair, tapping his pen on his teeth. "Why don't you just write them on Word and then send them to me and I'll…"

I gave him a huge kiss on his cheek.

"Excellent, I love you, Stu." I beamed at him, picked up my case and left them to it.

"This is a solid state disc. One hundred and twenty gig, Stu. Read it and weep, my friend. Read it and weep!"

Their voices faded away as did the smell of their conflicting aftershaves. I walked down the corridor, a spring in my step. I was a dinosaur. I'd tried, but if there was someone willing to do it for me… well why not? One more problem ticked off.

I arrived at my cover lesson and it was mayhem. I hate cover lessons. I don't know the subject, I don't know the kids. Sometimes my reputation goes before me, and the kids crawl behind their desks submissively, and sometimes it didn't. Today, it didn't.

Three kids, two girls and a boy were hurling everyone's bags out of the window. We were three flights up and nobody was looking out to see if there was anyone underneath.

More kids were using their mobiles (banned from the school), others had iPods plugged in (also banned in main school), and there was no sign of any work on the desk. Good old Simon. It was Cheltenham Races and if we looked carefully at the TV tonight, we might just see Simon, placing his bets.

"The last person to sit in their seats has a detention every lunchtime, for one week starting from today. You three go and collect every bag you have dropped otherwise I am phoning your parents straight after this lesson. And anyone who is seen with a mobile or iPod will lose it for one week."

"You can't do that." A sullen looking lad moved as slowly as he could across the classroom, in order to get to his place. I walked fearlessly towards him and leaned over to whisper in his ear.

"Just try me, sunshine. My lesson, my rules," I said, and then straightened up to give him a beaming smile. I scrutinised the rest of the room. "Right, that was done so quickly and so well that I have no need to put anyone in detention," I announced from the front of the class.

I took a sheaf of paper from the desk in front of me, and started to put one sheet in front of each pupil.

"Anyone who says they haven't a pen will miss their lunch time, so if you haven't got one, borrow." There was a frantic shuffling behind me.

I whirled round. "Women in Victorian England were expected to be the angels of the home," I said. "They didn't vote or work, unless they were forced to. They looked after the home and the children, and were thought to be inferior in intellect to men generally."

There was a general cheer from the boys and the girls looked mutinous.

"From your knowledge of Victorian England, write points for and against this statement, comparing it with our society today. We are going to have a debate in fifteen minutes. Make notes, and you lot," I glared at the bag-throwing miscreants as they re-entered the room, "give these bags back with an apology, or I'll give private lessons to you on good manners and respect every break time this week."

My mobile beeped just as I had got the class settled. They made various stupid noises which indicated that if they weren't allowed mobile phones, neither was I. I ignored them and checked my messages. There was one from Liz.

'Chris flew home this morning. Message from him. Says sorry he didn't have time to say goodbye. Wishes you all the best with new job and new flat. Will says to visit. Come round for tea before book club on Wed. R U OK? Love Liz.'

So he'd gone. My whole body seemed to sink down into the chair. Why was I so shocked? Did I expect that now he'd seen me again, he would want to stay? He had a wife and a son. I was no longer a part of his world and I hadn't been for years. I had to get a grip of my life and forget him. I looked up at the class and they looked back at me.

"Debate in five minutes," I said, throwing my mobile back into my bag.

The rest of the day passed relatively smoothly. I had lots of references to write for the sixth form. The head of sixth form had decided that I needed the experience, so I was given two hundred to do during the next month. He was taking a hand-picked group of Year 13s on a jolly to Cambridge for four days and so wouldn't have time. I sympathised, totally.

I met Alison on my way down the stairs. It was late and I had stayed behind to finish a backlog of reports, start the references and deal with two difficult students who wanted the social life of the college without doing the work. I gave her a fleeting smile. We'd come to some kind of truce.

"Are you going to see that lovely David?" she asked me. "If only I wasn't married, I'd snap him up."

The poor bloke couldn't afford you, I thought to myself.

"Maybe," I shrugged. "I'm not sure."

"Well," she said, looking over her shoulder conspiratorially, "I did see him in Luigi's last night with a rather stunning blonde, so I'd mark your territory quickly."

"You mean like a dog does?" I enquired. "You want me to pee all over him, Alison? Is that how it's done these days?" I couldn't help it. Alison did tend to bring out the worst in me.

"Your loss," she said airily as she set off up the stairs, high heels clattering. "I know what I would do."

"Check his bank balance," I said as I swung open the glass doors, noting with some satisfaction that they'd been cleaned.

I drove back to my flat, and pulled into my parking place. There were two swans gliding on the river, and I watched them for a while, before climbing up the stairs to my flat.

"Jill?" Jeff called from my bedroom.

I poked my head around the door, noting that Jeff had actually put some paint on the ceiling. "Yes. Were you expecting someone else?"

He climbed down the step ladder, and wiped his hands on his jeans. There were flecks of cream paint in his hair.

"Well," he said, walking through to the kitchen... Jeff didn't believe in working if I was around. "A woman called."

"What woman?" I filled the kettle with water as Jeff pulled a tray of odd-looking biscuits out of my oven.

He put the biscuits down, and turned to look at me. "She said she was your mother."

CHAPTER THIRTY ONE

Jeff was in no hurry to leave, as Jane was at her night class. So, ignoring my resolution not to drink on week nights, I opened a nice bottle of red and brought Jeff up to date with what was happening in my two lives, as well as filling him in on the details of my mother's flight. He nodded wisely while he happily cooked a culinary creation and my Johnny Depp apron became completely obliterated by Bolognese sauce.

I tried not to consider the fact that my mother may appear at any moment. I hadn't seen her for over eighteen years, since the day she walked out on us and decided the grass was greener in Hampstead.

Jeff put the plates on the table with a flourish. We ate in silence for a while.

"What are you going to do?" he asked, as he refilled my glass.

"About what? Which life?" I said, putting down my glass with a sigh.

"Let's take the present first, shall we?" Jeff wiped some sauce from his mouth with a napkin. "The bloke you've been in love with forever turns up, and you still feel the same about him, but now he's gone back home to his gorgeous wife in the US. So that's a no go. The guy who is helping you with regressive therapy wants to take you out, and you don't know what to do about that, so a decision has to be made, maybe at a later date. Now, your mother, who you haven't seen for eighteen years, turns up here wanting to see you. So the question is… do you want to see her? A more immediate decision there, I think."

"Yep, agreed and that's about it, for the present life," I said.

Jeff scraped his plate and then leaned back in his chair, patting his very slim, tight stomach as he did so.

"It seems simple to me on the outside," he said. "Bloke you love has a wife. This David seems like a decent chap, so give him a go, and then see what your Mum has to say for herself and take it from there. More wine?"

I smiled and shook my head.

"You women make life so complicated," he said, re-filling my glass again.

Listening to Jeff's philosophy on life, I was inclined to agree with him.

He put the bottle down and glanced at his watch. "Hey, must go," he said, getting up and picking up his car keys, "got to pick up Jane. Sorry to leave you with the washing up. See you Monday." And with that, he planted a quick kiss on the top of my head and was gone.

I'd just stood up to clear the dishes when his head appeared around the door.

"Almost forgot," he said, "parcel came for you. I signed for it. Toodle-loo."

I shook my head at him and smiled, then got up to stack the plates in the dishwasher and, as it was full to overflowing, I switched it on. After checking all was tidy in the kitchen, I made my way to the hall table, where Jeff always left my mail. It was a very small parcel and I didn't remember ordering anything. Not that that meant anything these days.

Inside there was a CD, no title, nothing to say what it was. Probably promoting something, I thought, as I slotted it into the CD player. It would amuse me whilst I packed my bag. I decided to go to my spiritual home. I was going to the place which energised and soothed me, where I felt close to nature and away from distractions.

The Lake District.

It was also a place to run to. I wasn't yet ready to face my mother, or understand what to do about my feelings for Chris, so I would leave first thing in the morning and be on the fells by 9am. I turned the volume up and walked into the bedroom. I opened the wardrobe door, and then I stopped dead. It couldn't be.

I ran into the sitting room and the sound flooded through the flat. I sank down against the sofa, my legs not able to support me properly. The pure harmonies of Simon and Garfunkel filled the room, the acoustic guitar pulsating through me. Kathy's Song.

Chris and I didn't have a 'song' like other couples do, but at university we spent hours listening to Simon and Garfunkel. Chris would play and I would listen and join in with the harmonies. He was a student of music, so our flat had always been full of instruments, sheet music and half composed melodies.

Kathy's Song. "I gaze beyond the rain-drenched streets, to England, where my heart lies… I stand alone without beliefs. The only truth I know is you."

I turned the parcel round and round in my hands. The postmark said New York. It had been delivered by FedEx, which is why it had reached me so quickly.

I leaned against the sofa and allowed the music to absorb me, and the memories to return. The smell of him and the comforting warmth of his strong body. He always smelt expensive, beautiful after-shave, crisp, clean shirts. He was meticulous in everything he did, but would laugh at himself and at me, and I adored him. Thick blond hair which glinted when the sun shone, long brown tapering fingers, and his smile. His voice singing to me, scraps of melodies as he worked at his piano, talking to me, making me laugh with his wicked sense of humour, filling up my world. The nearness of those blue eyes, an arm draped over me whilst he slept. I would spend hours watching him sleep, listening to his heartbeat, not wanting to waste a second of the time I had with him. Not believing that he'd chosen me.

Happiness like that may come once in a lifetime, or sometimes not at all. It's those brief glimpses of pure contentment that catch us unawares, colour all that we do and make us grateful for being alive.

I dropped the parcel and then reluctantly reached for it again through my blurred vision. A door slammed, my vision cleared and I was back outside Elizabeth's room, leaning against the iron banister, staring at the polished oak door. My legs were stiff. The dark wood floor creaked as I pulled myself to my feet. My feet felt tight in my little leather boots, and I smoothed down my skirts, staring at the door, wondering what I should do next.

The door opened suddenly and an orange glow of light seeped through the crack, which grew wider as the door opened fully. There was a murmur of voices and Jenny walked through the door and closed it quietly behind her. She gave a start when she saw me; her frilly cap was quivering as she put her hand onto her chest.

"Miss, you gave me such a turn," she said.

"How is her Ladyship?" I asked, hoping and praying nobody knew the truth.

She led me away from the door. "The Master is in there with her. She's had a shock, he said, so we've given her something to make her sleep. She isn't half crying a lot though, Miss. He's holding her so tight next to him; it fair makes me want to cry too."

I turned quickly away and raced back to my room, tears of shame stinging my eyes. I slammed the door behind me, walked over to my desk and sat down. I dipped the pen in the inkwell, drew out a sheet of paper from the drawer and started to write. The lamp glowed over the smooth ivory paper and all I could hear was the scratching of the pen and the gentle chimes of the clock on the mantelpiece. One of the tweenies came to light the fire, kneeling before it in her heavy-duty apron and coaxing it into life. The rain began to patter against my window and I caught the sight of my reflection, looking ghostly by the lamplight, smeared and blurred by the raindrops.

I wrote on, of my love for Elizabeth and the children, my life in the future, of my love for Chris and how I'd tried to recapture that by being with Charles, but how my love and respect for her was far greater than that. I begged her forgiveness with all my heart.

The fire crackled and sent flickering shadows across the room. I walked over to warm myself, reading the letter as I did so. I folded it and put it in the envelope I was carrying, sealed it and walked over to my desk again, to write her name on it.

I opened the door and moved out into the silent corridor. Candles had been lit in glass sconces which hung from the stone ceiling, and I made my way in and out of the shadows, across the floor which creaked and squeaked with each step. I reached her door and bent to slide the letter underneath. I felt numb and strangely empty, my senses deadened as though I was in shock. I made my way back to my room, to sit and wait for the outcome.

I sat by the fire, listening to the clock chime each hour. I was tired and eventually must have slept for a while, as I awoke with a start when there was a gentle tapping on my door. I looked at the clock. I was still in my past life and it was almost 3am. I rose unsteadily to my feet and opened the door.

Elizabeth stood in the doorway in a white nightdress and wrap, her beautiful hair loose about her shoulders. Her eyes were swollen with crying but she looked composed.

"I'd rather it was you," she said, her voice calm, but with the trace of a slight tremble. "I'd rather it was you than anyone else."

CHAPTER THIRTY TWO

I had no time to respond as I was catapulted back into my world by the sound of a bell ringing. I thought at first I must be in school but we had changed the bells to buzzers. It was the doorbell to my new flat. I was in the bedroom finishing packing. Clothes were strewn all over the bed. I was never an organised packer.

I knew with a kind of dread who it would be. I thought my escape to The Lakes would have bought me time, but it was not to be. I sighed wearily as I opened the door to an older, but still very recognisable mother whom I had not seen for over eighteen years.

She was suntanned and wearing the hippy-style clothes I remembered so well. Her hair was still long and swept up in a loose bun. She looked stunning, but that was my mother, she always did. There were lines around her eyes but she had that aging rock star glamour about her. Her hand was resting on the door lintel. She oozed style and self-confidence.

"Aren't you going to invite me in?" she asked in that husky voice of hers.

I opened the door wider and she stepped into my sanctuary. I followed her into the sitting room where she sat down on the sofa by the huge window overlooking the river. The sun was setting behind the trees and you could hear the ducks calling as though they were laughing at each other, or at me.

"Nice place," said my mother. "Aren't you going to sit down?"

I was nervous. I didn't like her being here. She'd invaded my private space and she didn't belong here. Yet she was sitting with an easy confidence on my sofa as though nothing had happened at all.

"Coffee? Wine?" I asked stiffly, walking over to the kitchen units which were on the far side of the room.

"Nothing for me, thank you," she had the grace to say.

"Then you don't mind if I do?" I said trying to keep the coolness out of my voice, as I poured half a bottle of Sauvignon Blanc into the largest glass I had.

"Go ahead," she said, waving her a hand airily, her many coloured bracelets tinkling as she did so.

I sat down opposite to her and took a long drink of wine. I was shaking.

She leaned towards me, an earnest look on her face.

"You must hate me for leaving you, Jill," she said.

I remained silent.

"Jill, you're not making this easy for me…"

"Should I?" I snapped. "Did you make it easy for us?"

She sighed. "You were seventeen when I left. I had to go. I had no choice."

I slammed my glass down on the coffee table and the contents spilled onto the table.

"You had a husband and two children. You just walked out on all your responsibilities, and then you just turn up after all these years of silence, trying to excuse what you did."

She shook her head. "I don't excuse what I did. I can't do that. I made a mistake. I married a man I didn't love."

I stood up. I was so angry that my legs were unsteady.

"Get out of my flat," I said. "How can you say such things about Dad? He loved you and was kind and understanding and caring. Get out and don't you dare try to contact him. He has someone else and he's happy. I want you to leave and never, never try to contact me again."

She stood up quickly, her easy confidence somewhat dented. I could see it in her face. She lifted her head up in a gesture I remembered so well. "I wanted to explain. I wanted to see you…"

I stared at her, my eyes saying it all, thinking about all the pain she had caused. I remembered Dad's look of bewilderment when he read her note. How he tried to be brave for us, yet we could hear him crying at night when none of us could sleep.

"Please leave," I said, more calmly. "I don't want to see you.

I have nothing to say to you. I don't know how you found me, and I don't care."

She looked as though she was about to speak but thought better of it, then she picked up her bag from the sofa and walked out of the room, towards the door. She opened it and turned to look back at me.

"You should never have married Dad if you didn't love him," I said. "You used him."

She hesitated for a moment and then walked out of the door. I could hear her footsteps echoing along the passageway.

I slammed the door behind her and locked it firmly. I plumped up the cushions and smoothed the beige fabric of the sofa as if trying to erase her presence. I picked up my wine and took a huge gulp of it. How dare she? How dare she marry Dad if she didn't love him? What kind of a person would do that?

I twirled the stem of my glass round in my fingers and breathed deeply, listening to the ducks laughing hysterically outside my window.

Her own daughter did.

I lay awake for most of the night, my thoughts of my mother, and of Elizabeth. I was surprised to wake up in my own time. I must have slept for about an hour and I woke at 6am. I showered, dressed and packed my rucksack. I would breakfast on the way and be walking on the hills by nine or ten. As I went to open the front door, I noticed a note pushed through the letterbox. It was from my mother and contained the words, 'Forgive me', and a mobile number. I was about to screw it up but thought better of it, and left it on the hall table.

The roads were quiet and I made good time on the A66. I turned off the main road and as soon as I hit the small winding road to Ullswater, I felt the concerns of the last weeks trickling from me. It was like shedding a skin. The power of the mountains and the beauty of the sparkling lake seemed to fill me up, leaving no room for private thoughts. Although it was still early in the year, I opened the windows. I wanted to experience the silence; I wanted my mind to be as calm as the lake.

I stopped the car in a lay-by, near to where Wordsworth was supposed to have written his famous poem, and made my way down to the rocky path. Snowdrops were bobbing and blowing in the wind from the lake and brilliant yellow aconites were opening like tiny suns amidst the rich brown earth. I sat down on my jacket, on a log next to the lake. I was alone with the beauty and stillness. Suddenly, the sun came out from behind the myriad of clouds which were hovering low and threateningly over the lake and shafts of sunlight formed blurry stripes down the sides of the mountains. Ribbons of waves were tumbling and rolling, relentlessly, hitting the jetty, gurgling and gulping and then gliding to the shore. Then the golden light darkened as the sun disappeared and the vividness of colour transcended into grey, the leaves turned silver and the sparkling water became dull and threatening. I walked slowly back to the car and headed for Glenridding, where I parked it by the information centre, and headed off for Helvelyn, my Wainwright in my hand.

I felt the wind on my face, and the firm earth beneath my feet. While I was stumbling and stuttering through my two lives, trying to make some sense of what was happening to me, the water flowed over the rocks and continued on. While all these stresses and uncertainties were filling up my head, until no space was left, the mountains remained steadfast and the rocks unchanged. Looking down through unending green valleys and feeling the strength of the rock beneath me, and the unchanging beauty of my surroundings, my body became filled with peace. As I climbed higher, all the specks of the busy world below me became small and insignificant.

I realised now that I had made the wrong choices in my life, but I must try not to blame myself for my mistakes. The choices had been right for me at the time, but I'd become stuck and rigid when I should have moved on. Self-pity had engulfed me so I'd erected a wall around myself for protection. It had taken my coming face to face with my past life that had changed my perceptions on my present one. I couldn't blame anyone, not Chris, not my mother, maybe not even myself.

I needed to learn to forgive and let go, and I knew then that I had to see my mother again. I also knew that however long I had left in my past life and whatever role I had to fulfil, I had to make things right with Elizabeth.

The wind whipped me savagely as I reached the summit and as I found a rock to shelter behind to eat my sandwiches, I realised that I didn't want to be alone any more. I wanted someone to share moments like this with. The wall around me was crumbling, and I felt suddenly lighter, freer. I visualised all my feelings for the past being blown away by the wind, and I started to smile. An old man with a black labrador came over the summit. The dog's ears were bouncing around in the wind, and she trotted towards me looking for crumbs. The old man tipped his hat to me and then stood leaning on his stick, surveying the vista around us.

"You realise," he said to me, a hint of a Cumbrian accent in his voice, "just what is important about your life when you come up here."

I nodded. "Yes," I said, stroking the dog's silky ears. "That's why I come here." I understood him perfectly. He tipped his hat again and I watched him as he disappeared over the brow of the hill, his dog bounding beside him. Although I felt at peace, I knew that Chris was still an important part of my life, and by sending me the CD, it seemed as though he felt the same way too. I couldn't think about it now. I wanted to absorb the peace and stillness this beautiful part of England gave me. I needed its strength.

I knew I was going back to my past life as I stood up and brushed the crumbs off my jacket. A mist seemed to swirl in from the valley completely obliterating Striding Edge. It travelled up towards me until I was enveloped in fog. I could hear Elizabeth's voice and she slowly materialised out of the fog and, as it cleared, I was again in my room, the fire crackling and Elizabeth by the door. My letter was in her hand. It seemed that no time had passed in this life whilst so much had happened to me in my present one.

I looked straight at her. "I can't do it," I said simply. "You're my friend."

She walked towards me, holding out her arms to me in that lovely generous way she had. I hugged her close and when we broke free, she still kept hold of my arms.

"You must," she said. "It must be you, I realise that now. I have spoken to dear Charles and…"

"No, no!" I broke away from her. "For God's sake, you're his wife! Look, surely you know that you can still make love without the risk of your becoming pregnant. Charles doesn't need me. He's got you. He loves you."

"And we both love you," she said.

I stared at her and she pushed me gently onto the small sofa and sat beside me. She turned to face me. "Let me explain something to you," she said. "Lord Charles's father, and your father were part of the Devonshire House set. Lady Georgiana was a gambler, and your father became addicted to the gaming tables. They were all in love with Georgiana and they couldn't keep away. Georgiana lived happily with her husband and her husband's mistress and everyone was content. Don't you see, it would be the same with us? Nobody would know, except us and we'd be discreet." She looked at me, and her eyes were shining. "It would make my husband happy, Alicia, and you are my friend and you would always be near me, and if you were here, you could help me with my causes."

I stared at her in disbelief, and gave a nervous laugh. "This is bizarre," I said. "Totally crazy. How can you do this? How can you even think about it? I would never betray my friendship with you." I stood up and started to pace the floor. "Look," I said turning back to her, "I'll always be your friend, and there are ways that you and your husband can… you know, please each other, without… Oh for God's sake, you don't need me."

She walked over to me. "Then teach him," she said.

She was in earnest. This woman was in earnest. *What the hell was going on with these two?* This was Victorian England and I was expected to give sex lessons. Wait 'til I told Liz about what her great-great grandmother got up to. She'd never believe it. *I* didn't believe it. It was like something out of a soap opera. I decided to change the subject and give myself some time.

I turned round to face her. "Have you read my letter?" I asked.

She shook her head. "No, I wanted to see you first."

I took her hand and led her back to the seat by the fire. "I think you should read it," I said, "and then we'll talk some more."

She opened the letter and I stared into the fire while she read it, my thoughts darting about in frenzy. Of course I wanted to make love to Charles, he was handsome and desirable and so like Chris, but it was wrong. It was bizarre and nothing she could say would make me change my mind. I was determined.

She finished reading and then folded the letter carefully and glanced up at me.

"My husband told me that you say that you are from the future. Even in this enlightened age, Alicia, I find this so difficult to believe. There are spiritualists in London and many of my friends have attended séances, but how can this be, that you are here with us and yet somewhere else at the same time?"

I sighed. "Because I believe that we have more than one life. We have lived a life or many lives before the one we are living now. One soul and many bodies. At this present moment my lives are running in parallel, some scientists actually believe that a parallel universe exists. I dip in and out of these two worlds. For some reason I have been sent back here."

She looked at me steadily. "Tell me about your life in the future," she said.

I gazed into the fire. "I'm a teacher. I was married. I actually lived with your great-great grandson and we had a daughter, Emma, who died. My best friend is called Liz and she looks just like you. We found out that she's one of your descendants. People who are part of my life in the future look like the people in my past." I turned to look at her. "In my time, the poor are looked after by the state, women vote and go out to work."

She gasped. "So it *will* happen!" She clapped her hands together, then she turned to me, suddenly serious. "Are you happy," she asked me, "in your other life?"

"I am happy here with you and your family," I said, "and I am learning to be happy and contented with my life in the future, but recently two people have come back into my present life who I never thought I'd see again. Just before I came back here, I was in the Lake District. I had gone there to sort out what I should do."

She covered my hand with her own. "And have you decided?"

I nodded. "Yes, I think so." I glanced at her.

"I want you to be with Charles," she said. "I understand now how it will be the best thing. You saved Emma's life. I know I was distressed when I saw you both together, but if he went to someone else, it would hurt so much more. I've thought about the situation all evening. Stay with us, Alicia, for as long as you can. Please."

I took hold of her hand in both of mine and we sat in silence for a long time, looking at the fire and content just being together.

"Alicia, there's something else," she said, after a while. She was gazing at the flames, and I turned to look at her profile.

"I am going to keep helping others," she said. "When I know that Charles is with you, I can continue my work and he will never know about it. Now that Miss Tibbs is not here with us, there is nobody to spy on me. I can work without fear of discovery."

I sighed. "Why don't you just give money to the charities?" I suggested. "Charles has expressly forbidden you to continue. You don't need to go out onto the streets. You're putting yourself in danger."

"Oh, but I do give money. Charles is very generous with my allowance, but I must carry on." Tears glistened in her eyes. She stood up and walked across the room, ringing her hands.

"Alicia, I have blood on my hands." She turned to look at me.

I was astonished. What had happened? Had she killed someone?

I stared at her in horror. "What on earth do you mean?"

She looked so small and delicate. I couldn't begin to fathom what she meant.

She lifted her chin and stared at me. "My father had a cotton mill. We lived in Manchester. We were kind to the people who worked for us, but when my father died, my older brother took over the mill. He employed children. He was a harsh man. Have you ever seen inside a mill, Alicia? It's full of cotton fibres which float in the air and get into the chests of people and they die, especially the children. The machines are dangerous, children get trapped, people lose limbs and they cannot work and..." Her voice broke and I saw the tears on her cheeks. "I need to atone for my brother's sins." She sank down onto a chair on the other side of the room and I went over to her, knelt beside her and clasped her hands in mine.

"You are not responsible for what your brother did," I said.

She lifted up her head. "Oh yes, I am," she said firmly. "I stood by and did nothing. I had no money of my own and no position but I did not fight. I swore that I would help children as soon as I had the means and the opportunity, and now I have. So whatever you or my husband say, I will never stop."

The clock chimed and we were both jolted out of our own thoughts.

"I need to check on the children," I said, glancing at the clock.

"No, Alicia, I will do that," she said, "then John and I are going to visit the workhouse across the river. My husband is expecting you after supper and whilst you are with him, I will continue with my work."

I looked at her. "Elizabeth, I really am not sure about this..."

She interrupted me. "I know you care about him. I know that you both want this to happen."

I felt a frisson of excitement when I thought of Charles waiting for me, but it still didn't feel right. I was not and never have been a person who sought out married men, and it was so odd to have the approval of his wife.

I sat down again. "*You* must be sure of this," I said, looking at her face for any sign of doubt. "The last thing I want is to hurt you, or for you to put yourself in any more danger out in the streets of London."

She rose to her feet. "I have told Charles that I am staying the night in London," she said, patting her hair while looking in the mirror. "You will travel down with the children and Nanny tomorrow."

"It's late," I said, trying to keep the worry out of my voice.

"I'll be safe." She gave me a quick smile. "And I can see that this little arrangement will help us all. Goodnight, Alicia. I look forward to you telling me more about the future." And with that she swept out of the room.

I stared after her until Jenny appeared in the doorway carrying a branch of candlesticks that cast long shadows in the hallway.

"Would you like some supper, Miss? You weren't at dinner. I can bring up some cold meat and cheese." Her little round face looked pale and tired, and her cap was askew. "Her Ladyship says I was to give you the housekeeping keys at breakfast tomorrow."

"Miss Tibbs hasn't returned then?" I enquired. So, I must have agreed to be the housekeeper too. I was going to be busy!

"No, Miss, and his Lordship wants to see you in an hour. He's with Mr Grimshaw at the moment. He sez to tell you, he'll see you here in your room."

I felt myself going scarlet at the thought.

"Thanks, Jenny," I said. "Before you go, you couldn't just give me a hand getting out of these clothes, could you?"

She blushed too. "But, Miss, you are seeing his Lordship..."

I could have bitten my tongue, so much for me keeping a secret and being discreet.

"But I need to bathe, Jenny," I said quickly. "Would you please draw me a bath?"

She beamed at me. "Yes, of course, Miss. I'm going to be your maid from tomorrow! Now you're the housekeeper, you need a maid, her Ladyship says."

Her Ladyship is a swift worker, I thought, as I gave myself over to Jenny to disrobe.

An hour later, after a good soak in the bath, I had drunk two glasses of sherry and was dressed in a long loose robe. I was nervous, confused and not quite sure how much of a say I had had in all these arrangements.

I decided to admire my new face and amazing boobs in the long mirror, wondering at the same time if it would be able to transport this more beautiful me into the future, when there was a quiet knock at my door. In walked Charles looking like everyone's dream of Mr Darcy, wearing a white linen shirt and fitted black trousers. I felt weak with anticipation and my high moral ground evaporated.

He smiled and I was lost. He took my hand and drew me to him, his hands undoing the ribbons that held my robe together. He kissed me gently and then with more and more intensity.

I closed my eyes and sighed, thinking that time travelling may be inconvenient but it did have its moments, when suddenly there was noise, so much noise, people chattering, laughing and calling out. I smelt food, and wood smoke, damp clothes and hair, and wet dog. My eyes snapped open and I was staring into the eyes of yet another labrador, whose head was placed lovingly on my knee. I glanced up and saw the familiar dark wood and burgundy walls of the Traveller's Rest Inn. As usual, it was bursting at the seams with hungry fell walkers who were tucking into mountains of food, or gulping down pints of Bluebird, their bright anoraks and walking gear making them look like a flock of colourful birds that had flown down from the fells to feed.

The labrador gave a long sigh and continued to look at me adoringly.

"Are you all right now?" came a voice from my left.

I turned, still tingling from my brief moment with Charles. My face was hot and burning. Why did I have to come back now? Just at the moment when things were getting really interesting? Damn it!

David was sitting next to me, and I was so surprised I didn't know what to say. He was holding two beers which he placed in front of us.

"You still look very flushed," he said, taking a sip and looking over the rim of his glass at me.

So would you, I thought. The other me would be having the time of her life and I wouldn't be able to remember any of it. What rubbish timing!

"What are you doing here, David?" I asked, finding my voice at last.

He put his pint down and grinned at me. "You've just been somewhere else, haven't you? Or you would've remembered. What were you doing?"

I opened my mouth and stared at him. "I was making a fire," I lied.

He nodded. "Not part of the role of a governess I would've thought," he said. "So, to recap. I've got a small house in Glenridding, and I come here most weekends, with or without my daughter. Mostly without, now she's discovered the opposite sex."

"Have we just met?" I asked, feeling rather foolish asking the question. "I mean… did we arrange to meet here or did we meet by accident?"

He smiled at me again and I noticed again how dark brown his eyes were.

"I was in the garden, and you walked past on your way down from the mountain, and here we are."

"Is this your dog?" I asked as the labrador continued to sigh and gaze at me.

"Yes, sorry. Jess, move." He tugged at the lead, and the dog trotted round to lay at his feet with another deep sigh.

"She's lovely," I said. "I don't think anyone has ever looked at me like that in my life."

"That's why I've got her," he said. "Ah, good, food's here."

"And it's on me," I said, as I coated my food in lashings of tomato sauce. "You still haven't let me pay for any of your sessions."

"And how is it going in Victorian England?" he asked, tucking into a healthy looking salad. No wonder he looked so good.

"I told Charles I was from the future. I had to. I was backed into a corner." I dabbed at my mouth with a napkin and looked at him.

He paused as he was about to take another mouthful of salad.

"Do you think that was wise?" he said. "People who make claims like that are usually put into straightjackets."

"I felt I had to explain," I said. "I thought I wouldn't be going back there any more, as I had stopped the tragedy."

David looked at me incredulously. "I'm not sure this is wise, Jill," he said. "I'm concerned that your presence in the past could change the future. You must be very cautious. If people you don't trust hear your claims, you could be in real danger."

"I'll be more careful," I said, thoughtfully. "But it just seemed the right thing to do."

My mobile phone bleeped. I was surprised as I always switched it off. It was a text from Chris, but I didn't remember giving him my number.

'Coming to England again next month. Can I see you?' it read.

All the calm of the walk in those beautiful mountains was immediately negated as my heart performed backflips again. I couldn't deal with this right now. I really couldn't.

"You look really flushed," said David, sounding concerned. "Are you okay?"

I switched off my mobile and threw it into my rucksack, nodding my head at the same time. Suddenly I wasn't hungry anymore.

"I must get back, David," I said.

"For what?" he asked, staring straight at me like he was reading my deepest thoughts. "You've just got your food, and it's only seven o'clock. You can either tell me what that text was about or go back to your hotel and worry about it all night."

Jess had found her way back to me so I had two of them looking at me now. I patted her head, and then picked up my knife and fork. The thought of a night alone didn't seem appealing anymore. I didn't want to think. I didn't want to make any decisions.

"So, how long have you got then?" I asked as I sawed reluctantly at my steak.

"As long as it takes," he said. "All I need in life is a beautiful woman, an adoring dog and a pint of Bluebird. I'm here for the night."

CHAPTER THIRTY THREE

David was good to talk to. He didn't set the world alight for me but I could feel a good friendship forming, and he was the only one who didn't look at me as though I was completely barking when I mentioned the time travel. We had a nice night. The log fire was roaring in the bar and the last walkers came down from the fells, tired, contented and uplifted, ready for a good meal and a pint of local beer. There was a real feeling of community in the pub. We all loved the Lakes and we were all here for the same reasons. We'd been close to nature all day, absorbing the awe-inspiring beauty which touched the spiritual part of you.

The food was warming, and the company and the beer superb. Two guitarists spent the last hour strumming and singing old songs, and most of the punters joined in, warm and happy with the pleasure of waking up to spend another such a day.

David walked me back to my hotel, and it was his turn to fill me in with his background which included a rather messy divorce. We parted on good terms, with no plans to see each other tomorrow. We agreed we both had fragile hearts at that moment, but we got on so well that we could see each other as friends. I must admit to feeling a little disappointed when he didn't suggest going back to his cottage, but who knew what might develop in the future. I was a more grounded person than when he first met me, and I liked him and wasn't afraid that he was going to hurt me. Maybe I would give him a call. We'd had such a nice night together.

However at the moment I was quite keen to get to sleep, hoping that I might wake up in the arms of Charles, not having missed too many of the activities. I also wanted to postpone any reply to Chris. I had decided that I would see him again, but on my terms this time. There was no way I was going to be hurt again and I wasn't going to be the mistress of two married men, that was for sure!

Sleep didn't come easily. Usually my best night's sleep was after a walk on the fells, but I tossed and turned. I gradually became aware of a creaking and jangling and the feeling that I was moving. It was still dark, so I stretched out my hand to put on the light, and at the same time the darkness cleared, and I was sitting opposite to Charles and his estate manager, Mr Grimshaw, who was scrutinising me with his piggy eyes. We were in the carriage, swaying and bumping, bowling through the streets of London.

"I must stress that I think this visit is not a necessary one, your Lordship. I think you will find that your tenants are happy and satisfied with their accommodation." Grimshaw continued to stare at me with his mean little eyes as he spoke, but I wouldn't be intimidated. I snorted in a most unladylike way.

"I promised Lady Swainby that I would see my tenants." Charles, dressed smartly in a long dark coat and shiny black hat, was staring out of the window. "I believe I have a duty to them and I have neglected them by leaving all the work to you, my man. If all is well, you have no need to be concerned."

There was a silence, broken only by the clip clop of the horses' hooves. I gazed out of the window, feeling Grimshaw's eyes on me, avoiding his relentless stare. The noise of the carts and carriages was deafening. The streets were alive, not with the suited and booted of the city I knew, but with rich and poor alike, all hurrying through the smelly streets, avoiding carriages, carts and animals. Shouting filled the stale air as on every street corner there were men and women alike, selling, bartering, bargaining. Suddenly, we began to slow down, the streets became darker and the smell stronger, and then we came to an abrupt stop.

John's face appeared at the coach window. "Two gentleman peelers to accompany you, my Lord. They are sitting up top with me."

Charles nodded, and tapped the roof with his cane. "Drive on," he said.

Grimshaw's sausage-like face became purple.

"M'Lord, why is this necessary?" he spluttered.

Charles looked at him sternly. "I have been advised my tenants live in a dangerous area full of pickpockets and vagabonds. We also have a lady with us. Do not question me."

Grimshaw's face was fading to a light puce. He glared at me and I felt a shiver. All his actions and words to me showed that he considered me to be his enemy. He ran a finger along the neck of his cravat in order to loosen it and his face started to glow with sweat. His eyes never left my face, even when the carriage stopped.

Charles leapt out and then offered his hand to me. I stepped down into the filth of the dingy street, lifting my skirts to protect them. As we moved away from the carriage, we became aware of scores of people, crouching by or leaning against the dirty wall which was running with greenish slime. The faces of the people showed humanity beyond despair, hollow eyes, sunken cheeks and mouths that knew neither food nor smiles.

The police pushed their way through, none too gently, clearing a pathway for us to walk.

"Which are my houses, man?" Charles snapped at Grimshaw.

"All of them, sir. You own the whole street."

Charles moved past him and guided me through behind the police escort. John stopped outside a familiar stained wooden door which was split and battered and coming off its hinges.

"This is my family's home," he said to Charles, his voice devoid of emotion. He pushed open the door and we bent our heads then walked into the gloom. The cold hit us before the smell. There was no fire. The children were huddled together on the bed to keep warm and their mother was breaking a piece of stale bread into pieces.

"Mother," said John, a crack in his voice. "Where's the food and the firewood I brought?"

His mother shook her head as she continued to divide the bread. "Stolen," she said without looking up.

John put a basket of food on the table and threw some blankets over to the children. In his other hand he had a bag of wood and coal. Without thinking, I took it from John's hand.

"I'll light the fire," I said. "These children are frozen."

I got down on my knees and scraped out the ashes, piled up the wood and coal and coaxed a stubborn fire into life.

"Maddy, Elspeth, go to the pump and get water." The mother seemed to spring into action. Two ragged girls took hold of the rusty pails which were standing empty by the fireplace, and then staggered out of the room.

Charles was still standing by the doorway, looking appalled at the sight before him.

"John, why did you not tell me?" he said. "Why did you not tell me? How could you let your family live like this?"

John looked across at Mr Grimshaw and I saw in his eyes that he was afraid of him. He said nothing. He didn't need to. Charles turned to Mr Grimshaw who was spluttering an excuse, but Charles cut him dead.

"Get out!" he said, his voice like ice. "Collect your wages, gather your belongings and go from my sight. Don't ever come near me or my family again."

I could hear Grimshaw breathing heavily, his face scarlet with fury. As he was walking out of the room, he suddenly stopped and turned to look at me. Charles had his back to him and was talking to John's mother. I could see money changing hands. Grimshaw pointed a gnarled finger at me and then drew it across his neck; then he was gone.

I was glad I was kneeling as I was trembling so much. There was no doubt what his intention was towards me. The fire was now bright and the children started to gather round it. I stood up shakily and brushed my skirts down.

"Alicia." Charles beckoned me over, and he turned to the policemen. "We must clear the street and re-house these people. These houses need sanitation and repair. Is there anywhere they can go?"

"The workhouse," said the younger of the policemen.

"No," I cried, "not there, they'll be separated from each other. Why don't you let them stay in the servants' quarters at Beaumont House? There are so many empty rooms there. They'll be warm and dry and we can feed them."

The older policemen gave a shout of laughter. "Half of these men are criminals," he said. "They'll rob you blind, sir."

"They probably steal because they are hungry." I glared at him, angrily. "We could organise just a few houses at a time," I continued, turning to Charles. "Oh sir, her Ladyship would so want to help with this."

"John, stay here with your family," commanded Charles, replacing his hat on his head. "Let them eat and get warm, then I will send the carriage back for them. We will start here."

He swept out of the door and I hurried after him, running through the slippery streets trying to keep up with him.

"Charles, wait!" I shouted as he stormed ahead, his coat flapping, ignoring the men who lurked against the dark walls. "Please wait!"

I stumbled and fell headlong amongst the slippery detritus of the street. I felt a strong arm grip me and pull me to my feet. I looked into the face of Grimshaw. He twisted my arm up my back and I screamed with the pain of it. The small group of men waiting by the wall laughed and made lewd remarks. Charles was nowhere to be seen. He pushed his face into mine and I could smell his rank breath and the sweat from his clothes. He bared his yellow teeth at me in an ugly grimace.

"You have lost me my position, little lady," he snarled as he twisted my arm further up my back.

"Please stop," I cried. "Please, you are hurting me."

He gave me a shove and I fell against the wall. He pinned me there with his hands, bringing his face so close to mine that I felt sick with the smell, and the fear.

"You get me my position back, Miss High and Mighty, or I'll come looking for you."

With that he brought his fist up to my face and I screamed and waited for the blow. It didn't come. He fell to the ground as Charles brought his cane down with a thwack against the man's back. Charles held me with one hand and with the other he pointed his cane at the neck of the prostate figure on the ground.

"You come near Lady Swainby and you'll be in jail or Bedlam. I'll see to it." And with that, he grabbed me by the hand and helped me into the waiting carriage which drove off so quickly that I was knocked against the seat, then fell, sprawling onto the floor of the carriage.

There was a constant ringing in my ears that wouldn't stop, and suddenly I realised it was my front door bell. I picked myself up from the floor in my sitting room. I'd fallen over my rucksack which I had dumped on the carpet. I must have just arrived home. I was still shaking from my encounter with Grimshaw. That man frightened me and he seemed to have no scruples. I was still shaking as I walked across the hallway.

I opened the door and my mother was standing there, a bottle in one hand and a bunch of early daffodils in the other. I leaned against the door frame feeling shocked to see her and frightened about what had just happened to me.

"Thanks for agreeing to see me," she smiled. "Can I come in?"

I took the wine from her and followed her through the hallway. I couldn't think of what to say. I'd had no time to prepare for this. My other self must have invited her. I gestured for her to sit down while I opened the wine. I poured out two glasses and sat opposite to her. I brought myself back to the present with a few deep breaths. Seeing my mother again was both unexpected and unwelcome.

"I think you need to do the talking," I said.

She nodded in agreement and took a sip of wine. "I've been working in Africa," she said. "I work with children, poor children who have nothing. I've been doing that for five years."

I looked at her in amazement. This was not the mother I remembered.

"Did you ever find yourself?" I asked, trying to keep the sarcasm out of my voice.

She looked at me and twirled the stem of her wine glass thoughtfully, her many bracelets jangling as she did so.

"I didn't like what I found." She gave a sad half smile. "I made mistakes and I don't expect you to forgive me. Paul doesn't want to see me and I have grandchildren who don't know me."

She looked at me with what seemed like regret, but I wasn't buying it. Too many years of hurt were buried inside me, and forgiveness was not immediately at the top of my agenda. I clasped my hands together, and stared at her levelly. "I went through a terrible time when you left and I so needed you. My life fell apart…" My voice broke. "Could you not have spoken to us about how you felt? You just went without even saying goodbye. I remember that night. How bewildered Dad was, his whole world was in pieces, and Paul and I sat on the stairs all night, watching the front door, waiting for you to come back."

She shut her eyes and I saw tears seeping through and gently coursing down her cheeks.

"I had to go, Jill." She wiped the tears away with the back of her hand. "I was so unhappy with the choices I'd made; I was suffocating, dying inside. I had to go, and I know if I had said goodbye to you, to my children, I could never have left. I just ran out of the house, escaped, and kept running."

There was a silence as we both tried to collect our thoughts.

"Why did you want to see me?" I asked eventually.

She put down her glass, and looked straight at me, her eyes swimming with tears. "To say sorry. People make mistakes and I've made so many. I don't expect you to forgive me or to see me again. I loved all three of you in my way and I still do, and that was my torture, but you get one chance with life and my mistake caused you all so much unhappiness, and for that I am deeply sorry."

I sighed. I felt emotionally rung out and worn down. Too much was happening at once, and it was difficult to cope with.

I drained my glass and placed it on the table. I folded my hands and looked at her.

"I've made mistakes too," I said. "So who am I to judge you? I still feel a tremendous hurt for what you did, but Dad has found happiness with someone else, and Paul is happy with his life, so it does seem as though things have worked out in the end."

"And you?" she asked.

I gave a short bark of laughter. "Oh me, well, how long have you got?"

In one elegant move, my mother swept her legs under her and

leaned her head on her hand, giving me her full and undivided attention.

"As long as you will have me here," she said.

CHAPTER THIRTY FOUR

When I closed the door on my mother it was almost midnight, and I felt almost halfway to understanding her. *I'd* been so quick to judge others when they didn't act the way I thought that they should, so I was open to listening. Granted, leaving a husband and two children took a bit of forgiving, but from her point of view we were grown up when she left. Apparently, she and my father hadn't lived technically as man and wife for many years and she felt that she was spiralling into depression. She'd moved to London and lived the highlife, thinking that was what she craved, but like any of us who envied the celebrity lifestyle, she was convinced by the photos, not realising that what she aspired to was transient and meaningless. A high powered job in advertising and a glamorous but stressful social life had led to an addiction to alcohol and drugs. Burnt out and unhappy she moved with a friend to Africa where she intended to travel, but she stayed and worked and gradually pieced the jigsaw back together.

I walked over to the kitchen for a glass of water. An interesting story from my mother, very unlike that of any of my friends' mothers, I must admit. However, her words stuck a chord with me; life is only a journey of self-discovery so long as you're aware that it is. I'd ring Dad and tell him that I'd seen her, but not just yet. Maybe I'd save it until I was sitting by the sea at White Rock with him, and I could break it to him gently.

My mobile bleeped again and I glanced at it.

'Arriving in England on Thursday. Lots to sort out. Can I see you? C'

I answered. 'Why?'

'I'd really like to see you. We didn't have time to talk much at Christmas,' he replied.

'Okay. Call me when you get here. J'

I threw the phone on the bed, and started to get undressed. It would be a closure between us. That's what it would be.

I brushed my teeth and climbed into bed just as I realised I'd probably have a pile of marking to do for tomorrow. A week or so ago I would have got up and marked until dawn. Instead, I just turned over and snuggled down the bed.

Who knew where I would be when I closed my eyes. Fighting with Grimshaw, bonking with Charles, helping the families move, helping Elizabeth with her causes? Whilst I was lying there waiting for sleep to come, I had a gradual realisation that my time was nearly over in my past life. It was a strange feeling that crept up on me unawares and unsettled me. It had occurred to me that the main reason I would stop going back was if I was dead. Was I about to face my own death?

I sat bolt upright in bed, feeling that creeping, icy feeling making my heart beat faster. I became frightened. I switched on my light. If the room was light, I may stay here where I was safe and not go back in time just yet, but was this a premonition or me, scaring myself? Dying in the past life wouldn't matter as I would still be alive in this one, but I was scared. Something was different, something was wrong.

I threw back the covers and wandered round the flat turning on all the lights. I felt really strange and my body was beginning to get so tired and heavy. I made my way back to the bed to lie down but I could hardly crawl back. I reached for my phone but a sharp pain in my back stopped me dead and I cried out. I inched my way across the floor, shouting out with pain as my lower body felt as though it was gripped in a vice. I could see the phone in front of me, but then there was a flash and all the lights went out. This had happened before in the flat. The fuses tripped easily and I *did* have every light on in the house. Suddenly the wave of pain was excruciating and I screamed out. Strong hands gripped my lower body, and I could make out shadowy figures at the end of the bed. I yelled and kicked and screamed at the top of my voice. The figures became clearer, and a candle burned low and lit up their faces.

"Push, one more push, my dear, come on…"

I gasped in horror. I was having a baby. The time had raced by in my past life and here I was, going through all the pains of having a child. It must be Charles's child. It was really happening too, as the pain ripped through my body and I screamed again. Suddenly there was a slithering sensation and then a blessed relief.

I heard a tiny cry, and after a while, a little bundle was placed carefully in my arms.

"A beautiful little girl," I heard a voice say.

There was a lot of clanking of pots and the sound of water, and then there was quiet. I looked into the little face which was still red and blotchy. A pair of blue eyes looked into mine.

I didn't expect this. I needed an explanation, and why had the time raced on like that? This had never happened before. Nine months at least had gone by without my knowledge. I glanced around the room and a round, red face appeared in front of me.

"I'll give the baby to the nurse," said a kindly voice, and then the little bundle was gone from my arms.

"Her name is Alicia," I muttered, half numb with shock. "Alicia, like me."

There was a gentle knock on the door, and Elizabeth appeared. She sat on the bed, her heavy skirts fanning around her, and she took my hand in both of hers.

"Oh, Alicia, she is so beautiful." She stroked my forehead. "You did so well."

"Where is she, what is happening to my baby? Where is Alicia?" I asked.

Elizabeth patted my hand. "She is being fed, she is well and strong."

I tried to sit up but felt too weak. Elizabeth pressed me gently back down. "You must rest, dear one," she said.

"Whose baby, why have I had a baby? What is happening?" I looked round trying to make some sense of it all.

Elizabeth continued to stroke my head. "It's yours and Charles's baby. My dear, why are you talking this way? You must be delirious. I'll send for the nurse." She rose to get up but I grabbed her arm.

"What will happen to my baby?" I asked.

She looked at me in surprise. "Why, she stays here with you, of course, and when you are married you can remain with us, as we arranged, as our housekeeper. Nothing has changed, dear Alicia."

"Married? To who?" I shouted as I tried to lift my head off the pillow.

"Dear, dear, don't worry, my husband is seeing to all that for you." She smiled at me. "All will be well, just as we planned."

Oh, so I'd planned this, had I? It seemed like a really good move on my part! And I was getting a blind-date-style husband to boot. I sank back into the pillows.

Elizabeth patted my hand again. "We'll get you home soon. Everyone thinks you have taken a few months holiday for your health. Then you'll arrive home with a new husband and baby and there will not be a breath of scandal."

"Where are we?" I asked.

She frowned at me. "Why at the Castle," she said. "Where else would we be?"

I pushed myself up on one elbow to look at her but fell back again, feeling quite weak and she immediately put another pillow behind me.

"Do you think people are really going to believe that I went on holiday, got married and had a baby?" I sighed. "And in any case, does it matter?"

"My dear Alicia, of course it matters," she said briskly, as she moved the pillow around to make sure I was comfortable. "We have your reputation and the reputation of the family to consider."

"No husband," I said firmly.

She stopped what she was doing and looked at me in horror. "But, Alicia, you must have a husband."

"He died," I said. "Fell over a cliff on holiday. Terrible tragedy, only just married. I'll go home wearing black and will have far more sympathy that way."

She gasped. "But my dear…"

"No buts," I said firmly. "Absolutely no husband and if you

276

don't want to tell Charles, I'll tell him. Now, can I have my baby back, please?"

I sank back into the pillows feeling as weak as a kitten. I hoped I would survive this. Some Victorian women died in childbirth or soon after and I didn't want to be one of them. I felt weak, but not ill and when the little bundle was put into my arms, I forgot everything; where I was and who I was. I just stared into those innocent eyes and talked to her and let her wrap her tiny hand around my finger, as I breathed in the newness of her. I was eaten up with love for this tiny creature. I wished I could remember how she came about but that was my loss and some very bad timing by whatever was controlling my life. However, I felt so peaceful and contented; I wanted to stay like this. It brought back memories of Emma, and I was determined, while I was here, to supervise Alicia's upbringing so she grew well and strong. The sun was shining through the tall windows onto the large four poster bed where we lay. It lit up her wisp of downy hair and made her blink and she turned her head away from the sunlight.

"No husband, Alicia?"

I looked up and Charles had come into the room. He smiled at me and I held our baby out to him. He would be a 21st century father so long as I was around.

He looked surprised but he took her and walked over to the window with her.

"My husband died whilst on holiday," I said. "Please accept my plan. I don't want to have a husband I don't love. Please don't make me do that. It wouldn't be fair on him or me."

Charles was still by the window, talking softly to his new daughter. I could see her little arms waving about.

"We'll talk at another time, when you are rested," he said, giving his daughter a kiss on the forehead and then handing her back to me. "I'll call the nurse. You must rest."

He bent and kissed me. "Well done, my dear," he said softly, then walked out of the room.

I was so tired. I could feel myself drifting off but I wanted to stay awake whilst my little girl was in my arms. I put my cheek against her tiny one. I could feel her soft breath, and feel her tiny heartbeat through my hand. "I love you so much, little one," I whispered.

The nurse came in as my eyes were closing and I felt her take my daughter. I wanted to sleep. The rich green hangings of the four poster bed started to go out of focus. I could hear the faint crackle of the fire and the distant call of the peacocks from the park. I had a daughter, a lovely daughter; she was alive and she was mine.

I was still smiling when I woke up, but there were no hangings above me, just Jeff's half finished ceiling. I could hear the radio from the kitchen and the sound of traffic in the distance. My spirits sank. I felt a huge sense of loss, emptiness without my little girl.

"Breakfast," Jeff yelled from the kitchen. "Time you were up, Monday morning and it's your assembly day."

"Oh, bollocks!" I flung back the covers and dived into the bathroom. That was the thing about this job, you never had time to dwell on anything, because you never had time to think.

Wake up and smell the coffee. That would be the day!

"How's the time travel?" asked Jeff as he flipped over the eggs. "Done anything exciting lately?"

"Yep," I said as I poured the coffee. "I've had a baby and made love to Charles, not in that order, only the latter was a bit disappointing as I came back to this time just as things were getting interesting. Also my life has been threatened. Apart from that, nothing much."

"When do you think it will end?" asked Jeff, as he slid an egg onto my plate. "Or do you think this will happen throughout your life."

I sliced up my egg. "Jeff, I don't know. I keep thinking it's coming to an end and then I go back again. All I am sure of is that I have to prevent a tragedy," I said. "And when that's done, I guess I'll stop going back. But I want to be there, Jeff, I have this beautiful daughter."

Jeff pulled up a chair to sit opposite to me.

"Have you ever thought of having any more kids?" he asked.

"You can't live in the past. Carpe Diem, my sweet. Life is about now."

"Actually, I'd like to have kids and I never thought I would feel this way," I said thoughtfully, "but yes, I really would. However, I've got to get the right bloke first. Must dash. Try to finish the bedroom ceiling today, will you? It makes me all disorientated when I wake up looking at the past and the present colours."

"Sounds as though you should be quite at home with that," he retorted.

I threw him a look and dashed out of the door.

I dropped my unmarked books into the car, and for some reason looked up. The sky was beautiful, one of those sights that stops you dead in your tracks. It was a mass of colours, pale blues and yellows with whirls of white clouds. At that precise moment, the sun began to move slowly from behind the clouds and it streamed down on me, lighting everything up, changing dull greys to luminous gold. The swans were back, gliding across the river, their pace of life stately and calm. The river sparkled with reflective sunlight. I breathed it in slowly, wanting to take it with me into the madness beyond. Carpe Diem. My assembly would not be about working hard to pass exams; it would be about seizing the moment.

I drove slowly to school, something I'd never done before. I usually tried to get into the rhythm of my day by speeding everything up as soon as I got out of bed, but today, I couldn't. I strolled leisurely through the clean glass doors and gave a beaming smile to the bursar, who looked back at me as if I'd created a public indiscretion. I walked into the hall which was filling up with those members of the sixth form who had managed to get out of bed this morning, and were hoping to catch up on an extra half hour's sleep in assembly.

The head of sixth form gave out various notices and reminders about the forthcoming exams, and then it was my turn. I was expected to give a short and pithy speech as back up on the importance of revision, but I left my notes in my bag. I looked out at the colourful array of fresh-faced youth at the start of the rest of their lives, and at the hassled staff who were checking registers and passing notices across the rows. I came out from behind the podium and stood right in the centre of them, in my new black suit and high heels, my hair swept up in a bun.

"When I was your age, I thought life would last forever," I said. The head of the sixth form gave me a quick glance, and then a smile. A thumbs up there then. I pressed on.

"I lived in the country, but I was too busy with my social life to see how beautiful it was. I didn't notice the change of seasons; I was too busy in the shops or on the phone to my friends. I didn't notice the first snowdrops because I was too busy complaining about the cold. One of the heroes of my youth was John Lennon. 'Life is what happens when you are busy making other plans,' he said, which is exactly how I spent my youth, so it passed me by. Now in this busy job of mine, I race to work, I don't notice anything. I can drive here and don't remember a thing about the journey. In the darkest times of my life, I didn't look for the good, so spent wasted years feeling sorry for myself instead of just being glad to be alive. Plan for your future, and if you want to go to university or start work after you leave college, work hard, but enjoy the process. Enjoy lessons, enjoy being with your friends, enjoy completing an essay, enjoy your life at home. Enjoy everything! Live in the now! Carpe Diem, seize the day. Let that be your motto."

I picked up my bag and walked out of the hall, my heels clicking on the polished floor. I climbed the stairs to my classroom and looked at it as though seeing it for the first time. The trample of feet on the staircase, the hum of adolescent conversation, always louder than generally required, grew piercing and more urgent as it reached the top corridor. However, this was my free period. Oh, the bliss of having a free period first thing on a Monday morning. I switched on my computer and put the pile of unmarked books on my desk.

Andy's head appeared round the door. "Hi, can tell you've been to the Lakes. Great assembly! The kids may not listen but the staff did. We're all talking about it. Alison has got 'Seize the Day' on her door already."

"She probably can't spell Carpe Diem," I retorted.

"Ouch!" replied Andy, grimacing. "And by the way," he continued, "wait 'til you see the Head, new hair style!"

"You are remarkably chirpy." I smiled at him as I took off my jacket and prepared for work.

"Seize the Day," he grinned, "and the twins are sleeping through the night."

I was just about to sit down when there was a polite tap at my door and the Head appeared. And I mean 'head'. She was transformed! A sleek new hairstyle, and no more curly perm. She looked fabulous and I told her so.

"Thank you." She gave a stiff smile, as it didn't do to get too chummy with the staff. "Your hairdresser is very good. And, by the way, could you deliver the assembly you just did to the Year 11s. Although the word 'seize' may be a *little* too dynamic for them."

"Of course." I smiled politely, and then I did a double take as she disappeared. Did she actually make a semblance of a joke there? I made a mental note to tell Andy, and to report on the saga of my hairdresser's card being thrown at her in anger, with a very positive result.

The room suddenly became dark as the sun went in and black clouds started rolling across the tops of the hills. Drops of rain started to patter against the windows and then streak their way down the glass.

I switched on the overhead lights and was just about to sit down at the computer when George Pettit, the boy I'd prevented from jumping out of the window, popped his head around the door.

"Hello George," I said. "How's things?"

"Great, Miss, thanks," he grinned. "I've been picked for the football team!"

"Great news." I smiled at him. "Did you want to see me about something?"

"Yes, Miss, a message from Miss Mooney, she's doing the cover list and she said can you go to the history room one, as the teacher has just phoned in sick."

My smile faded. Bloody Simon again, what was it this time, The Open? The Grand National?

"Thanks, message received," I sighed, turning off my computer, and picking up my bag. So much for getting up to date with my work.

I walked down the stairs to the history department, and on my way I met Charlie running up the stairs, obviously late.

"Hey, Miss!" he said, as he continued to run past me. "Did you enjoy the party? And my uncle Chris is moving to England. Isn't that cool?"

Moving to England? But how could he, his life was in America? I had no time to dwell on this. I heard the noise before I got there and it took a good few minutes to settle the class down. As usual there was no work left, so once more I was on a search in the history cupboard. It felt strange to be back here. This was where it all started in this musty, dusty room. There was the book, exactly where it was when I first pulled it from the shelf, the book that started it all.

Suddenly, my mobile bleeped. That was odd. People didn't usually text me at work. It was a message from David. 'Are you okay? Just felt I had to get in touch.'

I switched it off and slid it back into my pocket. Of course I was okay. Why shouldn't I be?

I looked at the book again. There was no work set and it was a good title. It would be perfect for settling the hormones of fourteen year olds.

I put my hand on the leather book and pulled it from the shelf. Maybe I could tell them about the child prostitutes. These children with their secure existence, maybe they needed to know, I...

My body was suddenly jolted and I felt as though I was falling. I reached out to grab something to stop myself. I was like Alice falling down the rabbit-hole, twirling and swirling, distorted shapes swimming before my eyes. There was a thud then a strong unpleasant smell. The mist cleared and I was looking into the eyes of Jenny from the bakery, her expression anxious under her frilly bonnet.

"Are you all right, Miss?" she asked. "You fainted."

I stared at her in horror. This is how it all started. Surely I wasn't going to run through my past life all over again. My hand connected with the same dank wall in the alleyway, when I had first gone back in time. I scrambled to my feet and felt a hand grip my arm and help me to my feet.

"You should not have come, Alicia, dear." It was the voice of Elizabeth. "This is far too soon after the birth. You are not well."

I gave a sigh of relief. It was not the same time. Elizabeth still had hold of my arm. Her head was bent as she brushed down my skirts and I caught sight of a little green feathered hat on top of her elaborately plaited hair.

"Jenny, take her other arm and we'll get you to the carriage. It's just two steps away."

"What happened?" I asked, as John held the carriage door open for me.

"We were coming back from the workhouse and you asked me to stop the carriage," explained Elizabeth. "You said you felt ill and..."

I climbed into the carriage as she talked to me, but there was already someone inside. It was Grimshaw. I gasped and tried to turn round but Elizabeth and Jenny had already stepped in behind me.

"Please, sit down, your Ladyship and don't make a sound or signal to your coachman," he said. "I have a pistol in my pocket, pointed right at your little governess. Rap on the roof and we'll be off, shall we?"

The three of us sank onto the seat opposite to him and Elizabeth reached up with her parasol to rap on the roof.

The smell of him was foul and he looked filthy. His pig-like face was sweaty and red, and his ragged clothes were covered in dust. Elizabeth, who was sitting in the middle of us, grabbed our hands. Her body was rigid, but she showed no fear.

"What do you want?" she asked, her voice surprisingly steady.

"Money. One thousand guineas," he sneered at her, showing his yellow-stained teeth. "Your little governess lost me my job. You tell that husband of yours that if he doesn't pay up," he brought the pistol out from his pocket and pointed it straight at me, "this little lady will be dead within the week."

Lady Elizabeth stuck out her chin defiantly. "How will we know where to find you?" she said. "*If* we decide to give you money?"

"Tell him to get the money and I'll find you." He rapped on the roof and the carriage lurched to a stop. I fell forward and he caught me neatly and stuck the pistol into my neck.

"Goodbye, little lady," he said, and then he laughed, and with one hand, threw me back against the carriage seat. "One week to live unless I get my money. You'll hear from me." Then he leapt out of the carriage and was gone.

CHAPTER THIRTY FIVE

The smell and danger of the man lingered in the carriage long after he'd gone.

Jenny had wedged herself into the corner of the carriage, her feet tucked under her. "Oh, Miss," she said, her voice trembling. "Keep away from that man. He is so evil. He means you harm."

"Jenny." Lady Elizabeth patted her arm gently, but I could see that she too had been affected by his threats. "We'll have to make sure that dear Alicia is never unaccompanied." She stretched out her gloved hand to help me up. "Don't worry, Alicia. I will talk to Charles. This man will not be allowed to harm you."

Jenny leaned towards me, her eyes wide with fear. "Miss, you must keep away from him. I've seen him before. He's bad and he'll hurt you. And you too, Mistress."

"Nonsense, Jenny." Elizabeth sat me down beside her and grasped hold of my hand. "This will never happen again. I will make sure that when we go on these visits, we have people to protect us."

"But, Elizabeth, your husband does not know about these visits. How can we tell Charles what happened?" I said.

"Alicia, dear, you will have to tell him that you were out on an errand with Jenny," she said. "*You* must tell him, but not mention that I was there."

I found my voice at last; I was shocked and stunned by what had happened. I could still feel the cold pistol in my neck. The man had terrified me. "Yes, I will," I said, "but are you sure you still need to deceive him? He is helping his tenants now."

Lady Elizabeth was looking out of the window, and she turned to me, a little frown between her eyebrows. "Yes, but it's not enough," she said. "There are so *many* people to help. You saw the conditions of the workhouse; you saw how they live, Alicia. You must help me to persuade Charles to employ people from there on the estate. *We* must help them too."

The carriage drew up to Beaumont House with a shudder, and we waited for the door to be opened. As the footman was getting the steps ready for us, Cook popped her head inside the carriage. "His Lordship has arrived home, your Ladyship. Unexpected. He wants everyone in the main hall."

Elizabeth gasped. "Quick, Alicia, Jenny, we'll use the backstairs."

Cook stood back to let us out. "I've got your nightclothes in the kitchen ready," she said. "Soon as I heard he was here. Now get yourselves down there and change so it looks as though you've been abed all this time, come on!"

We climbed out of the carriage and clattered down the stairs. The lamps were lit and cast eerie shadows down the walls. Cook brought up the rear and we could hear her puffing and panting and muttering to herself as she followed us down. Helped by Cook and two of the tweenies, we were soon in our nightclothes. We crept up the stairs to where everyone was assembling in the main hall. The whole household was there dressed in nightclothes with shawls or coats wrapped around their shivering bodies.

Elizabeth made her way through the crowd which parted for her respectfully. I followed close behind. Charles was standing at the top of the main staircase. He must have been looking for Elizabeth.

"My dear, whatever is the matter?" she called up to him. "Why have you summoned all the servants at this time of night?"

Charles started to walk down the stairs and then he stopped halfway down. He raised his hand for quiet and the buzz and hum of the servants' chatter suddenly stopped, and everyone turned to look at him.

He looked very pale. He gazed round at everyone until his eyes alighted on me.

"I have some very bad news," he said. And there was a collective gasp from the household and then speculative murmurs. He held up his hand again for quiet.

"I have just been informed," he said, his voice a little unsteady, "that at a few minutes before eleven this evening, our beloved Prince Albert, the Prince Consort, died." His voice broke, and then he looked straight at me, shaking his head so slightly that only I could see it.

"Our dear Queen, though overwhelmed by grief, is still in good health."

There was a sudden outbreak of emotion from the assembled party. Women were in tears, and were being comforted by the male servants who were themselves shocked and overcome.

Charles made his way down to us. Elizabeth stood rooted to the spot and then she turned and looked straight at me.

"You knew," she whispered. "You said this would happen."

"And on this date," Charles finished for her, as he reached us.

He walked past us and flung open the large main door to the house.

Ringing out across the streets and houses of London, from the stinking slums to the gilded mansions of respectable gentry, the dull boom from the bells of St Paul's cathedral sounded and filled each of us with a sadness and dread. I moved through the throng of people who were now standing silently, some even praying, and made my way up the steep flights of stairs to the nursery. All three children were sleeping the sleep of the innocents, curled up in their beds, a small shaft of moonlight peeping through the curtains and giving a faint glow to the room.

My little daughter was awake, watching me from her crib. I picked her up and held her to me, drinking in the fresh, warm smell of her newness. She nestled against me and I walked over to the window to look out onto the dimly lit square below, the boom of St Paul's still ringing out across the city.

"Alicia."

I turned to see Lord and Lady Beaumont standing in the doorway watching me.

"Now do you believe me?" I said. "I *am* from the future. No matter how crazy it sounds, it's true. I'm living two lives, one now and one in the 21st century. I was sent here to help prevent a tragedy. That's all I know."

They continued to stare at me and then the light began to fade and they became blurred and then they disappeared. The weight from Alicia in my arms faded to nothing and I was back in the classroom, perched on the edge of a desk, a group of children staring at me open mouthed.

"That is so gross," chirped up a girl who was wearing more make up on her face than I possessed. "Children as prostitutes? Young children?"

"Eeewww," chorused her friends, looking at each other in disgust.

"It was either that or the workhouse, and there was nobody to protect them. The Victorian age was full of hypocrisy. Respectability and scandal, wealth and dire poverty."

The buzzer sounded and I lost my audience in a stampede for the door. I picked up my bag, and as I walked back to my department, I sent Liz a quick text. I wanted urgently to see what she had found in the archives. Also I had to digest the fact that Chris was moving to England. I felt the butterflies returning to churn up my insides. So what was happening with him? Why was he leaving America and why did he want to see me? Maybe Liz would know.

I met Andy in the english office. His hair was still on end but there was no sick or anything else to be discovered on his jacket. His shirt looked as though it had been ironed.

"What, ho, Jill," he said, as he filled the kettle. "Some good news. All Year 10s are out on a field trip and they must have missed us off cover so we're free 'til break."

I put my bag down thoughtfully, and looked at him. We had a free period together; Simon's book was in the stockroom. It seemed like an opportunity.

"Andy, I want you to do something for me," I said.

He saw the serious expression on my face, and his smile faded.

"What is it?" he asked.

I sat down on a chair and looked up at him. "You know that I have been going back in time to Victorian England."

He looked at me doubtfully and was about to speak but I got there first.

I sighed. "It's true, and I don't think I have much time left to do whatever I have to do in my other life. You can believe me or not, that isn't important, but I want you to do something for me. I want to know what happens to me in this life when I am in Victorian England. I want you to be with me when I go back, so that you can tell me what happens to my body, to myself, when I am somewhere else."

He dropped into the chair opposite to me. "Are you serious?" he said, looking as though he expected me to break into peals of laughter and tell him I was kidding, but of course I didn't.

I stood up. "Listen, please listen until you have heard me out. It started when I pulled a book out of Simon's stockroom, and although it didn't happen the second time I did it, it just happened again a few minutes ago. I want you to be with me when I pull the book off the shelf again. I want to know what happens to me."

He was shaking his head slowly, a perplexed look on his face.

"I mean it, I'm serious. I think in my past life, I am going to die soon. I have been threatened. This could be the last time I go back. Also, if I die, I don't know what I'll be like when I get back here. I need you to be there for me. I'm frightened; I want you to be with me."

I saw him hesitate. "Please. I promise you I'm telling the truth. I would never waste your time; just go with it, please. I'll probably be away just a few moments."

He stood up, a bemused look on his face. "I don't know what to say, Jill," he said.

"Say nothing; just come with me," I pleaded.

The phone started to ring but we ignored it, and hurried down the stairs to the history block. There was a class in Simon's room who were giving hell to a new supply teacher. The air was alive with revolution.

"I'll be back in one second," said Andy to the harassed-looking women, who was being eaten alive. "We just need to get something."

We walked into the stockroom, Andy looking nervously around him as we did so.

I reached up to clasp the book.

"Are you ready?" I asked, looking over my shoulder at him. He nodded and I pulled the book down from the shelf. This time the transition was really forceful. I felt as if I was being catapulted through the air, and I landed with such a jolt, it completely winded me. There was an inky darkness around me which started to clear. I could feel the heat from a fire and I could see flames flickering. I was surrounded by faces who were peering down at me. I was in the kitchen and the scullery maids and tweenies were peering at me, looking very concerned; the little frills of their caps were bobbing as they looked at each other and then back at me. I was sitting on the floor near the fire, my arm resting on one of the Windsor chairs.

"What happened?" I asked them as I struggled to my feet.

"You fell, Miss," said the smallest one.

When I finally got to my feet, they had backed away from me and were staring at me from behind the table. The atmosphere had changed. I sensed hostility in the air from these people who had been so friendly to me. They were murmuring to each other in little groups and they looked first at me and then at Cook. She was standing next to the fire, her arms folded across her huge chest and her straightened hair tucked under her cap.

"What's the matter?" I asked, looking at them curiously. "Is something wrong?"

I moved towards them and they backed away. Only Cook stood her ground. I looked at her enquiringly.

"What's this about you knowing about Prince Albert?" she said. "What's this nonsense about you living in the future?"

I looked at them bewildered. How did they know? I knew that neither Charles nor Elizabeth would have discussed this with their servants.

"Who told you?" I demanded.

They looked at each other. "Miss Tibbs has been here, trying to get her position back but my lady told her to leave the house," said Cook, "but before she left she told us what she has heard. Young Alice here is her niece and she overheard you talking to them upstairs. She told Miss Tibbs what you said about Prince Albert. She also sez it was you that lost old Grimshaw his job."

I looked at her indignantly. "So you believe gossip then?" I retorted. "And you should be glad to get rid of Grimshaw, he was a crook."

"Crook or not, he looked after us down here, and he's always welcome in our kitchen. He's been with us this morning, brought us a brace of pheasants. We wouldn't have all those other mouths to feed if it wasn't for you interfering," Cook snapped, "and that's not all. Alice sez you've been carrying on with his Lordship, and you a friend of our lovely lady."

So Grimshaw had been here? Had he left or was he still here, and how much time had passed since he had threatened me? Was my week up? And how did they get to know about me and Charles? I felt that everything around me was falling apart, but I drew myself up angrily. "Mr Grimshaw has been dismissed," I said, "and so has Miss Tibbs. He should not be anywhere near this house and neither should she. And as for the rest, it's servants' gossip and you should be ashamed for believing it."

I started to feel a frisson of fear. The back of my neck started to prickle.

"Are you from the future then?" Cook demanded. "Young Jenny says you sees things."

The maids waited expectantly.

"No, of course I'm not," I said. "And I don't know why Alice should say such scandalous things."

"But Miss," squeaked Alice. "I heard you and the Master, and I've seen the both of you…"

"Alice, I'll have you dismissed if you say anything else that is untrue," I snapped at her, giving her my best withering look. "How can anyone be from the future? And as for being with his Lordship, firstly, that is none of your business, and if you want to know, I am really Lady Swainby, a friend of the family. That is why I am much in their company." Oh God, now I was starting to sound like a character in a Jane Austen novel. I was frightened and things were getting out of hand, and as usual, I was talking too much.

They continued to regard me and I had a strong feeling they didn't believe me. I turned away and began climbing up the narrow kitchen stairs to the house, feeling a real sadness at their treatment of me.

"Then, Miss Woods, Lady Swainby, or whoever you are," Cook shouted after me, "why should we believe you, when you never even told us your real name? Who's the one who's been lying then? And how come you were sitting talking to us plain as day and then you was suddenly on the floor. It's mighty strange to me."

I stopped and looked down at them all. Cook was in full flow, there was no stopping her. Her round friendly face was hostile.

"Mr Grimshaw says you is a spy. You spy on us and tell them upstairs," Cook continued, her arms still folded and her expression dark. "And you'll be breaking Lady Elizabeth's heart carrying on with his Lordship. We've got words for women like you. It isn't only Alice who's seen you, Mr Grimshaw has. He sez yous a witch, and should be thrown in the Thames."

The maids gave a collective gasp. Jenny was looking down at the floor, too terrified of Cook to try to defend me, even if she wanted to. I had no friends here.

I was astounded. How did Grimshaw know about me and Charles and how come they believed him and not me? I began to feel real fear. Was he spying on me? Could he still be in the house right now? I turned and fled up the staircase and along the corridor to Charles's study, but he wasn't there. I ran back down the corridor, my feet clattering on the wooden floor. I nearly stumbled, the long skirts getting in my way as always.

I climbed the next staircase two steps at a time, hoisting up my skirts and running for dear life. I flung open the nursery door. The children were at their lessons with their new governess. They looked up in surprise when they saw me, red faced and out of breath. Elizabeth was sitting with Alicia by the fire, humming to her.

"My dear Alicia!" she said in surprise. "Whatever is wrong?

Did you get the milk from the kitchen for her?"

"Elizabeth, I wish to speak to you in private," I gasped. "Please."

"Of course." She stood up in that elegant way of hers and tucked Alicia's shawl around her.

"Let's go to Nanny's sitting room. She is out shooting with Lord Kit," she suggested.

I'd never been in Nanny's domain before and it startled me with its lushness. Heavy, red brocade curtains hung from the sash windows and the dark wooden furniture was adorned with crimson silk. It was how one pictured the home of a well set up lady of the night, rather than a little old lady. Gilt mirrors hung from floor to ceiling and I gave a start as I caught sight of my reflection, dressed elegantly in a crinoline and tight bodice, my hair looped in plaits around my ears. Elizabeth sat down by the fire and indicated for me to do the same. She handed Alicia to me and I hugged her close.

"Elizabeth, Mr Grimshaw has been poisoning the servants against me. He's been telling them that I'm from the future. They all know, but how do they know? I've heard that some of the servants have been snooping but I know I've told nobody but you and Charles. They also know about Charles and me."

Elizabeth stared at me in astonishment. "We have told no one," she said. "No one. You must believe us. How is that man allowed into the house? My husband has strictly forbidden it."

"He's bribing Cook. He's allowed in the kitchen, and if he's allowed in the kitchen, he's allowed in the rest of the house."

I buried my head in Alicia's shawl, breathing in the soft innocence of her. "I'm frightened," I said. "He means me real harm. If we don't give him money or reinstate him as manager, I know he'll do me harm. I know it."

"My dear." Elizabeth left her chair to stand beside me. "My husband had the police searching for him since he threatened us. He will be caught and punished and then you will be safe. I have instructed the staff not to let him in the house and to keep all the doors locked. I will speak to Cook. She has disobeyed our instructions. You must not leave the house until this man is caught, Alicia."

I looked up at her, clutching my little girl even closer to me. "But he said a week, he gave us a week. Has he come back today to kill me? Is the week up, is our time up?"

I was getting hysterical. She didn't answer me. Instead she stood up and pulled the bell rope next to the fire. Jenny appeared almost immediately. I think she had been listening at the door. Her face was streaked with tears but Elizabeth didn't notice. I made a move to go to her, but she shook her head and pointed outside the door. I didn't understand what she meant.

"Jenny, I wish to see all the staff in the main hall after supper," she said. "In the meantime, inform John to check that all the doors to the house are locked. Oh, and I wish to see Cook immediately."

"Miss, your Lady…" Jenny began.

"Jenny, this is urgent, go now, go immediately!" It was unusual for Elizabeth to raise her voice, and Jenny was as startled as I was. After glancing at me quickly, she darted out of the room.

"I wish Charles was here," Elizabeth said as she paced the room. "He's so busy with the dear Queen. We must all wear black, I will order it done."

She continued to pace the room. "I am going out again this evening, Alicia," she said as she twisted her hands together. "I've organised a meeting with the Board of the Workhouse in Southwark. I wish to improve the conditions. I have given them a substantial amount of money and I wish to see it well spent." She looked at me. "Thanks to you, Charles's tenants are waiting for their houses to be cleaned and improved and we've found employment for nearly all the men. I don't think our dear Cook approves of all the extra meals, but it is wonderful to see the children look well. I cannot believe we allowed John's family to live in such terrible conditions. He must be a very evil man, Mr Grimshaw."

"Oh, you ain't seen how evil I can be yet, milady." A familiar voice rang out from the doorway. We turned in terror, and there he was, dishevelled, filthy, his face full of malice.

Elizabeth screamed and we ran to each other, shielding Alicia between us, as Grimshaw walked into the room, a shotgun over his arm, slamming the door behind him. He stared at us with a sense of triumph, his huge bulk blocking the doorway, knowing that he had us trapped.

"Time's up, my ladies," he grinned, bringing the shotgun up to point straight at us.

"Wait, please wait!" Elizabeth held up her hand, moving in front of us. "We have a child here, please don't harm her."

Alicia, sensing the fear in us, started to cry loudly. Grimshaw's smile faded but he didn't lower his gun.

"I don't harm young 'uns," he said, "just scheming women. Put her over there."

He jerked his gun in the direction of the sofa. Elizabeth grabbed Alicia, who was turning scarlet with crying, and placed her down carefully.

"Mr Grimshaw, please." My voice was cracking and I was shaking with fear. "Please give us time to do what you asked of us."

His sweaty face curled into a sneer. "Got me my job back have ya then? Got me my money? I'd like to know why the polis have been follerin me all week. Don't think that means I'm gonna be paid, does it? And you know the alternative, my fine ladies."

He raised the gun even higher and pointed it straight at my face. I could see Elizabeth out of the corner of my eye creeping round to the bell pull. I had to distract him.

"Mr Grimshaw, I promise I *will* get you the money." I was backed up against the table and if he concentrated on me, Elizabeth was out of his line of vision. Sweat was running in rivers down my back. I knew from the look on his face that he was deadly serious, and I saw his finger move on the trigger. I didn't want to die this way. Oh dear God, I didn't want to die at all.

"Please, Mr Grimshaw, give us one more chance. One day, please." I was down on my knees, crying and pleading for my life and that of Elizabeth. I saw out of the corner of my eye, Elizabeth pull the bell rope, but he must have noticed the movement of my eyes as his gaze swung to Elizabeth who still had the rope in her hand.

"What are you doing, you bitch?" he snarled angrily. "Set the polis on me and now you're ringing for help. Well Missy, you are just too late for that."

Then everything went to slow motion. I could hear the chiming of the clock, Alicia's angry screams. I saw him raise the gun and point it at Elizabeth. With every fibre and ounce of energy I had, I flung myself in front of her, and pushed her to the floor. Then I heard an enormous bang that echoed round the room. The force of the shot flung me backwards, and pain shot through me. I think I started screaming, but as my throat filled with blood, I began to choke.

I fell to the floor but not before there was another huge bang and through blurry eyes I saw Grimshaw crumple to the floor, a gaping, bleeding wound in his head. Lord Kit put down his shotgun, and I could feel Elizabeth's arms around me, and Alicia's cries getting fainter and fainter.

"Goodbye," I tried to say. "Goodbye." But I don't know if they heard me.

My past life was fading and I could feel both the physical and emotional pain severely. My face was wet with tears, and my mouth was full. I coughed and tried to speak.

"Look after my baby," I whispered. "Look after my baby…" Elizabeth's face faded from sight.

Andy's face appeared out of the gloom, and it took me a moment to realise that I was on the floor and he was holding me. A gaggle of kids' curious faces were framed in the doorway.

"Ooohhh, Miss, you all right?"

"There was such a crash! Miss, it was ace!"

"Shall I get the nurse?"

Excited voices filled my head. A distraction from normal lessons was always welcome.

"Scram," said Andy. "Get back to your places."

The heads disappeared with a few groans, but as they left, I could hear the faint sounds of someone sobbing. I looked around quickly but there was nobody there.

"What happened?" I tried to raise myself up. I could feel a sharp pain in my chest. My face was wet with tears.

Andy looked pale and distracted. He was trying to help raise me up.

"You were in the stockroom and I was trying to get some order in the room, and then you must have fallen."

"I was shot," I said, getting unsteadily to my feet. "In my past life. It really happened. I died. It's all over; I won't go back there ever again."

I brushed the dust off my black trousers, but as I straightened up I felt that sharp pain again in my chest. I doubled up with a sharp intake of breath. I was dizzy and disorientated. I didn't feel at all well. Tears were still seeping from my eyes and my vision was blurred.

"I'm taking you to the nurse," said Andy anxiously, as he took hold of my arm.

I allowed myself to be led down the corridor to the nurse's office, where after checking me over, she gave me the all clear. I was sent home, protesting and arguing loudly with Andy until he shut the school doors in my face. I didn't want to be alone just yet. I wanted to be with things familiar. I felt traumatised and ungrounded, not quite yet of this world.

I sat in my car and leaned back against the seat, closing my eyes. I was bereft, separated from people I loved. I didn't even get to say goodbye to Charles and I'd never know what it was like to be his lover. I'd never see my daughter grow up and I would never hold her again. The last sight I'd had of my dear friend Elizabeth was her eyes full of tears, tears which fell gently on my face. I'd seen blood on her hands, my blood. Tears of my own rolled in a constant flow down my cheeks and I leaned my head against the windscreen.

This was my life now. No going back. I had saved Elizabeth and now I had to save myself.

CHAPTER THIRTY SIX

I don't know how long I sat in the car with my eyes closed, but when I opened them the sun had come out. The bright crocuses on the grass in front of the school had opened up as though smiling with gratitude at the light. There were hundreds of them in a riot of yellows and purples. They looked so pleased to be alive.

I had my car window open and there was a bird singing above me. Its call was so shrill and the bird was so tiny, I was amazed it didn't fall off the branch with its exertions.

It's spring, I thought, as I started up the engine, *the time for new beginnings.*

I drove slowly to Liz's house, noticing the pink and white blossom along the hedgerows for the first time. I'd driven down this road hundreds of times but I'd never noticed the horses in the meadow, or the field of oak trees before.

Liz lived in a sleepy village but people from all over the area flocked to her little shop. She was so sincere and so knowledgeable. I could see her blonde riot of curls bobbing about in the window as she served people. I parked the car and bent my head as I walked into the old shop, the old-fashioned bell clanging as I did so. She looked up and grinned at me, and then her expression changed and she looked puzzled.

"Why aren't you at work?" she asked as she measured out an herbal remedy for a little old lady who was by the counter, leaning on her stick.

"It's a long story. Can I invite myself over for the evening? I've a lot to tell you. And I want a look at those archives you got from Chris."

Liz smiled as she handed the remedy to the lady and put the

money in the till. "Come round about seven and you can stay for tea. Pete's cooking!"

I looked at her and smiled. She was alive. My dear friend was very much alive and well. I wanted to hug her, but instead, I gave her a wave of thanks and left the shop, the bell clanging behind me.

As I felt the breeze on my face, I felt a calm determination, and thoughts and ideas which had been spinning through my mind started to form and settle. The familiar north east wind was gathering momentum as I climbed back inside the car. The daffodils on the village green were being tossed around, looking like miniature dancers shaking their heads.

It was growing colder, and I turned up the heater dial as I started the engine. As I made my way home, a thin drizzle of rain spattered the windscreen, and dark clouds scudded across the sky. The river outside the flat looked troubled, little waves criss-crossing its surface, moving in diagonal lines, and the ducks furiously bobbed about, squawking angrily at each other.

I ran into the flat, shaking my drenched hair as I closed the door. Music was coming from the bedroom and I glanced through the open door to see both Jane and Jeff, perched high on ladders, finishing the ceiling between them, music thudding out from a tiny radio which was perched on the window sill.

"You're home early. Finally got the sack have you?" said Jeff cheerily, as he waved his paintbrush at me. "I know you want this finishing quickly so I roped Jane in. There's flapjacks in the kitchen, if you want any."

I smiled to myself. I was still growing steadily, thanks to Jeff's flapjacks. I stuffed one in my mouth and went to run myself a bath. The steam filled the room and when I climbed in and lay down with a long sigh, I thought how different this was to the bath in Beaumont House with its clanking plumbing and sinking depths of water. Sadness and a sense of loss overwhelmed me. I'd been happy and needed in my past life, but this was now the only life I had, and it was up to me to make the best of it.

I fell asleep in the bath. Something I had never done before. My dreams were vivid and frightening. I saw Lady Elizabeth cradling

299

me in her arms, her body wracked with sobs. Charles was holding my hand, crouched down beside her, gently whispering my name. I could hear the wails of my baby daughter, and when I awoke, my own face was wet with tears. I looked around in confusion, as I remembered that I would never go back there again. I was here, firmly in the present time, a knocking at my door and Jane's voice calling my name from outside it. I scrambled out of the bath and pulled on a robe, turning the door handle at the same time.

Jane's face, spattered with paint, was peering at me, anxiously.

"We heard you call out. Are you all right?" she asked.

I nodded. "Yes, I'm fine," I said, pulling the robe around me. "I wasn't well at school so they sent me home. I'm feeling better now, thanks."

"Jeff's made a casserole for lunch," she said, as she tried to wipe the paint off her hands with a cloth. "It's ready now if you feel like eating."

Ten minutes later I was sitting down to a hearty casserole, made with the chicken I was saving for the weekend. It was then that Jeff and Jane broke the news to me of their wedding plans. We had a toast, then I sent them home, not wishing to risk Jeff finishing off my bedroom with a couple of glasses of champagne inside him. Their impending wedding put a thought in my mind, and I made my way over to my desk, cleared it of books and sat down. This was the beginning of the rest of my life and I wanted to get it right this time.

On a blank piece of A4 paper, I wrote everything down that had happened to me in the past, and carefully scrutinised each entry, trying to draw parallels between my lives, and trying to make sense of the significant moments which had changed my perceptions of my own life.

I spent the rest of the afternoon composing a letter to the Head, and as the day faded into soft twilight, I reached for the marking, the constant appendage of any teacher, and cleared the desk, stacking it into my bag, ready for the next day.

I opened my diary, seeing nothing in it but appointments and deadlines for the rest of the week. I wrote in large letters for Sunday,

'Chris', and immediately sent him a reply to his text, saying that I would come over to the Castle to see him. I made a list of all the people I had to call, and when it was complete I shut the diary with a snap, feeling a real sense of direction.

Grabbing a bottle from the fridge, I then made my way out of the flat and to the car. It was a beautiful evening. Everything was crisp and sharp, the outline of the hills against the red-streaked sky, and the black silhouettes of the trees. Somewhere above me, blackbirds were calling to each other and I felt a soaring optimism that I hadn't felt since I was a child, a sense of calmness and purpose.

When I arrived at Liz's house, I hugged her like I would never let her go, and we climbed over kids, animals and various bikes, trikes and scooters to get into the kitchen where Pete was stirring something in a pot. It smelled so good my stomach started to rumble.

We sat down at the scrubbed pine table, which was weighed down with breads and pickles and assorted salads. Various children and their friends came and went, and I felt warm and comfortable, being with my closest friends and being a part of the general hub of family life.

"Chris is back in the country," I announced, as Pete refilled my wine glass. "I'm seeing him on Sunday. Apparently he's moving back to England."

They both looked at me, forks halfway to their mouths. One of Liz's eyebrows almost disappeared beneath her curls.

"I'm just paying a friendly visit," I smiled. "I'm making quite a few decisions this week, and as my best friends, you'll be the first to know when they're finalised. Now, can we see the archives?"

"Sure," said Liz as she pushed back her chair. "I haven't looked at them since Christmas. There's just been no time. I think I left them in the sitting room."

We cleared the dishes away together, the banter comfortable and fun. Pete was in full flow, mocking me as he always had done, probably feeling more at ease with me now that I wasn't so uptight. We didn't mention Chris again. The subject had always been taboo since my illness. Pete had divided loyalties and he had found the situation difficult. He put his arm round me when Liz went to get the papers. "Good to see you looking so well, sweetheart," he said, giving me a hug. "We've been worried about you for such a long time."

Liz walked back into the room, shouting over her shoulder at her eldest boy who had his music blasting through the house. She looked flustered.

"Pete, where's the archives? I left them by the log basket."

"I don't know. No idea what they look like." Pete was opening another bottle.

Liz stood in the doorway, hands on her hips. "Pete! Pieces of paper, old paper. *Valuable.* I got them from Chris to help with my family tree."

Pete's head shot up, and red wine dribbled on the tablecloth. "Oh, shit!" he said. "We've run out of firelighters. I thought it was old paper the kids had been messing with. Oh shit!"

"Oh, Pete, you *idiot!*"

"I'll go and see if I can retrieve anything," he said, as he crept out of the room, trying to avoid Liz's gaze.

"Liz, it's okay," I said. "You know Chris. He won't care, but sit down and I'll tell you what I know."

She sat down reluctantly. I could tell she was still seething.

"Liz, Lord Charles and Lady Elizabeth, your great-great grandparents, and Chris's, were the people I worked for, in my past life. I became really close to them."

I looked up at my friend. "Alicia is not Elizabeth's other child." I swallowed the enormous lump that had appeared in my throat. "She's mine. That is, my other self's daughter. Lord Charles is her father. I was there when she was born. I held her in my arms, I named her."

Liz stared at me in astonishment.

"Liz, I know this is difficult to believe," I said slowly, "but in my past life, I was your great-great aunt. Not only are you related to Chris, but we are related too."

Liz sank down into the chair opposite to me. Pete had arrived back in the room. "Come on, old girl," he said, "you cannot for one moment expect us to believe that!" He sat down at the table. "Time travel is impossible. It's science fiction. You can't change history. You'll make yourself ill again if you keep having these fantasies."

"Pete, I've told you and I've told Liz," I said wearily. "Why would I make it up? David knows and believes me. He says it is against all the odds but possible. He's done regressive therapy on me and the experiences I have had are true. Unusual but true. Somehow I found a crack in time and slipped through, or I was sent there by what or who, I have no idea. I don't think I'll ever know. It happened to me. It was real."

They continued to stare at me.

"Okay," I said, "if I tell you some facts, you may find something which will convince you. My name was Alicia Woods, also known as Lady Swainby. I was governess to the children of Lord and Lady Beaumont, then briefly their housekeeper. I became the mistress of Lord Beaumont, with the blessing of his wife. She and I were close friends. I was killed by the manager of the Beaumont Estate, who hated me as I exposed him as a thief, and consequently, he lost his position. I saved the life of their daughter, Lady Emma, who must be your great grandmother, Liz. I died because I pushed Lady Beaumont out of the way. I was shot and I died. I had a daughter by Lord Beaumont who was called Alicia. They must have brought her up as their own daughter."

The two of them exchanged glances. "I remember reading something about Lady Elizabeth's death being unrecorded, which I thought was strange," said Liz. "So we won't know for sure if you saved her life or not. Perhaps Emma, my ancestor, would have lived without your help."

"Perhaps," I said, "but if she hadn't lived, the chances are you would never have been born."

"I managed to retrieve something," said Pete. "A small scrap of paper, so useless for lighting a fire. Can I just ask you? Do you know when you died?"

I nodded. "December, 1861. The same month and year as Prince Albert."

He held up the piece of paper between his fingers. "Your death certificate," he said. "15th December, 1861."

Nobody spoke. Pete handed the paper to me and I brushed away a stray tear. Liz said nothing but took my hand and squeezed it.

"Why?" she asked eventually. "Why were you sent back?"

"I think to learn things," I said simply. "To be given another chance at life, and as David said, to stop a tragedy. Perhaps I did save the lives of Emma and her mother, but I also think I probably saved my own life too."

Pete pushed back his dark hair and looked at me, a small frown between his eyebrows. He pulled up a chair and sat down next to me.

"Does Chris know all this?" he asked.

I shook my head. "I've made the mistake of telling too many people. I didn't think he needed to know. How would he react if I told him? No, I don't think so. It ends here. I don't want anyone else to know and I don't want to talk about it ever again. It's over."

He nodded and then I looked straight at him again. "Do you know why Chris wants to see me?" I asked, changing the subject.

Pete hesitated. "No, Jill, I don't," he said. "He hasn't said anything to me."

"Did *you* know he's coming back to live in England?"

He nodded. "I know he was thinking about it. He wants Will to be educated here, and Will is quite keen to come back. He likes the fact he has family here."

"And his wife?" I added.

"No idea." Pete moved his chair back and moved away from me. "Sorry, Jill, I've got work to do. Nice to see you, sweetheart." And with that he disappeared around the door.

"Exit with haste." I looked at Liz.

"He doesn't know anything, honestly." Liz pushed back her chair. "I just hope you know what you are doing. It's taken you so long to get over him. I really felt that you were making such progress, and you and David seemed to be getting on so well." She paused and looked at me. "Just be careful."

"I'm not the person I was even a week ago," I said as I folded the document carefully. "I think I know exactly what I want to do with my life from now on."

For a fleeting moment, I really believed I was looking into the face of Elizabeth. The likeness had never been so striking. I looked away and took a deep breath. The moment passed.

She gave me a brief smile. "Okay, Aunty," she grinned, patting my arm. "A cocoa before bedtime and then I want to know everything about your past life. I really do need to get my head round this. Tell me everything, especially about the affair! You minx!"

I laughed and gathered up my things. "No, Liz, I'm off. You may have noticed I've cut down on the drinking too, so I'm safe to drive home."

I looked at her, my friend with her unruly hair and her warm and generous heart. I gave her a hug with a promise to be in touch at the weekend, and I drove home, more ideas formulating in my mind as my determination to make the most of my life gathered more momentum.

When I arrived back at the flat, I made some phone calls and went to bed with a lighter heart. Next morning, my meeting with the Head went better than I thought. The weekend came around quickly. My life was so full of reports and parents' evenings that I didn't have a great deal of time to think about my meeting with Chris. Whatever happened when I saw him again, whatever he was going to say to me, I knew I had options and choices as we all do in life. However, the safe and controlled existence I'd been leading, with my head burrowed beneath the parapet was over with. Not only was I going to stick my head well above it, I was going to climb right out.

However, that night I slept badly. My dreams were of Charles, and they were so vivid that when I woke up, it felt as though he was still with me, lying beside me. I could almost feel the warmth of him. I showered and dressed carefully, spending longer than normal on how I looked. I had waited for this day for years, thinking it would never come, but it was a different me, a stronger me, not a victim anymore.

The drive to the Castle was so beautiful. Daffodils were dancing all along the roadside, shining golden in the spring sunshine. I drove through the villages with their warm sandstone cottages, and felt how glad I was that my home was in England. So many people knock our country for many different reasons, but when I see the English countryside in all its verdant splendour, it never fails to make my heart soar with the sheer beauty of it.

I arrived at the brow of the hill, just before the long straight road that led to the Castle. I reached the top, and there it was, high on the hill with the lake in front, the water glinting in the sunlight, the fields carpeted with daffodils. The tourist season hadn't yet begun, so I had to give my name at the gate. As I was waved through, my tyres crunched on the gravel, my insides crunched against my heart.

I parked at the bottom of the stone steps which led up to the main entrance. A young man in a smart suit ran down the steps and took my keys from me with a smile and an enquiring, "Miss Woods?" to which I nodded. He climbed in and drove my car around the back of the private entrance.

I walked up the steps, trying to keep calm and optimistic. The butler opened the door for me, and with a polite, "Miss Woods?" he led me inside. The hallway was filled with sunshine. The dome soared above me, its paintings of the elements faded with time but still beautiful.

"Please wait here, madam," the butler murmured. "I will inform his Lordship of your arrival."

I nodded and smiled, but turned immediately to walk into the long gallery. My feet clattered on the oak floor as I made my way to the marble fireplace halfway down the gallery. The room smelled of polish and a gentle breeze stirred the heavy drapes. Slightly off-centre, almost hidden behind a pillar, was the picture I wanted to see. I looked up into the eyes of Charles as he gazed down at me from the painting, and at Elizabeth, her sweet smile on her lips, looking so graceful and lifelike. And there, in front of Christopher and next to Lady Emma, was Lady Alicia, my Alicia.

I heard footsteps and turned to see Chris walking towards me.

I was calm but the sight of him so filled me up there wasn't room for anything else. I had no doubt at all the chemistry between us was still there, perhaps even stronger than ever.

"Good to see you, Jill," he said as he reached me, giving me a kiss on both cheeks.

I breathed him in.

"You too, Chris," I said.

He turned to the portrait. "So you are looking at Lady Elizabeth. Liz and I are related, it seems. We would have known more, of course, if my pyrotechnic friend hadn't burnt my family history."

I laughed. "Yes. He was mortified."

"And will be in the doghouse no doubt for many days yet."

We turned back to the portrait.

"An interesting branch of my highly eccentric family," he continued. "There's no record of Elizabeth's death, not here or in the church records. My grandmother believes she didn't die at all but was reincarnated. However, my grandmother was seriously crazy, as are a lot of my family."

I felt the hairs on the back of my neck prickling, but I simply smiled, willing him to continue.

"They had a housekeeper who they treated as one of the family," he continued, "but she was a lady, a family friend. Rumours are she was murdered in one of the rooms upstairs. She's the only non-Beaumont to be buried in our mausoleum."

I gasped. "She's buried here, with the family?"

He nodded. "Yes. Poor girl. There's also a portrait of her near the chapel."

My face burned with excitement. *A portrait, a picture of me?*

"Can I see it?" I asked.

"Of course. Anything else you'd like to know?"

I smiled. "I'm just interested," I said. "Quite a strange story."

We turned to walk along the long gallery, and I fell into step beside him, savouring the moment, hardly daring to believe I was here with him, and wondering for the hundredth time why he wanted to see me. As usual, we slipped into the familiar banter, but it wasn't as easy as usual, perhaps because we both had things we wanted to say, and couldn't.

He stopped before the stone steps which led down to the chapel.

"Here she is," he said, and stood to one side. It was a small portrait in a gilt frame. It would have been so easy to miss it. I didn't remember posing for it so it must have been painted when I was away from that life. It was me, there was no doubt. It was the woman I had seen in the mirror, slightly different features and infinitely more beautiful than me. I was dressed in dark purple so I must still have been in mourning for my father, but I was half smiling and there was a look of contentment on my face.

"This portrait hung in my father's study for years," said Chris. "He used to stand for ages looking at her. He told me that his great grandfather was in love with her. I moved it to here when I came back. She is too lovely to be hidden away. The public should see her."

I glanced at Chris, who was looking at me. He smiled at me, and I smiled back. It was so good to be with him again.

"Chris, why did want to see me?" I asked, eventually. "We haven't been in touch for years. I know that you're moving back to England, but I don't understand why…" I couldn't finish. My throat closed up. He was looking at me so intently I could almost feel the years falling away and it was just as it was then, the only time in my life when I had been happy, when everything had been right with the world.

"Shall we walk?" he asked, holding out his hand to me. "The gardens are lovely at this time of year. It's good to be back. I've missed England so much."

I took his hand and there was a feeling of the last jigsaw piece being found and slotted into place. There was a click and the world righted itself and settled. It felt so natural to be walking with him, our shoes echoing on the polished floor, just like my little leather boots had, so many years ago.

When we reached the Garden Hall and stepped out onto the stone steps, the whole vista of the gardens and the fountain and the lake below was bathed in sunlight. Everything seemed richer and more colourful, from the greens of the lawns and hedges, to the sparkling gold of the daffodils as they bounced in the breeze. It was as though nature itself was celebrating our reunion.

But I must not get my hopes up. He'd wanted to see me, but he was married and the heir to all this, and a lot had happened in the intervening years. I walked beside him taking little glances at his profile. This was a moment I wanted to treasure and to keep for all time, no matter what happened in the next half hour.

The sun, which had disappeared momentarily behind a cloud, suddenly appeared again and sprayed the mausoleum in golden light. The honey-coloured stone glowed and the sun's rays peeped out through the pillars. I felt the presence of Alicia with me, inside me, and I became strong. Chris stopped suddenly when we arrived at the little wooden seat by the fountain. He indicated for me to sit down but he didn't join me. I looked up at him expectantly, feeling much calmer. I would never tire of looking at that face. His hair glinted with gold lights as the sun caught it in its rays.

He looked uneasy, so I gave him an encouraging smile.

"Jill, there are some things I need to say to you." He looked serious and a feeling of dread filled my stomach.

I gave him a brief smile. "Go ahead," I said, clutching my hands together.

"I want you to know how sorry I am," he began. He looked uncomfortable, and I realised how difficult he was finding either the situation or what he was about to say to me.

He leaned against the fountain and looked straight at me. There was no looking away.

"Pete and Liz have filled me in about what happened to you when I left. I didn't know that my leaving would hit you so badly, I thought it was a mutual agreement that I would go to the States on my own and see how it went. As far as I understood it, we'd decided that we were far too young to make a lasting commitment."

My palms felt damp but I looked at him steadily, trying to betray no emotion. "It was a long time ago," I said as calmly as I could.

"We've both moved on, it's in the past. You're married, I've been married…"

"And our baby?"

Tears sprung into my eyes unexpectedly. I looked down. "Well, you know about that now. She died. She was three months old. One morning she just didn't wake up…" My voice cracked slightly.

"And you weren't going to tell me?"

"You weren't here anymore, and I knew you wouldn't come back."

There was a pause and I couldn't look up at him as the tears were welling up in my eyes. I looked down quickly and took some more breaths to calm myself down. The tears subsided.

"But I did come back," he said softly.

I looked up at him. The sun was right behind him and it was dazzling me.

"Well, bad timing, Chris. I was on my honeymoon."

"Yes, I know." He walked over and sat down beside me on the bench, looking out across the garden.

"I'm coming back to live in England. My brother has been running the estate, with my father, while I've been abroad, and it hasn't been the easiest of times for him. We have both suffered in our own ways from the kind of father we've had. Harry has bought property in France where he wants to live with his new wife. I am going to take over the running of the estate, and I can still do my song-writing from here. I have no need to be in New York anymore and I want Will to be educated in England. Will wants that too."

All I could hear was the splashing of the fountain. I looked up at the stone, now shades of grey and green, and remembered how new and fresh it had looked when I walked here with Charles.

I stood up and turned to face him. "Chris, I wish you well," I said to him. "I'm glad you're back. Please believe me when I say I don't blame you for what happened. It was my reaction to it. I just didn't deal with it very well, and when Emma died, I spiralled downwards, but that wasn't your fault. When you left, I never thought I would be able to love anyone like that again."

He glanced up at me. "And have you?" he asked.

I was startled by his directness.

"No," I said simply.

There was a pause.

"Me neither," he said.

We remained where we were, our eyes locked. We just looked at each other without saying a word. Neither of us knowing what to say, or what to do. I had been whisked in and out of time for so long. Now it seemed to be suspended.

A peacock called out shrilly and broke the silence.

I came back to reality with a jolt. "Your wife? What about her?"

He smiled ruefully. "Sophie and I haven't lived together for a long time. She lives in LA, and Will and I in New York. We just didn't have time for each other anymore. Work separated us and we just grew apart. I was busy with my music, she's always away filming."

I felt numb. What did this mean? Is that why he wanted to see me? He still loved me? Hadn't he just said so? Did he want us to start again? To be together?

As an answer, he took hold of both my hands.

"Jill, I realise my feelings for you have never changed but I can't presume that you'll invite me back into your life when you feel that I have hurt you so much. I do feel responsible for it, no matter what you say. I should have done things differently, and I'm so sorry."

I was so full to the brim with conflicting emotions that it took me a few moments to find my voice. This was everything I had ever wanted. I could hardly believe it was happening.

I was distracted by another shrill call of a peacock. I glanced over Chris's shoulder to see the mausoleum bathed in sunlight. There was a fan-shaped beam from behind the clouds which was directed onto the dome. Momentarily everything else was in the shade. I knew then what I had to do.

I took one of Chris's hands and held it against my cheek. I felt him stroke my hair. If this was the end of a film we would have clung to each other passionately as the credits rolled. But this wasn't a film, and our feelings were far too strong for any kind of sentimentality.

I kissed his hand and then held both of his hands in mine, looking directly at his face which held an enquiring look.

"Chris, I love you," I said. "I've never stopped loving you, but there are things I must do with my life, plans I've made."

He held my gaze, and I knew that if we stayed like this for much longer, or if he touched me, I would weaken, so I continued on before he could say anything. I was still holding his hands.

I continued. "If only you knew how happy you have made me, how much I love you and want to be with you, but I have made a bit of a mess of my life, and there are things I have to do to make it right."

He pulled me towards him and gave me a gentle kiss and then he let me go. He linked his arm through mine and we walked down the hill towards the mausoleum.

"Tell me about them," he said. "What are your plans?"

To stay here and love you for the rest of my life, I wanted to say, but with my eyes fixed on the mausoleum, I continued. "I've taken leave of absence from school for a year," I said. "I want to spend time with my father in Canada, and see my brother and his children. I severed all connection with them which was cruel and foolish. I haven't seen them for such a long time. When I return, I've arranged to join my mother in Africa, to teach children over there for the rest of the year, and spend some time with her. We've been reunited and I want to get to know her again. I'm renting my flat to my decorator and his fiancée, for a year."

I took a deep breath. We stood outside the mausoleum as the sun slowly moved away from it.

"That's not all." I turned to face him again. "When I come home, I want to adopt a child. I've started the process. I have no children of my own..." I stopped.

How could I explain the effect that Emma and Christopher and Alicia had had on my life? How the barrier I had erected since Emma died had crumbled? I looked once more into that beloved face, not knowing if I'd now lost what I held most dear, but I also knew that it was a risk I had to take.

We gazed at each other for a few moments. I was so aware of

everything around me, my senses alert to the warmth of the sun, the sharpness of the light, the beauty and scent of the gardens and to the energy between us, so strong that I felt if I reached out to touch it, it would crackle and spark.

I looked straight at Chris, taking in his slightly suntanned face, those beautiful eyes and the blue of his shirt, which matched them. His expression was unreadable.

Suddenly, he gave me that smile, the smile which had always melted me into a heap. "Your turn to follow your dreams," he said.

I nodded, feeling calmer now. "Yes," I said. "It is."

And with that he enfolded me into his arms, and I held him tightly, breathing him in, feeling his strong arms holding me, loving me, his lips on mine, on my face and in my hair.

He released me and looked at me with an expression that set my heart pounding. I could feel my body beginning to burn.

"A lot can happen in a year," I said.

He held out his hand to me as if we were an old married couple. It was so natural to take it, feeling the strength and warmth of him beneath my fingers.

"A lot can happen in sixteen years," he said, as we began to walk back towards the house. "Yet here we are."

I looked up at the honey-coloured stone of the house once again, feeling as I always did, that I belonged here.

Read more from Jan Hunter at:
www.janhunterauthor.com